CW01369606

THE SUN ON THE WALL

Other books by Ronald Frame

Winter Journey
Watching Mrs Gordon
A Long Weekend with Marcel Proust
Sandmouth People
Paris: A Television Play
A Woman of Judah
Penelope's Hat
Bluette
Underwood and After
Walking my Mistress in Deauville

THE SUN ON THE WALL

Three Novels

Ronald Frame

Hodder & Stoughton
LONDON SYDNEY AUCKLAND

William Faulkner quotation taken from an interview in *The Paris Review* by Jean Stein (Martin, Secker & Warburg, 1958).

The translations of Hebrew prayers have been taken from *Language of Faith*, edited by Nahum N. Glatzer (Schocken/Pantheon, New York).

Copyright © 1994 Ronald Frame

The right of Ronald Frame to be identified as the author of this work has been asserted by him in accordance with the Copyright, Designs and Patents Act 1988.

First published in Great Britain by
Hodder & Stoughton Ltd 1994

10 9 8 7 6 5 4 3 2 1

All rights reserved. No part of this publication may be reproduced, stored in a retrieval system, or transmitted, in any form or by any means without the prior written permission of the publisher, nor be otherwise circulated in any form of binding or cover other than that in which it is published and without a similar condition being imposed on the subsequent purchaser.

British Library Cataloguing in Publication Data

Frame, Ronald
The Sun on the Wall
I. Title
823.914 [F]

ISBN 0-340-60685-1

Typeset by Keyboard Services, Luton

Printed and bound in Great Britain by
Mackays of Chatham PLC, Chatham, Kent

Published by Hodder and Stoughton
a division of Hodder Headline PLC
47 Bedford Square, London WC1B 3DP

For my mother and father

'There is no such thing as *was* – only *is*. If *was* existed, there would be no grief or sorrow.'
William Faulkner

CONTENTS

I've Been Here Before . . .   1
The Sun on the Wall . . .   117
The Broch . . .   177

I've Been Here Before

ONE

A black cat picks its way along the top of a wall.
 A chandelier turns in a draught.
 A pair of opera-glasses are trained on the coded arrangement of clothes hanging to dry on a line.
 A gold filling glints in an informer's mouth.
 A blind accordionist changes tune as he hears the click of a certain pair of heels.
 A match struck on a wall. A star inside a circle gouged in the crumbling stone of a gatepost. A pavement artist's chalk painting streaked by rain, blues and yellows running for the kerb's edge.

I am the son of Decca Blane. Her name appears in the cast lists of a dozen films made in England towards the end of the Second World War and in the years just after. In *I Tell A Lie* her name features for the first time in the opening credits, among the six main supports.
 That was to be her last role on the screen. The young director's death also marked the end of her career. Subsequently she disappeared back into life. In the process she realised, sort of, that she was falling out of the rhythms of what had been her reality, having lost the truest form of happiness she had known.

Now I'm wide awake, in 1955, and through the windscreen in the middle of the night another England is being revealed to us, my mother and me, in the sweeping track of the car's headlights.
 It's dense with vegetation, inhabited by scandalised owls and scurrying verge-side creatures with luminous eyes. Sometimes an interrupted white line is laid along the brief distance of road, before the next corner, like a trail of white feathers leading into a forest.
 This other England has been here all the time, of course, but I've hardly been aware of it. I've become an urban child, and my experience of where

we've been living, London, is chiefly of a three- or four-square-mile box, from Chelsea to Regent's Park, from Kensington to Westminster. My mother thought it was where we belonged, and there we should be protected and safe. That hasn't proved to be the case, so we are on the run from London, or from whatever or whomever doesn't have our best interests at heart.

We seem to have swapped one source of hostility – which we don't talk about – for another. She won't discuss this one either, but she has to steer the car herself meantime, on all the tight bends and concealed corners. Here the hedges are high, and the trees so tall that it's impossible to see to the top of them through the windows; their uppermost branches float among the stars, and some of their trunks are gnarled with old carbuncles like alligator eyes. There are eyes watching us everywhere: from the lush grass bankings, from the trees that line these byways, from the other cars – few and far between – that have driven past us. The glass rubies sunk in the road are called cat's-eyes, but we only catch their gleam on the dangerous bends. Three or four times at the lit windows of cottages someone has heard the engine straining and looked out, into the night.

Earlier the wheels would squeal on the corners, until my mother got the hang of it. Now, though, she is starting to flag. Every so often she loses her touch for changing up and down gears, which may mean the tyres will begin to squeal again and burn rubber. The engine groans and whines; it has been driven hard, for four or five hours non-stop.

We continue to avoid the villages, driving round about them by following a signpost to another place further off, and when we have almost come to that other place we veer off again, towards yet another place. And so we go on, keeping clear of trouble, and seeing nothing very much except trees, hedges, and slithering animal life, the flustered flights of startled night birds, the trail of white feathers leading us always deeper into the forest. A full moon plays hide and seek among the clouds, and sometimes its light is like drifting blue smoke. The singing voices on the radio change to talking ones, and my mother turns the knob with a sharp flick of her wrist, and as the bulb gradually dies the little diagram of channels etched on to glass fades slowly, back into the camouflage walnut of the console.

The car's cabin as we speed through the night is warm, luxurious, rarefied. This is no more than my recent life has been educating me to expect is my due, but even now I can't wholly believe it, not in my heart, any more than when we were in London on our social circuit, as players in that fine game. Yet we *are* here, in this refined vehicle travelling so fast that the watching eyes are unfailingly drawn to our headlights, and nothing can be more real to me than this cream hide seat, the fitted grey carpet on the floor, the coachbuilder's walnut trim inside and steel silver-sprayed sleekness outside.

Sometimes the eyes are so drawn that the things, small birds and darting hedgerow shapes, are rendered helpless and they become our victims; they are sucked under the grille, but I try to ignore the occasional light judders beneath the wheels. Dead insects are splattered all over the windscreen; there's a thin crust of them where the wipers haven't been able to knock them clear. On corners I hear the swirl of leaves and dust as we create updraughts – a constant wash – in our wake.

Soon dawn will creep up the sky, from an invisible horizon. We've been driving since eight o'clock last night. We must be many, many miles away, with several counties between ourselves and Sussex, where we did our lying low.

I happen to catch sight of old, weathered script on a wall. The 'Somersetshire Cider Company'. So *this* is the distance we've come. It sounds very far away, although my geographical knowledge isn't what it might be, for all the money that has recently been spent on acquiring me an education. (And what of that? I try to picture myself back at school, in London, on the other side of this adventure, but I can't. I don't know how it might be arranged, and maybe it won't be. The future is impossible to see by the sweeping arcs of the car's headlamps.)

Somerset. Next to that is Devon. My mother has spoken of Devon, because once she went to convalesce there. She has talked about it less with affection than with a kind of wonder, that she really spent time there at all. She hasn't discussed it in any detail with me, because that is not her way.

My mother too is perplexed at this latest turn of events, which is returning her to the past. She stops, reverses, looks again at a signpost – considers for several moments – then pulls on the steering wheel, intending another direction for us both. More of the same follows. Thick, spreading, rampant vegetation, high steeped verges, the ubiquitous screens of trees. At some point ahead of us the red road narrows, to an uphill lane, the verges recede and the hedges advance. The lower branches of the trees come together, they fuse, and – intertwining – form a canopy. The hedges and the branches evolve towards the circular, towards the shape of a tunnel.

My mother's knuckles are white from clutching the wheel for so long. One hand drops to the gearstick. She makes a mistake. The gear slips, there's a wrenching sound. The engine stutters and the car jolts before the gear can be engaged. She eases the pressure off her foot on the clutch and pushes down on the accelerator. We take the hill at quite a turn of speed. There is no trail of white feathers. The hedges turn into trees, and the long branches weave together, in a continuous tracing of a round. I'm thinking of an open

The Sun on the Wall

mouth as we build up speed on our approach. A cry is released above us, and another owl goes gliding over the roof of the car. The trees lace together, like silver filigree in the headlights' shine. Faster and faster, to defy the backwards haul of gravity. Then one last hill, the hilliest hill of all, and a ramp of red road that goes vanishing over the top...

A blue lamp burning in a window. The squeaking of a wheelchair's wheels. An earring dropping down a stairwell, echoing down and down. Then the toss of a spinning silver coin. A coded message tapped out on a water-pipe. A letter inside an envelope left among the magazines at a newsagent's kiosk. One reserved table in a restaurant distinguished by a yellow, not pink, aster in the pewter vase. A telephone number traced by an intruder's finger in the steam on a bathroom mirror, behind the bather's naked back.

TWO

In those days – of the later war years, that is, and just after – several films would be shooting simultaneously in the Selsdon Studios. Through the corridors passed tides of technicians, production staff, actors: Elizabethans in ruffs and hose or hooped dresses, twenties flappers, Roman centurions, Boadicea's amazons, onion-johnnies, mudlarks and street urchins.

The story goes... My mother, with other extras, was walking off the set of a film dressed as a Cossack girl when one of the young turks among the directors, Benedict Matzell, chanced to spot her. He asked her name of a member of the crew, and was very specific. 'The pretty one with the blonde hair. Who looks so English.' He was casting his next film, to be called *A Tiger by the Tail,* and needed to find a girl who would report the disappearance of her father to a detective agency.

She landed the part, and played it the same week that she delivered a dozen lines in another film which was running late. In that she was dressed as a Heidi type in dirndl skirt and curling pigtails, a young cowman's wife who stumbles on a piece of nasty skulduggery taking place on a mountainside in the sinister Bavaria of 1935. There was no contest for her between the two films. She much preferred Matzell's novel vision of a not quite recognisable London to the mish-mash of fake Teutonic accents sounding so hollow in that plaster-of-Paris gully. She liked to see the sinister evoked on her very own doorstep, as it were.

Even knowing so little, she realised that Matzell was more talented than any of his colleagues. He used location shots, and alternated these with studio sets which he created to confer a deliberately stagey air. She hadn't encountered the boldness of such an approach before. Reality and theatre were intentionally confused, to tell the tales of characters caught between their imaginary freedom and the past's force of predestination.

Matzell worked quickly, but there was nothing of the slapdash in his methods. He thought authenticity was lost with too many takes, so he patiently rehearsed his crew and cast in all their moves beforehand.

Everything had been meticulously worked out in his mind, detail by painstaking detail. In a sense the film was already made, and all that was left for him to do was to let the cameras roll – no more than twice usually, and sometimes only once – and to head for a 'wrap' as soon as he could. She enjoyed the speed on *A Tiger by the Tail*, and the unique method of shooting in sequence; a sense of adventure was rushing everyone along as the narrative unfolded, carrying their characters with it.

He registered her enthusiasm, and gave her a more substantial part in his next film, *The Wheat and the Chaff*. This time she dropped from upper-middle-class to cockney office girl. Each film included a great range of types, and she recognised for herself how he set out to show society as an organism of diverse connections, which some choose to keep secret: all sections were linked by their dependence (most often self-interest or fear), from the very top to the very bottom, nobility to menials.

Matzell was a semi-aristocrat himself, on his mother's side, which must help to explain his success in those times when, in practice rather than by the enlightened theory, the traditional hierarchy was still acknowledged and respected. He was depicted in the press as the sophisticate with the common touch, and he had the linguistic dexterity to be able always to argue his own case very convincingly. His films were entertaining mysteries, but also – critics hinted, defensively and vaguely, as if themselves mentally shrouded in one of his filmic fogs – possibly a deal more than that.

Before my mother became Decca Blane she was Janetta Pickering. By a fluke there was another Janetta on the company's roll of actresses, otherwise it would have done quite nicely. When she was only in walk-on and non-speaking parts the coincidence didn't matter, but later it did. Matzell was the one who decided for her, in no more than minutes. He thought her surname should be shorter; he consulted a telephone directory between shifts on the set, starting at 'A', and settled first on 'Blair', then after reconsideration on 'Blane'. My mother was perfectly content that the choice should be his. She was christened unceremoniously over coffee in the studio canteen, but Matzell was very busy that afternoon and my mother found herself with new lines to learn for the following day, which Matzell had had written in for her especially.

One life was behind her now, and another was beginning.

When she first worked for him, Matzell was no older than thirty-two or thirty-three.

He was tall and bulky, with a thick waist and heavy thighs inherited – he claimed – from his father. Despite his mass he had graceful hands and a neat, precise motion of his feet. He wore his hair short, which only emphasised his size seventeen neck. The blackness of the hair and the thinness of his moustache were very much the fashion of the time. It was his mien that marked him out from the other merely fat cats of his business: the familiar jowl was accompanied in his case by spare ascetic lips, a narrow nose, and hooded eyes of a medieval cast. An abbot's pinched face on a friar's roly-poly body. The overall effect was rather severe, but professionally useful because it was also very distinctive. Plainness or handsomeness didn't come into it: he had physical presence, even if it was a little forbidding, and his background provided mystique, and that granted him charisma, which will always draw people even against their wiser judgments.

Some of Matzell's colleagues spoke of his charm and persuasiveness. Others referred to the distances he set up between them and himself. A few talked of his bullying methods in the studio.

Many liked him, and found his company inspiring to them. About as many said that working with him was an unnerving experience, putting them on edge, and that he was unsympathetic. Those who pleaded indifference were a tiny minority.

The effect exercised by the man was ascribed to his privileged background. Or to the intensity of his green eyes. Or to his way with words. Or to his professional reputation, and his connections in the business. Or to his money. Or to the contradictory opinions the world had of him.

He could take against people, when they failed to satisfy his expectations of them. But he remained loyal to those who remained loyal to him by acquitting themselves conscientiously, without 'self', in their studio work. His prolific output depended on his having a team of regular crew, and on his being able to call on particular actors familiar with his intensive method of working.

He was an *auteur*, but he took care to explain to everyone their individual contribution. Those who over-argued points or picked flaws or needed their egos gratified and who only slowed up the process weren't employed by him again. He turned people into devotees and sceptics, friends (more or less) and (no doubt about it) committed enemies.

At the end of *I Tell A Lie* my mother makes her final appearance, as yet another corpse.

She is an elegant one, in the murderous circumstances. She lies bloodied in a white silk nightgown, body spread sinuously across the bed's white satin sheets and silver satin coverlet. Her head and one arm are stiffened in space, suspended above a white bearskin rug smeared with blood trails. She is wearing diamonds – a necklace and drop earrings – even in bed, and her face is made up as if for a party. Her open eyes show nothing at all, not even a hint of the terror that must have presaged her death.

That blankness of the face is either a fine piece of acting, or it demonstrates a lazy failure to define the woman's last living feelings. It is either the coldness of death or occupational incompetence, and as Decca Blane's son I am in no position to judge which.

My first memory.

I'm guessing that the incident occurred sometime shortly after Benedict Matzell's death. A room turned upside down, rooms probably, their contents strewn everywhere. I don't know which room or rooms, in which flat or house – except that I realised the place was home. My mother is sitting on the floor in the middle of the mess, and she is crying. She won't stop, she never stops, but keeps crying, on and on and on, without end. It's hopeless. Our home is ruined. She sits there, helpless. She is angry, or afraid, I don't know which.

Here is the end of something. I understand as much from my own shock at seeing the damage wreaked on us. Everything before this point – which then, as today, I have no recollection of – is already past, it's over and done with, it's unsalvageable. From now on there are to be tenses in my life, and my education in people and things and what connects them is just beginning.

Afterwards she would only tell me that she had been ill.

'You were very small then. I wasn't feeling well, after your father died. I went away to get better, and my friends looked after you.'

I was three years old when a car crash killed Matzell. My mother's film career concluded at that point. Although we must have had quite separate accommodation arrangements from him, I sensed somehow that our home life couldn't now continue as it had been.

I have another memory, of a train like a steaming dragon drawing into a station one night, yellow eyes glaring in the dark. I can't remember who was with me, and why I was there. In the films trains were for ever arriving and departing, or rumbling 'off'. England was perpetually on the move, hundreds of thousands of people at any instant of the day engaged in their orderly transmigrations about the country.

I watched the fire dragon bearing down on us, panting and hissing, trailing sparks.

My mother's illness was a breakdown. Three months after Matzell's death she had to be taken care of, in a nursing home in Eastbourne. Her recuperation down in Devon was slow and difficult. She returned to Eastbourne for a second, shorter course of treatment.

I remember the train, and standing on a bridge of rickety planks above a brook, in a wood. (Not Eastbourne, not Devon. The Home Counties?) It *seems* to be a river raging beneath me, but I am a city child, and the bridge quakes every time whoever is accompanying me moves his or her weight. There must have been a rail or support, because I am looking straight down into the water. A rush of water, clean and clear and sparkling, running over stones. The sight and sound thrill me, and alarm me, and sadden me, all at one and the same time.

That's as much as I remember. In my imagination I drop something into the flow, run to the other side to watch it pass from under the bridge. I run back, drop something else – a twig, or a stalk of long grass – and then run back again. I hear myself, the trembling I set up in the planks. Whoever is standing by the rail keeping watch tells me to please stop. I don't see why, but I stop nevertheless, because this contrary pull of emotions is confusing. My perspective is of things hurrying from me. Not knowing when and how and why. But always carried away in the end.

My mother would divulge next to nothing to me about the past beyond her films.

Even though we hadn't lived with him, I was Benedict Matzell's son, I was left in no doubt about that. But she preferred that *she* should be unexplained, a mystery. She didn't want me to know where she came from, whose daughter she was, what her childhood had been like. Sometimes I asked, and she would say that I'd only be bored to hear, or that there wasn't time to go into all that, or that she had forgotten.

I stopped asking. I lost interest, as she must have supposed I would do once I realised there was no challenge in the business.

Then we went to live in a house, a large pink house with a thatched roof, situated in a flat garden on the edge of a salt marsh. My new father was the owner of the house: he had owned it for a long time, being a man of somewhere past fifty. There was a woman to work for us, and another to clean up, and life was rather dull in our quiet corner of that watery eastern county – my new father was often away at his business – but my mother and I were comfortably kept.

Things like shelter and warmth seemed to be important to my mother. Turning up the radiators, toasting towels and underwear on the top shelves of the airing cupboard, making sure I was wrapped up snugly when she put me to bed. Sometimes she lost her temper with me, and less often with her new husband. There were days that were good for her in that remote spot with its views of sunsets, while there were others – when the white mists came in, when the garden and the thatch sounded with unseen life – that scared the hell right out of her.

To give her something to do with her time, when he wasn't at home with us – which was quite often – my new father set his wife up in a shop. It was a small haberdashery concern which he had bought over. My mother didn't have a clue at first, but she started to learn.

The shop was meant to absorb her thoughts when otherwise they might have strayed; if an occupation provided her with a sense of self-dependence too, that was a calculated risk which my new father had taken. In the event she tended to perform the role of proprietress, perhaps because it seemed as unlikely an existence to her as it did to me. Its only verifiable reality was its sheer ineffable tedium.

The little town where my mother keeps her shop slumbers in the sun.

A church tower at the end of the street. The fishmonger's shop, whose window is an unglazed square in the wall: the unfinished walls inside the cold gloomy shop are as dark as rock, and the stone counters and floor are awash with water. The barrow outside the fruiterer's. The old mounting-stone from the days when people rode into the town on horseback. The Clydesdale, called Bonny, that pulls the dairyman's dray. A shadowy, unkempt garden behind railings that apparently belongs to no one, because the locals have forgotten whom. Other railings were melted down for the war effort, which has since caused neighbours to be falsely close to one another. A high, unsteady pavement on one side of the street, and a beaten track through weedy grass on the other, sunnier one. A lamp-post left leaning like a drunkard after an accident too many years ago to remember when. A wall of the native blue brick, with untrained honeysuckle tumbling over it. Sunlight sifting down from a great height through all the geometric riddles of a monkey puzzle tree. Every surface coated with dust or with the accumulated grime of life, the distillation of unexceptional ordinariness.

I had a bad bout of German measles when I ought to have been beginning school. I was late in embarking on my education, but I made up time by being taught at home. An elderly man, a hero of the First World War who had become a schoolmaster, provided me with all my instruction. Once I overheard him repeating to the new maid – who didn't know not to listen – some of the things he'd heard being said about their employer and the woman and her child who shared his house.

I've Been Here Before

The word 'woman' confused me, because shortly before this a stranger – a woman, and a good deal older than my mother – had appeared at the house. She was quite collected at first, and ladylike, but she gradually worked herself up into more and more of a lather, until she was banging on the windows and shouting through the letter-box at my mother after our retreat into the house. A few months after both incidents, the woman's coming and my overhearing my tutor's gossip, my new father collapsed of a heart attack on the street of the market town he was off visiting, and with no more ado he died on the hot pavement.

Only after that did my mother discover that Mr Kester had still been married when he married her, being the husband in law of the woman who had recently tracked us down. Subsequently my mother became as peculiar as our unwanted visitor, moving from calms to rages, chasing the staff away (including my tutor), refusing to open the shop, dressing at home in her underwear, removing small but valuable objects from the house and burying them in the garden but never remembering where when she went and tried to find them again. Letters came to the house which she didn't open; when some men in business suits drove up the driveway one day, she hid me in the pantry and wouldn't open the front door to them. When the two of us did finally leave, it was at six o'clock one morning, driving too fast through the curlicues of mist which were seeping in – as ever – from the marsh.

The first thing I saw when she opened her suitcase at the hotel that night was the envelope containing the old newspaper clippings about Benedict Matzell and his films, placed on top of her folded clothes. She saw me looking, and rubbed my head with some of her old playful affection.

'I want to show you the life I had,' she said. 'The one before.'

She called only Matzell 'your father' now; and although we stole the name of Kester, our recent provider was doomed already to the disgrace of her amnesia and mine.

We moved back to London. For a while we lived in a two-rooms-and-kitchen flat above a milliner's workshop in Pimlico Road.

I remember my mother pacing the larger room, our living-room and my bedroom, trying to memorise lines of dialogue from a sheaf of printed pages. She must have gone off and recited the lines somewhere; later I found the loose pages of the script discarded in the dustbin, under a mush of tea leaves and the food my mother had only picked at.

While I was at school through the day, my mother didn't stay in the flat. The rooms felt cold when I got back, and I noticed that sometimes my mother's cheeks had a flush as if she must have run from wherever she had been, in order to get back there before me.

The Sun on the Wall

* * *

My mother bought postcards of famous paintings, from boxes laid out on the Chelsea Embankment at the weekends. She liked to decipher any handwriting on the backs, no doubt imagining that the messages referred to deeply involving love affairs. She placed the cards on the mantelpiece, the ones that were in better condition, and the others that she'd bought on an instinctive response to some detail she stood up on the shelves in the kitchen.

I have seen the paintings many times since, in books and even where they hang in galleries. I can summon them to mind without a moment's hesitation, because in the dull moments of our Pimlico existence I used to be transported to those sylvan glades and rocky shores, as an invisible observer. I would fix on them, from a supine position on the thin mattress of my fold-away bed, and in a sort of trance of attention each one of them would become as familiar to me as the room where I was.

Each painting told a story begun in one of the classical ages and fated to be uncompleted all through time, which is enacted by every living generation in turn. Daphnis and Apollo, Cupid and Psyche, Echo and Narcissus, Venus and Adonis, Diana and Actaeon, Pygmalion and Galatea. The legends of love and seduction. The contest of desire and reason. Statuesque poses, with sometimes in the background a half-concealed impish face, or a curious knot of shadows which to the eye is not validated by the perspective.

Several publicity stills from the films and a few Brownie shots of ourselves were kept separate from the film clippings and honoured with storage in a cardboard box that had accompanied us to Pimlico Road. A round white box with fluted edges. A royal blue band printed on the lid; in silver cursive script, the name 'La Maison du Chocolat', and an address, 'North Audley Street, Mayfair'.

I knew that box well. I'd been told that the chocolates had been a present, from my father. Chocolates were now a rare luxury in our lives, and I pictured a more splendid time, just before I was born, when my mother had known advantages. I regretted my ignorance, and was jealous of the mystery of those earlier days, even though I did belong to them as my parents' son. From the material fact of a box of superior chocolates, I conjured up a feeling of life then – the privacy of taxi cabs, the supple fit of gloves, the heat of a roaring hearth in winter – and even if I didn't understand anything about, say, champagne or oysters I had lived already in fairy tales and could imagine the sensation of being enveloped and protected by concern as my mother suggested, of submitting to affection like the force of a river in spate.

I've Been Here Before

* * *

In the little flat at night my mother would read magazines, the sort that chronicled the lives of rich Londoners, which supplemented the morning staple of the William Hickey diary in the *Express*.

She kept scrapbooks, filling the pages of coloured blotting-paper with photographs of glamorous partygoers and snippets of information about how they conducted their lives, at which luncheon rendezvous and in which supper-clubs. I remember a jeweller's advertisement, showing a blue opal bracelet clasped over the wrist of a pencil-line forearm. There were fashion designers' sketches of ball-gowns, and more artists' illustrations of cocktail and afternoon dresses being worn on a catwalk.

One or two evenings in a week she would fetch the scissors and glue-pot and sit down to the task. She debated carefully what to cut out, and would consider this against that, and plan the layout of a page before starting to snip and paste. Music meanwhile wafted out of the wireless speaker, one of those small orchestras that played in the West End hotels. A couture evening gown, styled by Victor Stiebel perhaps. An ensemble of faces caught in the aureole of a flashlight. The canopy above a restaurant doorway. The controlled frenzy of another film première, an electric atmosphere crackling along the pavements of the street crowded by fans.

Then suddenly we moved away from Pimlico Road. And exactly simultaneously I was introduced to my mother's new friend, a youngish-looking man by the name of Metcalf.

The coincidence of both events seemed to me a destined matter, like my mother's silence about how one and the other had come about: our finding ourselves in a furnished flat – 'chi-chi' would have been the word for it – in a block in a desirable corner of Kensington, and my mother's entertaining this personable and alternatingly charming and solemn stranger.

It was he who asked me to call him not 'Mr Metcalf' but 'Uncle George', and my mother appeared surprised and bemused by the request but also determined to be practical about it. He became 'Uncle George' to me; I was agreeable, because he was the only uncle I had, and one was any number of times better than none.

All my life had been change. This was merely the latest instalment. I liked our luxurious new phase, very much indeed, and I enquired very little about it. I was adapting with a facility that baffled even myself. Soon I was quite certain, at seven going on eight years old, that I didn't want to or mean to regress from here, from this unexplained condition of grace, back on the gravity slide to the lesser end of Pimlico Road.

THREE

I am a man in my middle forties. When I recall the London period of my life, I am also a boy of seven years old.

Remembering, I am neither one nor the other, but both. The man reverts to the boy's height, he occupies his physical space; the boy seems to be precociously aware that each new stage of his life is temporary, that it will pass, and that he is pledged to detail as much of it as he can, as well as to retain its essence, its *perfume*.

The man is disposed to explain, the boy to describe. I cannot disentangle who I am now from who I was. This is *my* story, and my mother's: a chronicle of events, and also a reaction to them, lived through from one day to the next but viewed with the chastened hindsight accumulated in the forty years since.

I realised early on that Uncle George was not included in the social activities which, magically, were opened to my mother and me. He was very interested in everything she had to tell him, however, and he never lost an opportunity to learn more. Most days he would phone my mother, and as often as he could he would drive round to our flat. I wondered if I was about to acquire another new father, but my Uncle George didn't seem to be getting very far with his vague fumbles and cuddles. My mother would shake him off and slide away from him. She had too much else to think about in these heady and novel times.

I would pick up the telephone receiver and recite the number. Whoever was phoning wanted to speak to my mother. I learned to recognise their voices. Lady Coniston, Hugo Rathbone, Sybille Surtees, Bobby de Villeray, the countess.

When we were living above the hatters', we hadn't had a telephone. Now we were indulging ourselves with our extravagant toy, a white model with a white flex. Our new acquaintances weren't to be informed about our recent deprivations, though: I already had an instinct for what was to be told and what not.

'I'm so sorry to have kept you waiting –'

My mother would breathe the words in that intimate, actressy way she still had, folding one hand across the other to hold the receiver as close to her face as she could.

'But, your ladyship, I should be delighted –'

Bruton Street.
   Wilton Crescent.
   Monmouth Square.
   Burlington Gardens.
   I didn't need a map to direct myself to where in Belgravia or Chelsea or Mayfair or, closer to home, Kensington the cars and taxis were taking us. I knew how long the journey would be each time, because I soon had a memory for all the occasions on which it had happened before.
   Hans Place.
   Brook Street.
   The Boltons.
   St James's Street.
   My mother jotted down the locations in her diary, and the times of the rendezvous. When she didn't take me with her, I had the company in the flat of Mrs Turpin, from Pimlico Road, who brought her work with her – dresses she was running up for customers, which required pernickety bodice work in silver thread or sometimes coloured sequins. While Mrs Turpin sewed and held her breath at the difficult moments, my mother was out on the town, sitting at a supper table or sipping her drink at one of the cocktail bars her group frequented, to report it all back to her faithful listener Uncle George sometime later.
   Hanover Square.
   Hyde Park Gardens.
   Charles II Street.
   Tregunter Road.

All my mother's new circle had known Benedict Matzell. That seemed to be what they all had in common. Any friend of his was automatically a friend of theirs, so they accommodated her very happily.

'I wasn't a star or anything like that.'

My mother didn't want to establish any false pretences. The term 'film actress' granted her a certain allure, sufficient for her purposes. Self-deprecation in an actress was an event in itself, and made her only more worthy of notice.

People searched in their minds, determined to recollect her.

'But you won't remember, really.'

The films were familiar to some of the company. Several of them were able, in muddled fashion, to recall odd details.

'The characters were part of the ambience,' she explained confidently enough but using someone else's words, Matzell's or a critic's. 'They drifted into one another, like smoke.'

It sounded an authentic, considered judgment. No one was a film buff and could know any better: and, after all, *she* with her personal experience was the one in a position to pronounce.

Not a star. Modest. Intelligent, perceptive. She tantalisingly confuted initial expectations they might have had of her. The ease with which she adjusted and fitted in was the subtlest sort of confirmation of her past life. The films were a long while ago now, she always insisted so: but those small skills she had acquired to pass herself off as the form of the woman only silhouetted by the script, they were as ingrained in her as that most neutral and placeless of unaccented accents she spoke with.

I was the only child I ever encountered on that circuit. I was a curiosity. I believe that had less to do with myself than with those resemblances the others caught in me to someone else, my father. It wasn't ever my mother's looks they recognised, but Benedict Matzell's.

Adults generally treated children as nuisances. I enjoyed this contrasting boon of attention. I could have exploited it, but I don't recollect that I did. One of the prerogatives, however, was their also knowing when to leave me alone, on their games evenings for instance or when there was some dancing, so that I was free to sit and watch them all in silence. Being alone meant there was less onus on me to behave properly, and to smile, and to ingratiate. I merely sat there in our friends' homes and I watched, from beyond the pools of light, out on the fringes, unconsciously memorising that time to bring back when it should all be over.

Now I remember, seeing through the boy's eyes.

The bulky chiffoniers and escritoires, the clock-cases and marble-topped side-tables, they all helped to provide the huge rooms with some definition, otherwise they would have seemed endless. A tapestry shrank, hanging on one of those walls; paintings were well above adult eye-shot, and vases elevated on unreachable mantelpieces; a carpet was swallowed up by the expanse of floor all about it.

I've Been Here Before

The interiors were as often lamplit as not when we saw them, which left the chandeliers redundant and threw up further mysteries with our crisscrossing shadows. Corners of the rooms remained dark and out of bounds: some rooms I never did set eyes on by daylight, and I remember them as cavernous and unfinished, somehow *escaping* at their edges where the conversation and the laughter petered out. My mother and the others sat on low pouffes before the fire to play backgammon or mah-jong, or they sank into sofa cushions with their coffee cups and balloon glasses, and – as I supposed – they might have been in a campfire clearing at the heart of a great gloomy forest. On some evenings there was bridge, when they played on upright chairs at baize-topped games-tables, and their concentration was so applied – both that of the players and those standing behind them – that from where I sat, with a jigsaw on a tray placed across my knees, they were like castaways on an island oblivious of everything else except trying to work luck from the cards played to them.

We listened to records, and that way I was introduced to composers and performers who would be explained to me by my mother's acquaintances: Bach and Mozart – Casals's sonatas, and the string quartets – and, at the other extreme, Django Reinhardt and Lionel Hampton. A few of them would dance to the jazz, while the rest of the company looked on with practised good humour. When the big band struck up, my mother would get to her feet and shake out her dress and be first to solicit the co-operation of a partner. She was a very able dancer, with supple ankles and neat darting feet that could keep out of the way of her clumsier companions'; her eyes took on a shine as she entered effortlessly into the verve of the music, spirited to us over the years from a Left Bank cellar or a dance hall in Chicago. When they'd finished, when some refreshment or other was being served, the music played on in a disembodied way, and suddenly they all failed to notice how incongruous one milieu was to the other. Someone other than myself must have had an ear for it too, though, because the music would be changed at last, to something more sedate: one of the Passions, or Menuhin playing a Mozart concerto. We settled ourselves again to that seemly and refined tempo.

Nothing from outside reached us, in those dimensionless rooms with their heavy dragging drapes that muffled the sounds of traffic, of the vulgar world going about its commercial business, during the run of months my mother and I were seduced by our good fortune.

In summer outside awnings of stretched canvas were pulled down at the windows, to protect the furniture and fabrics and floor coverings.

Sometimes, when the sunlight was especially strong, the shutters and curtains inside would be half drawn as well. The interiors of the rooms grew warm but never hot, saved by their height and the presence of cooling marble. Even so, iced drinks would be served in mid-summer, and there were electrical fans for the most extreme conditions.

We might be tempted out into the gardens on those evenings, but only because there was shade. We sat about on loungers, deckchairs, bamboo garden chairs, teak benches, on the edges of mossy balustrades, or on worn crumbling terrace steps. The backgammon or mah-jong boards would be brought outside, and the bridge or bezique cards cut, and books and magazines opened. There was always talk, of course, and the music playing on a gramophone indoors – quietly, so that the occupants of neighbouring houses shouldn't be disturbed. There would be exits and arrivals: someone going off to the opera, another person who had come on from a drinks party. We would eat informally, as the term was understood: usually from a buffet service of chilled soups and mousses and cold meats and cheese and fruit, and – in the other seasons – simple vegetable soups or consommé, a bird or a roast, perhaps salmon or trout, and a light pudding or a savoury. The standards were fairly consistent but went uncommented upon, it merely being presumed that there was a cook or hired help behind the scenes to organise the hospitality.

Reciprocating was made a little easier for my mother. Since home was too confining for purposes of entertainment, she became known as one of two specialists in devising picnics, for indoors or travelling as well as outdoor occasions. She made liver pâtés and jellied fish moulds and seafood tartlets, which she vaguely suggested were prepared by someone else to whom she gave instructions. Because picnics weren't the norm, she got off relatively lightly, and because when a picnic *was* organised everyone provided their own hamper and crockery and silverware she could concentrate on the prettiness of the food itself.

Once the clocks went back we remained indoors. The curtains were drawn early, and the table-lamps lit. The fires were banked high. Glasses and tumblers were replenished, and there might be a hot punchbowl. Cigarettes appeared from monogrammed silver cases, gold lighters proffered flames. The fire crackling in the grate became the central focus of the room, unless the room was equipped with two. Furniture receded into degrees of gloom, and the proportions of every room could only be guessed at. With a blazing fire, a storm seemed to roar in the chimney, and the shadows of flames scaled the silk and damask walls. At Archie Rathbone's, the unlit glass chandelier turned with every draught that blew into the house off the heath and the slivers of crystal would sweetly chime; in Lady Coniston's townhouse, the great piano on which Liszt had played lay at the back of the drawing-room like a beached whale; in the Countess of Charminster's apartments, held on royal lease, the dragons on the Chinese lacquered screens had been supplied with firestones for eyes, and these glinted wickedly in the murky privacy of their lairs.

The life I'm describing should have been a lie, but it wasn't. So many people's London in the first half of the fifties was bleak and seedy, but mine was not. My mother's friends had shut themselves off, to protect standards. They talked sometimes about politics, in knowledgeable fashion, but I presume that over the years the discussion had become more abstract. They tried to inject the exchanges with some humour, which tells me the talk had probably lost a good deal of its point. They may well have been aware of what life was like for the majority, but what might have concerned their consciences once – as the mentions of rallies and soup kitchens testified – now seemed to matter less to them. When the board games began and the bottles were opened and the radiogram built up throttle, their use of words like 'regeneration' and 'reconstitution' had an undirected feel: to my listening ear now there was a hackneyed element, as if they were fumbling for meanings, in a vocabulary of fine-sounding otiose generalisations.

They mentioned new books, new plays, concerts they'd been to, talks they'd heard on the Third Programme, but their intellectual interests were surface concerns. They had no precise judgments of their own when it came to 'culture': the same opinions would emerge from different mouths in the course of an evening, and most probably they had been memorised from notices in newspapers or the weeklies.

Their conversation was a ritual of politeness and calm, never contentious enough to be disruptive. An air of sophistication was everything, and no egos were indulged. There were no debates over 'better' and 'best'. They all spoke their common cultural language, and it's that I remember rather than the little details.

The last of the rations didn't affect us, I never understood why.

We lived in circumstances of great plenty. Whatever my mother needed to prepare her picnics would appear in the kitchen of our flat. I may have enquired once or twice, but after that I think I became afraid that I might break the spell if I asked any more questions. Superstition won, and a deep silence developed around the subject.

It didn't embarrass or shame me to realise we lived quite differently from most other people. I was becoming aware from my own experience that life is a sweepstake, and winning and losing is accidental. My mother was too relieved at our change of fortune to let guilt bother her, and I followed her example. It didn't mean we were heartless. (My mother would remember to remind me every so often that I should be 'grateful'.) Rather, we were phlegmatic about the injustices of life, and knew to seize our chances whenever they came. There was a talent in not letting luck go, until it decided to let go of you.

We continued to see Uncle George, of course.

He had told my mother, and she passed the information on to me when I asked, that he worked in the offices of a shipping line. When I asked *him*, he told me it was dull work. 'South America,' he said. 'South Africa. Those sorts of places.' And then he became confused between the two Capes, Horn and Good Hope, and the subject just fizzled out.

He seemed to have an amount of free time at any rate. Every second day or so he would drop round to our fancy flat, usually mid-afternoon. He continued to phone us as well, once a day and when he couldn't get away, to hear again about our shiny new lives.

When he called in person, he would bring my mother silk stockings, the very top sheer quality. She built up quite a supply of these: a small parcel would appear alongside the other gifts he plied her with, and she would thank him without opening it, without asking him any questions. George Metcalf too was part of this charmed world of abundance, which had no truck whatsoever with the privations and restricted choices of ordinary folk. I felt that if I could only stop thinking of their routine manner of life, a kind my mother and I had known ourselves, then it would never be able to claim us, and we should always belong instead to this context of careless favour, among the saints in light.

FOUR

The others had known one another for varying lengths of time, but most of the acquaintanceships – I hesitate to say friendships, since there was often a degree of formality involved which puzzled me at first – dated back to the years just after the war: none was more recent than eight years old, which meant that the community – to call it that – had been established in the form in which we found it by 1946 at the latest.

It was Lady Coniston who organised our social activities – or, more correctly, it was her secretary Miss Deegan who attended to the minutiae of appointments on her employer's behalf, where and when we should next meet.

Lady Coniston I still find hard to fathom. As a young woman, thirty years before, she had been a famed bluestocking. She continued to show flashes of that impressive intellect, or maybe those remarks only seemed impressive by contrast with her general scattiness. She was very forgetful on occasions, and became bothered by it, and couldn't recall what it was she was trying to remember, and so lost the thread of why she had begun. At other times she forgot to censor what was on her mind to say, and she said it, and then – realising from the little pulses of shock – had to start apologising for something uttered which hadn't seemed at all exceptional when she was speaking it.

Widowed but titled by birth, Perdita Coniston was tall and very thin, bony-shouldered and long-armed, drop-breasted and wasp-waisted. Her neck and face looked emaciated, while powder was applied so thickly that it resembled a plaster cast. Her clothes succeeded in being ethnic and soignée at the same time: oriental tea gowns and kimonos and North African burnouses expertly 'readjusted' by her dressmaker, worn over silk and cashmere separates of a 1930s cut but always, apparently, in mint condition. A silk bandana in a primary colour concealed her brow and pushed her crinkly hyacinth hair back and up in approximately tribal fashion. Her jewellery had a primitive originality: combinations of bone, silver, wood, ivory, copper, coral, gold. A slash of fuchsia lipstick on her harlequin face invariably stained her teeth, and her mouth gave an appearance of unravelling. The words that emerged had to be decoded into understandable English from their arcanely mannered accenting: elasticated vowels, chipped and honed consonants, perverse and absolute stresses.

Sometimes her starved face grew long and lantern-jawed or the bandana exposed thick black eyebrows, and on those occasions she had a mannish, almost transvestite appearance which the rattle of jewellery only exaggerated. Then she would revert, the bandana would drop into line with the tops of her eyelids, her chin would be drawn tighter by the weight of necklaces, her litheness would be svelte not muscular, her mauve eyes acquired an intensity and zeal, and you could imagine she might have made numerous conquests in love in a prior and fuller-bodied epoch of her life than this one.

The best-known of the inner circle of eight or nine was Leofric Anstey, the archaeologist.

He was just into his fifties, silver-haired and -moustached, monocled sometimes, and on cold days sporting an astrakhan hat indoors. His outsized floppy bow ties were his trade mark with the public. All his London clothes, as distinct from those he undressed to on his digs, had an Edwardian cut.

He was apt to sit in very studied poses, most commonly elbow on chairarm and chin propped on one elegant hand and dark brown eyes gazing up into a far corner of the ceiling.

Although we never had an opportunity granted to us to see inside his bachelor rooms, they were photographed for *Tatler*, where I recently found them again: stuffed with portrait paintings of formidably statuesque, bosomy grandmothers and maiden aunts, crammed with furniture in the baroque spirit, all the surfaces covered by trophies of his travels, including – although it went without mention in the caption – what I can guess now to be an elephant pizzle, at least eighteen inches long and thrusting to its point like a twist of stalagmite rock.

The magazine article coyly referred to the 'Ladies' Hour', when chosen company was 'invited to take tea' with the fashionable self-publicist. The bed was a high-set, fully double four-poster of Georgian provenance, but the bathroom for all its many prints of unclothed classical statuary was functionally up to date.

I recognised Sonja Hellstrom from a cigarette card of 'Heroines Of Our Time'. In fact her 'time' had been the mid-thirties, and the cigarette card was one of a batch, a job lot, which my mother had bought for me in a bric-à-brac shop when we were living in Pimlico Road.

She was two decades older than she appeared in the colourful, not very expert illustration, but it was easy to imagine her as the famous aviatrix. She was tall, still athletic, still with her blonde hair plaited on either side of her head like earphones. Her eyes, sapphire blue just as the illustrator had shown them through her goggles glass, often took on a rather manic purpose. She talked in great galloping bursts, she never rose slowly from a seat when she could jump up, and she unfailingly gave the impression that she was in a rush to get somewhere – although it wasn't at all clear where, since in the event she would be one of the last to make her departure into the night.

Clarita Valdés-O'Shaughnessy, the restaurateuse, wore the chicest little fur jackets to the midriff: of mink, or silver fox, or wolf, and trimmed in an identical style with decoratively stitched tweed borders. She liked to leave the jackets open and roll the sleeves along her tanned arms to the elbows. Her hair was of a suspiciously even brown hue (like her fellow luminaries, she was safely into her middle age); it was scraped back and tied into a pony-tail. She had Latin colouring and an unflawed complexion, large dark Spanish eyes, a perfectly regular nose but a mouth with a dissatisfied, even cruel cast. She smelt of both expensively elusive oils and the fiendish Turkish cigarettes she smoked.

My mother was in undisguised awe of her, of her glamour and her disdainful southern beauty. In the flat I saw her tucking up the ends of her cardigan in front of the wardrobe mirror, and I watched how critically she sniffed the contents of her own bottles of eau-de-cologne and bath oil and crinkled her nose afterwards as if she couldn't find anything among them to please her or which would be likely to please anybody else either.

My mother had her own 'look', though, and a number of times I saw Mrs Valdés-O'Shaughnessy inspecting *her*.

Her definitive outfit was a waisted alpaca jacket with navy velvet collar; a white silk shirt; corduroy pants; loafers; a velvet bow, usually black, in her hair; a pair of pearl studs. She had one evening gown of her own, and borrowed others from willing sources. She owned a cocktail dress, and a shantung suit for afternoons, but the 'outfit' – with its variations of colour – was the one which showed my mother to best advantage, as she realised quite well. It was theatrical, vaguely aristocratic, English but stylish, formal but just a shade louche at the same time, just right for that calculatedly casual way in which she would stand smoking with one hand on her hip.

The Sun on the Wall

* * *

Mrs Curtain must have weighed considerably more than twenty stones. Her age was difficult to determine – the middle forties perhaps. She wore voluminous beaded and fringed gowns with matching stoles, and on her remarkably neat feet beneath the thew-like calves and ankles, velvet harem slippers with pointed toes. Her swollen wrists and vast, bulging forearms clanked with bracelets. A sparkly net was thrown over her hesped hair. She spoke a polished version of a north London suburban accent.

Her claim to fame was her psychic powers. She didn't fritter her time telling fortunes by ball or card, which was the terrain of lesser mediums, but used her gifts for grander ends – to correspond with alien forms of life wishing to communicate with earthlings. To earn her handsome living, she would proceed into trance to predict the future for such as prominent businessmen and senior politicians, who could visit her consulting rooms strictly incognito. Her abiding passion – 'my obligation', as she termed it – was to apply her mental faculties to the reception of extra-terrestrial thought-transference, to read the texts of lives already recorded in the future.

By comparison with Phyllis Curtain, my mother was easier even with the pianist, Dame Helena Winthrop, notwithstanding her (once very well-known) appearance.

She was built in the manner of a Greek tragédienne. Tall, broad shoulders. Wide hips. A hypnotic, sculpted face, one whose expressions were capable of alternating between great moral sternness regarding others and of less critical, more indulgent sensitivity concerning her own feelings. A fine, straight nose. Strong hands, with a man's spread. An olive complexion. Low eyebrows above eyes blacker than Mrs Valdés-O'Shaughnessy's. Grey-flecked black hair, coiled up in a French roll. The suggestion of a moustache. White carnivorous teeth. A determined chin. A long and sturdy neck.

How odd, then, that her playing when she could be persuaded to offer us a humoresque, a 'lollipop', should prove to be so hesitant, so pianissimo, so very *apologetic*.

The Rathbone twins were ineffably refined. Although one had attended Sandhurst and the other Dartmouth and both were said to have explored the upper reaches of the Orinoco in their earlier years, although Archie had a spearman's scar on one cheek and Hugo slightly limped owing to enemy shrapnel still lodged in his knee, they appeared now in their fiftieth year of brotherhood and bachelordom like nothing so much as paragons of a superior kind of lounge lizard.

Always, without fail, they would be seated side by side on a sofa, one in a white tuxedo and the other in a black dinner jacket, with their movements in unconsciously synchronised alignment: so that even when A crossed his legs and B did not, their bodies would twist to left or right in the same fashion, and their torsos would be set at a corresponding angle on the cushions. They both had the family hands, long and tapering, and held their gold-tipped cigarettes – each of them was left-handed – in the same supremely languid pose.

Archie admitted to playing the stock market and living off his investments and playing a great deal of Real Tennis. Hugo was director of a bank in the City, and maintained a separate office in Pall Mall, but like his brother he also had the leisure to socialise and always to be able to quote from the gamut of the American and European press. All the time they sat nursing their malts and managing to tip the cusps of ash from their cigarettes into an ashtray *just* in the nick of time, they gave a semblance of being about nothing very much – and yet both were alive to each and every nuance of conversation in the room, especially to things that weren't quite being said.

Lady Coniston was inseparable from her secretary, Miss Deegan.

Miss Deegan – I never learned her christian name – dressed twenty years older than her probable age. Long pastel cardigan, baggy tweed skirt, flat laced shoes. She spoke of her mother and maiden aunts. Her accent was one she might have acquired by correspondence course: an Essex inflexion kept breaking through, so that her pretended neutrality wavered and wobbled. I sensed that she was unused to children, because she was awkward with me. She allowed us to imagine a background of matriarchs, and elderly occupations, and yet there were moments – usually when she had to show a reflex, if an object dropped or a door was about to bang shut – when she betrayed the quick and agile movements of a younger woman. With her yellow-grey eyes, the colour of a cat's, obscured from us behind the narrow lenses of her swept-up blue spectacle frames, it was hard to get to the truth of her.

On the little finger of her right hand she wore a monogrammed signet ring that had been her father's, and I can remember wondering even then if she regretted that there had been so few men in her childhood. She now displayed a clumsy flirtatiousness with the sex: when she smiled, a dimple formed to the left of her mouth, and I couldn't match it with the prim matter-of-factness of her behaviour with Lady Coniston. In her employer's company she could even be quite sharp, seeming to chide her for letting something slip her mind. The swept-up glasses and the cropped cut of copper hair only played down her femininity, as if – I see it now – as if she was afraid of admitting an aspect of herself she mightn't be able fully to control.

Miss Deegan didn't as a rule join the others, even though she made herself privy to their affairs through Lady Coniston. It would have been presumption, of course, to sit eating or drinking spirits with them, although she might have been useful as a fourth at the tables. But – somehow I sensed it – she was quite in favour of the arrangement; it gave her a perverse satisfaction to accompany Lady Coniston but to sit in one of the other rooms made available to her, sewing or writing letters. When we went to Lady Coniston's country establishment, Weatherhill Lodge, things were a little different, because then Miss Deegan would always be a hovering presence: she wasn't *with* us, certainly, but whenever a door opened she was to be glimpsed attending to some little matter and placed within clear hearing range of us.

She unfailingly made a special point of smiling for my mother, I noticed. She asked her little questions about nothing of any consequence, in her affectedly 'correct' accent. She would turn the questions into smiles at their conclusions. When she stood especially near I could smell rosebud sweets on her breath, that and the slight acid trace of perspiration. Sometimes there would be tiny beads of it above her upper lip, where a shadow like Dame Helena Winthrop's seemed to lie on her skin. When she had a hard light behind her, peach furze softened the sharpness of her front profile, which narrowed to a pointed chin. Now and then she brought her face so close to mine that I could distinguish the pores and follicles. Through the narrow lenses of her spectacles I could even see myself reflected in the cornea of her golden cat's eyes. The orange, waxy lips would pull back in another of those confidential smiles that seemed to ensure intimacy. The dry, purplish back of her tongue would be lying on the floor of her mouth, curled at the tip behind the lower front teeth. It was when she moved in so close to my mother and me, all politeness and affability, that I detected she was being more unrevealing about herself than ever.

FIVE

'That damned clock,' my mother would say, when the hour struck and the cuckoo shot out on its spring. She would wonder aloud if anything could be done. Tape over the mechanism? Stuff a sock inside?

In the last minutes before the hour, and if she remembered, her eyes would fix on the little door above the XII, behind which the cuckoo was mustering its strength for another assault. There was always the possibility in my mind that *this* time it might just happen to forget: or be late: so that I too, when I remembered, sat beneath the clock – at the kitchen table – in a state of gathering, quite pointless excitement, anticipating what might not occur when the long hand jerked upwards at the very end of the fifty-ninth minute.

We were getting ready to depart, and the company's coats were being fetched. The last topic of conversation had been my father and his knowledge of the turf.

'Oh, there's so much I could tell you about Benedict,' Sonja Hellstrom said to my mother, who was standing next to her as she frequently seemed to do. Instantly, at the mention, my mother's eyes shone brighter.

'Please tell me –'

Miss Hellstrom smiled.

'I shall –'

'You must.'

'– oh, I *shall*.'

'What can you tell me?'

'Another time, Decca.'

'Not now?'

'A proper story-teller spins her story out.' The woman raised her eyebrows, as if she were really phrasing a question. 'She knows how to make herself appreciated better.'

My mother glanced down at me before smiling back at Miss Hellstrom.

'Yes,' she said. 'Yes, I quite see. What you mean.'

Miss Hellstrom nodded, still smiling but still with one eyebrow raised, as if her question were only half answered for her.

Leofric Anstey would explain to me what lay under our feet, so to speak. All the layers of history that we didn't see. Elizabethan theatres, medieval bull pits, Saxon sacristies, Roman temples, pagan well-heads, Iron Age foundries, mammoth traps, fossilised forests, volcanic ash, ocean floor.

I also pictured our own age covered by those of the future, ages being created by ourselves. I wondered if just now, the moment of picturing so, could send up little echoes, little waves to the time that was still to come. And if you could pull back the skin of the earth *then* and listen, would the burbling voices you heard be coming from this 'now', or from tomorrow, or yesterday, or last year or last century or some ancient epoch.

The Countess of Charminster, our most elderly companion, suffered from occasional incontinence. When she rose from the card table, sometimes a patch of dampness would be left behind on the seat of her chair. The sofa cushions absorbed more, although the evidence would be clear in the darkening of the velvet pile or the flowered pattern. Nobody thought to mention it to her, and I didn't even hear the subject brought up until my mother let slip a remark to Mrs Curtain.

'I can't think what you mean, m'dear.'

'The countess.' My mother nodded towards the bergère chair. 'You know – her little problem –'

'Oh,' Mrs Curtain said, with a warningly confidential smile. 'Does the countess *have* a problem?'

'Doesn't she?'

The smile stayed resolutely in place, secured by ample folds of flesh.

'But haven't you . . .' Noticed, my mother was intending to ask, without using the verb.

'I don't really think the countess has *problems*, m'dear. Persons in her position don't usually, do they?'

My mother looked flustered by the reply.

'Noblesse oblige, Mrs Kester.'

'Oblige?' my mother repeated after her, sounding a little sceptical.

'That's why it's a long-lived family, you see. They leave the worrying to other people. Us hoi-polloi.'

Mrs Curtain sighed, with an implication of genial envy. The two women of one accord turned and looked towards the countess. Her embroidered and monogrammed evening bag hung from the chair's arm, and she was adjusting the floss of ostrich feathers on the neck of her bodice. Her face in private repose was more eagle-like than ever. She was sitting with her knees placed strategically apart beneath the ankle-length tasselled gown, spangly and disguising where it mattered, on the seat. She lightly grunted, and twitched her lips. As she did so she raised her heavily lidded eyes. In a split second they had seized upon my mother's, since she was the newcomer. My mother coughed into the back of her hand; an untidy, confused spluttering which managed to sound not very ladylike. Bracelets jingling, Mrs Curtain gestured with her sturdy hand to signal recognition, as if she had only just caught sight of their aristocratic companion.

Uncle George continued to bring my mother flowers – unseasonal varieties, arranged by a clever hand and wrapped in paper and ribbons imprinted with the names of expensive florists she recognised. He presented her with corsages, of orchids or gardenias, which she wore for her nights out – not with him (he tended to disappear in the evenings) but with her friends.

Other gifts assured her of his thoughtfulness. A pair of suede gloves that perfectly matched the celadon green colour of an outfit; cakes of a certain soap from Fortnum's she'd once enthused about and which his nostrils had helped him to memorise; a box of pretty silk handkerchiefs patterned very palely with butterflies or their ghosts. She let him see her pleasure, and once she wrote to him about it in a letter, using the thick creamy notepaper from Smythson's which he'd given her and trying out his birthday present to her, the gold fountain pen that was the most beautiful I had ever seen, like a monarch's or president's intended to sign grand and solemn charters.

He cossetted her with little intimations of luxury. As a result she started to lose some of her recent suspiciousness; she came to smile more, she said coy things, and flirted with him. She appeared in this interlude to be happy, and I wanted to be so also, for her sake.

I too became accustomed to the gifts: the wooden box of coloured pencils, a model garage in which to keep my Dinky cars, and at Christmas time, the grandest of all, the Hornby-Dublo model train set. My mother tut-tutted, in a way that she seemed to expect of herself. She only once showed active disapproval, when I unwrapped from its tissue paper a Swiss army-knife. I thought it must be because I wasn't sounding grateful enough, but when I tried again she took the knife from me and returned it to its provider.

'No,' she told him, 'no, this isn't right.'

She meant, I believe, that the choice of gift was wrong, and not the fact of the gift itself. We were both of us too vulnerable and too marked by experience to look into the mouth of a gift horse so generous as this one.

So the Swiss army-knife and its eight folding blades was taken away, with a show of grudgingness from Uncle George as from me, but in its place I was provided with a bamboo box kite of multi-coloured cotton panels and trailing ribbons. My mother could have no objections to that, although my own first reaction was that I should have preferred the knife. But in time and with practice I came to appreciate the pleasures of kite-flying. It was a tougher construction than any of the others we encountered on our expeditions to Hampstead Heath and Alexandra Park. It needed a proper wind, and then it would ride those healthful draughts with astonishing grace for its size and solidity. Envious eyes would be drawn and continue to watch. All down the strings were silk bows, pigtail-fashion and authentically of China, which was where I was told the kite had come from, put together by folk who knew all about these things. The factory-made English specimens were poor, ungainly imitations, thrashing about tetchily and collapsing in pique whenever they dragged on the branches of trees. I learned with Uncle George's help to soar clear of danger, although I felt that the kite must be willing itself at the same time, with its oriental disdain for our small and cramping English perils. It turned in the gusty, watery blue skies of north London like a splendid dice, rolling gold over emerald over scarlet over turquoise. I became much more adept than I'd been – Uncle George said I had a talent for it – and my mother approved, because it took me out of the house and put a healthy shine on my cheeks.

The kite-flying brought us together, literally speaking. Uncle George stood beside me to show me how, enclosing my hands with his. My mother, wearing the Grès silk scarf he had given her, watched the two of us as much as she did the kite and its ladder of silk bows. I didn't feel that he and I were becoming a great deal closer, however, except in this physical sense. Several times he placed a hand on my head, but I guessed from how my mother would look at him that he had to signal first for approval with his eyes. She continued to smile at me in a manner she must have meant to be cajoling, but which seemed to me infected with vagueness, or with some anxiety maybe.

We took our cue when to leave from her: she would start to stamp her feet with the cold, and sometimes she would shiver. Back in the car I noticed there would be hesitations – appraisals – between the things that were being said. After we'd ventured west we started visiting the same curious tea-rooms out at Richmond, housed in a rambling twenties cricket pavilion embellished with mock cross-timbering and lozenge-leaded windows. Inside there were curling rugs on the highly polished floors to trip the unwary and cut pride down to size. At the table Uncle George smoked, and my mother would eventually do the same, and the tea would be cooling forgotten in its pot while only I was left drinking. 'Help yourself, Merlin,' Uncle George would say, offering me the cake-stand while my mother faintly tut-tutted. She knew to be not even tempted by the baking; he took a single slice of Bakewell tart or coffee walnut cake, and I attempted to limit myself to two or three items, including my favourite coconut macaroon. The waitress would mention each time how little we'd eaten as she wrote out the bill, and my mother would smile embarrassedly in the same way and Uncle George would say 'Just too much of a good thing, I'm afraid.'

So it was. And I imagined it would carry on just like that. Even the strictly inexplicable can be constructed into the form of a ritual. I supposed I should become perfectly used to the contrast of bluff wind and fussy warmth on these afternoons, taking change only as it must come to us, slowly and gradually. The waitress's stout shoes clattering across the wooden floors. Our dim reflections in the battered silver plate of the tea service. The trail of steam from the pot of hot water. The murmur of conversation from the other tables, and our long silences. My mother's vigilance with her eyes, speeding round the half-timbered room and into the one beyond; Uncle George's quiet and enigmatic smiles, the litter of cigarette stubs – mostly his – in the ashtray. Visible through the diamond leads in the windows, between the curtains of fading chintz, his brand-new Riley Pathfinder parked apart from the other cars in the gravel yard. The brisk movement of clouds in a restive sky, which means fine weather for raising a kite.

My mother glanced at her watch.

'Yes,' she said. 'Yes, I could come over. If you're alone. When do you –'

She looked across the sitting-room to the windows.

'There's Merlin,' she said. 'But I'll think of something.'

Someone was found to look after me, and my mother left. Later Uncle George rang, asking for her, so I knew it wasn't him she had arranged to see. My minder had been long gone by the time she got back, just before morning. I heard her key in the lock. I got out of bed and tiptoed across to the door. I opened it.

My mother had switched on the lamp on the hall table and was standing in front of the mirror, staring very hard at herself. She pulled off her coat and dropped it on to the chair. She stepped out of her shoes, looked down, and seemed to remember. From her handbag she removed her stockings, one and then the other, and placed them on top of the coat.

She went through to the bathroom and ran a bath. I heard her take the scrubbing brush to herself, and turn on the shower attachment for several rinses of the shampoo.

She was in the bathroom for three-quarters of an hour altogether.

I heard her come out. The next sounds reached me from the sitting-room. A bottle, a glass.

The Sun on the Wall

In the morning I found her lying asleep on the sofa, where she'd fallen back in her towelling robe on the cushions. An unfinished glass of whisky had been placed on the floor, on the parquet beside the rug. Her face as she slept wasn't quite expressionless: her mouth had taken on a slight twist, and there were two deep creases on her brow, over the bridge of her nose. Her breasts rose in the deep 'V' where the sides of the bathrobe had eased apart. One arm was laid across her abdomen, as if in her dream life she had an instinct she must protect herself.

'Would you act again?' Uncle George was asking, supposing I was asleep in the back of the car.

My mother shook her head, watching the traffic on the road ahead of us.

'Why not?'

'I couldn't get back into it,' she said. 'For one thing.'

'And for another?'

'Oh...' She brought up her arm and placed her elbow on the door sill. She pulled loosely at her hair. '... it's a pretty stupid sort of job to have.'

'Is it?'

'For a grown-up person, yes.'

'Why?'

'It's just putting off real life. Real living.'

'Everything's real,' he said. 'In different ways.'

She sighed into the back of her hand before she spoke again.

'If I hadn't done the parts, someone else would. Filled my shoes. It doesn't take enough skill for people to notice.'

'But they employed you. *You.*'

'It was my moment.'

'There you are, then.'

'But it was just an accident.'

'It meant as little to you as that?'

She sighed again, into her sleeve. With her elbow still raised, she placed her hand on the back of her neck. Then she must have remembered me, and half turned round to look into the back.

I pretended I was still asleep. When I heard the creaking of leather on her seat as she straightened herself I opened my eyes again, just a little, to slits. Staring right back at me, reflected in the driving mirror, were Uncle George's green eyes, distrustful but – because I immediately closed mine shut again – exonerated.

Even when she was alone with me in the flat, my mother would sometimes walk into a room projecting the mannerisms of an actress. She would pause, as if to establish herself, looking about her to pick up her cue from this chair or that lamp. In company her playing could be just as pronounced. Quite often I caught a blankness in her face which might have been a panic that she wouldn't remember what to do or say. When she stood like that, holding the pose of one of those mannequins who paraded through department store restaurants in that era, what she was doing as well as affirming her elegance was delaying: calculating an effect, considering her options. Someone would then speak to her and she would start slightly, from relief possibly, and also because it was her own spry trade mark, to make herself *appear* spontaneous and youthful and just a little naïve. I don't know how many truly believed in that air of charming, quirky innocuousness, but I can't doubt they found it very attractive – a *divertissement* – to watch.

From one of the sitting-room windows I observe my mother's departure from the building. She is wearing a new musquash jacket and court shoes, and a pert little hat with a veil, as if she is doing no more than going out to have lunch with one of her friends.

But today there is no car waiting outside at the kerb to collect her, no taxi either with its engine rattling and passenger door ajar. My mother walks off briskly but somehow too concentratedly stepping along a very exact line on the roadway from one pavement to the other and looking to neither left nor right. An older man whom she passes turns his head and looks back at her, studying how craftily and precisely she picks her way along the pavement, stepping around any flagstones which might catch her heels and unbalance her.

At the corner, another busier road intersects with ours. Cars and buses flow past. She stops. She is looking about her. When the few other pedestrians take advantage of a break in the traffic to cross, she remains where she is. She tips back her cuff and consults her watch. She adjusts the hat perched on her head and resettles the veil. She stands there for maybe only a minute altogether, but it seems a much longer interval of time. At last she raises a hand; a wave of recognition to someone, a woman: I can't see whose face behind the upturned collar of her fur coat, a scalloped ankle-length fur coat. My mother steps purposefully out into the road, crosses one lane of traffic, and waits on the island until it's quite safe to proceed to the opposite pavement. As she reaches the kerb, she skip-steps up on to the level. She is suddenly transformed: she is lighter-looking and younger on that other side of Peebles Road, and it is for that I shall have to work so hard in the future to forgive her.

My mother, expertly trained at it by now, 'played' the telephone.

I would be reminded of someone performing on a violin as she stood with the receiver resting on her shoulder and her fingers flicking through her engagements diary. She knew exactly how to project her voice into the mouthpiece, how to modulate it for every inflexion she required to make, how to move in and out of the mouthpiece, how to stage-manage supposed distractions which allowed her a vital second or two's thinking time, how to be forceful or non-committal or girlish or even erotic, how to listen and how to suggest and how to remain mute at the strategic moment.

She could seem to give all of herself or equally to volunteer almost nothing.

I was fascinated to watch and listen. It was theatre, and afterwards she could be left quite drained or, alternatively, high on adrenalin and without an outlet for her zest.

'I don't know how you're going to fit it all in,' Uncle George whispered. 'As the bishop told the actress.'

My mother brought her lips together in a disapproving way. She shot a sideways glance across the sitting-room at me, and my noticing and not attending to my jigsaw seemed to be a further irritation to her.

'Well, that's about the size of it. Ditto. What do you say?'

'Ssshh!' she hissed back at him.

'Kitten—'

'Don't call me that. I've told you before.'

Uncle George nodded, and now it was his turn to take a furtive oblique glance at her.

My mother, doubtless aware, dropped her eyes to her glass and sighed.

'What, wrong time of the month for jokes, is it? You should warn me about that kind of thing.'

The fact that he had to enquire surprises me now, when I acknowledge the implication. I might have supposed them to be closer. When we sat in the John of Gaunt tea-rooms, my mother might have been passing herself off as another wife, placid but a little bored. Love, or the memory of love, ought to have excited more brio than she was in the habit of showing to Uncle George. He was quite a good-looking man, but in the end he may have exhibited too little true *gentillesse* and tact for my mother. She must have had her physical wants, of course, but she also had standards and ambitions. After Benedict Matzell, George Metcalf was never a plausible contender for her affections.

My mother was congratulating Lady Coniston on the pheasant, asking for her compliments to be passed on to the cook.

'It's Miss Deegan you should thank.'

'Not Mrs Holt?'

'Her father's ill, she had to go off yesterday, left us in the lurch pretty much. Thought I'd have to call it off, but Miss Deegan—bless her—set to. Found her in a cloud of feathers slitting the things open as if she'd done it all her life. Took the shot out clean, gutted the things, amazing.'

Lady Coniston laughed.

'All in the line of duty, I expect,' my mother said.

'Oh yes, she'd run the whole ship if she could. But there's –'

Lady Coniston stopped. I looked over, in the direction taken by her eyes. There was Miss Deegan in customary cardigan, checking the levels in the bottles and decanters on the sideboard. Whatever Lady Coniston was going to add, she didn't add. Miss Deegan picked up a bottle to scrutinise its label, apparently attending only to that. Very probably her knowledge of wine would have surprised us all too. So my mother's expression seemed to say; she didn't speak any such thought aloud, though, as if she had a premonition that the woman's hearing might be super-efficient also.

We were in the Riley one Saturday afternoon. Uncle George was talking. My mother idly picked up the mention of something, a somewhere.

'Wodeham Place?' she asked him. 'Where's that?'

'I was reading about it.'

She shook her head. 'I was thinking of Cookham Place.'

'Not Wodeham?'

Silence.

'Should I know,' my mother asked, 'about it?'

'I just came across the name. In an article. It said it was requisitioned during the war. A lot of country houses were.'

Silence.

'Taken over?'

'Oh . . .' Uncle George made an attempt to remember: or else, was letting us see that he was trying to recall what he'd read.

'Counter-intelligence work, I think. Domestic intelligence. You know?'

'Oh.'

Silence.

'I thought you meant for evacuation. A school maybe.'

'Much more hush-hush than that.'

'Oh,' my mother said, incuriously.

When we got out to fly my kite she was saying even less than she usually did. Her thoughts seemed to have carried her further away, not to Wodeham but to another of those houses in her litany of them, Cookham. Her thoughts were carrying her further than the distances spread beneath Richmond, further than the eye could see, to where neither Uncle George nor I could conceivably follow her.

SIX

When my mother came home one afternoon, I noticed she was wearing a different perfume. I recognised it at once. It was the same one Miss Hellstrom wore. I was certain, because it was quite distinctive: a thick sickly aroma of roses which would stick in the back of my throat whenever the aviatrix came too close.

My mother had applied it more discreetly, on her wrists perhaps, but it was the identical perfume. Again I felt it starting to put me off-balance, a queasy sensation in the pit of my stomach. Even a very little of the stuff made drifts in the air after she'd passed through, and suddenly the flat wasn't so intimately ours any more.

It was only now that I realised – realised properly for the first time – that nothing was actually ours. We were tenants, moving in to these furnished quarters without explanation, owning none of this. The unnerving perfume seemed to be colonising the place more distinctively than we could do with our quiet comings-and-goings and our reticences when we were together, my mother and I, only ourselves.

I saw in the crystal clarity of a terrifying few seconds just how shiftless we were, and shifting, how helplessly mobile.

Then, slowly, I came back to my senses. That other vision dimmed. I caught my breath and also the tempo of my thoughts. Even so, though, I was left with a sensation of floating, of haphazard drift, somehow crucially at the centre of myself.

I would still hear them discussing our friends, Uncle George and my mother.

Apparently he had met the Rathbone brothers; a friend of his had once taken him to Weatherhill Lodge, and someone else he knew knew the countess. My mother had asked him why he didn't do something about joining them himself if he was so fascinated. But I think she also understood that he hadn't the nerve, and not the Matzell connection, and that she could tantalise him with her snippets of gossip by disclosing as much or as little as she chose to.

Sometimes she was amazed he was so earnest about it. At other times she became wearied or impatient with the questioning. Her coyness with him had only been temporary, and now she had reverted to indifference. I guessed that there were occasions when he wanted to stay on, overnight, but she was sharp with him about that. I heard her telling him once that it wasn't allowed, it wasn't among the terms of her 'lease', and she laughed not very warmly; she told him, anyway what about Merlin, and when he said that he doubted if I'd either notice or mind she replied that I was a bit too observant for my own good. That must have given him something else to think about when he'd gone, but when he got round to the matter again – the next time – all my mother said (between diplomatic smiles) was that the arrangement was fine as it stood, thank you kindly.

Miss Hellstrom always seemed to know more about us than anyone else did. She knew about the little things, the most domestic: how many others lived on our floor of the building, the trouble we were having with the hot-water tank, the mysterious bubbling noises the radiators made, the model and date of manufacture of our refrigerator, the confusing manner in which the bathroom door could be locked from both inside and out, even the silly business of the cuckoo clock – and its sillier conclusion when my mother poured hot custard into its workings and silenced the beastly Kuckuck for good.

I thought Miss Hellstrom must have a very retentive memory, to recall so much of what my mother – presumably – must have told her. I didn't understand how my mother had the time to tell her these things, because she was obliged to mix with all the others too. I would watch the quondam great aviatrix watching my mother when she was occupied somewhere else in a room, and I'd wonder if her hearing was for some reason more acute than anyone else's, even Miss Deegan's. Her smiles for my mother were compassionate, excusing; my mother would respond with toned-down smiles of her own, but only after taking a fast check of the activities of the other eyes in the room first.

My mother woke late one morning. When I went through to her room she was still asleep.

Spread out on the quilt were her newspaper clippings. She must have been reading them before she lost consciousness. Some had fallen on to the floor; I picked them up.

They were reviews and articles, all referring to Benedict Matzell, my father, and the films he'd made. There were several fly-on-the-wall shots of him in the studio or out on location, as well as publicity stills from the chocolate box.

I peered at the photographs, until I heard my mother stir. She seemed to sense a shadow falling across her, and she had started to smile before she opened her eyes. When she saw it was me waiting beside the bed, her eyes reacted in advance of her mouth, showing a degree of puzzlement, even pain, which I couldn't connect with the ordinariness of her saying 'goodnight' to me only the round of the clock ago.

I happened to be standing at the window one day when a car, a swanky white American one, dropped off my mother in the road. I knew that Miss Hellstrom drove a Chrysler. When my mother came in she explained to my minder that she'd been shopping and had taken the Underground back. Which was why she was late, with the walk from the station. And what not.

She smiled at me as she breezed past. There were no constraining blushes at the lie: she was being a consummate actress, I realise now, even in her uncommonly well-provided-for retirement.

I smelt that fragrance again, the pungency of those blowsy over-ripe roses.

'I can't see it,' Lady Coniston remarked one day, fixing on me.
'Can't see what?' Miss Deegan asked her, a little testily.
'The resemblance.'
Miss Deegan allowed her impatience to show. '*Which* resemblance?'
'To Benedict.'
Miss Deegan's eyes widened and she looked between Lady Coniston and my mother.
'Well, damned if *I* can see it.'
Miss Deegan lowered her voice to snap back at her. 'Of *course* there's a resemblance. It's clear as day.'
'Can't see –'
'You've said that already.'
'I don't know what everybody –'
'Frankly,' Miss Deegan cut in, 'I don't know what you're talking about.'
My mother seemed shocked by her curtness.
'We can see the resemblance,' Miss Deegan persisted, 'because there *is* a resemblance. I can't think what you're going on –'
'I remember him better than you, though.'
'Well, no better than the others. And *they* remember.'
'Benedict and I –'

I've Been Here Before

'You forget a hell of a lot, may I remind you.'

Miss Deegan's face was reddening with her irritation. My mother put an arm around my shoulder, as if meaning to draw me away from this undignified exchange.

'Forget what?' Lady Coniston asked.

'So much. What things used to be like.'

'I remember Benedict.'

'Just now you do,' Miss Deegan replied. 'Or you think you do. You remember his name.'

The telephone interrupted us. Miss Deegan went off to answer. Moments later she reappeared in the doorway, summoning Lady Coniston to the adjoining room.

When our hostess had gone, her secretary smiled her widest smile; her top lip hooked on to both top incisors.

'I do apologise.' Somewhere not too far away, very probably the suburban sprawl of Essex, was calling blithely through the contrived neutrality of her accent. 'She – she's wandering again. Disrespectful as it is for me to say so.'

'I quite understand –' my mother began.

'I don't think you can.' Miss Deegan placed a slim but sinewy hand on my mother's arm. My mother smiled awkwardly. 'She's getting worse, I'm sure. She says things, and I prefer to think she doesn't mean them. It's just silliness. She can't see it for what it is. How children open their mouths and say –'

She smiled down at me. It was a smile at half the wattage of the other, because I was only a child, even with the father that I had.

'She gets confused, you see. She can't make connections. Between then and now. It's sad, of course, but I have to be practical.'

My mother nodded.

'Oh yes,' Miss Deegan said again, banishing Essex at last and turning the ring on her little finger, the distinctive gent's signet ring. 'I have to be practical.'

The repetition of the words was jarring.

'Your son is the image. Everyone says so. It's important too.'

'I'm sorry,' my mother said in the silence, sounding curious. '"Important"?'

'Mr Matzell was the mainstay. Of the set. The Weatherhill set. You see, we call it that, and yet Lady Coniston . . .'

She let her voice trail away, as if words wouldn't express her meaning. But behind her scrolled blue spectacle frames she was being fully attentive; viewing them from beneath, I watched how closely her eyes were staring at my mother for a reaction, without blinking. My mother was embarrassed, and stood passing her own eyes over the fine objects in the room: almost as if she were trying to memorise them, as if – who was to know? – this might be our last opportunity.

It wasn't, however, because Lady Coniston forgot the occasion: or rather, she must have been made to realise from Miss Deegan's admonishments that she had been indiscreet, and vaguely apologised to my mother on another occasion for a social misdemeanour she had no recollection of committing.

My mother shook her head, put out again. She was only too ready to forgive.

Miss Deegan looked on, all the while twisting her father's signet ring on her little finger. Her toothy, dimpled smile was timed for the moment when my mother, after a slow turn of the head, glanced past Lady Coniston's shoulder in her direction.

It was like the Pope's signing of the cross. The harmonies were restored.

My mother would ask me sometimes, 'Are you happy, Merlin?', saying it quickly and with her voice light, as if the question was of no real significance. She always waited for me to answer, though, and left me to muddle about with the words. I meant to tell her 'yes', and I thought it was the answer she was counting on hearing from me. She pretended to be convinced, and nodded her head, but she was careful not to look at me just then, in case she saw a doubt betrayed on my face.

I think I guessed for myself what I know now, that happiness is unquantifiable: if you are happy you're too swept up in the feeling to be objective about it, and if you have been happy you only realise so afterwards, when the circumstances aren't the same ones that helped to bring that amount of pleasure about.

If I'd hummed and hawed more than I did, I shouldn't have been lying to her, but I must have thought she would suppose so. Lies, I somehow intuited, were the currency of so much human exchange.

For a while my mother was the only woman with whom Leofric Anstey, ladykiller of no little repute, didn't play the flirt. To her it was probably an omen of his true intentions.

Later I came across the two of them in a corridor – at Hugo Rathbone's converted oast-houses in Kent, I think it was. My mother was pulling her wrist out of the grip of his hand, and he was making an absurd show of consternation.

'It's too complicated like this,' my mother was saying.

I've Been Here Before

More display of astonishment, more huffing and puffing. For some reason my mother was invulnerable to his charm, and he couldn't understand why. She wasn't directly dependent on him for anything, however, and that – if he could have realised – was her incontestable advantage.

She was trying to let him down gently, to cool his earnestness.

'It's too much, Mr Anstey. Much too much –'

Sometimes I would wake up in bed and hear my mother walking through the house. Even when she wasn't wearing shoes I heard her, from the shifting pressure on the floorboards. Whenever I woke up, the silence had an intensity it hadn't had earlier. It might have been two or three o'clock, and I knew that in the morning my mother would deny that she had been up and about at all.

She would open the curtains and steer herself about the rooms by the light from the streetlamps outside, with some help from the moon when it obliged. I listened for more sounds, aware that I'd had a reason for waking. A chair might be moved, feet scraping on the floor. Or an ornament lifted up and set down in a different place. A newspaper shaken out. A magazine dropped on top of others. The kettle didn't boil, and the tops stayed on the drinks bottles, because my mother wanted to sleep, even though she couldn't. But being up, even in the darkened rooms, was preferable to suffering the spectres that prey on insomniacs in the horizontal position.

Keeping vertical, she could maintain the illusion that she was participating – cognisantly – in her own destiny.

A moving shadow on the earth. In my dreams Sonja Hellstrom takes again to oriental skies. A white silk scarf flutters behind her, the sun dazzles in the glass eyepieces of her goggles. Merchants on camels point to the progress above them, as do sailors on dhows. Beneath her, sand dunes drift and porpoises leap.

Once, it seemed to me, I opened my eyes in the middle of the night and there she was in our home, in the flat. Not wearing goggles but a figure in a long luxurious fur coat, with a white silk scarf swathed round her head. She and my mother were tiptoeing from the room, talking in whispers. In the hall Miss Hellstrom took my mother's hand in hers, her other arm passed across my mother's shoulders. The whispers became the rustling of leaves in a forest, and overhead the bi-plane skimmed the branches of the tallest trees, while two suns dazzled in the glass of the goggles and a white silk scarf like a pennant fluttered behind.

Miss Deegan was talking to my mother on the front steps of Weatherhill

Lodge as we were all taking our leave. I hung over the old mossy balustrade, forgetting my manners but just relieved to be out of doors again.

'Working for Lady Coniston is my whole life.'

'Ah,' my mother replied, at my back.

'I don't think there's anything I wouldn't do for her, Mrs Kester.'

My mother started to descend the steps.

'That,' she said, 'that is – great dedication.'

'*Is* it?' Miss Deegan put a spin into her delivery.

'Yes, certainly,' my mother replied in her steadier vowels.

'But what else might she expect of me? After eight years?'

'That long?'

It might not have been the reply Miss Deegan was anticipating; or perhaps she misheard the tone of my mother's voice.

'But it seems no time at all.'

'Her ladyship,' my mother said, 'is very fortunate.'

'I do understand so much about her. It's just like telepathy, Mrs Kester. I know exactly how her mind works.'

'Ah.'

'And what is most suitable. For her *peace* of mind. So that she shouldn't be disturbed. Or taken advantage of.'

'Merlin!' my mother called back at me.

When I pulled myself upright and turned round, Miss Deegan – but a second or two too late – remembered to direct a smile at me. Her top lip pulled back over one incisor. The orange lipstick always seemed to have been freshly applied, no more than minutes before. Or perhaps she simply took greater note of her appearance when my mother was around.

We were being driven back to town. My mother tapped my shoulder, indicating that I should get into the car first.

'This,' I heard her tell Miss Deegan, 'has been most pleasant.'

'Lady Perdita will be gratified to hear that.'

'I *have* thanked her. But if you'd care to –'

'Of course, Mrs Kester. That is my job.'

From the back seat I watched Miss Deegan's smile fade to half its original brightness as my mother approached the car. She took off her spectacle frames to wipe something from the lenses, and in those few seconds I saw her eyes with adequate long-sight travelling from my mother's hips to her feet and back again. When we were ready and the car started to move off, on the tail of the one in front, my mother leaned forward and unnecessarily straightened the mat at her feet, which was quite straight enough. But stooping meant that her eyes were averted from Miss Deegan and the inevitable wave of the hand which was the final element in the ritual.

I've Been Here Before

Some moments later my mother dropped back into the seat. I turned and looked out the rear window. The two women, Lady Coniston in gaucho poncho and her secretary in spinsterish woollens and tweeds, stood on the steps watching our departure. While Miss Deegan fussed with her crop of copper hair, her other hand reached out and attached itself to the upper arm of her employer. Lady Coniston turned round and began to climb the steps; she seemed to be going to look back again, but the hand insisted, and with no more delay she was directed towards the doorway under the firm, determined guidance of her putative subordinate.

SEVEN

'Do you never get confused?' Lady Coniston asked my mother. 'With your names?'

'My names?' my mother repeated.

'The name you use. And your real name.'

'Kester? Or Blane?'

'Pickering.'

My mother's eyes fixed.

'How – how did you know that?'

Miss Deegan appeared from nowhere.

'Benedict Matzell must have told you, Lady Coniston. Didn't he?'

Her employer seemed confused.

'Of course,' Miss Deegan said. 'he would tell us about his work –'

My mother seemed just as confused as her ladyship. Many years later I was to be informed, reliably, that Matzell had always introduced her as 'Decca Blane', and that even his closest friends were under the impression that that was the only name she'd ever had.

Miss Deegan was zealously pummelling scatter cushions with her fists. My mother had forgotten the cigarette in her mouth, and started to cough; she removed the cigarette and paddled at the smoke with her hand. Lady Coniston was looking suddenly very absent-minded.

It was only a momentary occurrence, and one not witnessed by the others in the house, but it was quite sufficient to sow some essential seed of doubt in my mother's mind: not surely about Benedict Matzell, but about her hostess.

A car's side-lights passing behind trees. They're reflected in puddles, or in the bodywork and chrome of other cars.

Something about the steady, deliberate speed must have disturbed me. I realised that a pair of side-lights had accompanied our arrival or departure on other nights. The car appeared to be gliding: such an easy passage along the stately streets and crescents that comprised our social geography.

In the afternoons I couldn't be so sure. One car's movements were difficult to distinguish from the general flow of traffic. I didn't know what I was searching for. My mother noticed me looking, and asked me what the matter was. I couldn't give her an answer; she put a hand on top of my head and, amiably and without over-emphasising the point, she turned me round to face forwards.

The feeling didn't leave me, though. And the side-lights were there the next time we left Hugo Rathbone's residence after a protracted afternoon tea, with dusk slowly coming down. They glimmered behind the plane trees on that serpentining Kensington avenue, at walking pace as the car trailed our progress along the pavement. My mother glanced back; perhaps she had a presentiment herself this time, because she didn't ask me what was interesting me so much. She took my hand. I was grateful to have it held inside hers, imagining that now I must be protected and safe.

My mother sat balancing the ashtray on her knees. She waited until Uncle George had turned the last page of the newspaper before asking.

'What do you know about this Deegan woman?'

'Me? Nothing.'

My mother started at the suddenness of his reply. She sat inhaling on her cigarette. A little cloudlet took shape in front of her face, then dispersed.

'*Should* I know?' Uncle George asked her back, folding the newspaper and leaning back in the chair with the semblance of ease.

'You know so much else,' my mother said.

'Enough.'

'I thought you might know about her too.'

'Doesn't follow.'

'No? You told me your friend was quite a chum of theirs.'

'Of Lady Coniston.'

'They're very close. She and Miss Deegan.'

'Decca, she's just a damn secretary.'

'Is she?'

Uncle George laughed, in a rather forced way.

'Well, isn't she?' he said.

'She always seems to be about, I've noticed.'

'So . . . ?'

'And sort of watches over us.'

'She takes her duties seriously, I expect.'

'I don't know.'

My mother inhaled again. While she glanced down I saw Uncle George's eyes narrow as he studied her. Everything my mother had said was registering with him.

'Does it matter?' he asked.

'Probably not,' my mother said.

'Does she bother you?'

My mother shrugged.

'Then forget her.'

She smiled at him, but in a loose and disengaged way.

'You ought to, Decca.'

My mother looked over to where I was sitting on the floor, with an edition of the *Children's Newspaper* spread out in front of me. It was too advanced for me, but she bought a copy whenever she felt guilty that she was neglecting me, and I didn't tell her that I should have preferred a comic.

We met Leofric Anstey in Knightsbridge. He hadn't been in evidence for several weeks. My mother blushed when she caught sight of him. He was signing an autograph for someone, but called out to my mother to please stop.

He was his usual charming self. He lifted his hat, patted my head, and told us only that he'd been in London all this time, that he'd had a difference of opinion with one of our number who should remain nameless.

'Will you be coming back?' my mother asked him. 'To join us?'

'Should I take that for an invitation?'

My mother blushed again, more deeply than before.

'Rest assured, Mrs Kester. I am standing on a principle here, although' – he tried to make a joke of the matter – 'although it may look to you like a street corner.'

My mother responded with a circumspect smile.

'No differences of opinion in Matzell's day, Mrs Kester. Did you know he was going to do a short film about me? It was all planned. Terrible tragedy, the car smashing up. Things have never been the same since.'

He may or may not have realised that that was the surest way to break my mother's reserve. They spoke for a while about my father, standing at the intersection of those two busy, noisy streets.

'Why not the same?' my mother asked, raising her voice a little against the traffic.

'He saw what we might be capable of. Each of us. As figureheads in our areas. You know? I think – I think he respected us.'

'But – but why shouldn't he?'

'Words of poison in the ear.'

'I'm sorry?'

'With a gentleman – with the likes of Matzell – you know where you are, Mrs Kester. When you are of the same mind, I hardly need add – as we were.'

They both nodded. Then they each turned and looked at me. At that moment, and standing between them at the crux of Brompton Road and Knightsbridge, I could imagine – absurdly, of course, but genuinely – that I was positioned, oh, at the midpoint of everything, of everything important, at the very least at the heart of an empire.

'Do help yourself, Mrs Kester.'

Miss Deegan appeared – again – from nowhere. She was holding a salver of petit-fours and chocolates.

'Thank you,' my mother said.

'I can recommend the chocolates. They're quite excellent.'

My mother's hand hovered over the selection. Her eyes must have been attracted by the brightest foil, the gold, pleated to hold the chocolate.

'A very wise choice,' Miss Deegan said.

'Oh, good.'

'They're from La Maison.'

'Ah.'

'Do you like crême oranges?' Miss Deegan asked, with a clumsy French accenting.

My mother smiled. 'Very much.'

'They're your favourite?'

'I...' My mother nodded, approximately, and smiled. A self-conscious smile.

'I shall leave you to enjoy it.'

I was invited to pick also, but my favourite sort was not enquired after. The salver was placed at an awkward height in front of me, and I sensed that Miss Deegan had better things to do than indulge *me*. I made a grab for a chocolate with a sliver of hazelnut on top, and she said nothing. The salver was whisked away on a strong wiry wrist, high over my head, and with one of her special four-inch-wide smiles for my mother the woman was gone.

Perhaps, I thought, she hadn't liked to be carrying round the salver, like a glorified maid. She got rid of it soon enough, but maybe only so that she could concentrate better on keeping my mother in her sights.

The shop, La Maison du Chocolat, is no longer there. The building still stands, but an insurance company occupies most of it; and where the shop once was, a foyer and reception area gaudily overwhelm with pink terrazzo and gilt fittings.

The Sun on the Wall

There was marble in the shop: white marble counters and shelves to provide cool and tempting surfaces for setting out the chocolates. The wood panelling on the walls and the underside of the counters was as dark as the plainest, bittersweet *amer chocolat*. A few chairs with narrow bamboo and cane frames and scarlet velvet cushions were distributed about the shop for the relief of customers. Raked mirrors above the height of the tallest shelves made the shop appear busier than it was: the *chocolatier* did very good business, but discreetly so by way of the order book, and the serving staff were never in so great a hurry that they forgot their reputation for imperturbability and courtesy.

The chocolates were mostly of the shop's own manufacture. The business may have had a French name, but the owner was a native Briton. He had learned his trade in Vienna, under the tutelage of two brothers called Adalbert who operated cafés in the Graben and on Budapest's Kossuth Lajos and on the rue Royale in Paris. In Harkiss's Mayfair establishment a famous range of chocolates was available, including *bûches* (filled with green almond paste), *rochers* (filled with toasted almonds), blackcurrant or raspberry or cognac slabs, exemplary noisettes and pralines, and luxurious candied chestnuts dipped in *mi-amer*. Customers returned with the regularity of addicts. London-domiciled Austrians, Germans and Hungarians were faithful patrons. Vans with a spruce livery of silver lettering on a royal blue ground delivered to the most select addresses in the metropolis. Harkiss still oversaw production in the small factory and packaging rooms, and kept several steps ahead of the competition by avidly following up developments in manufacture he happened to hear about via the Adalbert connection. As a reward for his industry he drove a two-tone royal blue and silver Bentley which was replaced every year – a 'mint' model, so to speak – and commuted between work and a small maisonette in Halkin Street and an Elizabethan manor-house just south of Haywards Heath.

Up on the cinema screen a cup of coffee is steaming on a table top. The camera shifts. A woman sits staring out through the window of the workaday café. The window is covered with rain runs.

At a noise from the kitchen the woman is distracted, she turns from the window and lowers her eyes to the table in front of her. She reaches forward for the handle of the cup, already crooking her index finger. As she touches the handle with the pad of her finger a man's voice speaks a warning at her shoulder.

'I shouldn't, if I were you.'

She looks up. The man is walking smartly away. She opens her mouth, as if she means to call out to him, but he is already at the door. He pulls the door open, and the sounds of the street tumble into the room – tyres hissing on the wet tarmacadam and splashing through puddles, a car's horn, a newsvendor's cry – so that he couldn't possibly hear her anyway.

She stares at the cup. She removes her finger from the handle, uncurls it. Her hand straightens. She lays it on the table top. She sits staring at the cup for a long time, at the surface of cooling coffee, until the scene fades out.

My mother left the kitchen and immediately let out a little scream.

I followed the tracks of her eyes, to the front door. A figure was standing behind the panel of frosted glass. A silhouette, a black outline against the time-switch light on the staircase.

We both stared at it. Then the bell rang, and each of us jumped, nearly out of our skins. The finger remained on the button, for three or four seconds, and the ringing shuddered all through the flat, seemed to be pulsing through the floor.

'Answer it,' my mother said, 'will you?'

She pushed me forward. I heard her take a step or two back, towards the door of the sitting-room. I walked slowly down the hall. I clutched the cold brass door knob in one hand and undid the snib with the other. I opened the door with the chain still in place. I looked through the crack.

A delivery man was holding out a parcel. I removed the chain, to be able to open the door. I took the box from the man. It was round and flat, wrapped in shiny royal blue paper tied with silver ribbon. I stared at it.

'Ask him where he comes from,' my mother was saying. I turned to look at her, over my shoulder. 'Ask him who sent him –'

When I turned back to the door, however, the delivery man had gone. I saw his head between the banister rails as he made a quick departure down the staircase. I opened the door and stepped out on to the landing.

'Excuse me,' I called after him. 'Excuse me –'

Even if he heard me, he didn't stop. I listened to the sound of his footsteps on the tiled front steps.

'Never mind,' my mother said. She held the door open for me, then closed and snibbed it and replaced the chain. She took the parcel and turned it over. She returned with it to the sitting-room. She untied the ribbon and started to unwrap the sheet of royal blue paper.

The round white cardboard box with fluted sides carried the signature of La Maison du Chocolat. My mother removed the lid. Inside was a luxurious array of dark plain chocolates arranged in alternating gold and silver foil pleated boats.

Her eyes stared at them, then at the name on the lid. She lifted the box and looked beneath it. She took out a chocolate and examined its base and the dainty container of foil.

'He didn't hand you a card with this?'

I told her, no.

She asked me to describe his uniform. Just navy or black clothes and a cap with a peak, I replied. I hadn't thought to look more carefully, and anyway he had been standing with the electric light fully behind him.

'It was a strange time to deliver it,' my mother said. 'In the evening.'

'Are they from Uncle George?' I asked her.

She shrugged, probably because she thought they couldn't be.

She placed the box on top of the sideboard, with its lid on, and from where she went to sit she turned her eyes every so often to look at it and to consider. Her brow corrugated into folds of concentration. She lit a cigarette, and wreathed herself in the familiar blue smoke of thought.

We had one chocolate apiece after supper. I took a triangular noisette, and my mother chose – not an orange crème – but a slim oval with crossed lozenges of lavender sugar on top.

I was able to tell a good chocolate from an indifferent, and this was definitely a superior sort. There was a bitter nippiness to the taste which intrigued me.

My mother had seemed restless since the delivery man had come to the door and rung the bell so shrilly. She couldn't settle, but these days that wasn't so exceptional. She got up and down, opened one magazine and then another without reading more than a few lines on any page, riffling quickly through the pages of photographs. Now and then she would meander, by way of the surfaces of the room, towards the white telephone, as if she was expecting it to ring. I waited in uncomfortable anticipation that it would, and so I couldn't really settle either, being unmethodical in putting together my Airfix kit of a Wellington bomber because I'd skipped the parts of the instructions I ought to have read.

I wasn't offered another chocolate.

I watched my mother's eyes pass from myself to her magazine, and between the magazine and the telephone and the box of chocolates replaced on the sideboard. Me. The telephone. The magazine. The box of chocolates. The magazine. Me again. The box of chocolates. The telephone.

Up on the cinema screen a shot rings out in the night.

Then a second.

A shape, a human form, slumps down on the greasy cobbles of the street.

A window is raised, a man's voice calls out.

Blood trails trickle into the grooves between the stones. The camera follows their graceful progress. The scarlet ribbons reach a pool of gaslight, where the camera stops, fixing on the pale object that dams the movement of blood. It's a woman's pearl-handled revolver, gleaming with a sinister beauty.

A couple of days after the delivery I found a box of chocolates just like ours crammed into a dustbin in the lane behind the block of flats.

Only two of the chocolates had been eaten. Then I realised it *was* our box. It must have been stolen... But why then had the culprit not wolfed down any more of the chocolates?

Back in the flat I kept trying to think of a way to ask about what had happened. At school we were taught to be passive, under the guise of extreme courtesy, never presuming but always waiting to be spoken to. I was already taking my expensive lessons to heart, although not infallibly.

Could it have been Mrs Turpin's doing? Or was my mother more likely to think that it had been mine? Already a little hard crust of complications was forming on the situation.

We were sitting in the John of Gaunt. It had become our regular stopping-off place on Saturday afternoons. Uncle George would have taken my mother for a walk by the plantations, while I was left quite happily flying my kite. Windblown usually, we would retire to the tea-rooms to be revived.

We were sitting there one otherwise unexceptional Saturday afternoon. My mother had gone off to the Powder Room, so I was alone with Uncle George. I was telling him about something or other. When he didn't reply and I looked up, I saw he was staring ahead. Staring, with his lips pressed tightly together and his fingers picking the petals from the yellow aster in the posy dish.

Three or four tables away a woman sat by herself. She was chic and collected: maybe ten years older than my mother, she was dressed down to a younger woman's look, a studied form of casual wear. Green-spotted white chiffon blouse, soft white jumper draped around her shoulders and sleeves tied in front, blue jeans. She was holding her teacup in both hands, elbows up on the table, but she wasn't drinking. Instead she was looking straight back at Uncle George, staring at him without blinking. Most particularly at him.

Those several seconds seemed to be lasting very much longer. Time was pulled long like elastic. Everything meanwhile turned on that stare being exchanged between the two of them.

There were only seconds in it, though. Then the thing was over and done with. Uncle George coughed into the back of his hand. The woman turned her eyes away. I watched her cradling the cup in her hands. She had a sharp face, with a thin nose and a pointed chin. She smiled to a passing waitress, smiled insincerely, and an inappropriate dimple appeared between her mouth and her cheek.

Uncle George had difficulty brightening when my mother returned. Today she was looking for an excuse to hold back from him, and she found it now quite easily. Outside, on the way to the car he started to whistle, tunelessly. My mother kicked at a gravel chip on the brick path, and it went rattling along in front of us like a reproach.

Lady Coniston was a devotee of Scrabble, and playing was an obligation. At some point in the proceedings three or four tables would be set up in the drawing-room, and guests were expected to participate.

One evening when my mother had taken me along to Wilton Crescent, while I was sitting at a jigsaw there was an interruption to the adult play. We all dutifully trooped outside to witness the arrival of the first grouse from the shoot on a cousin's Perthshire estate: gunned down mid-morning, and despatched on the two o'clock train from Perth. Once Lady Coniston had received the trophies, and when Miss Deegan had appeared on the area steps with the cook and a girl to take the birds from her, we all made our way back inside.

I was placed near my mother, so I saw the expression on her face when she sat down at the table to resume play ahead of her partners. She was staring at the letters set out on her rack. The smile of just a few seconds before had turned to a grimace; her eyes had set like stones.

Suddenly she stood up. She pretended her hand had merely caught the rack, to send the pieces slithering to the floor. The others were returning to the room. I meanwhile was down on the floor picking up the letters where they had fallen. I had just gathered them all when my mother tugged at my sleeve telling me we couldn't stay any longer. She pulled me to my feet and I hadn't time to put the letters back on the table. Outside in the hall I felt like a thief and crammed the bits into my trouser pocket. My mother was offering her excuses to Lady Coniston. 'Merlin is very tired, I really shouldn't take him about with me like this, but –' She sounded as I knew she hated to sound, ungrateful, but she was still shocked and didn't quite understand what she was saying. 'He doesn't sleep well, you see.' That wasn't true, and it was illogical, but she wasn't thinking straight.

Back home she didn't make me go to bed. She hardly remembered me at all. She tried to call Uncle George, but he wasn't there to answer. She sat down with the envelope of newspaper clippings about my father and his films. She got up and poured herself the first of several drinks.

When I went to the sitting-room door to say 'goodnight', I had to repeat myself twice. She looked up from the spread of cuttings on the sofa cushions.

'Oh. Yes. Goodnight, then –'

Briefly her eyes scrutinised me. I hovered. But then her eyes dropped again, back to the islands of newsprint on the chintz and a life I knew so very nearly nothing about.

ONHRUTSWC

I still have eight of the nine scrabble letters. One has been lost in the subsequent uprootings of my life.

With the eight I can make a name, a surname minus one letter, plus an initial. UNSWO(R)TH, C The surname isn't rare, but it's out of the ordinary. While Scrabble is only a game of chance, it occurs to me that the coincidence was likely to have been something more than coincidence.

The name Unsworth appears in the title credits of several of Matzell's films.

'Assistant Sound Engineer . . . . . . Colin Unsworth'

Someone must have placed the letters there on the Scrabble rack, whether in the full and proper order or not. Finding them was intended to provide a shock. It was a confession to my mother of another person's knowledge.

But whose? And, after the intervening years and after all my mother's efforts of concealment, why now?

The news of Leofric Anstey's death came to us via the wireless.

We were in the kitchen. My mother's head jerked up when she heard. Her eyes stared straight ahead.

'It's over,' she said.

She started shaking her head. I thought she meant that the man's life was over, that there would be no more conversations like the one we'd had on the windy street corner. Even though his previous disappearance had been a preparation of sorts, I felt very sad. I knew we had lost my favourite eccentric.

Our group was deeply affected, and talked of little else for a while. A kind of paralysis set in with us. It was discovered that there had had to be an autopsy, and a newspaper duly reported that death had resulted from an overdose of barbiturates in whisky. Certain acquaintances – but none from our set – were quoted as saying that they had found him latterly in very low spirits indeed.

Uncle George was driving us somewhere. I had no means of knowing that

The Sun on the Wall

this was to be the last journey we made in the Riley, and with Uncle George.

My mother leaned forward and opened the glove compartment. Uncle George was facing the other way, waiting to join traffic at a roundabout.

Some moments later he turned and looked at her. Looked away again. Did a double-take.

'Hey, what're you doing?'

My mother had taken a letter out of an envelope and was reading it.

'Decca—'

'Where did you get this?'

'Please, Decca—'

'It's addressed to me.'

'I can explain—'

She pushed the envelope in front of his face. 'D'you see?'

'I know what you're thinking—'

'This was meant for me.'

'Give it to me, Decca.'

He reached out and tried to snatch the letter from her. The sheet of paper tore.

'It's mine!'

He made an effort to grab the rest.

'Mine, George!' she yelled.

'You don't want to read—'

Instantly she laughed. A bitter, mirthless laugh.

'It's all quite simple—'

'Are you out of your mind?' she shouted at him.

'I wouldn't presume to know. About that sort of—'

'Stop the car,' she said.

'What?'

'Stop the car. *Now!*'

'Decca—'

'I mean it.'

She tugged at the handle and started to open the door. Immediately he lifted his foot off the accelerator and turned for the kerb.

'Please, Decca, I can explain—'

'I don't want to hear your explanations.'

The door swung open and she put out her feet when the kerb drew close.

'Get out, Merlin. We're not going any further.'

I had to wait while she stood up, then tipped her seat forward. Uncle George put his hand on my arm but she yanked roughly at the other one and won that point as I was propelled forwards out of the car.

I've Been Here Before

'You steal my letters,' she shouted down into the car. 'You – you break confidences. You tell me I'm crazy –'

'I didn't say any such –'

She slammed the door as hard as she could. She glared down at him, looking daggers. Then she leaned forward and pounded on the window with her fist.

'I never want to see you again!'

He was mouthing something, a plea. He began to wind down the glass.

'D'you understand me?'

'Decca –'

'Never again. I'm finished with you.'

She seized my hand and led me away. We were in the middle of nowhere, but that didn't matter to her. Just so long as we weren't in the car, in that car, with *him*.

After twenty yards she was in tears. He was calling after us. She wouldn't look back, though. I heard his footsteps and turned round, but she pulled harder on my arm.

'No!'

The footsteps stopped. I listened, hoping for them to come running after us, but all I heard were our own, her heels scraping on cement and my crepe soles squeaking as I half ran to keep up with her.

A black cat streaked across our path and vanished.

I could feel my mother's anger, transmitted through the pain of my hand clutched so tightly inside hers. Forget acting, I knew quite well that all this hurt was for real.

She had the locks changed on the doors of the flat. The telephone rang several times, but she didn't answer it. Eventually she took the receiver off the cradle. She mentioned to the locksmith the possibility of having locks put on some of the windows. Or would that be expensive? The matter was left in the air: she said she would call him back when she'd made up her mind. When he was gone she tested the locks on both doors, front and fire escape. She went from one to the other, half a dozen times. She made sure she was quite familiar with the procedure, reassuring herself about the speed with which she could double-lock the mechanisms.

I had supposed at first that the locks were changed to keep out Uncle George, in case he had a key. But then I wasn't so sure. I heard my mother trying to call him, dialling his number. There was no reply. She went through the exchange and asked the operator if she could help. The woman rang back, but only to apologise and tell her she had no news.

The Sun on the Wall

After the call my mother forgot to switch on the lamps in the sitting-room. I found her curled up in an armchair, in darkness. Maybe she'd been sleeping, or just thinking, or even crying. The room felt cold. A room that belonged to other people, not to us. I made out a smile, the gleam of teeth: whether a brave or defeated smile I couldn't tell. Just a smile, and mysterious.

The telephone rang at last. My mother hurried to it and grabbed the receiver.

'Hello? George?'

She moved the receiver, holding it an inch or two from her ear.

'Hello?'

She turned her back to me.

'Hello? Can you . . . can you hear me?'

She listened.

'Is anyone there? George?'

There was no reply. She listened for some moments longer. Then, slowly, she replaced the receiver.

She turned round. She saw me watching.

'I think it was a telephone box,' she said. 'There must've been something wrong with it.'

She kept in careful proximity to the phone for the next half-hour or so. Her eyes grew tight and tired. When it did ring again, she was caught out. She ran through from the bathroom, managing to catch her foot in the braided flex.

It was Uncle George, calling from another telephone box. She repeated the word 'hotel'.

'Where are you? George? Why on earth – ? Yes, I'm listening, yes, but –'

She wrote down what he told her. She nodded, then realised he couldn't see.

'Yes. Yes. I understand. Can't you tell me – ? All right. Yes. I'll stay here. You'll call me?'

When she'd finished she put on a show of normality. Picked up a magazine. Shook a cigarette out of the packet. Asked if I could help her find a box of matches. Alighted on another magazine to read. Went through to her bedroom and changed her shoes. Returned. Sat down, got up again. Went through to the kitchen and started to prepare my tea. Turned the gas on and realised some moments later that she'd forgotten to light it. Had to open the window to clear the air.

He didn't call again that night. In the morning my mother was putting on a different act. Now she was dissatisfied. Put out. Bored. Why should a man suppose?

I've Been Here Before

She still couldn't settle. She opened all the other windows, although there was no smell to be got rid of, either gas or perfume.

In the middle of the morning she rang up the hairdresser's to make an appointment. Then she returned to her vantage point at the window. Nearer lunchtime she told me she was going out, just for a couple of minutes, down to the corner shop. It was there she bought me my sweets and cigarettes for herself. I volunteered, supposing there might be something in it for me, but she told me she needed the fresh air. I think she meant, rather, she needed a little space for herself, and the time to consider.

She had been gone no more than five minutes when the telephone rang. I recognised Miss Deegan's voice before she told me who she was. Did I know, she asked, where she could get hold of my mother's friend, Mr Metcalf?

I was surprised. I hadn't known that she knew him, or anything about his being a friend of ours. He hadn't been able to answer my mother's questions about *her*.

'Uncle George?' I said.

'Is that what you call him?'

'My mother was speaking to him.'

'When?'

'Last night.'

'I'm trying to find him, you see. It's awfully important. But I want it to be a surprise. A surprise, Merlin. Even from your mother.'

I was flummoxed. But she made me feel I was in a position to help her, and I suppose I was flattered to be treated so by an adult. Then I remembered the slip of paper. I told her, and when I'd found it I read out what was written down, stumbling over my pronunciation. Godalming. The Pheasant Rising Hotel. Ashclere. Third past. Then a telephone number, in brackets. I faltered over that, and she had me repeat it. She had me check there was nothing written on the other side of the piece of paper.

'A surprise, Merlin. Your mother isn't to know.'

I was still puzzling over her knowing Uncle George when he wasn't an acquaintance of hers.

'No one's to hear about our having spoken. Do you understand?'

She tried to put a smile into her voice at the other end of the line. I wasn't fooled, although I told her yes, remembering that pointed cat's face. I seemed to catch a whiff of rosebuds, and to be feeling the warmth of her breath on my neck, in my ear. She pretended she hadn't caught my reply –

'Yes,' I repeated.

'Promise me.'

'I – I promise,' I said solemnly.

'Good. You've been very helpful to me, Merlin. Very helpful indeed.'
There wasn't a trace of Essex now in her voice.
'My mother,' I told her, 'will be back soon.'
'Of course she will. I'll say goodbye then, Merlin.'
'Goodbye, Miss Deegan.'
'A secret, remember. You've promised me on your word –'
'Yes,' I said.
'*Good*bye.'

The emphasis rang false. I recalled that later, when – eventually – I did tell my mother, after four days had passed. By then our circumstances were different, quite different, and I realised I couldn't hold anything back: certainly not to preserve a secret given to Miss Deegan, a woman I now appreciated I didn't care for and never had.

When my mother got back from the shops, smoking already, she didn't ask if anyone had rung, presuming – because I didn't say so – that they hadn't.

'Now lunch,' she announced, with only some pretend optimism forced into her voice, bending down to open the oven door.

If only I hadn't told Miss Deegan . . . If only she hadn't chanced to phone just then . . .

But how much of a part does mere 'chance' play in any of our affairs? The timing couldn't have been any accident.

There was a telephone box on the corner of the road, at the other end from where the corner shop stood. Her call might have been made from there, in that vital interim between my mother leaving and returning. No time had been wasted before the subject was introduced. 'I've been trying to get hold of your mother's friend, Mr Metcalf –'

I've been here so often before, at this impasse, asking myself questions that won't yield definite answers. About that afternoon, and the drive to Godalming, about everything that led us there and to the interval of days afterwards, where it seems to me – when I concentrate very hard – that the opportunities are granted to me to untell our story, or to tell it differently, to invent a fresh conclusion before all the tape is played out on the spool.

Somebody was supposed to be coming to look after me, but at the last minute she had to cry off. When my mother rang our neighbours' doorbell to find a substitute, there was no reply.

'Well, you'll just have to come with me.' She exhaled a heavy sigh, so that I should be able to appreciate the inconvenience this was causing her. 'Ten minutes, then we'll go. Can you get yourself ready?'

She searched around for her bag.

'Chop-chop, Merlin!'

I was waiting for her. We locked up, went outside, and got into the plush car, an Armstrong Siddeley which had been delivered that morning from a hire firm. ('If you're going to do something,' she'd told me, referring to the car, 'you might as well push the boat out, go the whole hog–') An elderly gentleman who lived across the road waved over, as he always did, but this time my mother looked away instead of acknowledging him.

I asked my mother where we were heading for. She told me, just wait and see.

We left London at speed.

We took a road to Leatherhead, then another to Guildford. After that my mother followed signposts to Godalming. I remembered the name written down on the piece of paper, in my mother's handwriting, along with The Pheasant Rising and Ashclere. My conversation with Miss Deegan was also called to mind, and I felt a twist of pain in my stomach, sensing that I had pledged myself to her in a way that it wouldn't please my mother to know I'd done.

We pulled into the car park of a hotel. I was startled by the name on the signboard, even though it was what I was expecting to see. A colourful pheasant was depicted, wings spread, in gainly ascent. The building was large and false-timbered, a fake: I was reminded of another Tudor pastiche, the anachronistically named John of Gaunt.

My mother opened her door.

'I want to check if someone's here.'

'Uncle George?'

She turned her head sharply and looked at me. I hadn't set eyes on him since the afternoon of the letter in the glove compartment, when my mother had exploded with rage, but since then I'd been aware that he was in the thoughts of both of us.

'Is it him?' I asked.

Her eyes lost their sharp focus.

'Well . . . it might be.'

She got out and shut the door. She walked off, without looking back.

She reappeared at the entrance of the hotel after only a couple of minutes inside. A man was pointing out a direction to her. She nodded, said something in thanks, and walked back to the car.

She smiled in at me, not very confidently, then opened the door and lowered herself on to the squeaky leather of the seat.

'We'll have to go somewhere else.'

She started the engine, snatched at the handbrake, and then we were off again.

We had to travel out of the town to find what we were looking for. At last she recognised something specific: a red post box set in a wall, among straggling creeper.

A lane turned off the road. It wasn't made up, and for the first few yards – until my mother slowed – the car's tyres sent the scree ricocheting under the chassis.

My mother leaned forward, examining to left and right through the windscreen. We passed several cottages. We came to a small area of common land, with cows grazing. The lane became bumpier after that. Our tyres fitted into two tracks. Hedges, a broken wall, a headless statue entwined with convolvulus. A couple of cottages. And then after fifty or sixty yards another cottage appeared, looking like an estate property this time, with some Gothic touches: small tracery windows, barley-sugar twist chimneys, a peaked front porch supported on pillars hewn out of tree trunks.

My mother wound down the window. No name was written on the latch gate, but that too seemed to be what she was reckoning on finding.

She turned the steering wheel and we rode up out of the tracks on to a verge of neglected grass. She braked, and switched off the engine.

'I may be a few minutes,' she said.

'Can't I come?'

'I want to see your Uncle George by myself.'

'*Then* can I?'

'I don't think so. Not today.'

I was going to ask her why not, but she interrupted me.

'I'll let you know if I'm going to be longer.'

She got out. She reached back in for her bag.

'I'll tell you. Then you could go for a walk or something.'

She didn't look as if she believed that I would want to walk, not in this gloomy and overgrown spot. I nodded, complicating a lie.

I watched her push on the gate. It rattled shut behind her. She looked up at the upstairs window, which was open. A curtain had blown against the wall and was stuck to the stonework.

She stepped into the porch, searched for a bell, then lifted the knocker and rapped on the wood. When there was no answer, she tried again. And a third time.

She backed away, out of the porch. She looked up at the open window. She started to make her way along the little gravel path, towards the side of the house. She briefly hesitated, then she turned the corner. After that she disappeared from view.

I've Been Here Before

She was away for several minutes. I sat playing with the controls on the dashboard in front of me. I had switched on the radio, so I didn't hear her footsteps at first. Then I did hear them, running over the gravel. The hinges of the gate shrieked.

I looked back. My mother was leaning against the gatepost. Her hand was covering her mouth. She was bent forwards, peering down at the ground. She was swaying slightly on her feet. I had never seen her face so pale.

She didn't return to the car for another couple of minutes. She stood trying to get her breath back. Something had to be wiped from her hand with her handkerchief; she pushed the handkerchief – vaguely – back into her bag. She looked up the lane, and down, both ways, several times.

Back in the car she said nothing. Her face had a greenish underwater tinge, and her eyes couldn't hold. She pulled on the steering wheel, lifted the handbrake, and we rolled back. The knuckle of her thumb was smeared red, as if she had cut herself. She started the engine, found reverse gear, pressed her foot on the accelerator, and we slithered back into the tyre tracks, but facing the way we had come.

'Aren't I to go for a walk?' I asked.

She didn't hear me. She rammed the gear stick into first and we went skidding off, towards the open area of grazing and the smoking chimneys of the cottages beyond. At the lane's end she hardly slowed before swinging out into the road in third. An angry horn blared at us from behind, but she moved up into fourth gear and in only moments we had lost the car.

She barely spoke at all on the journey back. The radio was left switched on, and impeccable voices smoothed over the silence between us. A discussion about the pros and cons of snails in the garden. A news broadcast. A talk on the delights of Beirut. A lecture with sound illustrations on Bach's 'The Art of Fugue'.

My mother's face was still bloodless. Now and then she would rub at her eyes or blow her nose. Outside Epsom she parked the car to go into a hotel. She came back with her face freshly powdered but with her eyes red. I thought I caught a sour whiff of sickness on her breath.

The lights were going on in London. We coincided with a pale blue twilight. People stood about on street corners, and at pub doors. Dogs lay dozing on the pavements. Windows were open to air the narrow houses.

Even in our own road some of the window-sashes were raised, but no curtains had blown out and stuck to the walls. The friendly gentleman who lived across the road was making his way back home; now he hesitated before raising his arm to wave over to us. My mother ignored him again, but seemed unaware that she was doing so. I tried to respond, opening my hand

and spreading my fingers, sensing that I was doing some wrong not obvious to me. A gas man in blue overalls got in the way, so I couldn't be sure that he'd seen me.

In the flat something happened to my mother, being back in these rooms that had never been our proper home. They were closing in suddenly, and she lost her command of the situation. Maybe she had still been in shock on the drive back from Godalming. Several tumblers of whisky started to unnerve her. She didn't seem to know what to do. I caught her high tide of panic, needing to have in front of her some lines written down on a page to memorise. I had become used to her restlessness of late, but not to these shiny eyes in the dark and the intermittent sound of a sob being choked back.

She appeared with two suitcases.

'We can't stay here,' she said. Not having the nerve to stay meant making other decisions. 'Put your things into one of these, will you?'

I didn't ask why. She stared at me as if she was only waiting for me to do so.

I went off to my room.

The telephone rang, twice. The second time the ringing continued for six or seven minutes. I forced myself not to ask her, why wasn't she answering. It was as if by staying silent I was willing this not to be happening, refusing to be complicitous.

I delayed, even though I was ready. When I came out of my room she had switched off all the lamps. She let the front door close behind us. She didn't double-lock it as she always did now, so I guessed – had a premonition – that we might not be coming back here. I wasn't as sorry as I wanted to be, although I lingered on the staircase; I was only halfway down by the time she reached the front door.

'Look sharp there!'

I let the bottom of my suitcase trail on the stairs. It bumped, bumped, bumped. She turned her back on me.

I kicked at a silver sixpence someone had dropped; it disappeared under the banister and fell echoing down the stairwell. My mother halted mid-step, back tensed, before continuing.

On the floor beneath I thought I heard movements behind the Fergusons' door, and it was only that which caused me to pick up speed and go scurrying the remaining distance to the front steps.

In the car my mother seemed determined to ignore my awkwardness. She smiled at me, to encourage me, before catching her reflection in the windscreen mirror. Seen apart from her mouth, her eyes looked sad and hopeless.

I've Been Here Before

It was the sight of that confusion, and the bravery of her concealment, which brought me to my senses at last.

My mother's fingerprints would have been left behind in the cottage. Someone would have spotted the Armstrong Siddeley passing down the lane and then back again; for several minutes it was parked outside, up on the verge. Without an inkling that we did so, we were only giving ourselves away.

We spent the next couple of nights in a hotel somewhere on the outskirts of London. It was sited on a main road, and the other guests were businessmen and reps. Outside was a suburb constructed of the same red brick as the hotel. I worked on the five-hundred-piece jigsaw of the Trooping of the Colour which I'd had the foresight to bring with me. A good deal of my mother's time was spent in the telephone booth in the downstairs hall, plugging coin after coin into the box or waiting for her calls to be returned. I supposed it must be Uncle George she was talking to.

I asked her, 'Are we going to the sea?'

'What?'

'Is it a holiday?'

'A holiday?' she repeated. She stared at me.

'I just wondered –'

'Hardly,' she said.

And that was that.

I hung about the corridors and listened outside room doors. I watched the cars driving past. We went for a walk outside, along some less busy roads called 'avenues', past little gardens behind rickety wooden slatted fences and low privet hedges grimy with the traffic dust. I saw my mother looking about us with a kind of queasy concern, then with mounting alarm. Clearly all this domesticity appalled her: she had no understanding of what it added up to. Two women with shopping baskets turned and looked at her and spoke quietly to one another, and they might have been discussing her as if she were someone famous, or who had once been a 'face'. I think she realised too that they might be, because she slowed her pace and dallied briefly, with her jawline raised and her head in profile to the pair. We walked on, and the matter wasn't explained, it was left behind us in the dusty, rather airless warmth of that suburban afternoon on the fringes of everything.

'Miss Deegan?' my mother repeated. 'Miss *Deegan* rang?'

'Yes.'

'You're sure it was her?'

I nodded.

'For God's sake, Merlin, why didn't you tell me?'

'Because – it was a secret – she made me promise.'

'Oh, promise be damned!'

She stood staring at me. Her face was fury. She looked as if she wanted to hit me.

Something stopped her, though.

She shook her head again, for the tenth or twelfth time. It meant she was incredulous with the situation, with me, and with herself. And it meant there wasn't a thing, not a bloody thing, that either of us could do about it now.

EIGHT

In La Baule, where she was living in the late 1980s, she was using (as she always had done) the name of her now late husband, Mrs Charles Cornelius.

The words were placed at the very top of the plate of residents' names beside the lobby doors to the apartment block. I discovered when I enquired at the concierge's desk that Madame Cornelius occupied the building's duplex penthouse.

When I was shown into the main reception room with its two entire walls of picture windows, I found La Baule ranged beneath me. The décor was dramatically white and pastel, but at the same time it felt discreet and unflamboyant.

The owner entered the room silently. When I turned round she was there. A small neat woman, between seventy and eighty, wearing immaculately cut grey flannel culottes and café crème silk blouse. Her eyes were clever and cautious.

After the formalities she took me out on to the terrace. She invited me to sit on one of the lemon-cushioned loungers. Drinks were served to us by a maid. Suddenly everything that I wanted to mention to her seemed very far away indeed, on the other side of a deep chasm and enveloped in one of those pea-soupers we used to suffer in London. In the bright August sunshine, in its full glare, even our shadows faded on the pale terrazzo, and I felt that the people I wanted to talk about were still less related to substance than those shadows.

But she remembered; or at any rate she was versed now with a few facts. She had considered my letter, she said, quite long and hard. She had gone looking through her husband's papers (unpublished, notwithstanding the interested offers she had received) to uncover whatever might be there. Which wasn't a great deal, she admitted to me.

'But I understand very well why you need to know.'

And little and late, we agreed, must be better than nothing and never.

* * *

Ben brought along the girl he's been telling me about. She's called Decca Blane. I see what appeals to him. All through lunch I sat thinking, you could believe she's innocent and guilty at the same time. I'm not sure what it is about her. Maybe her eyes and mouth don't correspond in the way other people's do: her brow and her hands, or whatever. She's full of disputes inside but she's charming when she talks. Shouldn't we be wary of her? Her eyes open wide and it could be vulnerability, but perhaps what she's doing is remembering everything, every single damn thing . . . She has slim expressive hands, full of strength as well. With some fine tuning – a little elocution work, advice on her clothes and her face – she could get away with playing a duchess. At the office she reads something Ben gives her, which flusters her a little, but she's okay. Ben is impressed, and I can see he's puzzled by his own caring what happens.

'Did *you* know them, Mrs Cornelius?'

'I met your mother once or twice,' she replied, angling herself a little more out of the sun.

'What sort of impression –'

'She was very polite. Remembered to say the right things. But I think we intimidated her a little. Charles invited them down to the house, you see, a couple of times. The first time, I showed her about. She seemed very interested. I can see what Charles meant, though – about your not *quite* knowing where you were with her.'

'I beg your pardon?'

'She had a kind of – well, wondering look about everything. But it was all going in, I could tell. She was memorising it all, storing it away. Like a camera.' For emphasis Mrs Cornelius closed her eyes, like a lens shutter, then opened them again, with myself for their subject matter. 'The surface of her was very charming, certainly. And that deflected you, rather.'

I nodded.

'And my father?' I asked her next. 'Do you remember him too?'

'Your father?' she repeated. She appeared muddled. 'I thought – it was your mother –'

'Benedict Matzell.'

'Your mother was Decca Blane –'

'Yes,' I said, 'of course.' I couldn't understand this muddlement at all. 'And I was their son.'

'*Their* son?'

'Decca Blane's and Benedict Matzell's.'

Her shrewd eyes stared back at me. Her head was quite still. Not a muscle moved on her face.

I was mystified. What could I have said to disable her like this?

'That was why,' I began, 'why I came. Because you knew them both. You and your husband. When I wrote to you –'

'Yes,' she said, sounding very remote. 'Yes. Your letter –'

'I've always wanted to know.'

'About Decca Blane?'

'Yes, my mother.'

'And Ben Matzell?'

'That's right.'

'But – didn't you say – ?'

'My father,' I said, nodding.

She tilted her head off the straight, blinking several times as her eyes tried to hold their focus on me. Behind them she seemed to be making rapid-fire calculations. About what I might be in a position to know and what not.

She dropped her eyes to the white terrazzo, fixing on some point in the pattern. She looked at the floor for fifteen or twenty seconds before raising her eyes again. They examined my face, searching it for any details of appearance that might be familiar to her. Again I was back in those dream-like rooms of a certain portion of my childhood, being scrutinised by my mother's friends for evidence of a further past.

'They weren't married,' I said. 'And he died. When I was very young.'

Mrs Cornelius still said nothing.

I cleared my throat.

'You're not shocked?' I asked her.

Mrs Cornelius straightened herself on the lemon yellow cushions of the lounger.

'If' – she cleared her throat – 'if it's true –'

I interrupted her.

'Oh yes,' I said. 'It certainly is.'

'Your mother told you?'

'Yes. Of course.'

'I – I'm not shocked. Morally speaking, I mean. God, no. But – but yes, I *am* very surprised.'

Pause. Freeze-frame.

'Why?' I asked her, supposing simplicity the quickest route to a reply.

'He said nothing. To us. We saw him right up to the end.'

'With my mother?'

'Not with your mother, no. Not at the *very* end –'

'He said nothing?'

'No, he didn't.'
'But you did see him together with my mother. You saw how they were.'
'Oh yes,' she said. 'We noticed that.'
Pause. Picture-hold.
'And – and you thought what?'
'That your mother – she fascinated him. Although not half as much as *he* fascinated *her*.'
'But he *was* in love with her.'
'Your mother must have thought that. If that's what she – what she needed to believe.'
'Yes, of course.'
'And *you* believe what you're telling me,' she said. '*You*'ve convinced yourself that it's the truth.'
'Well, isn't it?' I couldn't help the question. It was starker than I meant it to be. 'Isn't it true?'
'I don't –' She lowered her eyes from my face to the arm of my chair.
'Tell me,' I said.
She was going to shake her head.
'Please. You must tell me –'
Her eyes returned to my face.
'I don't know if you mean that,' she said.
I nodded vigorously.
'I do mean it,' I said.
'It's easy enough for me sitting here,' she said. 'It was another place and time, all that. A mixed-up time.'
'Then it can't matter,' I said. 'When it was so long ago.'
'It's your history, though.'
'I don't know,' I told her, 'what my history is.'
'You *think* you know.'
'If it's a lie,' I said, 'I don't want it. Do you understand?'
She was reluctant at first. Then she did nod her head. Slowly, solemnly. While all the white light of high summer dazzled around us – on white plaster and white woodwork, on white terrazzo and lemon fabric – and with the bay of Nazaire sparkling under a filter-lit blue sky as summers do in films and in the memories of childhood lived before the fall.

From the windows of Leighston Park, from every window on the front and sides of the house, the boy can look out and know that what he sees is Matzell property. He has been brought up with every conceivable material advantage in life. It is no consolation to him, however.

He tries to read, in the silence of the library that is like a tomb's. His own boredom reminds him of his mother's, which is the disease of her enervated class. Some days the smells appal him, the dust of dead time and the books' leather bindings – skins peeled from hooked cow carcasses – until there's no air left to breathe in that sealed enclosure and he has to get up and run, skidding on the polished floor, for the door.

From the windows at the back of the house he looks down on the kitchen, the scullery, the larders, the ice-room, the boiler-room that used to be the dairy, the garages, the old stables. He can still hear his mother's heels on the cobbles as she hurries across the yard towards the stables and the archway under the stopped clock. Later none of the staff will be able to remember a thing, except for a maid who blurted out to him that she wasn't supposed to say, because they'd had to promise not to, and because they'd all felt sorry for madam.

A car would be waiting, and his mother would be driven off, dressed for a fancy lunch somewhere. His father meanwhile would be with the factor, or buying at a livestock auction, or out with the hunt: he had taken to the country life with a vengeance, to prove himself worthy of the aristocrat's daughter whom he'd had the gall – as a mere broker in the insurance market, however successful, and third generation of Catholic Swiss-Italian émigrés – to marry. If the servants secretly thought him vulgar, they made up in their loyalty to his wife.

Benedict as their only child recognised he was the synthesis of two experiences and two cultures. *His* loyalty was a much less straightforwardly decidable matter to him.

Mrs Cornelius tried to explain.

'The trouble was, you see, they didn't meet in the ordinary world, your mother and Ben Matzell. It was films. God knows, life was grey at that time, and everywhere was run down, so that those stage-sets seemed somewhere very special. It was just chipboard, though, and lots of bright paint and smart clothes bought in wholesale. And those hot lights, they're so brilliantly bright but it's a cold light they give off. It might have seemed a better place to be, and it *had* a sort of reality, of course: but it was only partly true.'

Mrs Cornelius hitched herself a little more upright in the lounger.

'I felt it had put a spell on your mother. Maybe she knew it had and didn't care, or maybe she didn't realise after all and she really was – disorientated. She spent so much time there, even when she wasn't needed. She had friends among the crews. Charles told me how she would sit and watch, she used to have everyone else's lines off by heart. I tried to find out if she had friends outside, but I don't think she did. We had her to the house, of course, because she was with Ben – I told you that, didn't I? I noticed how she liked to touch things, just lightly – the furniture, the curtains, the walls – as if she was checking that they *were* real. As if she'd forgotten they could be.'

In the little silence that followed I put together the words to ask, what exactly had been the relationship between my mother and – (I saw Mrs Cornelius's eyes starting to narrow in anticipation, so I sidestepped the term 'father' that so unsettled her) – between my mother and Benedict Matzell?

'I knew they were going out together. I thought of them as companions for a while. With a touch of the Svengalis about it, I have to say. It must have been – well, intimate too. But I don't think I ever considered it as *serious*. For keeps, I mean. Ben's wife had just left him. Your mother was an amenable girl, approachable, lots of curiosity. She didn't much resemble Catherine. I'm sure Ben was just savouring all the differences between them –'

'Could anything have come of it? Anything permanent? I was their child, after all.'

Mrs Cornelius's eyes narrowed again. She was looking for some way to steer about the same obstacle as before.

'He wanted to educate your mother. In the manners of the world. To give her something, in return for the comfort she had given him. Once he had shown her how, she would know for herself. She would know how to knock on doors, and which tone of voice you need to talk in to make sure you gain entry, and then how it is you make your entrance.'

After the divorce the boy's father removed all the evidence of his mother that he could. Occasionally a newspaper would slip through the defences and in it would be a photograph of the new Mrs Goldberg with or without husband, gracing yet another pukka social function. The most hurtful aspect of all was that she looked younger than she had before she made her getaway: younger, healthier, and now happier, ready with an indefatigable smile turned towards the lensman.

The Goldberg variation.

Louis Goldberg wasn't the archetypal Jew, which made matters worse for the boy. He had been expecting a hooked nose, the sharply-etched lips, a Levantine complexion, and oily black hair. Instead, name apart, Goldberg might have been taken for normal – for gentile, more or less. He was without any of the generic excesses, spoke with a delivery halfway to a clubland drawl, and was distinguished principally by his suavely English appearance and sophisticated talk and good manners.

For some reason it came to seem a more insidious business than ever to the boy, a dirty Jew trick.

I've Been Here Before

* * *

His father didn't marry again.

In future a gap persisted at the centre of their lives: an absence, a reticence. A gloomy silence prevailed in the rooms of the house, and it was always to be there, beneath the hum of any conversation there might be.

The photographs disappeared from the frames, but the ciné films remained in their tins, overlooked. The boy taught himself how to operate the projector, and sometimes if his father had reason to be somewhere other than at home he would play them back, either on the screen or on a wall. When he tired of the forward motion he put the spool on to rewind action and watched the past unravelling. He could believe then he might have saved them from what had overtaken them, by spiriting them back to their essential selves – wherever he stopped the films – at some picnic or on a beach in his childhood, or even earlier, when his mother strolled elegantly pregnant in a garden that was unrecognisable to him. When he played the films forward he searched diligently for clues and indicators, for omens, but couldn't find them. His mother smiled or looked becomingly pensive; his father had eyes only for her, surely done in humble admiration and not in anticipation of her one day deserting them.

'Decca could have gone on to become a character actress,' Mrs Cornelius said. 'That's what they called them in those days.'

'I see,' I said, although I knew nothing about it.

'That's what the demand was for.'

'Your husband,' I asked, 'would he have gone on making films with Matzell?'

'If we hadn't gone to Hollywood, I'm sure he would have done.'

'The public's appetite might have changed.'

'Quite possibly. The films suited the times. They were escapist, but they came out of our lives then. It was an uncertain, mysterious age: directionless.'

I nodded again, and this time I did understand her. Triumphalism that couldn't celebrate. A period of great poverty, financial and political, when people took solace in imagination. Bankrupt Britain. Austerity and Utility. Matzell caught the mood of a population living bored lives and intermittently experiencing a kind of hysteria, poised between a past they couldn't shake off and a future that was refusing to take shape.

From a rooftop terrace in La Baule it all seemed so far away. It ought to have been inconsequential by now. But my own story was entangled with those of the principal players (notwithstanding my informant's claiming my mother had had a future as a character actress), and I realised I shouldn't be able to glean the significant clues I required if I failed to unpick that skein of destinies.

Matzell's early short films were made under the aegis of the old Sundial Studios out at Purley. It was Herbert Kolb himself who had first spotted his potential and encouraged him. Kolb had come to the fore working in Fürstenwalde and Starnberg-am-See with fellow Expressionists: Reiff, Litzmann, Herz, Ganghofer, Dehmel, Brüll. Matzell was to meet a number of them on travels overseas with Kolb. Kolb had a German distributor, and a number of Matzell's films were shown (dubbed) as second features in the cities. Kolb, a half-Jew but a committed pragmatist, had already involved himself in setting up a documentary film unit for the National Socialist Party.

Kolb's wife was English. It was through her, or through friends of her friends, that Matzell met the woman he married: an archetypal English rose, who only later revealed a degree of thorny will – to have children – which the soft bloom of her appearance gave no good indication of. From the beginning she allowed her husband's working life to remain a fuzzy matter to her, just as if he had been a lawyer or banker; a pragmatist also, she recognised what her function was, namely to be as different as possible from any of *that*, and with her quiet ladylike pastimes to be the antithesis of those others about whom she expressed so little interest. She ably fulfilled her role, while unbeknown to her her husband drifted into faster and deeper social currents, where his new friends spoke – from all their complex motives of envy or ennui or altruism or revenge or derring-do – of trying to change the world.

Mrs Cornelius filled her eyes with the glare of the sun.

'Things could have gone any way. At that time. With the country in Queer Street, money-wise. There was a great vacuum. That bad winter of '46 into '47. I remember the cover of *Picture Post* in the spring, Brandt's photograph of Stonehenge under snow, and the caption. 'Where Stands Britain?' The stones were stark and lowering. Mythical in a way you couldn't quite get to grips with. What did it mean? Winning a war and then seeming to lose the peace, because it had cost so much and our freedom was all we had to show for it. The country was ripe for taking over. I don't know what stopped it happening. Maybe chance. Or maybe there's a sort of lethargy in the British, they've too little emotion, at least for violent nationalism. Enough for the Royal Family, though, for their sort of pastiche of aristocracy. It was because they seemed more upper-middle class, that's why they didn't seem so remote from the people, maybe it's what saved everyone in the end. Edward the Eighth would have caught on to some new Mosley's coat-tails, but that was all too much fuss. England was Girl Guides, and gymkhanas, and the two princesses, and the Queen with that handbag, and poor George with his stutter. It couldn't be rallies and goose-stepping, we would have been much too embarrassed. Our weaknesses, you see, they were turned into virtues. We were our own best reason why the takeover never happened.'

Matzell's world was one my mother only knew about from reading the society pages in newspapers.

Nightclubs. Supper rooms. The cocktail bars of the big hotels. Even a racecourse or two. A few afternoon regattas by the Thames.

She was introduced to a selection of Matzell's friends. Some of them were his colleagues in the film business, others not. Up in town they wore dinner jackets and silk cocktail dresses, and for the country blazers or tweeds and jersey separates and fur trimmings. A number of those she met looked at her dismissively, or condescendingly; most, however, showed interest, either on her own account or because anything that Matzell did intrigued them.

She was living her new life to the rhythms of a Cuban band or the rippling harmonies of a cocktail pianist, by the coral glow of pink-shaded table-lights or in the muted, sieved daylight of a racecourse or riverside marquee. She travelled about in comfortable cars when she wasn't in taxi cabs, and ordinary lives slipped past quickly and a little dreamily to her. There might never even have been a war. She wasn't quite sure how she found herself on the inside of this most congenial myth. It had wrapped itself about her, and she let herself be swaddled without a thought of demurring.

'We'd always known he had another side to him,' Mrs Cornelius told me. 'That he had political leanings.'

'Which were...?'

'Pretty far right, I think we could say.'

'He discussed it with you?'

'No. But we heard things. After the war there were various new outfits. About the time of the "Crisis" talk. They thought they knew the way forward.'

'He was quite interested?'

'Oh, quite involved.'

'You knew for a fact?'

'Not so much while he was alive. Charles met someone afterwards who claimed Ben's films weren't about what they appeared to be about. That they were full of bits of code. Which would be useful to an enemy.'

'He did do some propaganda work as well, though? For the Ministry of Information.'

'A little. That was earlier. It was to give him some purchase – you know? –

so he could do his other films. Claim his credit. Not that his feature films *seemed* to be very patriotic. But he shot London so well, he gave the place so much atmosphere. I think the powers-that-be felt it was the next best thing. Making the audiences see it as something unique, as their own, *worth* saving at all costs –'

'And the coded bits?'

'Oh, I don't know about that. Charles said if you were determined to find such things, find them you would.'

'Your husband didn't believe what he heard?'

'I don't know. Possibly, yes. Ben was supposed to have helped set up some periodical. The *News of Albion* was it? – something like that. But Charles respected Ben as a fellow-workman, a real craftsman. That more than anything else. It made him blind about him in one or two respects. But *he* would have said those respects weren't the important ones.'

'Not even – what? – treason?'

'Ben was dead. Charles felt it was an awful tragedy. He wanted to leave it at that. Apart from keeping the work in circulation, that is.'

'And you, Mrs Cornelius?'

'I'd always seen something else in Ben. Something colder, deeper down. Do I mean "colder"? Very detached, then. What's the line in the song? "The smile beneath my smile." He – he disconcerted me sometimes. Oh, I realised how charming he must have seemed, but I wasn't depending on his favours the way some people were.'

(Momentarily I found myself recollecting the dapper and promiscuous form of someone now long forgotten by his public, Leofric Anstey –)

'Like my mother, for instance?'

'She believed in the things she felt, I'm sure. She was persuaded. I had my own life, and Charles, and our child. I wasn't looking to see any of those things. I saw too much in another way perhaps. But I'd had a different life from hers –'

She sat forward in her lounger.

'I wouldn't have blamed her,' she said. 'Not for any of it.'

'Or blamed Matzell?' I asked her. 'With his fascist lot?'

She pursed her lips.

'And the company he went on to keep?' I said.

'Well, at the time it was secret. From us especially.'

'But that wouldn't have made his treason any –'

She interrupted me.

'His misplaced patriotism,' she said.

'– or whatever,' I countered. 'Anti-semitism?'

'That was part of it. One part.'

'Do you think my mother knew?'

'I doubt it. If she did know something – she didn't let it trouble her. She was far too much in love with him.'

'And he? Was he in love with her?'

'He would have been aware of her feelings, to some extent. But . . .' She pursed her lips again. '. . . but he had the films on his mind. Everything was riding on those.'

'He would have let her think her – her love – that it was reciprocated?'

'It didn't work like that.'

'How then?'

'He prided himself that he behaved as a reasonable man. That's what he was in his own eyes. Your mother, I think –' she hesitated – 'her feelings, they began to bypass reason. He wouldn't have been able to pick up on them, you see. If he had, then he might have been able to *do* something.'

'Do what?'

'Tried to save her from herself.'

It was a life away from La Baule, but it had the capacity to haunt me. When I was so far from it, I was implicated by my own guilt.

'How did Matzell die? The newspapers said his car crashed.'

'He was in a car.' Mrs Cornelius folded her hands on her lap. 'And it crashed. He was driving back to Selsdon.'

'It was an accident, though?'

'He'd been drinking before he left for London. Charles told me. To get up his courage.'

'Courage for what?'

'It was like one of those moments in his films. He had an appointment with a doctor.'

'What sort of doctor?'

'I don't know what they're called. They deal with fertility problems. His wife wanted children. When they learned they couldn't have them, she looked elsewhere.'

'*Who* couldn't have children?'

'Ben.'

'What?'

'He told Charles once. When he was deep into his cups.'

'His wife, surely – he meant *her* –'

'No. He meant himself. They'd both had umpteen tests done. Then more tests on Ben. Courses of treatment. I don't know all what. It was pretty much pioneering stuff in those days. Clutching at straws too, because Ben knew how things stood. But sometimes that's just the way of it. Not being able to do what you most want to. You can have so much else in life –'

'You're sure of this?'

Mrs Cornelius smiled brightly, confidently.

'Oh yes. Yes, I'm quite sure. And Ben was quite sure as well. He *knew*.'

'That's why he'd been drinking?'

'This was a second opinion he was going for. Well, probably a third or fourth by that time. It was a rich man's game. But he must have predicted what the answer was going to be.'

'He needed the drink to be able to take it?'

'And he probably had more to drink afterwards. That would have slowed down his responses in the car. It *might* have been an accident –'

'Or it might not, you mean?'

'It depends how depressed he was feeling. Having to face certain people at the studio the next day. Getting a poor notice in the press, or a run of them. Although that hardly signified, not against knowing he would never be able to father a child of his own. Anything could have helped to swing it, I mean. Atmospherics. How the light was in the sky, or that awful feeling you get when the summer's really gone and you smell autumn in the air. Something incidental like that could have seemed overwhelming, even just for a few moments.'

Her smile now was sympathetic rather than sad.

'How many others knew?' I asked. 'That he was . . .'

'Infertile?'

'Yes.'

'Very, very few. Scarcely anyone, I dare say. Catherine was discreet: she was desperate for children, of course, but I'm sure she was tactful. Charles had known Ben for ages –'

'He told your husband about that – but not about his political affiliations?'

'Films were Charles's life. I hardly remember him making a remark about politics. Sometimes he might say something about a politician, when they seemed intent on making things difficult for film-makers. Ben told him about the other matter because Catherine and I were old friends, but he knew Catherine wouldn't tell *me*. He realised we couldn't understand about the marriage falling apart, and that we never would if he didn't let us in on it –'

'And – there's no question of doubt at all? About any of this?'

'The accident in the car? Oh yes –'

'No. The infertility.'

'Oh no. Absolutely not.'

'Someone else could have found out about it, though? Whom he'd said nothing to?'

'Well, only if they'd been spying on him, I suppose. Spying very hard.

Following his movements. But no one would have been likely to do that, would they?'

'I can't say,' I replied.

She hadn't intended the remark as a question. Her head was now tilted enquiringly on to one side.

'You think – ? Who on earth?'

'If he was involved in politics, Mrs Cornelius –'

'Shenanigans? Oh, that was just in films. Maybe you've been watching too many recently?'

'You said – about the doctor – the melodrama spilling over into life –'

Her head tipped on to the other side. She might have been suppressing a philosophical smile.

'Hmmm...'

In the fog, up on the cinema screen, a solitary female figure stands on a bridge.

It could be either day or night.

A car's headlights briefly curdle the fog to swirls of smoke. Tyres sizzle on the roadway; then they're gone, and silence returns to the scene.

Even inside the silence, though, there are very faint sounds to be heard. Water slapping on stone. Echoing drips. The faraway rumble of a train. A muffled steeple bell.

The figure moves, starts to walk. Heels – a woman's heels – strike cobbles. The silhouette alters shape momentarily as the arms are raised and the headsquare is shaken out, then retied in place.

Behind, just visible to the camera's reach, a car's headlamps light up, like a pair of yellow ogre's eyes.

The woman walks on, without noticing. Her heels grow a little fainter, scratching on the stone.

Churning fog passes in front of the car's headlights.

Hidden water eddies into a tunnel. Drips sound eerily beneath the unseen arches.

Another train rolls out of earshot, into the distance.

For the reason that she was obsessed with him, my mother probably knew something about Matzell's other company, if not about the Weatherhill set's League of Albion.

When she met George Metcalf, he opened a door she had purposely kept closed until then. He prompted her to take the steps she wouldn't have dared to take if he hadn't suggested it. He urged her to clarify the past, and in the process he redirected her back there, into the trauma of her unrequited love for Benedict Matzell. Metcalf was doing her no favours – the favours were all intended for himself, to serve his own undeclared ends – but she could imagine that he was sincerely meaning to help her.

Her pain was only the obverse of a young woman's naïve joy and inviolable sovereign hope, which she couldn't have dreamed she would ever experience again. She would have forgiven my Uncle George anything: after all he had been the means of her testing the efficacy of the one great enduring and transcendent romance of her life.

NINE

We had stopped at a lay-by and my mother had dropped off for a few minutes. When she woke she stared about her, trying to remember where she was.

Then it came back to her.

She opened her door, twisting her legs round, and got out. She pulled herself up straight, took a few steps forward, looked at the view over the fence.

I switched on the radio. It warmed up, and from the speaker a man's voice emerged through the crackles, sharpening itself. He was reading the news. About General Péron's resignation. About a train accident in Belgium. About Princess Margaret Rose's speech to Girl Guides. About a white tiger that had escaped from a circus. Then I heard the words 'near Godalming' . . . 'in a cottage' . . . 'the body of a man' . . .

From nowhere my mother's arm suddenly reached in front of me. The voice faded back into the walnut fascia.

'Didn't I tell you I was tired of the news?'

She snapped the words at me, balanced on her knee on the seat.

'We – we could listen to the music,' I said.

'What?'

'The music –'

She stared at me.

'Sometimes there's music,' I said.

She looked away. Then, to take the weight off her knee, she slithered round on to the cushion of the seat.

'Not now, Merlin.'

She turned the ignition key.

'When?' I asked her.

She shrugged.

I sighed, as if that were all it was about: music or no music, a voice or its disappearance behind the burnished wood of the console.

Ignoring me, her eyes found the other woman's eyes in the driving mirror.

The Sun on the Wall

* * *

Our destination was deepest Sussex, a wooded lane on a gradient at the back of a village.

It seemed at first sight a handsome house, but after a day or two I was changing my opinion. Of twenties vintage, it would soon be overrun by creeper, by the trees whose roots had buried themselves beneath its foundations, by the gloaming half-light inside that felt more natural to it than the bright daylight of noon. Its roof was like a stove hat pulled down low; the upstairs leaded windows were eyes, either sly or wounded eyes, the broad eaves were the hat's brim or furtive eyebrows, and the sloping gables on either side were the building's shoulders sadly hunched in resignation.

The weather vane spun so easily that I supposed a part of the mechanism was loose, so that its prognostication – fair weather or foul – didn't seem to signify a great deal.

My mother called them my 'aunt' and 'uncle'. Aunt Kitty and Uncle Leslie. They were the only relations I had ever met.

She told me on that first full day, after I'd been conscious of her watching their diffident movements about the garden, that she meant – of course – that they were my great-aunt and great-uncle. *Her* aunt and uncle. I wasn't to hear her call either of them 'Aunt' or 'Uncle' herself, but since I had no experience of family I couldn't be sure that she should have done.

We had no staff, no domestic help at all, which such a sizable property in those days would normally have required. I supposed that Aunt Kitty and Uncle Leslie must have had help until recently, because they seemed awkward with the house and the work that needed to be done each day. Sometimes Aunt Kitty grew petulant, when she broke a nail for instance: even though Uncle Leslie was good-humoured and even though my mother assisted all she could, my aunt clearly regarded the household tasks as demeaning. In her crystal diction she told my mother that I should be pulling my weight too, doing this or that, and my mother would – a little hesitantly – agree with her. My Aunt Kitty didn't treat me with any of the sympathy I was used to from women, there were no fond and coy mentions of my handsomeness or sturdiness. To her I could be 'a damned pest', 'a wee brat' – as she called me when she thought only my uncle was there to hear her – and rather than being angered I was left completely nonplussed as to why she should think any such thing. I didn't feel I could have changed much since London, but her hostility expressed a counter-opinion.

'He hasn't improved any, Les,' she remarked ominously.

Nor did she like me playing too close to the windows. She complained about her migraines, and if I didn't actually cause them she fixed her eyes on

I've Been Here Before

me as if she needed a focus for her discontentment. She started every time she heard the front gate rattling and footsteps approaching on the gravel driveway, and she had to steady her nerves with a top-up from the Gordon's gin bottle. For a sixty-two-year-old my uncle was very nimble at getting to his feet and making for the more shadowed portions of a room where he could look out without being seen. My mother by contrast was unmoved: or should I say, she held in her breath and froze in her chair whenever she heard an intruder, or on the few occasions when the bell on the telephone rang out.

The house seemed to be full of surprises even to my aunt and uncle. They were for ever opening drawers and peering into cupboards, only to appear mystified by what they found or didn't find. I wondered why that should be when I'd been told this was their home. It was a big house certainly, and frequently dark, with creeper at the narrow windows and dim light-bulbs under the fringed shades; hands would fumble on the panelling to find light switches, and at night my aunt – who had 'nervous trouble' that affected her bladder – steered herself along the upstairs gallery to the bathroom carrying a torch.

After lights-out the house was racked with sounds. Upstairs the beams cracked behind the walls. Birds flew in and out of the roof. Behind a skirting board a mouse trod in boots or rearranged its furniture. I could have sworn I heard the kitchen clock muttering beneath the floorboards, and I only fell asleep at last by imagining that glinting eye of the brass pendulum swinging against the apricot-painted wall. When I woke in the night, which I frequently did, the sounds were still there, becoming louder the longer and harder I listened. They were joined by other sounds outside.

The branch of a tree tapping at a window.
Wings being shaken out in the trees' height.
A fox barking across the fields.
The screech of a game bird.

By day doors were shut on me as I passed rooms, and I heard combinations of voices being lowered so that I shouldn't overhear. So I took to the garden instead, running about the baked yellowing grass or hiding in the trees or constructing dams in the stream, and only when it rained did I go up to my room and build with Meccano or, better, plan a battle with the lead soldiers Uncle Leslie found in boxes in the attic and of which – when I enquired – he seemed to have no recollection. 'Just like old times. Isn't it, lad?' he said, confusing me hopelessly.

I liked to go into the wood at the back of the house and stand on the bridge of rickety planks above the brook. I would lean out between the spars on the side and look straight down into the water, imagining a river was raging beneath me. A rush of water, clean and clear and sparkling. The bridge would quake every time I moved my weight, and the flimsiness delighted me.

I would drop things into the flow, and run to the other side to watch them pass from under the bridge. I would run back every time, drop something else – another twig or stalk of long grass – and then run across again. It felt not at all an unfamiliar pastime to me ... I heard myself, the trembling I set up in the planks. So much freedom! All, however, is not bliss. Being thrilled and alarmed and saddened are all mixed up for me. I keep dropping odds and ends, running to the other side of the bridge and waiting for them to appear. My perspective is of things hurrying from me. Not knowing when and how and why. But always they're carried away in the end.

No one objected when I kept to myself. For me, putting up with my own company was preferable to trying to appease Aunt Kitty when she was in one of her fretful, handkerchief-twisting moods. Once I heard Uncle Leslie suggest to her that she was 'over-reacting to the situation', and she replied with a glacial silence more to the point than any words would have been.

But sometimes things were a little better, when Aunt Kitty thawed and Uncle Leslie remembered jokes. It was a fortunate coincidence, I felt, that their own background should have turned out to be a theatrical one, like my mother's. I realised that it must be a very small world, because for my mother the names they used in their story-telling didn't require explanation. Several times their experiences exactly matched, and I understood that they and my mother had been somewhere or other at the same juncture, in a touring play or in a film.

The suppers would become long with talk, with my uncle's mimicry and the others' laughter, and I'd feel my head growing heavy with tiredness, but it was an enjoyable sensation – the mutual recollections, the whoops of laughter, the sounds of Sussex birdsong outside, an occasional straining of a car engine in the lane behind the hedge. Something too about my aunt's and uncle's voices, so utterly familiar and convincing to me although my mother had introduced them to me as strangers ...

The windows remained open, and candles were left lit upon the table, and we might have been on a stage-set ourselves. I didn't even wish to be in the throes of an imaginary battle with my lead troops then, I was quite happy as I was, taking a delight in this tranquil truce. These evenings were my favourite parts of our days and at least I had the sage instinct to perceive it then, when it surely mattered that I did.

I've Been Here Before

* * *

On day eleven, without any warning, my mother sent me upstairs to pack. Her face was wan and serious, grim even.

'As quickly as you can, Merlin.'

I couldn't understand the reason for such speed. And at the end of the evening like this, so soon after our late supper. Had it something to do with the car headlights Uncle Leslie spotted earlier, travelling up and down the lane behind the beech hedge, delaying the preparation of our meal and taking away my mother's appetite?

'There isn't a minute to lose,' she called through between our rooms, and I wondered how she could be so certain. When she came through for me, she was short of breath.

'Now – are you sure – absolutely *sure* you've got everything?'

She scanned the room from the doorway, but there were too many corners to have to see into.

'Come on, then.'

Aunt Kitty and Uncle Leslie were standing downstairs, waiting for us – she checking her appearance in the hallstand mirror and he holding our coats in his arms. The eyes of both were wide in their faces. My mother gave them a dry, tight smile as she received her llama jacket and I my gabardine school mac. The wall-bracket lamps against the fumed oak panelling lent the muffled atmosphere of a club.

Suddenly my mother said her goodbyes, and she tugged me by the arm I was holding my school coat with. My aunt astonished me by aiming a kiss at my forehead, and my uncle clasped me manfully on the back of my neck.

'Keep in touch, son.'

His voice was without its usual rich, fruity timbre.

We walked out to the car, my mother prepared in flat heels not high. Uncle Leslie slung her suitcase over the lip of the boot, then he took my lighter one and placed it on top. The lid was slammed shut.

'Ssh –!' my mother warned him, too late.

I got into the car after my mother, and we closed our doors quietly. My mother lowered her window and waved to my aunt, who was standing in the vestibule with a blue light behind her. She lifted the handbrake and we freewheeled down the gravel driveway only on side-lights. My uncle opened the gate for us and we passed through, out into the lane. My mother, starting the engine, waved again. Uncle Leslie said something through the window, about 'keeping mum'.

'As we decided,' my mother called over her shoulder. 'By the script.'

My uncle said something else, perhaps repeating her. She blew him a kiss.

He came out and stood on the road – I saw him in the side-mirror –

watching us climb to the top of the hill. At the summit my mother switched on the headlamps, dipping them. Then she slammed her foot down on the accelerator, grabbed at the gear stick, and we were off.

There they are, in Matzell's *Famous Last Words*. It's 'Uncle Leslie', in clerical garb, performing a baptism at the font of a country church. No wonder he looks a little surprised himself at his calling. 'Aunt Kitty' appears later, as the haughty lady of the manor: frights overcome for the nonce, resolves perhaps stiffened with a gin or two in the dressing-room, she can concentrate better on maintaining the airs and graces demanded by the role.

Yet I think their skills were just as keenly tested afterwards, when in return for some past favour done them by my mother they were chivvied into helping conjure up an atmosphere of 'home' – to evoke something like it out of an assemblage of strange and unfamiliar props, for the doubtful end of convincing a child that there was still a normality left to him.

TEN

Who were they all, our 'set'?

Twenty, thirty years later I pieced their lives together.

What the facts themselves weren't able to tell me, I have had to suppose. The essence of others' lives is elusive, *perfumed*, and amounts in the end to guesswork. The best we can want to do is to try to understand.

Sonja Hellstrom, the aviatrix, had a deceptive name. She had been born in Bexhill-on-Sea, to parents as English as steak and kidney pudding, and christened Sonia. In later life she was to marry a Swede called Hellstrom; she kept the surname after they were divorced and even after she, briefly, was a wife for a second time. She wasn't properly a 'Miss' therefore, but that designation was the one to her liking. So 'Miss Hellstrom', whether for aesthetic or darker reasons, she remained.

She had become famous for her flying skills and her intrepid spirit. To journalists her glamorous sort of heroism was a godsend, flying solo to the improbable places that she did: Siberia, Tibet, the rim of Antarctica, across the Sahara, over the Inca cities of the Andes. Her fame had come to her in the late 1920s and early to mid 1930s, when these exploits were more unusual and harder to achieve. They brightened up the gloomy years. She had scrubbed good looks, an athlete's physique, and a chignon of auburn hair she let down for the photographers, arranging it so that it trailed beneath the tonsure of her strapped leather helmet.

In the fifties she was in demand chiefly as a fête-opener, invited to judge bottled jams and garden marrows; not so long before she had been judging bathing beauty competitions and belle of the ball parades, where earlier – in her prime – she had been invited to distribute the prizes at aeronautical shows and also to drop the 'off' flag at Brand's Hatch and to fire the starting gun at the racecourses of Europe, at one of which she had first made the acquaintance of Benedict Matzell. What changed days these now were.

She might have kept flying but, quite inexplicably, her courage had gradually deserted her. Maybe in truth she had tired of it, or had run out of destinations she actually wanted to fly to, or the wealth inherited from a sheep-farming Australian uncle had softened her. She wasn't a sentimentalist by nature, but she had since taught herself to turn her exploits into fables and to illustrate them with lantern slides. With time she had come to resent the indignity, yet she also wished her courage to return, even though it patently would not. She found that, without fully meaning to, she was wrapping myth about her like some extravagant cloth, like one of the sumptuous Samarkand silks she hadn't had the storage space in the bi-plane to allow herself to buy when she was physically, authentically, there.

Her relationship to the past became complicated. She hated it for causing the turmoil of feelings whipped up inside her head which she couldn't bring herself to confess to anyone. She wanted to soar above this present time, to go off in quest of her former courage. On the few occasions when she *did* get airborne again, the de Havilland Hornet Moth shuddered and groaned with age, and she felt that whereas she had once been able to tame its horsepower, now that mechanical strength was a malign force tugging at her arms and rattling her skeleton as she tried to steer the infernal contraption. A light cocaine snifter only complicated things further, it wouldn't release her mind as it was supposed to. She became horribly muddled about directions and wind currents, and she worried – woozily – that she might stray into a flight path. Away from the commercial air lanes, she felt, she might well be a different woman, if left to her own devices and pushed back on her own resources: but because modernity cramped her and confined her, she didn't have a chance of flying far enough away to discover for an indisputable fact.

Leofric Anstey had been among the first modern populisers of archaeology. He treated it as something between a science and an art, and possessed the singular virtue of allowing the readers of his books or the listeners to his wireless talks to feel they had benefited from the experience and become more learned than they'd been before.

He recounted his exploits as an adventure story. History wasn't so much lying dormant beneath the surface as compelling you – *you*! – to discover it. The man's cultivated tones took on a tremor of excitement as he described his digs, their fulfilments and mysteries. He let a penumbra of enigma pertain to the ancient past, as if to suggest that our knowledge about it can never be complete.

At Cambridge his fellow-dons were divided into his supporters and his detractors. Certainly he was a showman, but a legitimate innovator also. He bought a Legonda sports car, to travel the distance in term-time between his college set and his country house, a commodious rectory out beyond

Newmarket. In the vacations he went off about Britain or abroad on his excavations, with a band of young disciples in tow, both students and (he tirelessly worked on the arrangements) their fiancées and sisters. He assumed a liberal, egalitarian manner: it went quite against the grain with him, he claimed, that women should not receive the same opportunities as men, even in such a physically demanding area of practical study as his own.

Rumours did the rounds concerning those excavation jaunts. The photographs of Dr (not Professor, although journalists commonly called him that by mistake) Anstey that would appear in the newspapers had acquainted the public with his dashing handlebar moustache (it was gradually clipped back with time), the sleeked hair, his colourful waistcoats for town, his suede shoes, and – not least – the bright gleam in his rather small, close-set eyes. It wasn't too difficult to imagine... Why else should some of his female excavators have proved so absurdly loyal to him on their return and their male colleagues so reticent?

He himself remained as productive as ever. Books and broadcasts were churned out for the duration of the war, and his accounts of work on Arthurian sites had fired the British imagination as even his Persian and Syrian uncoverings could not. There was a patriotic tone in his writing now, as well as the mystical hypothesising of before. His books were bestsellers and taken up by the book clubs, while each new wireless talk drew an audience of seven or eight million listeners.

When the post of College Master fell vacant, only weeks after the war's end, Leofric Anstey let it be known to those in whose gift it effectively was that he was offering himself as a candidate. He had the pride and confidence of his public popularity, and must have felt he was advertising the fact that *his* candidature was of a more beneficially high-profile sort than that of anyone else tempted to put himself forward for consideration by the electors.

As events very curiously transpired, he did not receive the consensus of support he had calculated he would, and found himself beaten to the post by more than a pip. His confidence took a severe drubbing, but his pride was only intensified.

Thereafter he continued to hold his position in the college, conducting tutorials in his rooms and lecturing in the faculty building as before. He became a more public figure than ever. Patriotism still informed his wireless talks, his newspaper articles continued to intrigue readers. Fleet Street photographers, anticipating the treatment Miller and Monroe would receive, liked to juxtapose him in their shots with pretty young women. In the flashbulbs' glow at whichever function he was attending there was a twinkle in his pentagenarian's eye and just the hint of an old man's leer.

The Sun on the Wall

* * *

The year following his rejection by the college's selection committee, Leofric Anstey attracted second-headline coverage for discoveries made during his latest excavation project. Under the grassy ramparts of an eighth-century fortress at Sandlestock in Wiltshire, a burial chamber yielded what Anstey declared was the lost treasure of Avalon. These included, among the gold and silver totems of power, several skeletons buried inside elaborately ornamented lead sarcophagi. On the ribcage of one of the skeletons was found a crown of white gold inset with semi-precious stones: not the king's actual crown, but – Anstey deduced – its exact replica in secondary materials, as the Egyptians and Aztecs had equipped their own sovereigns for the journey to the afterlife.

The newspapers had a field day, literally enough. Mention of the business was made in the House of Commons and recorded in Hansard. At a time of (unofficial) national crisis, King George was able to include a reference or two in his speeches. His brother enquired from Paris whether it might be possible to purchase any of the artefacts, should they be bound for auction, and Cartier were informed. Ted Heath and his Band recorded an instrumental piece called 'Avalon', which became a popular hit in the following weeks. American *Time* treated the story, and photographs published in *Picture Post* were syndicated to newspapers across the United States.

Anstey had the finds offered to Cambridge University. They hesitated, and a decision was put off until the following term. For Anstey, thin-skinned in this respect, their insulting procrastination was tantamount to a refusal, and he withdrew his proposal.

He had planned an addition to be built to his own college to house them, the Anstey Wing. Now the destination of the finds was of no concern to him. Museums fought over the treasures, but he remained aloof from their disputes. Close friends of both sexes claimed he had lost some of his old familiar sparkle, and seriously doubted that it would return as before.

No one had properly known what Mrs Curtain's background was. With her bulk she was almost an abstract person – a great rotund question in a fairground 'Guess the Weight' competition. She was included in the group because of her psychic skills. She operated at a more mundane level with *éminences grises* in business and finance, anticipating their futures before it happened, yet her influence went far beyond that.

Mrs Curtain, uniquely, was in frequent communication with aliens, with those extra-terrestrial beings hovering just beyond our own globe in inner outer space. *They* used the medium as their exclusive agent in dealings with humankind. She had 'gone up' herself three times, and had seen and learned some quite astounding things.

What Mrs Curtain 'knew' could have had devastating effects on numerous institutions if allowed to enter the public domain. Religions would have been discredited, most significantly, and since those were the pretexts for wars and insurrections, the justification for régimes and dictators all around the globe, whole systems of life would have been thrown into further turmoil. Certain governments in the world depended on factional upsets affecting their neighbours, and would have been compromised themselves. Panic upon panic would have ensued, at all strata of society.

Mrs Curtain was aware of these implications. She had been consulted at regular intervals by go-betweens who reported back to high government officials, even to Cabinet. She had more than once received in her rooms a high-ranking visitor from one of the Eastern European embassies, who can be supposed to have liaised with his masters in the Kremlin. Super-Reubensian, gargantuan, Hendon-spoken Mrs Curtain was a woman with her megalithic finger on the pulse of intercontinental, interdoctrinal politics, which were motored by the primal emotion of fear.

It would have been hard to believe from the external evidence. A pleasantly smiling, rouge-cheeked titaness, upholstered in beaded shifts and shawls, with a glittering black net cast over her hair and two armfuls of bracelets chiming cheerfully to outdo Lady Coniston's. She would cross her paradoxically dainty feet in their velvet harem slippers, elbow herself a little more room against the armchair's resistance, and all would seem to be straightforward and innocent enough in the world she colossally occupied. Smile after smile. The chair would creak under its burden, of course, and the owner's eye would return nervously to the spot, but no one would have considered offering a word in the hapless chair's defence. Mrs Curtain's social inviolability was wholly assured, as the stars – and their beady-eyed green travellers – foretold it must be.

Dame Helena Winthrop may have looked like a Greek tragédienne – statuesque, black-haired, black-eyed – but in fact she was one of those persons whose appearance owes almost nothing to their line of ancestry. Her parents had been Welsh folk of no more than middling height, with brown hair and rather vapid features and unsunned skin. Yet she had been born as she was, and invested from that first day of her life – and earlier – with her prodigious talent and all that it would achieve.

Her mother and father had been a little musical, but in an amateurish way, so that her skills when they first manifested themselves were a wonder. However, no one cared to dwell on their source: everybody, and the child

Helena most of all, was determined to make the very utmost of them, as if superstitiously afraid that they might fade and vanish if not lashed into the discipline of practice, practice, practice.

The early years of arduous training were rewarded with Helena's growing fame in her mid-teens. She performed all about the land, in the chilly public halls of market towns and the quaint music-rooms of venerable foundations, at London venues where the audiences sat intently, and even (when requested) at private aristocratic functions, where the trappings of high birth delighted her notwithstanding that tongues wagged and mouths suppressed yawns above receding chins. She made herself wholly available, and her only conditions concerned her sizeable fee.

She married a composer, and when her reputation eclipsed his, they mutually separated and were divorced, and she married for a second time. Her new husband was an elderly industrialist who collected rare and precious objects. They got along together very well, shaking down much better than people had supposed they would, and when he died she found herself somewhat at a loss, except financially. Her third husband was a highly sexed music scholar, who also became organiser of her itineraries: but he worked her very hard, and in the end he absconded with a heavy whack of the proceeds plus the young girl who had regularly sat by her side turning her pages, and – without a clue as to his whereabouts, and lacking the legal means of disentangling herself – it proved a most unsatisfactory business altogether.

Then, however, the war came, and she was visited with the true fame that was to be her fate in life. The free recitals she gave to raise morale became legendary the length and breadth of Britain. (The recitals were sponsored in effect by her second husband's will, which provided her with an embarrassingly generous monthly income – without stipulations, since he had never supposed that he should die or she marry again.) She very adroitly spread herself, from Penzance to Inverness, and also hired the services of a canny, enterprising publicist. Photographs of her playing about London out-of-doors – on rubble sites, wearing a Schiaparelli gown and a blue fox jacket and with a gas-mask case placed within snatching-up distance on the lid of the Bechstein – entertained and cheered those of the nation's public who could only hear her on the radio. The war *was* her moment, the summation of her talent. When it finished, she herself – never mind Britain – considered that she belonged to it, was woven into the woof of the history of that time, and in the future must fail to possess as much authenticity as she had done then.

That proved to be the case. Her own playing was never to sound so dextrous or as apt as when she had played to tearful, still-shocked locals on the more photogenic sorts of bomb-site. In concert halls her skills had acquired a tinny echo, and an uncontemporary touch, even an air of artifice. She couldn't quite understand why; she thought she was playing in the same way, and then wondered if she ought to be. But without her expensive sheeny gowns she felt she must be like everyone else, of more mature years, and she was afraid of hazarding ordinariness. Her father died, and then her mother, and she couldn't be persuaded to try any of the more recent music because modernity put her in mind of both her third husband, the music scholar, and her treacherous page-turner. One evening in Birmingham she looked down from the stage and saw the pair of them sitting with broad smiles in the front row of the quarter-filled auditorium; her confidence deserted her, and she muddled through the recital, with fistfuls of wrong notes in the final passage of Grieg. In the dressing-room she finished the bottle of whisky she had taken two tumblers from before she began, and waited for a knock on the door that never happened.

After that, and to cut an inglorious story very short, it was downhill – declining arpeggios – all the not very pretty way. Butterflies, palpitations, the vomiting beforehand. A last steadying drink, to try to calm shaking hands. Losses of memory in the middle of a piece. Sticking to compositions with *tunes*. Moving into and out of different tunes because composers will bloody well repeat themselves or else plagiarise. Hearing pins drop in an audience, waiting for the hacking cough which would cause her to lose her concentration again. The coldness of those halls like barns, the darkness beyond the stage, the heatless light from the spotbulbs. The heaviness of her gowns; the occasional, perplexing stiffness in her wrists; some sluggishness which actually seemed to be *inside* her hands, slowing up the fingers. The idiot grin of the ivories every time she opened up a piano. Hearing one wrongly tuned note, but as soon as she thought she'd located it discovering that it had jumped up or down an octave. Feeling the chill on the keys that lay out of her usual range. Sensing the hostility of the pedal mechanisms. Imagining the height of the stool was sinking and perhaps having to end up striking the keys with that chin which she wished wasn't Grecian and tragic and old-womanly as it was. Visualising herself recklessly tearing at her gowns one evening on stage and throwing off all her clothes, to be free of this whole goddamned burden that her life had become. Running from the laughter of astonishment for the velvety shadows at the sides of the stage, taking literally to those wings and rising clear of everything, flying high through the proscenium arch and out through a tiny window up beneath the ceiling somewhere, out and into the starry and forgiving night.

Clarita Valdés-O'Shaughnessy was *the* 'Clarita' who had owned and managed the supper-club of that name in Old Compton Street. I was to find photographs of the place; the décor was ethereally done out, in white and pink and pale blue, with murals by Rex Whistler on the walls that showed sea views through arbours of yellow roses and greeny-blue vine leaves. It was the apogee of sophistication, in its time. A pianist played at a white piano, and on certain nights of the week a small band was provided for dancing. Clarita's was very well known, to those who had discriminating standards: its appeal was to a clientele who didn't care for ostentation or flashy fashion and who valued discretion and quiet good taste. The best tables had to be reserved weeks in advance, and Clarita's own favouritism was of a very ordered kind.

Everywhere has its day and Clarita's flourished between 1932 and 1939. The lady continued in business in Soho throughout the war, but by the later stages the restaurant had the appearance of a lost, nearly innocent age. It might have become popular again, but that would have taken another couple of decades, until its quaintness could be appreciated by, say, the sorts who frequented Biba's Rainbow Room. Mrs Valdés-O'Shaughnessy sold out to another restaurateur called Belloumeau, bombed out of King Street and an earnest rival of a fellow-Frenchman well established in Greek Street. The delicate décor was dispensed with and replaced by burgundy velveteen walls, salmon-tinted mirrors, black leatherette banquettes and cartwheel centre-lights with lime green shades.

Clarita's became a memory, of better times, to those who had been in the know. Their own lives seemed to have been more fulfilled then, or at any rate more optimistic. Because the supper-club had been relatively short-lived, its reputation for posterity appeared all the surer. Clarita's hadn't had the chance to outstay its welcome, and certainly didn't make the mistake of opening its doors in the harsher, unromantic glare of lunchtime daylight.

That hadn't been quite the whole story, however.

For the discerning patrons, 'those' and 'such as those', the attractions extended beyond the social and culinary. On two or three nights out of each fortnight, the supper-club while to all appearances 'open' had in fact been 'closed'. On those occasions no chance customers would have been found on the premises.

In the second dining-room, behind a partition of tapestried Second Empire screens, a number of roulette tables would be in operation. Clarita herself supervised, proving especially solicitous to the high spenders. The croupiers were extremely efficient, and had been poached from establishments in Mrs Valdés-O'Shaughnessy's beloved second home-town, Monte Carlo.

The activities were, of course, to remain unofficial. Over the years, from her experience in other supper-clubs, Clarita had made acquaintances drawn from many walks of life: some doubtless more carefully sought out than others. Among those who appreciated life's finer things and enjoyed them unrestrictedly in Old Compton Street were one or two of the big shots from Scotland Yard's top echelons, for whom the club was within easy travelling distance of work on one side and home on the other. They became regular customers, and could only have done so with the proprietress's express approval. She made a particular point of gracing their tables when they came, but as if only to engage in politesse. Mrs Valdés-O'Shaughnessy was a wealthy woman in her own right, and if money can 'talk' then why shouldn't a dialogue have been possible with those similarly blessed?

Throughout her career, Clarita's colleagues and enemies would have agreed, she had known how to serve her own interests best, under the guise of friendship. Where friendship wasn't quite enough, she'd had another weapon at her disposal – bundled into rolls and held by elastic bands and tucked into a large, plain, sealed envelope. She had become a successful entrepreneuse because she had understood never to drop her guard for a moment, never to stand still and be tempted to look back over her shoulder the way she'd just come.

Clarita Valdés-O'Shaughnessy was now, in the mid-1950s, part-owner of two other restaurants. One was French and one North African, but they were businesses rather than enthusiasms. All that would satisfy her would be another club, where the mixers would be enabled to mingle with the shakers. It was far less a matter of the expense of the outlay than of picking her moment, when the public would want it and more importantly so would she. It had to be her life, a devouring passion. As with her fellow-members of the Weatherhill set, the future always promised better than the recent past; for her as for them, it would be a consummation. Like them, she was only biding her time – making ready, preparing the (high-rent) ground.

ELEVEN

And George Metcalf.

I can't be so forgiving of him now.

Who was he?

Not an employee in a shipping line office, surely.

A journalist? I haven't been able to locate articles in any newspaper or periodical of the time written by George Metcalf. The name may be a pseudonym, however.

If not a reporter, then perhaps he was an investigator of some sort. An official one? – or a freelance, collecting his information to sell to an interested party at the highest price the market would sustain?

In August 1958 – I have the dates and details on computer disc now – a report appeared in *The Times* that Leofric Anstey's literary executors had alighted on several blackmail letters – anonymous, of course – among his correspondence.

Three weeks later a much bigger story broke in the general Fleet Street press, and set everyone talking. The revelations disclosed that Anstey had tampered with the finds of the dig at Sandlestock. This effectively exploded the myth of 'Avalon Rediscovered'. Even the famous artefacts were shown to be resoldered hybrids of varied and very scattered provenance, Persian and Syrian among them: the white gold of the crown was in fact buffed bronze. Anstey had in person engineered (that is to say, fabricated) the greater part of the purported 'evidence'. The skeletons inside the sarcophagi were now claimed, with anti-romantic licence, to be those not of ancient warrior-princes but of Victorian derelicts dug out of their paupers' common graves.

There were subsequent accusations laid against the Cambridge authorities that they had contrived to ruin Anstey's reputation, which elicited from them very strident denials. Accusations were delivered against individuals in the same line of archaeological research as the late Leofric Anstey, who might have been presumed to hold grievances; but they too repudiated charges of involvement, and there was a deal of talk banded to and fro about libel proceedings.

Yet the notion persisted, that only a party with a grudge would have acted to uncover this web of misinformation which the populist Anstey had so sedulously concocted to support his 'Avalon' theory. The exposé could not have happened for no reason at all. A journalist revealed that although Anstey had been comfortably off he was 'obliged' to sell various archaeological items quite legitimately in his possession to cover unspecified 'costs'. His banks were approached in the hope of some light being shed, but their reticence was judged to be less a matter of discretion than a genuine inability to trace any system of payment through their records. The financial speculation prolonged the story's newsworthiness.

Going out of circulation. Our accidental encounter. Blackmail letters, from person or persons unknown. A fatal cocktail of barbiturates in whisky. Press interest. The strenuous denials of certain individuals and professional bodies, threats of libel actions in the courts.

Secrets that couldn't be kept secrets, which broke their seals.

A newspaper hoarding which I saw summed it all up. SUICIDE LATEST: BURIED SHAME OF TALL-TALES PROF LEO.

Eventually, decades later, I succeeded in tracking down a photograph of personnel from the period when Wodeham Place – a fact my Uncle George slipped into the conversation one day, to be met by the intensity of my mother's silence – was operating as a Home Intelligence centre.

A couple of dozen staff are arranged in semi-formal pose, seated or standing on the steps of the front portico. Some of the men are in uniform and others in tweed sports jackets; the women mostly wear civilian dresses. One woman is accoutred in trousers: they're smartly cut, and paired with stylish two-tone shoes.

Uncle George is easy to spot, standing with arms crossed at the back. He is little different from the man I recall. The woman in trousers puzzled me for a while. She seems to have set herself apart from her female colleagues, in her ensemble of dark trousers and striped blouse and jumper casually knotted around her neck. The others remain faithful to cardigans and skimpy wartime jackets, but she is more ironic perhaps, halfway to joining the men and able to make a woollen look *sportif*.

What is it about her?

I'm perplexed by what I see, or by what I'm not seeing. For days I ponder the matter. What is it that I'm failing to recognise about her? By what association do I find myself remembering those hollow-sounding tea-rooms out Richmond way, latticed with ersatz beams and called the John of Gaunt?

I had the black and white photograph magnified several times.

'Up again, please.'

Then 'Once more, can you?'

The faces started to blur. Metcalf, Uncle George, was on the point of slipping away, after my triumph of having salvaged him from the records.

But it was less on him that I was concentrating than the woman in trousers, who sat perched at the base of one of the columns, straight-backed, ankles and feet crossed.

There was something about her...

She presented herself attractively, but she was self-contained. A sharp face with pronounced cheekbones, or merely a clever manner in make-up. She had blonde hair, fashionably bobbed. Slim hands.

She was smiling, but only as a gesture, for the camera. The smile pulled a dimple in her left cheek.

She wore a ring on one of her little fingers: it was just recognisable as, yes, a signet ring.

She was about as far from the appearance of Miss Deegan as a woman of the same build and proportions could have made herself. The trousers with the clean creases; the modish two-toned shoes; the oh-so-casually knotted jumper draped about her shoulders; the go-anywhere hairstyle. This gad-about-town read fashion magazines, was up to the minute, but set out to make her *own* look. Although she was sitting down, I guessed she must be of average height at least. She had poise, but the pose – was I right? – seemed somehow unsympathetic, as if calculated to distance her from the others.

My recognition of her at last was inspired rather than reasoned. Could it actually *be* her? The face tapering to the point of the chin...

My eyes kept passing between the two figures, the man and the woman, trying to hold them – one superimposed on the other – in a focus that would help explain to me just what it was that I needed to discover.

Once they had known one another. They had been colleagues working for the common patriotic good. The headquarters were housed in a grand country house, but it wasn't the size of a public institution in a city, so there could have been no avoidance. At the least they had exchanged communications, passed in the corridors; they had eaten the same food in the same canteen, and maybe they had been included now and then in the same round of drinks bought in the local pub.

I sat for long periods in front of the photograph, trying to read the past through the bloody conclusion that had befallen it.

A biography of three English film-makers of the forties, including Matzell, was published in 1984.

Concerning Matzell, the book was disappointingly perfunctory, and although litigation was unlikely the author steered well clear of controversial matters. The author may have lacked sufficient proof of Matzell's active political sympathies; mention was made of European friends – German business men of a certain age, titled Italians bereft of former privileges – and of regular private visits to the Black Forest and to Montecatini.

One of the photographs was taken on board the Prince of Polignella's yacht in late 1945. Capri is visible in the background. One person of the group of a dozen fellow-travellers intrigues. A woman. Of thirty or so. Plainish, and in her tweed skirt and cardigan much less elegantly dressed than the others. Hair darker than fair, to judge from the black and white dots of print. She is holding a pair of spectacle frames in her hand: the glass in them appears to be clear, not tinted. She's smiling, and a dimple pulls in her cheek. Her chin is pointed. She wears a ring on her little finger.

It's another Miss Deegan, an earlier prototype model. The cardigan sits loose on her shoulders. The hair has changed colour, but is not yet worn close to her head like a helmet; that, however, is a small detail of her appearance to alter, and she's working on it. The accents – phonily suppressed Essex and clumsy, uneducated French – are also in the experimental stages. But the physical outline is already there, the pose and the attitude – briskly attentive and insincere, 'Smile, say cheese!', mouth dutifully pulled back over one incisor, and that tell-tale dimple showing, only waiting for the photographer to be done.

Benedict Matzell was killed less than two years later. Only a little while after that, Lady Coniston lost her husband and gained a social secretary, so 'Miss Deegan' originates from – at least – that troubled juncture, if not before. The other household staff were to remember her as efficient but domineering, stand-offish when she chose to be but versed at winkling out the facts of everyone's history. They in turn had learned almost nothing about her, presumably because she'd been quite determined that they would have no chance to find out. Increasingly she had made herself indispensable to Lady Coniston, and edged out the others from her confidence; there was no family to question her intimacy with the woman's affairs. Whatever her intentions were, she encountered no opposition, or too little to deflect her from her purpose.

* * *

From her wartime work she would have had access to a great deal of incriminating evidence against individuals who subsequently achieved high office and influence. She had known about the League of Albion in its formative stages, but that was small beer compared with the possibilities presented to her later by the thrusting ambition of those with past lives to be kept secret.

She practised her gentlest blackmail on the members of our group. They were all wealthy in their own right, and she could persuade them that their generosity was necessary to preserve the League. (Only Leofric Anstey refused at last to play along and pay up.) She may well have tried to keep the idea of Albionism in circulation among them, to hold them together. The Weatherhill set's principal usefulness to her was in providing her with a base of operations. From the outset she'd had bigger quarry in mind.

Success and wealth are commonly synonymous. That was a premise of her continuing interest in the careers of men, and women, whose names – gracing the pages of *Who's Who* and society magazines – had once appeared on classified lists of those engaged in activities considered not conducive to the public good.

Matzell's involvement was of particular interest to her.

She knew how to locate much of the material she required, and how to cover her own tracks, but her approach to her researches re Matzell was more personal than with her other subjects. She'd had leads on him since his days with Herbert Kolb, which was why she had set out to make his acquaintance when he first went to work at the Selsdon Studios. Disguise had always come easily to her, and even though her Miss Deegan of those days had been a younger and less extreme version, no one would have had any cause not to suppose that she was who she appeared to be.

Who was she finally, though? Was she any more the well-groomed *bon ton* figure in slacks and knotted jumper than the one I became familiar with at Wilton Crescent and Weatherhill Lodge, in her uniform of long cardigan and shapeless tweed skirt?

More questions.

What was the connection between George Metcalf and the woman who called herself Miss Deegan? Was their time at Wodeham Place the last occasion when they had worked together? Could they have met since, to pool the information which they had each collected? Subsequent to that, might a falling-out have occurred over the steps of their future policy?

Once they had worked together, as colleagues. That was as much as I could be certain of. If they had been closer, they were no longer so. She had lived so far inside her disguise that it had become a bona fide identity: an identity defined by the woman's will, and this will was dedicated to her own protection. Too much was at stake, and one man with an imprecise curriculum vitae and indeterminate loyalties didn't have the right to imperil her standing within the group of Albionites. He couldn't be allowed to signify, not against what it had taken her so much careful contrivance and years of vigilance to sustain.

The outer life of history is a scarcely credible pantomime, and our smaller lives – to distinguish – seem like a crude and highly coloured melodrama. Coincidences and recurrences; hypotheses and predestinations. Round and around, and as tedious as a twice-told tale it is, this knot intrinsicate. But there it is: and here we are. So what more is to be done, except to trace the patterns in the flow?

For my mother it was the prospect of a future when there seemed little else, only Pimlico Road and trying to lose the recollection of Mr Kester. Benedict Matzell had taken her up not so much because she had a talent for the job as because she evinced a quality she might not have realised she had, or didn't have: an interior emptiness. She allowed him to impress upon her the features of type in a world of drifting types, a kind of personality Plasticine-modelling.

In the films she acts capably but no better than that. She was useful to Matzell because she was essentially faceless and forgettable, and because she could credibly become the unwitting instrument of fate in other characters' lives – and so incidentally in her own character's too.

She fitted later into the group because that was her instinct. She had me with her, and I was her justification, because I was Benedict Matzell's child. She believed that, I'm sure, because (as Mrs Cornelius suggested) it was so important to her that I should be his child. The studio gossip may have got it right, that her boy's father was one of the stalwarts of the sound crew, but she had determinedly turned a deaf ear, and tried to put it from her mind, tried to . . . She had only truly loved Matzell, even if he hadn't been able to love her as much as she'd wanted him to, and when she lost him she temporarily lost hold of her reason also. She recovered it no better than partially, because there was always to be the memory of both the fine time *and* the bad, and the contradiction was irresoluble to her.

Some critics, the more grudging, view Matzell as a diiettante, because they want to make a political point about his background. Others, working from more detailed cinematic arguments, see him as an adventurer in style. A few call him a subversive, because on screen he reduced society to systems of programmed behaviour with individuals functioning as ciphers, directed by frustrations and wants they have inherited from lives lived before their own. To that third school of critics the films are cold games, furnished with techniques learned from the German Expressionists, where emotion is some kind or driverless car: intellect, in the British fashion, occupies – so to speak – faded and shadowy back rooms, like a mysterious tenant who gives no precise clues to others of his designs.

The films are seldom shown on afternoon television nowadays, not being considered quaint enough. Some aspect – a negativity, of an approximately existentialist sort – fails to make them comfortable viewing. The ambience of menace in this shadowscape isn't always explained, and the endings eschew happiness.

When the films *are* given an airing, it's in the early hours of the morning when buffs can record them. They are a young man's work, and part of the pleasure they afford involves our speculating where his talents might have taken him once he had narrowed his eager experiments with form to structure a wholly recognisable language of his own, with a 'message' and his specific 'something to say'.

The Anstey case became quite a scandal.

Of the others in the set it was Hugo Rathbone who later held the public attention, indeed gaining notoriety for himself.

In 1960 a scam was exposed, and Rathbone sent for trial and found guilty. For ten years he had masterminded a skilful fraud: the estates and pension policies of certain persons had continued to be drawn upon after the (unacknowledged) deaths of those individuals. The business had required fastidious diligence in the details, a sixth sense for potential inconsistencies and contradictions, and a hypersensitivity to financial conditions that might have caused unwelcome attention from legal representatives and insurance companies. While Rathbone had continued to hold a position as associate director of his bank, with access to privileged insiders' low-downs on markets and also personal accounts, he would spend at least half his working day employed in his imaginative exercise of deception, breathing life back into the dead by means of reams of authoritative-seeming, expertly forged paperwork.

To have evaded detection for ten years was a considerable achievement, which may have helped him sustain his esteem during his ensuing incarceration at Her Majesty's Pleasure. He had confined himself to extorting comparatively modest sums in the cases of each of the deceased, and he had been cautious in selecting only those individuals who had led solitary or (in respect of London) geographically distant lives. He had not indiscriminately – or even greedily – plundered: he had lasted the course because he had known precisely what he was about.

The end came suddenly, through an accident of circumstance which he could not have foreseen. The long-lost brother of one of those he considered his 'clients' came to light smallholding in the scrubby backwoods of an African protectorate; a third party brought him to London with the purpose of establishing a claim to the family inheritance. The services of the estate's administrators were dispensed with, but only after they had assisted some officers of the law in their enquiries. The third party believed there was good cause to pursue matters still more vigorously, and instigated legal proceedings. Threads of connection were followed back, through all the distracting fankles and complications which the wily Rathbone had devised, and further and further back. Even when the persons charged with handling the investigation were confronted with a series of aliases and addresses of convenience, connections continued to be made. It was an arduous and time-consuming process, but a team of young eager beavers found their appetites whetted, and the more so the longer their search lasted.

The press would have been better pleased if Rathbone could have been proved to have acted more selfishly than he had, to line his own pockets. However, a proportion of the ill-gotten funds had been diverted to the promulgation of the doctrines of a small right-wing nationalist group, styled the League of Albion, and that had made less gripping copy. The group's own literature was reproduced, in censored form: hectoring pamphlets with a jingoistic tone, but carrying also a racist, anti-semitic undertext. To hard-boiled journalists with a nose for next day's news, the story already had an old-fashioned – very nearly nostalgic – ring to it, concerning issues that had been of consequence one or two decades before but not now, not in this age of supposed plenty and personal opportunity.

The newspapers concentrated upon the crime of extortion rather than its ends, namely the dissemination of political theories that had had their day. Photographs appeared showing the bachelor felon's residence in The Boltons and also his country place, the converted oast-houses down in Kent. His domestic habits were described from a cook's or chauffeur's point of view, and the names of his friends were paraded in print (included among them was 'Maître' Cyril Harkiss, proprietor of the epicurean La Maison du Chocolat), as were the marques of car he used to drive and the vetting policies of the gentlemen's clubs he would presumably be blackballed from.

* * *

A two-toned royal blue and silver Bentley was found parked three miles outside Eastbourne, in a flint lane leading to the sheer chalk cliffs that crest the sea there.

The car's owner, one bearing the name Cyril Harkiss, was reported as missing. The East Sussex constabulary weren't able to obtain any word of a sighting, and no body was ever found that positively answered to his physical description.

A relative took over the running of the business in Mayfair. The name La Maison du Chocolat was changed, which was considered a foolish decision, and an augury of altered recipes and financial decline. The firm was taken over in the mid-sixties, and for many years the most faithful of Harkiss's high-society customers were to regard the selling as a betrayal of a loyalty much more personal than commercial.

One of the two brothers from whom Harkiss had learned his trade in Vienna, called Adalbert, was arrested as he travelled between his apartment and café-cum-*chocolatier* establishment in the rue Royale, in Paris. A famous Viennese self-styled 'avenging angel', stalker of war criminals still at liberty, had provided the French police with a file of information. They regarded the evidence as unequivocally damning enough to act upon. Adalbert was sent for trial in the city where, as it was proved, he had carried out his collaborationist activities, Rouen. A fortuitous overdose of – once again – barbiturates in alcohol, mysteriously ingested somewhere between prison and the courtroom, deprived the prosecuting authorities of claiming belated justice for the souls of the persecuted.

TWELVE

I woke in the morning with a valley spread out beneath us. The lowest parts were still shrouded in mist. Above them, on the steep rises, was a jigsaw of hedged fields. Red soil. Green pasture. White cut corn. Blue smoke trailing from a cottage chimney.

My mother was lying across the two front seats. She was curled on her right side, facing me, asleep. She was breathing quite regularly, and her forehead was clear. I didn't want to wake her.

She woke soon after, though. Maybe I disturbed her, or a sixth sense detected she was being watched. Eyes still closed, her brow wrinkled with concern. Her eyes suddenly opened, fully, before I could retreat behind the seat back. I remained where I was, fascinated, and a little frightened. She stared up at me with momentary terror in her eyes. Then she started to remember.

'What time is it?'

I looked at the little clock in the fascia.

'Quarter past seven.'

'Good God –'

She turned further round, so that she could push up on her hands. When her head was at window height, she blinked out at the view of valley.

She didn't speak. Her eyes filled with the prospect, and she seemed to be remembering from much longer ago than just last night.

She pulled herself upright on the seat, swinging her stockinged feet down on to the floor. She raised one hand to an aching shoulder and rubbed at it. Her feet stepped into the shoes. She shook her head at the thought of something. She placed her other hand on the door handle, as if she meant to open the door. But she must have changed her mind.

The soles of her shoes slapped down on the pedals, she turned the key in the ignition, and the engine rasped back to life.

The road through the windscreen was red. It snaked its way downhill, towards the valley floor, where the mist lay. It carried us, when we descended at last, between high hedges and flowering banks of meadowsweet and wild chervil and goose-grass. Everything was dewy, and hung with trailing silver spiders' webs. My mother was still adjusting her focus, and plants and twigs scraped against the doors and windows as she drove in too close to the verges.

We passed one signpost, and then another, but she didn't look at either of them. It was as if she now had her directions quite clear in her head, and instinct would prompt her.

She told me we had reached Devon. The tilled soil was the colour of old, dried blood. The cottages had dirty bulging walls and untidily thatched roofs, and I could imagine the swathes of creeper as their russet beards. Somewhere near the valley bottom, cows being driven out cantered ahead of us along the road: my mother didn't allow herself to become impatient, but kept an even distance and a quiet engine as she followed behind the herdsman. I thought this augured better for us. I felt that she must have a surer sense of our whereabouts than just the map inside her head, that our journey now had a definite end in sight.

The bungalow we'd rented, called Talaton, was reached by a private road of flint and sand and grass. None of the intersecting roads in the place was made up, even those to the more expensive properties on the fringes of the golf course. Some roads had gates across them, and the rest – like ours – had gateposts without gates. There was no pavement, but the road was broad, with two long mounds of grass between the grooves worn by tyres, and ample space beyond the tracks for pedestrians to keep clear of any passing car.

The straggling community, somewhere between a village and a town, had an unfinished look generally. It was very doubtful that proper roads would ever be laid now. Here and there pavements *were* provided: however the flagstones were raised troublingly high, and old folk had difficulty climbing up and down wherever the pavements stopped and just fell away, back into loam and vegetation. There were hedges and bushes and wild-seeding flowers everywhere, and infestations of weeds and nettles. Some had blown into gardens over years; the result was an air of not unpleasing casual neglect, except in the most fussed-over gardens. Teigncombe Sands couldn't have been mistaken for suburbia, with spiky New Zealand palms and seaside fuchsia shrubs and spreading sea holly insinuating itself into beech and privet. Gull droppings had propagated peculiar sproutings of pinks on mossy roof tiles and yellow gorse from chimney pots. Hydrangeas grew with a lush abandon I haven't seen anywhere else, whatever conditions caused it – the proportion of sand in the loam, or the simple fact that nobody appeared to care about them very much.

I've Been Here Before

* * *

'I've been here before,' my mother said.

'*Here?*'

'To Teigncombe.'

'When?' I asked.

'When – when I wasn't very well. I was brought here to get better.'

I tried to think of a question to follow with.

'Is it – is it the same?'

'Oh yes. Oh yes, I think so.' I heard her sigh. 'It's just the same.'

'Why – why did you want to come back?'

'Oh . . .' She might have been going to reply more honestly, but then she seemed to change tack.

'Don't you like it?' she asked me.

'I *quite* like it,' I said. 'But we'll be going back to London, won't we?'

She smiled, gently enough. In her eyes, however, there was a look of dread, at the very impossibility of such a thing.

She stopped on our way back from the Stores at a poster on a noticeboard. Itced was advertising a film being shown in a town a dozen miles away along the coast.

A man in a mackintosh and trilby was holding a frightened young woman close to him. They were just out of a searching track of torchlight. The woman's eyes gazed up to the man's imploringly, and it was difficult to tell where the greater danger lay for her, with her craggy-featured protector or with the person or persons raking the brick walls of the alleyway with torchlight. The pretty face was filled with alarm and it was also filled with awe, panicking at the nearness of fulfilling her dream of love.

I had brought my kite with me, folded and packed away in my suitcase. My mother found me putting it together in the garden. She stood watching me, but she said nothing, which was how I knew it shocked her to see the thing again.

I went with her to the dunes to fly it. There she would turn away, and look either towards the waves and the flying spray or uphill, in whichever direction the wind was blowing from, and away from the flapping box with its long, trailing silk pigtails.

Love and fear and death.

In several of the films my mother becomes a corpse, gracefully draped over a chair with the telephone receiver still in her hand, or spreadeagled on a staircase with her handbag open and the contents rifled. In *Talk To Me* she ends up slumped on the back seat of a car with the doors locked from inside and a pearl-handled revolver in the furious grip of her dead fingers.

The Sun on the Wall

* * *

To get us both out of the house for a while, she took me walking up on to the windy headland.

We would stop on the turf where we always stopped, at a hole gouged by aeons in the rock, descending two hundred feet to the sea, by way of which smugglers used to be lowered and raised on ropes to escape the law's lookouts. I'd venture to a point three or four feet from the fissure, close enough to hear the waves rushing into the caverns and to catch a cold up-draught of salty air on my face.

Half a mile further on there was a pig farm. Even though it stank, I would linger by the pens, until my mother called at me to hurry up or she was going on without me.

Up there, among the few slanting thorn trees and the thistle beds and yellow broom thickets, we were quite alone. White clouds scudded carelessly across the mildest of blue holiday skies.

On our walks we picked wild flowers to take back home – tamarisk and mallow and wild mignonette – and because we did I supposed that my mother must be intending we stay here for a while, which suited me quite well.

My only problem was that I should have liked to go down to the beach more often than we did. We only went first thing in the morning and – sometimes – in the cool of the evening, when my shadow preceded me across the sand as I ran to take my chilly dip in the surf. My mother would wait for me in the dunes, wearing her raincoat and a headscarf knotted under chin; I guessed she was dressed like that only so that she could keep warm, and didn't realise that she must also have been trying to elude any stalking eyes that might have remembered her from a few years before. She would wrap the towel around me when I ran out, and help dry my shoulders and back, and then turn the other way as I clambered into my clothes. With the breakers singing in our ears, we would set off for Orchis Road, first slithering down the dunes to the flat of spear grass behind and then following the beaten right of way that led by stiles across the fields.

She had quickly rediscovered her way about the place. At the quieter times of the day she tuned back into the familiar, almost effortlessly, as if she was steering herself about by means of radio waves. Teigncombe and its environs might have been crossed by aboriginal songlines, so surely did her feet obey the directions she was keeping in her head.

The walls of the bungalow were hung not with paintings or their reproductions but with maps: Ordnance Survey in the hall, antique cartographers' work under glass in the sitting-room and dining-room, and some framed sailing charts in the other rooms.

The largest was in the dining-room, above the sideboard. It was a seventeenth-century illustration of England, which resembled a bloodily pink item of offal lying on a butcher's slab. The paper was unevenly faded and spotted about its surface with little rust marks, but the size and age of the map were both impressive. When I sat at my corner of the table I sometimes forgot about the food, letting my eye trace a progress around the nibbled shoreline. Sitting opposite me, my mother would look too – with an odd mixture of curiosity and irritation. When the sun shone directly through the oriel window at lunchtime, our two reflections in the glass of the frame got in the way and England disappeared beneath us, sinking into its curdy yellow sea.

In my bedroom hung a sailor's chart, of all the shades of mid-blue. No land was shown at all. The gradations of colour indicated lesser and greater depths. Italicised numerals were current speeds. A sandbank obtruded into the bottom left-hand corner, and was rendered in pale saffron beside the name Doom Bar. Other names indicated reefs and light-ships and, scattered about, ship-shaped hieroglyphs marked the sites of wrecks. It was a monotonous and unengaging piece of work, yet my dreams for five or six nights included an undue amount of sea and sensations of floating and drifting: not, I think, of foundering and preparatory drowning, although in effect that is what our time then consisted of.

'This isn't the first time –' my mother told me again.

But, bizarrely, I now had a sensation of reacquaintance myself after our first ten days.

'–I've been here before . . .'

I looked past her when she'd told me, over the shoulder she was rubbing some persistent ache from, to the selection of postcards she'd placed on the kitchen shelves. Hero and Leander, Iris and Morpheus, Daphne and Apollo. Myths and legends. Ideals and exemplifications.

I stood nodding my head, even when she'd gone from the room. I looked outside. Our clothes were dancing the can-can on the washing line, turning somersaults in a gust. Overhead, a fast blue Atlantic sky. High, streaky mare's-tail clouds. A hawthorn tree tilting tipsily from side to side. Again I had a sensation that I was recollecting this place as well as experiencing it at this moment. There was something very nearly tactile, and yet I couldn't reach out my hand and touch something that – so frustratingly – wasn't actually there. I knew and at the same time I didn't know, and I couldn't resist the fancy that I was following in my own footsteps and that my movements had all been acted out before, in another layer of time laid gauzily beneath this one.

THIRTEEN

My mother looked up from her deckchair.
 'You're not thinking of going to the beach, are you?'
 I nodded.
 She let the newspaper she'd been reading fall on to the grass.
 'Not now, Merlin.'
 'Why not?'
 'Can't you play in the garden?'
 'I want to go to the beach.'
 I watched the expression on her face change. She looked hurt.
 'I wish you wouldn't.'
 I shrugged, but got to my feet nevertheless.
 'Not today, Merlin.'
 'Why not?' I repeated.
 She sighed.
 'Later – maybe –'
 'Why did we come then?' I asked her.
 The corners of her mouth flexed with irritation.
 'It gets cold later,' I said.
 'But there are fewer people about –'
 '*They* go in the afternoon.'
 'I'd prefer you to stay here.' Her delivery was firm, and not spoken in the pally voice she'd been using earlier. After her quiet contentment at lunchtime, she suddenly looked tired and strained.
 Perhaps I knew I was the cause of it, but I hadn't the good sense to limit the damage I was doing. It must have seemed to me too much like a victory.
 She got up and she followed me into the house. I stood in the kitchen feasting my eyes on all the room's red surfaces. I gloated. Red was not one of my mother's colours, despite its theatricality. A curious thought came into my head – that I'd only once seen her blood, if it was her blood, in the car

leaving Ashclere. I had never seen her blood flow as she had seen mine do.

'Why are you – why are you being so awkward, Merlin?'

Her voice had a little crack in it. She looked taken up with the problem of my obstinacy. The skin around her eyes was grey; it was then that I did see blood, tiny bursts of the stuff trailing in the white at the corner of each eye, by the duct.

She stood staring, but it was as if she wasn't really seeing *me*, or any of this here and now. She had been brought to this point before, in the same place but in another time. The resemblances may have shocked her, but when she started to nod her head slightly I knew she was accepting the inevitability of the situation. It could only be the way that it was.

The vexation started to drain from her face, and I watched. She dropped down on to a chair. She lowered her eyes to the red linoleum on the floor.

Her face was slowly emptying of frustration. Maybe, I wondered, maybe now its proper colour would come back, and she would begin to look as she used to look.

She sat for a few moments placidly inexpressive. She didn't speak, didn't even glance over at me.

At the time I made the mistake – the terrible miscalculation – of supposing it was because she didn't care. That it was now a matter of indifference to her what I did.

Which made it easier for me to decide what to do next. It was hardly a decision at all, though, since I was only submitting to a want. I couldn't accept that I was simply pleasing myself, so I trusted instead to the cold justice of the deed.

I left the room and a couple of minutes later I left the house, in a huff, without speaking one more word.

I heard the sound of an explosion from the beach. It sounded like quarry-blasting, and I only halted for a moment or two on my skittering slalom run across the ribbed wet sand.

When I heard the fire-engine bells I stopped again. I was standing in the sea, with water up past my knees wetting the cuffs of my shorts. I turned to look back, over the dunes towards the hillside. A plume of black smoke was rising from behind trees; I supposed it must be coming from somewhere about halfway up. The smoke continued to rise.

I came out of the sea, shaking the legs of my shorts. I trod heavily on the squiggly worm casts left in the damp sand. All the time the bells were ringing, and those bells were joined by another sort, at a different pitch, which might have been an ambulance's. When I looked again, the smoke was denser, and turning into a mushroom cloud.

Then I did begin to feel apprehensive. I took the chill from the beach on to my skin. Goosepimples. A faint aching hollowness in my bones.

I found I was standing still. Something kept me from moving. It was more than the deep numb of the cold. A slow knotting in my gut.

I couldn't think for several seconds – I couldn't focus on a thought – not while the bells rang and the mushroom began to consume itself. Gradually I could smell smoke. It was then that I kick-started myself and broke into a run, up the beach towards a gully between two dunes. My feet sank into the soft, fine dry sand but I propelled myself forward. Past the dunes I stepped into my plimsolls and set off again with a second wind, following the sandy track worn through the spear grass. I was running too fast to care about the scratches and the thistle-stings. I passed the finger-signpost and the first stile ahead, and beyond it the bridle-path tramped around the edge of the cows' grazing field. From the top of the stile I looked uphill, over the second field of corn stooks, towards the source of the smoke rising behind rooftops and trees. I could smell fire and burning dust, and noticed briefly the glimmer of orange flame.

Panic was growing and growing inside my chest, so that I didn't know how I could hold it all in. My ribs hurt under the pressure. My throat was affected too, it tightened all the time and I had to open my mouth to swallow air to breathe, just so that I could keep running.

I reached the last stile, and on the other side had the flintiness of unmade road beneath my feet. Ahead of me smoke blew through the trees, shredding on the branches. The bells were so loud, they seemed to be ringing inside my head.

I took to the network of lanes and tracks between the avenues. It was ground I would cover in my sleep. In my dreams particular bushes and tree trunks and garden fences had a touch, a smell, a way of dropping their shadows on to the ground at my feet for me to jump over. Now I was oblivious to all these intimate features as I sped past, brushing against hedges and shrubs and ducking under branches and pushing myself off brick walls and creosote screens. I ran with my senses shut off. A great black nimbus of presentiment obscured sounds, smells, touch, glazing my eyes so that I was only seeing to my journey's end.

When I reached the gateposts at the end of the road, two fire tenders were already in operation. Hose-pipes had been attached to a hydrant, and water was gushing into puddles like lakes. The doors of an ambulance stood wide open. The smoke was rising straight up, and only descending again lower down the hillside. Someone tried to hold me back, but then they must have recognised me and the restraining hand was lifted from my arm. I walked on, knowing what I should find when the smoke cleared enough for me to see.

Half the bungalow's roof was missing. The windows had all been blown out and wet scorched curtains clung to the outside walls. Smoke was belching out of the rear of the house. A chimney pot, I noticed, had fallen into the side-bed of blue tea-roses. Bits of red kitchen cabinet littered the back garden, along with brick, plaster, wooden timbers, metal utensils, even ripped and charred laundry.

There was a vast stink of smoke and dust and gas.

I started to cough and cough.

Other hands reached out to me, and I felt myself being directed – under all that condolent authority – from where I'd been standing to somewhere else entirely, a neighbour's garden. Dining chairs were set out upon the lawn, and two firemen lay back in a couple of them with their tunics loosened and their faces blackened, and with their eyes fixed and blank. I was seated, with my back to them: or I may have been meant not to have in my sights what I very briefly did, the ambulance driving off, swaying along the stony potholed road with its axles heaving.

I was being spoken to, but there was nothing I could be told which I didn't know already for myself. I just nodded my head and looked down at my feet. I was conscious that I was being unnecessarily muted: I can't have been wholly in shock, but – I suppose now – I was very largely so. I picked out words from the talk that reached me. 'Gas', 'kitchen', 'destroyed'. Nobody said 'killed', but maybe that was implicit. I didn't ask from my comatose silence, although I must have had an instinct that someone would have found a way of sparing me if my mother had survived. But no one said anything for several minutes, while every so often a hand would touch me on top of my head, on my neck, my shoulder, my back. They wanted to be kind, meaning to do the best for me; they found they lacked courage, though, and justified themselves by not overburdening me with more than they thought I could be expected to deal with for the moment.

Their tact was misplaced. I already understood. I started to cry, and selfishly, I cried chiefly because of how I'd left her, because now my poor mother would never have a chance to know how sorry I was. It had only been a few seconds of mischief, but the effects were going to last all my life.

The voices and the clamour fell away. I don't remember what happened next, except that everything shrank to a whisper in my ears and memory-flashes resurrected the past in the most fleeting glimpses. Goodbyes and goodbyes... Later I was sitting not in the garden but in someone's living-room, in an armchair with a rough moquette cover and an antimacassar pulled down behind my head. When I thought to look at them, the faces about me became agitated as each pair of eyes turned to confer with the others. What could they say to me? A hand attempted to smooth the antimacassar where I had rumpled it, straightening the dainty crochet work.

My mother had used up all the script.
  No lines were left. No directions.
  There was nothing more, nothing at all.

No one knew what happened. That is to say, they knew that there had been a gas explosion, but they couldn't have any final means of deciding if the explosion had been accidental or willed.
  I was asked, many times, for my impressions of my mother's behaviour in the last few days of her life. I told them in all intended honesty that she had seemed to me much as always. They didn't enquire any more closely as to what precisely that usual condition was.

Sometimes in the Kensington flat she would walk into the kitchen shaking a cigarette out of the packet in her hand. It was easiest for her to light it from one of the gas rings, if she was cooking, or even to open the oven door. Once, on another of her off-days, she left the oven door open – something distracted her and she forgot to close it – and the gas flames, turned down very low, blew out in a through-draught she had inadvertently set up when she returned to the sitting-room and raised the sashes of the windows. I was there in the kitchen to notice the gassy odour, so I was able to alert her and no harm came to us.
  I was an adult before I fully remembered the incident. Now more clearly than ever I see myself, the obdurate little boy wading in the sea with my back turned to Teigncombe's hillside. I see the kitchen of the bungalow: the red fittings, the red lino floor and, against one wall, the bulbous cooker with its panels and grill the luteous colour of the richest clotted cream. I see my mother dressed as she was on that last day in a simple candy-striped sleeveless summer frock, looking into the little square of mirror above the draining-board, telling me she'll need to make an appointment with the hairdresser, the one who does his rounds in a van.
  Would she have said such a thing if she'd had any intention of taking her life?

She stands fumbling with a packet of cigarettes. She stands there for ever. She's meaning not to look at me, hoping there is some way I might begin to understand her anger and the impossibility it is to her to explain why we are here, why she doesn't want to let me out of her sight.

The script is all used up.

I've Been Here Before

* * *

Accidents happen. Tragedies happen, and there is surely more likelihood that they will in circumstances that aren't properly familiar, on a road taken at the wrong speed or in the perfect hazard-prone anonymity of a stranger's rented house –

No lines are left. No directions.
  There is nothing more, nothing at all.

Then a woman in a bungalow nearby said she had spotted a gas repair man in the road only the day before. She hadn't seen where he was going to or coming from. She had recognised him by the type and colour of overall he was wearing. A blue boiler-suit. 'From the Gas,' she was sure. That is, he looked as if he was.

No one else in the road to whom the police were able to speak mentioned making a report about any fault found in their gas connections. The local gas offices had no record of repairs being undertaken in Orchis Road or its immediate environs at that time. In my imagination the rumoured gas man still haunts the spot, however, another question who persists in begging an answer.

Matzell's camera takes the personal angle, watching from windows over the characters' shoulders: discreetly watching, at the curtain's edge, just out of range of watchers' spying eyes. Streets and pavements slant across the screen on corresponding diagonals, into the distance. A figure walks off, recognisable but made to seem different by the nervous excitement that keeps the person walking away, in high heels or steel tips, in a fur stole or gabardine mackintosh. Even pillar boxes and phone boxes and the most workaday lamp-posts are all viewed awry from this unorthodox bias: as if they have all along harboured some arcane significance in respect of what is now happening, like old friends turned sudden traitor.

Departures in the middle of an afternoon, or at dusk, as the streetlights flicker to life. On the rim of the lens's frame, almost out of shot but not quite, a taxi or car stops, and the person's journey assumes a different nature, showing that it is no spontaneous event but carefully planned if not wisely considered. The shoes, courts or Oxfords, disappear from view, and a car door is banged shut. Cut to window and watcher's face. Cut back to road, to car's rapid exit or to vista of empty street reaching to its vanishing point, to thin air painted on a backdrop.

The Sun on the Wall

She is the age to be his mother. Forty-three or forty-four, she has to think about it. His face is unformed; he is still flitting between possible selvves. She has used up all her own opportunities to change.

She hears herself talking. She listens in for a while. She imagines how a young man with academic pretensions could be impressed. Her manner of talk carries so many echoes of her late father, and he was judged a sophisticate, a culturist. Her American companion will return to his mid-Western university with his fine impressions, and with a few more humorous private observations about her at their restaurant lunch which he'll share with his friends, and she wouldn't be able to recognise the resulting little myth of herself.

She shakes a cigarette out of the case. A silver case, with her father's initials engraved on the front panel. She pauses momentarily as she always does when she sees them, intertwined like serpents. She'd started smoking at school, and only did it openly at home after Father's accident, when he had no means of – literally – taking the cigarette out of her mouth. Ladies don't smoke, he had always told her, but he knew that she did, so what point was he really trying to make?

Her companion offers her a light. A throwaway plastic lighter. She smiles acknowledgment, inches her head forward, catches the flame, inhales.

They haven't mentioned Father directly for several minutes. She has been listening to her own descriptions of Oxford. To him it must sound an exotic set of circumstances, but then *he* hasn't had to live here. Since Father's death the year before last she has realised how much they were kept afloat by others' company, which has subsequently drifted away from her. The college has named a meeting-room after him, and endowed a scholarship in his memory, and some of his books are now housed in a collection at the faculty library, and a Festschrift publication is planned, and in these small ways he is bit by bit being appropriated by them and taken away from her.

The Sun on the Wall

It occurs to her that she hasn't spoken for some moments. That he has been sitting waiting, in expectation. And now *he* begins, offering her in return a few more details about his own history.

She isn't really interested. She switches off. Suddenly, instead, she is seeing herself as her neighbours must, on ordinary days unlike today. Riding her bicycle along the road. Defiantly wearing denim jeans and a clingy rollneck which only accentuate that she's starting to lose her figure. And her looks. Her hair in a pony-tail, as she has worn it since she was six – how her mother bunched it, when she went to sit on the edge of her bed during those last months of her illness. She recently exchanged her gold-rimmed pebble glasses (for longer distance) for large plastic frames with a pinkish tinge, but these somehow only make her face look bigger too. And pinker. On a squat neck. Normally she opts for squashy moccasin shoes for comfort's sake, but as she pedals the wide, tree-lined residential streets she longs for heels, for frivolity. Only the wrist-watch she bought herself is in that league, the case and face made of what is purportedly Italian Alpine marble, without any numerals or even marks to indicate hours and minutes, an empty round except for the thin gilt hands.

She has dressed up for today, but unfortunately for dinner not lunch. However . . . (that adverb and conjunction is the leitmotif of her life) . . . it's too late to start apologising, and she senses that a lady wouldn't. But a lady ought to have known. Her father had an unfailing instinct for social etiquette, so canny and informed about the skills it takes to assure and deceive from the outside in. Such a clever and astute man, but twice as subtle and calculating as her smiling and inexhaustibly respectful companion from Middle America could ever begin to understand.

She had cut out all the newspaper obituaries of her father, and stapled them together. She had kept them, although two or three times she'd held the envelope in her hands over the pedal-bin in the kitchen. But something had stayed her hand, she didn't know what. The obituaries were proof of some worth that it had been considered necessary to commemorate.

The photographs printed alongside had been taken in the forties and fifties, when he'd been in his prime. A certain brooding severity which none the less had a dashing, romantic quality. Virile, Heathcliffean. Clear gaze fixed on some distance well out of camera lens range. Women might have felt butterflies in their stomachs at what they saw, and maybe some of his male students had puffed a little harder on their pipes with envy.

Occasionally she tipped the envelope's contents on to the kitchen table. Moved them around on the old knotted pine with her fingertips. Skimmed the public details of the past with her eyes. Tried not to engage with those eyes in the photographs – but they weren't looking at her anyway, they were directed towards window light, into implied antiquity. That far and ancient past had been his perfect disclaimer, his excuse from responsibility – he had meant to be untouchable there, inviolate. He was a man, and such ambitions were credible for men. She meantime had only been able to experience Italy on the surface, in its immediate tensions, while he deeply pondered the past with the ablest of his hand-picked students – just as in Oxford she was fated to bob about on the current of life like flotsam, without the confidence or appetite to plumb any depths for fear of what might be there. Running the house had kept her mind distracted, and her secretarial duties were another millstone she wasn't ungrateful for. She'd had to keep looking forward, not sideways and least of all back.

The obituaries were always returned to the envelope and the envelope was locked away in the bottom drawer of the bureau, pushed beneath folders of legal papers and yet placed exactly where she would know to find it the next time she had the demeaning, self-defeating compulsion to look.

In the restaurant she examines the redcurrant stains from the summer pudding on her fingers. She tries to lick away the redness of the berries. The colouring persists, though. She dips her fingers into the tumbler of water. The water clouds, just a little. She wipes her fingers on the napkin on her lap. She wipes and wipes until she can see a definite improvement. The rest will come off at home in hot soapy water, but nowadays she tends to put the immersion heater on just for short bursts, which is no saving really but she can't follow the Electricity Board's Economy 7 literature. Her existence is filled with illogicalities, she knows so, but when one person has the running of a house the size of hers then something – consistency, or common sense – has to give.

She stares at her fingers. She turns them to the light, then curls them back into a fist. She will often sit with her fingers bunched, but she has to surprise herself doing it. Then, of course, it is no surprise to her, but only too predictable. She can't go changing the burden of the song now.

If her mother hadn't died...

But she had. And all the rest that followed, it could only have resulted from that.

It was a miserable death, of cervical cancer, about which there was nothing to be done. Disease should have served no part in their immaculate life in north Oxford. At the time it was difficult not to believe that some shame was being attached by others to her illness, *their* illness. Too many people didn't want to confront it, and her mother had to suffer doubly by being spoken of in hushed tones, and then later by not being spoken about at all.

It was assumed that her husband would marry again, for their daughter's sake, but he didn't. No reason was ever forthcoming. He was considered good-looking in a man's man's way; he had style in his dress and talk; he held a senior college position, he was clever as well as learned, and was getting to be known among a wider public than classics scholars for his radio talks on Greek and Roman civilisation that went out on the Third Programme. He had some money to his name, and he entertained and travelled. His daughter was mostly quiet and well behaved and offered no major disincentives to potential partners, other than her being there in the first place. It can only have been, therefore, that the consciousness of his late wife dissuaded them, scared them off, for nothing to have come of his several and quite public dalliances.

He settled into widowhood. She deduced even then, young as she was, that he didn't really want to change out of his widower's ways. He could be content in his well-worn rituals. He had gone halfway back to the selfish pleasures of being a bachelor: only halfway, of course, because there was her own presence to remind him of how his life had, temporarily, been shaped to quite a different pattern.

The women came and went, all deemed eligible but lacking some final, authentic dimension for him. He didn't sorrow over any of them afterwards, because it wasn't properly a loss to him. She sensed quite well as a child of nine or ten that he accepted this arrangement, their living together, as his new normality.

Two helpers on a rota kept the house between them. She stayed on at the small preparatory school for girls a mile from her home, where she mixed with others of her own kind, the daughters of dons, diplomats, army officers, a few businessmen to whom the school showed favour. The loss of her mother gradually became less of an awkwardness – it was an inconvenience, rather, but not frequently so. Since she didn't know what to call her – 'Mother', or 'Mummy' – she preferred to wait until her father spoke of 'your mother' (when he did) before she made a reference to 'she' or 'her'. It was silly, but more than that it was necessary: without being able to clarify the situation to herself, she obeyed an instinct of heart which she mistook for a response of her brain.

When the time came, Aunt Andrina, her father's sister, tried to explain to her, but not at all cogently, the reason for the fruit stain dampening her

The Sun on the Wall

knickers. She didn't quite like to have some of the details gone into. She caught the general drift of it all, and she appreciated that the business was bound to be a bother to her every so often, but she wasn't terrified as she later discovered some of the girls at school had been, supposing their insides were falling out.

On the morning when she was told, the sun was shining. She was wedged in a corner of the window seat with her knees drawn up to her chin; she was watching their neighbour 'the Bohemian', who was out on her balcony, standing on her hands. She thought she must be able to cope with what every girl had to, that she would continue to feel the heat of sunshine on her skin, and that good days – bloodied or not, in Oxford or anywhere – would always seem just as hopeful to her spirits as this one.

She grew up assuming that those enclosed college gardens her father took her to were the real world.

Rolled lawns, clipped border-edges, weeded beds, the tallest pink hollyhocks only half the height of the grey stone walls. The dons tiresome or straining after eccentricity. Their womenfolk entirely practical or nervously fluttery. The students wound up for those conversational obstacle courses. And no one ever seeming to say what they intended, as if they were awed to evasiveness by the skyline's soaring spires and pinnacle serrations.

The heat became trapped in those hideaway gardens, secreted only yards and feet away from the narrow cobbled lanes that threaded the web of the city: *her* city, that two-square-mile confinement. The gases hovered above the primped flower-beds and danced along the tops of the walls. The sun, multiplied by dozens and scores, dazzled in the leads of mullioned windows, or fell as ink spills at her feet through stained chapel glass. Voices chimed mellifluously, about their own small concerns.

While somewhere else the rest of the feverish sixties, the disillusioned seventies, and half of the egotistical eighties passed them all by . . .

In the gardens the students wore suits, even the most informal and anti- of them, and – looking back – it seemed to be the hairstyles that marked the progress of the years. The voices continued to tinkle, and the soft laughter burbled into little distances beyond each knot of talking heads, and sometimes a gate opened in a wall and there was another arrival or departure, and bees droned among the godetia and antirrhinums, and a bicycle went creaking along the lane close by bounced by the cobbles, and a bird might have the temerity to sing above their heads, and the uniformed staff muttered to one another about dirty glasses and last buses, and the sun sank into a long slow decline in the sky – one gargantuan sky in her recollection, amassed from so many lesser ones – until it had dropped behind the domes and cupolas and mossy gables, until firstly the light turned a little misty in the garden and then was tinged with blue, so that the flowers stood out with exceptional, fully three-dimensional clarity. Father and she had always left for home by the time the stars appeared, but not before the moon had risen – it altered from one recollection to another, in all its metamorphoses between invalid's pale fingernail and ripe yellow cheese – hoisted high on a wire, and the sky an obligingly absurd, melodramatic swathe of azurine or blush velvet.

There was always one perfect student – an identikit model *par excellence* – who was composed of all the best parts of the prototypes whom she had discovered, with a disappointment that turned to tedium, to be flawed. She made him up, and knew that his existence was owing chiefly to her at the same time as she became confused by traits of physique or character that gave positive proof of resemblance to this or that former favourite disciple of her father's.

He dated back to the early sixties, but as he had developed he remained indifferent to the decades. His age didn't change, and he seemed most at home not in the college's gardens or its low-beamed sets where she must have met him but in their own lofty drawing-room with its two bay windows and view of grey-brick florid Victoriana to front and the oblong, dark garden of yew and juniper at the back. He spoke wittily, although she could never be quite sure what it was he said that his fellow-guests considered so consummately amusing, she tended to lose the words or their sense. He had a habit of melting away out of her line of vision, even though she was meaning to direct all her attention at him – as she felt he was all eyes and ears for *her*.

It was infuriating that she couldn't completely lock him there with her senses, that they invariably let her down at the moments in her dwelling on him – snatched from another of the unavoidable tasks in her day – that promised to be most auspicious, to be about to lead them both to an understanding: something short of a commitment as yet, but – even so – a mutual triumph of will.

Long long ago, when she was still doing her school prep, her father would come and stand behind her.

His hand would drop on to her shoulder. Then it would attach itself to the back of her neck. He held her only by his fingers, but she'd find it difficult to move her arm to turn a page or to use her pen.

He would sit down beside her, and ask her how he could help. Sometimes she didn't need assistance; sometimes, however, she did.

The Sun on the Wall

Whatever she asked him to explain to her, he could explain, and slowly she would begin to understand what she had failed to earlier.

Remembering her manners she would thank him, but saying the words quietly and rushing them a bit, in case he should imagine that she depended on him totally for putting her right.

Breathlessness.
Breath. Less. Ness.

Suddenly. It would happen. Even in a restaurant like this. For no good reason. Reason she could think of. Something. Thing in herself.

This silly losing, losing hold. The nuisance of it. Socially, that is. The sheer vexation. Not the worry about herself. What it meant. Might mean. To her health.

She had to wait. Until her breathing steadied. Gradually. By itself. Of its own accord. Until she could fill herself, fill her chest with it. In, out. In, out. In again, out again. If she closed her eyes – then she could do it. Focus, concentrate. The concentration, that would carry her. Carry her all right, to the other side—

When she opened her eyes, everything would have quietened and fallen back into its proper outline and shape. The room recovered its equipoise; the furniture was still again, the objects were only themselves. The revolution was quelled. She wasn't choking on her panic; the hazard had evaporated into the high ether. The air was left a little dusty, and a little familiar, and she breathed on it, in-out, in-out, and she was surviving.

Nobody knew why it happened. Over the years doctors had been consulted, specialists; what one said would contradict the theory of another. She continued to be a mystery to them, and she deduced from their expert-sounding ignorance that she was the only person who had a hope of being able to help herself.

She sits on the swing in the garden, squinting into the sun. Nanny Chisholm is asleep in the basket chair. Her father is standing at his study window. He lifts an arm and waves. She takes one hand from the rope and waves back. Her feet skim the grass, to and fro. She lifts her head and looks backwards, up at the sky, a fine summer sky, at blueness so wide and deep that her mind could soundlessly drown in it.

They used to play games of tig up and down the house, her father the eligible widower and she: boisterous games with a competitive edge, which ended up giving her a headache and tight eyes.

The tig sessions didn't stop when the other games of her childhood started to embarrass her. Her father wanted to play, and if she was left feeling – for the game's duration – older than him at ten or eleven, it was an easier matter to show willing: easier than to find reasons why not, since untruths had a way of advertising themselves on her face, imprinted in pink heat-botches. So instead she reddened her face with the effort of sprinting up and down the stairs and running for the cleverest cover she could find.

Her father would whoop sometimes, and then she knew it was one of their just-like-any-other-day days, when he meant to jolly their lives along with his bonhomie. But at other times, when they were running and hiding, he would hardly say a word and he'd be furtive about his movements in the game, and the seriousness of his face would be at odds with what she still imagined *ought* to have been a frivolous pastime.

Meanwhile the breath accumulated in her chest, it stuck in its basket of bones like a stone. The game was also one of honour, and she couldn't – purposely – allow herself to be caught, so somehow she had to find the means to keep running and then pick her place of concealment, bundling up her shadow and holding in the pain in her chest – an ache that seemed to be cracking her ribs – until he should either have run past or become tired of standing there stock still outside the door, able to swallow down his breath and with his eyes stealthily scanning the dark for clues of her.

One afternoon, though, she forgot about the shadow, and that was how he found her, in the smaller of the guest bedrooms.

She had the sun behind her. She felt it starting to warm her where she was half crouching, in the gulch between a dressing-table and the corner of two walls. The sun came slanting low and wide on one wall, but not so low that she could avoid being betrayed by the shape of her obverse black double – or the lower half of it – lying supine on the carpet.

She heard his sly, breathless approach in the silence. Silence like an old marble tomb's.

She was hoping that the mirrors on the dressing-table would confuse and divert him. Reflections of sunlight were dancing across the ceiling, like rippling water on the surfaces of a sea-cave. She held her breath too for these moments, until all the ribs in her chest were hurting.

The silence grew, swelled, it seemed to be reaching far back into antiquity, she was thinking she must have encountered it before, surely, it felt so lulling and beguiling even under the pain, so curiously comfortable in its own way . . .

The silence, the jewelled light, the heat, the elation of no air at all circulating in her body.

The Sun on the Wall

He struck in an instant, and she screamed, once. Hands on her shoulders. His strength lifting her up.

He was holding her now by the waist. She wanted to let out another scream, but it wouldn't come. Then he started to turn her, like a ferris wheel, something that had never happened before.

The room went spinning.

The floor was sliding into the ceiling.

She stretched her arms out to push herself off, but she was anchored. Turning and turning.

She was conscious that her dress was inside out and hanging down, that she was showing what she shouldn't be. Bizarrely, though, while she hung vertical and straight for several seconds, she was exhilarated by the sensation of abandon, by the rush of blood to her head and the unfamiliar airiness between her legs.

Her protests went trickling back down her throat, she wanted to laugh instead. A giggle did spurt up, or down, her throat, it dropped out of her mouth, on to carpeted ceiling that was really the floor. While on the new floor, when she raised her eyes, the sunlight still flickered like sparkling water.

Above her, or beneath her, her hair fanned and winnowed, she touched it with her fingers, a halo of soft harvest straw. She wanted to laugh again, but that was when she started to turn, the other way, with the room tilting in the opposite direction.

This time it was a scramble. Her hair fell down, and the material of her skirt caught, and she felt herself struggling against gravity. Her father's face came into view, both serious and smiling together. His mouth pulled back in a grin but his eyes were watching her with such an intense and earnest stare.

She held on to his shoulders, gripped them hard in case she should lose her balance. The muscles flexed through his pullover and shirt, and she was – briefly – intrigued.

His eyes were only inches from hers, so close that she could even see the flecks of darker colour in the blue of his irises. His mouth was still worked into the shape of a smile, and ought to have reassured her, but she was aware that she wasn't convinced. So she smiled instead, to help to make up for it.

When he saw that, his own smile relaxed. He forgot about it and it was left stranded on his face while his eyes narrowed to concentrate on *her* eyes. He remembered in another few seconds although it seemed much longer to her. His lips pulled back, over his teeth.

He was holding her upright in front of him, maybe a couple of feet from his face. She dropped her gaze, down to the carpet on the floor, which was really the proper floor at last. He lowered her, and she stretched her toes out to get a first touch of the ground.

'Found you,' he said. '*I* won.'

She could feel his voice warm against the skin of her face. He spoke gently, but she could tell he was excited. Or tired. A vein was throbbing on the side of his head, like a little sunken twig.

She didn't speak. She watched the vein out of the corner of her eye while she stood on the floor, getting her balance back. She was fascinated, but didn't want to admit it to him. She hadn't asked to be spun around, even if it *had* been an interesting experience. She felt she should be insisting on her dignity just a little at least.

She stepped back. Took several steps. His smile snagged over one of his front teeth.

In the mirror she noticed her skirt was still hitched up at the back. Suddenly flustered, she tugged at it to pull it down.

He was watching every movement that she made. Now, she didn't know why, she couldn't smile; it refused to form.

In the central panel of mirror she saw herself apparently in a fall of sunlight, but it was light thrown off one of the side panels. Only her middle portion was illuminated in the harsh track, from her neck to her knees, not her face or her shins and feet. In fact it was hard to place her eyes at all, and when she found them in the room they weren't her own but a timid animal's, staring warily out from its cover in some great gloomy forest.

'Do you like when Daddy plays with you?'

'What?'

'"*Pardon*", Hermione.'

'Pardon.'

'When Daddy plays his little games with you—'

She shrugged.

'I suppose so.'

'I'm sure you do, yes, take my hand now, won't you, like a good girl.'

Nanny Chisholm always ran her words together when she was flustered or excited about something. She had a habit of gulping down her breath, as if her thoughts were racing ahead of her and she had to sprint after them, so to speak, in pursuit, just to keep up.

They had tea in Elliston's department store one afternoon. Sweet Russian tea and sticky buns. It wasn't Nanny Chisholm's way at all. The questions came thick and fast. She responded between swallows and bites. At one point she noticed Nanny Chisholm looking across the room with her eyes wide and making little nods of her head, as if she was signalling a message to someone. But a mannequin was passing among the tables and she preferred to look at her instead, imagining that this was her mother – who hadn't died after all – but who was still tall and slim and beautiful and smiling like this, and magically preserved in her youth.

They discuss her father's work, she and her lunchtime companion, the young American. Over the past year she has had several such conversations with interested parties on the subject.

She finds she is having to simplify because he doesn't appear to understand certain points, obvious points surely.

(She places her elbows on the table, a cardinal rudeness, so that she can shield her eyes against the sun with her hand, that bloody sun.)

He is adrift in the subject, although he smiles encouragingly when she offers him an answer, and now *she* is confused. This isn't how these conversations are supposed to go.

'He died a couple of years ago. And—'

'You've stayed on?'

'What's that?'

'Here, in Oxford—?'

He leans forward. His hand touches her other arm. She feels the air stiffen. She looks away, still with the elbow up on the table and her hand protecting her eyes. The sun dazzles momentarily, it slices between her eyes, a rapier point—

She clasps her hand to her brow. He is talking to her, talking again, in that smooth and pleasant instant-whip tone of voice he makes sound so inconsequential. How Dr Herzl lets his voice wash round about her, in that warm room where he queries his patients, with the venetian blinds drawn against the workaday morning sun strafing the leafy road outside. Talking over her silences, meaning to quell her into words, like a hypnotist's ruse, in that room kept at blood-heat where the clock – Viennese workings inside a painted Swedish case – chips away at the same hour every Thursday morning, grinding time down. Herzl too knows a little about the ancient civilisations, because he was obliged to for his job of work with her, and he will still direct her that way while he scribbles on white lined index cards and tries to win her confidence, to put her at her ease, during each Thursday round of the clock she spends in that stripped-pine-and-dhurrie room at the front of the house in Tivoli Road.

But now the sun is naked and unashamed. It screams about inside her head. She can hear the ticking of the young man's watch, remorseless beneath his soft words and the ebb and flow of other voices and cutlery sounds in the room. In the kitchen at home she never wears a watch, she doesn't hear any of this as she places her left arm on the table top and shields her eyes with her hand. The arc of sunlight is creeping along the kitchen wall. Urgent white on cream. It reaches the bottom of the shelves. The potter's crock of spatulas, draining spoons, mashers, whisks. The electric plug socket. The hook where she ties the rope of the clothes pulley. The rack of spice jars.

It's at that point, after the last of the jars, ginger, nutmeg, cinnamon, saffron, cayenne, paprika – after red paprika, when it reaches the top of the long crack in the plaster like a river in the Deep South, an inch short of the dried death-trail where she swatted a moth weeks ago – it's always then that despair will overwhelm her. Everything, she realises, is useless and without reason. The sunlight is the searing white of absolute nothingness. Now there's no one to see or hear, and her command just snaps, she's dropping down and down into herself, layers deep, tumbling head over—

His hand is on her wrist. She jerks her arm away, pushes her weight against the back of the chair. His hand is left marooned on the pink tablecloth. Her own arm is resting in a pool of sunlight.

She immediately pulls it away a second time, folds it over her waist and holds it there, caressing it as if she's been scalded. She catches the look in his eyes. They're not irritated, they're bemused, even *a*-mused. She doesn't know where she is with him. In a restaurant, of course, but no more than that.

She realises she is jabbering away. About restaurants. About the ones in Italy and Provence she used to visit. With her father. How much he appreciated good food. Wines. Cigars too. She wants to stop talking about him, this man called her father, but she finds that she can't. It all just gushes out of her, because she has had nobody to tell, even though it's so bland and tells nothing whatsoever – about her father, about herself – and is just pap, an excuse to talk and keep talking to cover the silence that might then come roaring back at her.

But he smiles. (What *is* his name again?) She knows, however, not to put her arm back down on the table. She won't give him a chance. Not a goddamn chance.

In her most persistent dream she is sitting in a café in a hot city. The arches outside drop brief shadows into a siesta square.

She sits alone, reading a book, a novel. She is engrossed. She doesn't notice that a man has placed himself on the bench next to her. He taps her on the arm, and she looks up. She has to refocus her eyes after the close-work of the text. He is older than herself, and handsome. He doesn't speak, but she knows that he is not one of her compatriots. Very politely, but without speaking, he takes the book from her.

He peruses the page she has reached. The book is in English. Can he understand what he's reading?

Her unspoken question is answered. He removes a propelling pencil from his pocket and proceeds to underline a word. He hands the book back to her. She sees that he has underlined the word '*I*'.

She smiles, nervously. She says nothing, and lowers her eyes to the page. She cannot concentrate, of course, not now. After half a minute or so she finds his fingers are resting on the top of the book. She gives it to him again. As politely as before he takes it from her. He uses his propelling pencil to underline another word he looks for on the page: '*want*'.

It goes on like this, in silence. He returns the book. She makes a pretence of reading. He requires her to give him the book. Another word is underlined.

He constructs a sentence.

'*to*'

'*make*'

'*love*'

'*to*'

'*you.*'

She is alarmed. Doesn't know what to do. Is starting to perspire. Looks past him, as if for guidance. He takes the book for the last time and inside the back cover he writes out an address. He hesitates, then adds '– *The other side of midnight*'. Then, with a final cryptic smile, he stands up, collects his briefcase and the books placed on top of it, and departs.

Not a single word has been spoken by either of them.

She finds a block of flats at the address. The concierge's door is closed and the blind pulled down. A noticeboard indicates where all the apartments are located.

She gets no further than the lift finally. An old-fashioned cage-lift, with modern controls. When it stops at the third floor he is standing there waiting for her. He steps inside. He presses the button, and the lift starts to move.

They are proceeding upwards. The shaft is open, inside a grille, with a staircase winding up on all four sides of them.

He begins by kissing her. The lift stops. He presses the button again. They go down. He is undressing her. When the lift stops, he reaches back without looking and the lift is in motion once more, travelling up and up. She loses track of when it comes to a halt, but she does eventually notice, from the carpeted floor where she lies almost naked. This time the cage remains where it is. They could be seen, only too clearly, but the building is silent.

Swiftly, easily, he moves into her. She forgets the circumstances – the building, the possibility of someone discovering them, her being hijacked by design between floors. Later, when she has been swept away in the frenzy of what she can believe is love, the lift ascends again, and then it descends. A sensation is transmitted through the gasps and contractions which have seized hold of her. She finds she is occupying the horizontal and vertical planes both at once.

And still not a single word has been spoken by either of them. Inside their cage they have the only vocabulary of desire which they require. Up and down, she is turned inside out, head over heels, until – deliriously – she starts to lose consciousness, clasped inside the circle of a stranger's muscular arms, with words – the agents that contrived to bring them together in the first place – so patently inadequate to the task of conveying meaning. In unceasing hydraulic motion they have reached their destination – the fourth dimension of the senses, where the air is immaculately thin and pure.

A waiter pours coffee.

Now she's tired of talking. She only wants to think. To herself. Maybe if she thinks hard enough, she will think it all out of her head and, in time, she can start to forget. At last.

When she was young people would use the term 'pretty' to describe her. Then they started to forget, or she came to forget the responsibility that prettiness confers, until stage by stage she lost it, she lost the clue to it, and it was gone.

Her mother might have kept her up to the mark, they could have become rivals. Instead... In mirrors she came to see how everything that was extraneous to her being was deserting her: prettiness, smiles, the effort of sociability. What she was reduced to was her eyes: primed to the moment, hiked up to twenty/twenty vision, and without the hazard of an expression in them to betray her.

From about the time in her childhood when Nanny Chisholm's services were dispensed with, her father took her with him on his summer travels.

Adjusting to the heat became *more* difficult as her age reached double numerals. By the time she was twelve she seriously wondered if she could continue.

Nothing changed, things only worsened. Eight, ten, twelve years old...

The Sun on the Wall

* * *

In Italy, in Greece, the sun was everywhere, only a few hidey-holes behind rocks escaped the intensity of the spotlight.

Her eyes would ache with the constant glare all day long. Her head seemed to have an iron band clamped to it, which would tighten and tighten by degrees. Sun thrashed around her, baking her inside her skin. Lesser and greater distances fused together, to form one blazing continuum of crystalline golden light. Her vast surroundings would extend mistily to an invisible horizon.

Each time she would grow tired, sick, sated of this shimmering richness and splendour. All the talk of time gave her vertigo, and bound the iron clasp still tighter about her head. When she stayed in her room the sun invariably found a way of slicing under the slats of the shutters and forcing multiple entry, so that the shadows lightened until she couldn't define them as shadows any more. Days were endured as ever to the trilling of cicadas and the lethargic grinding of propeller ventilators (where they worked, that is) on hotel ceilings. More ripping and slashing sounds inside her head as the rickety shutters of yet another room were penetrated by the sun.

There was no escape, but she couldn't think to submit either, not with her increasingly English complexion and her developing instinct for small, exquisite order.

Nature was rampant here, and knew no bounds, and it left her afraid and humiliated.

She couldn't get rid of the headaches. Her sense of taste was flattened, and her nose was unable to distinguish smells so carefully as at home. Every summer she felt herself becoming dulled in sensation, sluggish in her thoughts, and even – in her appearance, when she looked in a mirror or surprised her unfurled shadow on the ground, like a thin paper cut-out – starting to shed one of her dimensions.

When she was eleven or twelve she was first able to believe she was spectating from a standpoint outside herself, she was encountering this person in a book. She would swoop down on the figure from above, incurring no resistance, realising – when she was a few years older still – that this imitation of herself was exposed and defenceless. She might have been inclined to be sorry for her if she hadn't thought she recognised such a wilful stupidity in the girl.

In the restaurant where she sits with her attentive transatlantic companion the sun serrates the top of her head, cuts it off clean like the dome of a boiled egg. The shadow of a sharp knife lies across the wall. She feels her thoughts are all being tipped out, on to a plate. No, on to a saucer. Hot sunlight washes around her, it simmers and bubbles. Her back, though, it's cold with perspiration. She realises suddenly how tightly she's holding on to the arm of the chair, how sore her own arms are with the pulling of old rusty wires inside them.

Laughter. It isn't hers, it's from across the table. She's afraid to lift her head and look over, to see who's there. It might surprise her, but there again might not. She crosses her wrists on the cloth. She lays out her hands; they resemble delicate fauna. The fingers itch to get away, but she pulls them back. She keeps them in her sights. They trail like floating river weed, like sea flowers in a swell. The sun coddles them through the depth of water beneath the surface.

He, her father, should have been more used to the heat. To her it was always a fiery furnace of discomfort. It prickled everywhere, including now – with her body on its first messy change, at thirteen years old – the private places meant to be kept secret, and she blushed with her utter embarrassment. At times she couldn't look people in the eye, she was so uncomfortable with the heat rash between her legs and spreading like fire across her sprouting breasts and the top of her chest and up to her neck. Her face was daubed with those bumpkin's red blotches. Her arms and legs were like lead to move; there was little point anyway, because her co-ordination had gone, oh, all to pigs and whistles.

It came out of the blue, out of the azurine blue of the August sky, in Arles. On a dry, hot, windless siesta afternoon, four months after her thirteenth birthday.

He had come into her room about something or other. She was lying on top of the bed in her slip and knickers, after a shower, weary and half asleep. He didn't turn and go out again, as she'd supposed he must. She had turned away herself when she felt his hand on the small of her back. So gentle, so sure, as he'd always been when she was smaller. She tried to remember how long ago that had been.

Curiously the stroking didn't stop. His hand passed up and down her spine. Then to her bottom, one cheek of it and then the other. She thought that he must understand what he was doing. Her famously clever father.

She didn't move. Beneath her slip, his fingers were resting in the space between her legs, at the top. Then they pushed beneath the gusset of her knickers. She felt them fitting, with complete ease, into the gully.

A new, utterly enveloping sensation reverberated through her. The cotton knickers were loosened. One finger applied more pressure; his thumb returned to the crack of her bottom. The strangest pleasure pulsed through the rest of her body, so intensely that it was *that* which alarmed her, not her father's freedom with her. Everything thrummed, like electricity, from her scalp to her toes. She had to open her mouth for breath, and she gulped it down. She must have turned further over, because the hand inserted itself deeper into the crevice between her legs.

She couldn't breathe, so she couldn't speak. She had an instinct – this was important to her later, weeks and years later – that she should be telling him 'no'. But when she lifted her eyes to the window she saw an unfamiliar view, so she knew only that things were not – or could not be – as they usually were.

Still she didn't move, didn't speak. Somewhere a dog was barking. Nothing stirred otherwise, in the torpor of heat in the streets. Maybe only the dust did, smudging the distance yellowy white.

Her eyes filled with it. She was aware of the gradual load of his body on the bed beside her. The springs in the mattress sang. The pillow behind her sagged.

Perhaps – she was to tell herself in the far future – all she was thinking, all she was capable of thinking, was – he wants to rest, Father, in all this awful never-ending heat. And so that was why she had allowed him—

Unless, when the next thing happened, it was heat madness that had been inside herself too. She hadn't stopped him, or offered more than a gasp of shock, enough – she concluded long afterwards – to have excited him even more. He had always been the person who'd loved her best in her quiet and privileged but depleted life. Love was his forte, and maybe also his due. It hadn't seemed right to deny him now. And he did the things so tenderly, she wasn't to forget that. Even when, in time, they became routine, he never lost his loving touch.

At one point, though, there was an awful hurt, somewhere at the tops of her legs, and reaching inside her, but she was also floating high above it, her head like a zeppelin in the heat. She was covered afterwards in fruit stains, and she stared at the mess on the sheets, forgetting for a few moments what Aunt Andrina had told her in her clumsy way and supposing she had cut herself. Her father only nodded his head when she pointed. He took the sheets from the bed and carried them over to the basin. 'Lemon,' he said, 'is good for blood. We shall try lemon juice.'

He had it wrong, of course. Salt in cold water was for blood. The sheets wouldn't wash. He exchanged hers with his and told the chambermaid, in her language, that he had jabbed a pair of scissors into himself. The girl stared closer at the marks. Even allowing for difficulties of dialect she seemed not inclined to believe him. Her father mimed exasperation with himself. The maid folded the damp sheets, and in the course of the business examined one particular patch more intently, where there was no blood but an ivory smear. She held the sheet up to the light from the window. A faint smile appeared, and she bowed her head as if she thought she might keep it hidden.

Afterwards they went to a café. Her father bought her an ice-cream. Three scoops of assorted flavours. She couldn't swallow any of it. She played with the spoon in the sundae glass. Her father read a newspaper: or pretended to.

She knew they shouldn't have been sitting like this, and yet here they were.

It was so simply done, the outward form of it.

She felt hollow and sluiced out inside. She didn't look up at anyone, and continued to toy with the spoon in her glass. Outside in the square some children squealed as they darted in and out between the columns of the arcade. The sounds worked their way upwards, through the height of the room, to the ceiling: conspiring against the principle they'd learned about at school, gravity. She could hardly even hear the tinkle of the spoon on the side of the glass.

The change in only hours, between the morning and this afternoon, seemed to be absolute.

It continued in Oxford. It felt different there, even though the window of her room (always *her* room) was left a little open to try to cool the sullen, marshy, claustrophobic heat.

It was being treated as a custom, but it was an awkward one. They never discussed what went on, just as they hadn't spoken of the happenings in Arles when they went out on their sightseeing excursions afterwards. While she felt sunk deep inside herself, he presumably had the excuse of thinking she was only as quiet as she invariably appeared to be, that he didn't want to interrupt her thoughts. The excuse was a rotten one, but she gave him no pretext for not holding to it.

The most unbelievable aspect to her would always be that they hadn't talked about it, that she couldn't remember having once spoken to encourage or to repel him. She recalled the incidents of that time as being played out to a soundtrack of human silence, only birdsong and occasional traffic and sometimes a dog barking, or a bell ringing in their city of clustered spires. And, at some required stage in the proceedings, cotton and elastic yielding on her skin.

How could it have happened?

Only too easily.

Through mutual misapprehension, perhaps. The mental misapplications of a passably attractive but strictly ungregarious girl of thirteen years old and a father successful in his line of work, who was lonelier among all his friends, acquaintances and acolytes than she could have supposed such a gifted and striking-looking man to be.

There was so much scope for so much misunderstanding. There was also so much need, and – notwithstanding the college's demands on her father's time, and his commitment to his research – too much in the way of opportunity.

So wise in hypothetical explanations after the events, and so numbed and desensitised of feelings there and then. She hadn't resisted; the first time she had even placed her arms around his neck, as she had always done when she was especially miserable – or happy. But after that she had given him no indications at all. Inside herself she let the heat of Provence fill her with its glare and dazzle. She stared up past his hair-fuzzed shoulders, over the balding crown of his head, to the sun on the wall and the ceiling. There was no dapple or ripple, only the purest white of white. In Oxford the effect was different, because the sun was fitful, and the wallpaper continued to be visible through its shine, the same boring stripes and pattern of fleur-de-lys. From their neighbours' gardens she could hear latch gates clicking open and rattling shut, certain cars sounding familiarly on the road outside. The furniture in the room was being stoically non-committal, and the dolls in the collection her father had helped her to start when she was younger might have been holding their breath, some with their eyes wide open and others with them narrowed to slits. The water dripped in the storage tank upstairs and hissed in the toilet cistern next door, and everything was so tediously recognisable to her. She knew how any heat they had in that late summer would sound in the hidden fabric of the room, causing the joists to creak as they expanded and contracted, and she thought she might die suffocated by the excruciating predictability of it all.

Her single bed, she was certain, was developing a dip on one side which it hadn't had before. At night, when she was left alone, she could easily have rolled into it, but she struggled with herself not to. At night he never came, and – shockingly to her in her later life – she managed to fall asleep quite easily. Sometimes her dreams were crazy, and lowering, but she would sleep right through them until morning.

At school she sensed quite well that she was becoming more withdrawn than before, but for a while her work carried her, and none of the mistresses thought to fault her. All she was to them was gauche, and some light social tuning would surely improve her performance in that department. In her retiring and undemonstrative fashion, she temporarily succeeded in passing muster.

The Sun on the Wall

* * *

She developed a cough: a persistent, dry, scratchy wheeze she was always trying to clear out of her throat. Aunt Andrina on visits wanted her to go to see a doctor, but her father insisted no, that it wasn't necessary. Aunt Andrina continued to argue her case, but her father was equally determined that she should not go.

In the end a chemist of Aunt Andrina's acquaintance suggested a remedy, and the cough became less troubling to her. It took months to get rid of completely, and even so she was left with a vague sensation of some undefined delicacy in her throat. She preferred to keep it covered on cold days, and when the weather was warmer she still had an instinct that a scarf was in order as protection against she didn't know what.

He didn't hurt her. He was gentle, and she was gentle in return. A simple touch would bring all the original physical agitation back to the surface, so that she thrummed again all over. He would envelope her in his strong arms.

So little was required of her by comparison. He needed her, that was all, and in only a slightly different way from how he had before Arles. He had always made himself available to her, and she didn't see how now she could even shy away without seeming ungrateful. If she was to let him down, then surely she wouldn't be his little girl any more.

Lying like this with him over that year and the next one and the next one after that, she felt it was bringing her closer to her mother, closer than any previous amount of wishing had ever done. Absorbing herself as she was in her mother allowed her, during that process, to forget everything else.

She would float into the image of her, the mannequin-image of Elliston's restaurant, and the present time would fall behind, unbelievable and forgone and shrinking so fast that it might never even have been.

Her father and Aunt Andrina quarrelled about her, but as courteously as they could.

She overheard them. Her father said the comings and goings were disruptive, and Aunt Andrina said she was only thinking of Hermione's well-being, and her father said she needed stability, and Aunt Andrina said that was just what she was trying to provide, and her father said, but she wasn't really.

After that she didn't see so much of Aunt Andrina. She knew she hadn't been abandoned by her, and that it was her father's wish there should be fewer visits than before, so she knew not to listen for the taxi stopping and her aunt's heels scraping on the pavement and the latch gate stuttering open in that uniquely hesitant way.

One situation had evolved into another, no more than that, and somehow the girl had understood. When one door closes, the adult woman would finally have the experience to fathom, somewhere else another door closes too.

He bought her clothes. A watch. A crocodile skin travelling-case. Anything she might have wanted.

But she was uncomfortable in the new clothes, because she couldn't get the stiffness out of them – or out of her own limbs. The watch was too expensive for her to wear with confidence. She was afraid of scuffing the travelling-case, so she left it at home.

Anything she wanted, she could have had, for the asking. She knew that it was for a reason. She might have taken advantage, but that would have implied she thought it was deserved.

She pushed the stiffest of the clothes to the back of her wardrobe. She kept the watch coiled inside its ridiculous chamois-lined presentation box. The travelling-case gathered dust underneath her bed.

She didn't want his ludicrous gifts. It didn't interest her at this point to look sophisticated beyond her years.

Yet she kept an eye on herself in the mirrors, in shop windows. She couldn't help noticing. Out of the corner of her eye, over her shoulder. She stared at girls or women who had the courage of their good looks; she was aware of whomsoever her father looked at, as if every time he must have a cause. Threads of significance webbed every room they walked into, cat's-cradled the narrow pavements and cobbled back lanes of Oxford. She tried to miss nothing, but sometimes – passing into and out of shadows – she couldn't be sure that her jealousy hadn't failed to pick up something. A single clue could be vital, she mustn't let anything slip, she had to be constantly vigilant. It was a strain, having to keep all her senses primed, but she needed to be certain there wasn't another world entirely going on, how she used to picture to herself when she was younger and closed her eyes in bed at night: one world for her, and another for everybody else, when she couldn't see and had fallen asleep.

Sometimes she would catch her father's eyes moving between her and the one oil portrait of her mother, or the favourite framed photograph on top of the walnut bureau.

When he superimposed one image on top of the other, hers and her mother's, did he see the same face? Or perhaps the same body?

The Sun on the Wall

A deep silence would descend. He seemed oblivious then to what she might be doing, even to the fact that she was watching him. He was here, and he was not, and the contradiction confused and unsettled her. You *should* be somewhere, or alternatively you shouldn't be, and not be in two places at the one time. A few moments later he would notice her, and shift his eyes somewhere else. She would become caught out by that, and feel that she was deceiving him with some guile of her own.

Around her the air in the room seemed to thicken, congealing with complications.

If it had happened earlier, she might have thought nothing of it, that it was only what a father did. That every father began by pushing in with his fingers and showing his daughter how to help stroke his bits and pieces. But there were other names for those parts, and she had heard the cycle-shed gossip at school, so she knew there was much more to it than that. She knew it was what wives did, and if not a wife then there was bound to be a scandal.

It had come too late, and maybe most of all this was what she couldn't forgive him for.

Other people used the word 'shy' about her. 'She's not really,' her father's voice would reply, telling no more than he said. The others were unpersuaded.

Sometimes she wouldn't meet their eyes, his colleagues' and friends'. She would look everywhere else, but not at their eyes. When she caught sight of herself in a mirror or a window, she realised that her own eyes had somehow withdrawn from the rest of her face. They were her most vulnerable feature, the give-away: preoccupied, and sad. With the rest – her mouth, her chin, her brow – she could probably cope. Probably. No, it was the eyes, always the eyes. She couldn't trust them, her own any more than anybody else's, and she would have to look away or close them tight. Even the buses on Cornmarket Street were conspiring against her, carrying her reflections in the window glass as they careened past leaving her tottering on the pavement's edge.

Then it stopped.

In the third year it stopped and was never to start again.

She fretted about it. She couldn't ask him, why not? She stared harder at the faces that came into their house. At the faces in Elliston's, on the pavements of Broad Street or the High.

If she was different to him now, she didn't know how. Everything to her felt exactly the same.

The Sun on the Wall

She concentrated on doing the small tasks of her life just as she had done them before it stopped, to see if she could wind her way back. Making her bed in a certain order of movements. Folding her clothes in a certain way, using this coat-hanger for this dress and that one for another. Replacing her brush and comb on precisely the same spots on top of the chest. She wondered if she ought not to have been more careful with *things* all along, with objects, if they might not have expectations of her and accordingly feel pique or even malevolence at her thoughtlessness. Their ingratitude might become rampant. So now she had to make twice as sure. Checking that the tongs and shovel and brush hung comfortably on their brass stand in the drawing-room hearth. Not letting flowers in a vase brush against a wall. Satisfying herself that a chair's legs stood exactly on their indentations impressed into the carpet. She would ascertain again that all the picture frames were quite straight before she left a room.

But, even so, her new-found scrupulousness failed to alter the situation. Nor did it seem to make any difference when she took more deliberate care dressing, and in managing her personal toilette, how thoroughly to shampoo and rinse her hair or clean her teeth or soak every inaccessible nook and cranny of her body in the bath.

What had happened didn't happen again. She expected that it would, that it must. When it didn't, she forgot to feel relieved; too much had taken place for her to submit to levity lightly. It could all begin again, and she didn't know if she might not be relieved then, to be returned to circumstances as she'd been used to having them. It had been easier to drift in that numbed condition, to let her mind sleep on. Now she had to assume another kind of unconcern.

The weather was bleakly autumnal, which didn't help: damp, but with the smell of bonfires in the air. In the next garden flames turned to smoke, and sometimes children exploded chestnuts in the embers, and their laughter seemed not just yards but several miles away. Whenever they came out she had to stay indoors, and she watched them through her own furtive reflection in the window glass. The October and November sunshine had a miserly, unfriendly feel to it, and made her shiver. She noticed how it reached particular points of the house at very nearly the same moments in the day, and she would be there – before or after school on a weekday – waiting for it. On Saturdays and Sundays her father found himself with more social calls to make than he ever used to have, and so she would sit alone in the kitchen in the mornings reading, lifting her eyes to stare out from under her fringe at the weather, her mood-barometer, somehow failing to remember that the weather must be the same for everyone. Sunshine should have helped to buoy her up, she felt, but it was wind and fast mare's tail clouds that did that. The sun cruelly picked out the blemishes on her face and caused her scalp to itch, and if she'd drunk too much tea it marked more wet circles under the arms of her cardigan. She felt she ought to be responding to it as their neighbours did, cheerily, but she heard their bright *Good Mornings* and was more than ever conscious of her solitude in the house, with or without her father.

She had eavesdropped on their Mrs Drinkald discussing her with the char next door. Sometimes she came right out with a question. 'Why don't you invite some of your pals from school, Hermione? Your dad wouldn't mind.' She didn't want them here, though, in this house that was thick with solitude like a gum. (Mrs Drinkald sensibly hurried to get her work done quickly and then off home, away out of it, back to Wolvercote.) She waited for invitations to the homes of the girls in her class she was most comfortable with, but the invitations weren't repeated after the first, and new invitations were forthcoming only from the wrong girls. She was quite used to restricting those acquaintanceships to school. She didn't want to have to introduce her contemporaries to her father, and then to avoid watching their expressions and his, dropping her eyes as she knew she did when she was received (in politely wary fashion, as if her reputation went before her) into other girls' homes.

If her mother hadn't died . . . But she had, and that was exactly the point of everything. One thing leading to another.

It was afterwards that she encountered her little problems, 'little' as her father was always assuring her they were, able to be dispensed with by the flourish of his signature on a cheque.

He offered each time to drive her to Tivoli Road and back, although it was so little distance by way of North Parade, but she always walked. She realised that he trailed her, so she would go there by a long route, via the back of the matching Edwardian crescents of Park Town where cars couldn't pass and along the right-of-way by the Cherwell.

In her expensive clothes, in her hand-sewn shoes, she would perch on the edge of the chair in the front room – the consulting room – of the deadly still house, looking across to the Dutch gable of the red brick neighbour across the road. It was joined to the house next door, but was pretending in its grim way that it wasn't –

This might have been merely a social visit, but she saw how complicated the system of locks was on the front door. A discreetly placed azalea bush hid her from the view of anyone who might be passing along the pavement, so that they shouldn't have any suspicions. There was no brass medical plate on the front door, or was a psychiatrist – a mind doctor – not entitled to show one?

Dr Herzl had the manners of the Hapsburg era to which his severe, silver-haired mother housebound upstairs was a living witness. These were overlaid – in spite of his name – with the most pukka of accents, so that she sometimes had great difficulty making out his questions, before she could even begin the task of eluding him with her answers.

He wouldn't have believed anything she might have told him. He had known her father for many years, and he very clearly remembered her mother, to whom he would refer. She was here because her father had told her he was obliged to send her: because her school had rusticated her for a term because she had stolen some make-up from a shop and been apprehended (with more than enough money in her purse to pay for the items), because she had removed some books – all by or including contributions from her father – from the study's shelves and wrapped them up in newspaper and dropped the parcel into the dustbin, where Mrs Drinkald had found it.

Several years still in the future she would return to Dr Herzl, by her own choosing, when she found herself coping with an invalid at home, but mercifully all that was uncharted territory to her as yet. Later she would have the need of his voice, lapping up the silence and sounding so oddly consoling to her whereas once it had merely irritated her.

In those early days he kept a wad of case-notes by his side but he was only hazarding a path with her, through the mental undergrowth. He wouldn't have accepted for a moment the stories she could have told him, so she didn't start. One of the reasons for her being here was that she was supposed to be a fabulist, a dealer in the fantasy life.

She could never win but only, over and over, be the loser.

She would dream in her sleep of the stones in the garden.
 Lifting stones.
 In Tivoli Road, only two or three stones' throws away from home, her inquisitor could hardly believe his luck. 'Amazing stuff,' he told her, but she didn't see how. Then his face clouded over, as if he realised, perhaps she's trying to put one over on me.
 Perhaps she was. But the dreams were real enough, and if they were textbook copy they remained just as real never mind that she shared them with troubled dreamers across the world.
 'What kind of stones, Hermione?'
 'Just stones.'

'Can you...'

She fixed him with her eyes. 'Slimy stones.'

'Excellent!'

No, she couldn't describe to him what was underneath when he asked. No, she couldn't even hint at it as he wanted.

She was greatly shocked in turn. Couldn't he even *guess*?

For a spell dating from her middle teens, after she became more conscious of her appearance and other women's, she was a smart dresser.

There had always been money for clothes. She was able to use the Elliston's account, and the Harrods' one, and a lame Hungarian woman living off the Iffley Road had such deft hands for her dressmaker's work that she might have been bewitched once, back in the gypsy-haunted land of her youth.

She wasn't unduly extravagant, but she was encouraged not to stint. Her taste, she found, was now inclining to whatever was a little beyond her years. Perhaps that was inevitable, given that she always had the example of her mother in mind – from what she saw in surviving photographs, and from what she imagined of the life that people spoke so sketchily about. She had grown up with the proof of her mother's eye for quality in the house's furnishings, the fabrics, as well as the few clothes she had left behind in the wardrobe. She grew taller herself, and a size larger, so that the clothes wouldn't fit: but the image of herself in the mirror, on the afternoons when she had the house to herself and tried the clothes on, that gave her sufficient clues.

In her late teens she liked not knowing everything about her mother. She felt she had space to think all round about her, and even if the picture was hazy it did provide her with several different angles on the person. Her own memories were so vague, they might have been imposed upon the past, conjured out of that nebulous absence of impressions. But she couldn't be sure, she didn't mean to be.

She dressed in memory of her mother, in what she hoped might be the proper spirit of her. At that time of her life, so far from certitudes and when she could believe clothes actually had some statement to make about a person, she wanted to be a testament to her mother's elegance.

They continued to go abroad every summer, to conferences her father was speaking at or to clue up on archaeologists' site-work.

They moved about, from hotel to hotel, now occupying their separate single bedrooms. Was it merely an accident that they were invariably located on separate floors of the building?

She was nineteen when they visited Montecatini Terme, in Pistoia, for the first time. Her father was relieved to be done with his public speaking engagements, having delivered his addresses wholly in Italian this year, and she was relieved to be postponing thinking of her future for a while longer. Most likely she would start a secretarial course the following spring, and she wondered why she persisted in clinging on to home, and why she was so unconcerned about what to do with her life, so fatalistic almost, like a proverbial rabbit caught by car lights and stunned into helpless immobility.

Her full name was Contessa Anna Eleonora Marghieri Di Borzovari-Tribucce. The woman would call herself 'Contessa' on the telephone, which seemed a vulgar thing to do. Was it a sign that she lacked confidence? She wasn't the lean, long-limbed sort of aristocrat, all crisp thinned angles, but was solid and well built, the build of a hockey-player in fact, and more bovine than equine about the face – large and slow, rather stupid eyes, and too fleshy lips. The explanation was that, widowed a couple of years before she met Father in Montecatini, she was a contessa by virtue of her wedding ring. Being unmarried again and still in her forties, she'd had to make a strict market evaluation of herself: as a snob she would have spotted a (largely) genuine English gentleman like her father by instinct, notwithstanding her modest IQ. Father, skittishly over-dressed for the resort in his bespoke London clothes, was a man apart even for Montecatini, noticeably drawling a little more than usual and making a public display of his quaint manners. (His holiday reading matter, quite suitably and as if to provide a refresher course in the sort of social deportment he made a speciality of, was Henry James: vintage middle-period, *The Awkward Age* and *The Sacred Fount*.)

    The contessa dropped her umbrella at the moment they were passing her in the hotel's foyer, surely by no chance. Father picked it up and returned it to her. Time warped, in the pink marble hallway of that awesome anachronism like a sweetmaker's nougat and marshmallow palace, and they were immediately caught – snared – in an elegantly confected fiction of seventy years ago.

The Contessa Eleonora Etcetera had been left comfortably off. She was seeking stylish and stimulating companionship after her trying years of marriage to a dull and stingy, much older man. She had the experience to know how to beguile and enmesh the younger sort, and Father presented himself to her as another potential victim of her wiles. Things did indeed go far in consequence, but maybe further than she had intended, during their sojourns in the spa that June.

The Sun on the Wall

* * *

The next month she showed up in London. In August Father had to go off to Paris on some alleged matter of business. In September she evidently walked into the very same restaurant in Rome to which Father had persuaded his colleague Professor Galletti to take him.

They all met up in early October when the Contessa invited them both, her 'English knight' and her 'favourite English rosebud', to her villa in the Marchigiano foothills of Umbria. Father and she were collected from the station and driven to their destination in a fast, sleek car. Their rooms were ready for them, spotless and scented with pine from the fires banked in the grates; the linen sheets had already been turned down, whiter than a nun's shroud.

'My dear Hermione, I want you to treat *my* home as *your* home—' So the woman assured her. But she seemed more intent on arranging her absence from the property.

A bicycle was provided for her amusement, and an elderly artistic acquaintance called Signor Ceracchini was summoned to provide some meek instruction in watercolours which coincidentally took her out to some of the local beauty spots, leaving Father and their hostess together in the house.

She complied, because in the still and fervid heat of that second little summer she couldn't think how she might resist. She ate the contessa's food, drank her wine, sank into the soft cushions of her armchairs, replied to the woman's determined causerie with her own sparer sort. In her room at the back of the house she switched off her bedside light last thing and listened for movements, doors opening and footsteps, and when she heard them she seemed to have no choice but to let them happen.

She felt irredeemably a foreigner here, a stranger. The house was run with clockwork efficiency, the routine obeyed its own internal tempo, and nothing she could have done would have made an iota of difference to any of that.

The contessa had pressed upon her books about the local fauna and insect life. They didn't interest her, but they were an excuse to be alone, although not quite in the way – or to the ends – which the woman can have meant. She used her solitude increasingly to keep to her room, not to roam the fields, and when she was upstairs by herself she dwelt almost exclusively on what was taking place behind her back, directed by the contessa's brand of cleverness that outdid her father's. The two of them, helpless Inglesi, they were becoming trapped in the story of this dreadful déclassée woman's life.

As well as the books, the contessa provided some of her late husband's most prized possessions to try to keep her young guest entertained and outward-bound. A microscope, glass specimen slides, a magnifying glass mounted in tortoiseshell, a butterfly net, blotting paper and pins for staking out her catches, a flower press. Anything and everything that might just keep her occupied and distant but all of it so annoyingly, so damnably obvious.

One afternoon of worse sultriness than the others, she kept to her room when she supposed that they thought she was out. A door opened somewhere. Footsteps. Then she heard them, the two of them, quite blatant and unashamed this time, on the staircase close by. At their hanky-panky again. She sat on the edge of the bed and covered her ears with her hands, but the sounds she'd been listening to – groans, whoops, limbs slapping on the walls – spread and spread as echoes in her head. When she unplugged her ears, after a couple of minutes, they were running upstairs – *running* – the woman squealing like a silly tease half her age, but a witch in the things she knew to do. Father was being merely obedient, because she had him wound round her squat little finger – because men to the contessa were no more than a species of mechanical dancing toy.

She moved to the table by the window. She hated the view of blue heat-hazed distance, the deckle-edge of the cypresses, the prissy quilted hillsides. She hated being here, by one person's will and command, and she hated the contessa for that and hated her father for having the stupidity of a cerebral, academic man which prevented him from seeing the selfish game of manipulation the woman was playing, for her own wanton pleasure, right in front of his nose.

She opened one of the count's books, with a coat of arms in faded gilt-work emblazoned on its leather cover, and found herself confronting a diagram of spiders. She turned the page quickly, and then another, went flicking through the rest of them with her thumb.

The sounds from upstairs had stopped, which made her suspicious. She looked across at herself in the mirror, and bit at those straight lips in that sun-scorched face.

The sun was shining full through the window, on to the desk top. Some of the books' covers were buckling. Hatred was causing pain in her chest; it made a bitter, rancid, yellow taste in her throat that trickled under her tongue. She didn't know why she was caring so much, it should have been nothing to her what they got up to, those two.

How little did she signify to them, that they supposed her intelligence so low as not to let her guess what was going on?

She stared at the collection of books on the table. At the microscope slides. At the tin box of watercolour paints.

She didn't know why she should be doing one thing rather than any other.

The Sun on the Wall

She lifted her eyes to the view. Umbria outside, out there, it terrified her with its remorseless causes and effects, its appalling apathy. She saw nothing remotely picturesque or agreeable in any of it. Lizard-land. Dead things in ditches and dropped down wells. Decay and disintegration. One thing leading to another, all the time, on and on.

She picked up the magnifying glass, for the want of anything else to do. Perhaps only because it was fated for her to do so. She hated fate too, but she didn't think she had enough of the emotion left in her to apply it so widely and so deeply. Fate was beyond her reach.

She held the magnifying glass in her hand. She turned its lens a little away from her, so that it was angled to the source of light. She watched the sun's reflection in the convexity of glass: the sun melting, a white pupil in a mad eye.

She held the glass quite still, listening for sounds. She sat like that for a minute, maybe two minutes, without moving.

She smelt singeing before she noticed – with eyes widening, fixing – the first tiny plume of burning gas from the page of the book.

A little brown flare.

Becoming gradually darker.

The edge of the page curled. Folded back. Started to char.

She watched, rigid with fascination, but feeling her heart's palpitations.

Here was only more of nature's work, after all. An actual scientific process in operation. A beginning working to an end. And perhaps to another, new beginning.

Her right hand was shaking now, but by power of her own volition she managed to hold the magnifying glass in place. The true-tortoiseshell handle felt like hot steel.

With her left hand – as if she had two minds working – she collected the other books together. What would happen would happen.

When the first book was alight and burning, a flame detached itself and – as if by some ordained force of attraction – leaped to one of the companion volumes.

After that she had nothing to do except leave nature to do its work.

Following the bonfire of books, a curtain succumbed. It was like a ladder to the flames. Then the pelmet started to burn, and the other curtain, from which sparks dropped on to the cream linen cover of an armchair.

And after that, she supposed, there would be no impeding the progress of the fire, although she didn't stay to watch. All that furniture in the heat of the room, all that accumulated vainglory of generations, and this was what resulted.

Doom and damnation!

The Sun on the Wall

She started to smile on her way downstairs, and didn't stop even when one of the domestic staff appeared at a door, concerned, eyes travelling past her upstairs. Oh yes, she wanted to say, oh yes, I know about *them* all right. And I know more than you think I do, although it goes back a long way, over years...

She was smiling as she stepped outside. But she remembered that nature sometimes needs some sympathetic prompting, so she summoned the housekeeper's husband whom she'd just passed – she very politely called out to him – and pointed down the valley, to the painter's house.

'Can you take me, please?'

'*Si, signorina.*'

He nodded towards the Lancia. She didn't have her easel or paper or paints with her, but the man said nothing about that. In the car, sitting in the front passenger seat, she felt quite relaxed. She wound the window down several inches and breathed in the scent of tamarisk, and then the pine – which always put her in mind of the tales of the Brothers Grimm. She lowered the windscreen visor to protect her eyes from the glare of the sun. The whole sweep of landscape appeared to be quivering, shifting, with the energy of pure white light. The heat danced above the road in front of them; a trail of dust behind the car screened her from the villa, formerly so proud on its elevation, now confronting its apocalypse.

Her father and the contessa jumped naked from the top floor to escape the flames.

The contessa was badly burned, but lived. Father lived also, but he broke his spine in the fall and for the remaining twenty-four years of his life was confined to a wheelchair.

The problem of her future was therefore solved at a stroke.

Her father would only say that he remembered very little about what had happened that day.

She looked into his face for clues, for the hieroglyphs of fear or hatred. She saw nothing there except grimaces of pain which he attempted to play down. He was occupying himself with getting better, or with learning just to cope with his injuries.

One thing, she wanted to explain, had only led to another.

To begin with, she tidied up his room in hospital. She covered the other smells with the perfume of bunches of flowers, the most aromatic she could find to pick in the contessa's scorched garden.

Back in Oxford they restricted her hospital visits to once a day, for half an hour. She was piqued. She didn't know what he might be saying when she wasn't there. She also sneaked in when the nurses were too busy to keep tabs, until from on high Sir Somebody Something-or-Other in person read her the riot act.

She had organised the house into apple-pie order for his coming out. Every memento of the contessa had been removed.

During his first days at home he didn't go further back in his talk than the hospital in Perugia. She adroitly reminded him that he was supposed to have forgotten almost all about what had taken place in Umbria. She noticed his surprise at her ability to cope so well with the practical details of his convalescence. She hovered about him, not molly-coddling him but letting him understand she had the aptitude to be an extension of his five senses. If she should only choose to be.

He was mild-mannered with her, and didn't scold her for anything – even though he was experiencing constant, solid pain. They both behaved, by and large, impeccably. It was the third great silence of their lives; they were very practised by now and duly proved it. Sometimes his mouth might shrink – at the recollection of any of the three sacrificial victims, she presumed – but some dire panic in him ensured that the corners of his mouth didn't turn down for longer than a second or two.

His face slowly healed of its light burns. His spine and back could not be coaxed beyond a certain point, however, and after one operation that was successful and a second that was not he effectively lost the use of his legs. The surgeons explained to her with the aid of X-rays and the illustrations in medical manuals. She nodded her head. Between experiments with short skirts (thighs too big) and dark silk stockings (too nursy, not like Suzy Wong at all) she kept singing to herself, although her father might just have been capable of overhearing, odd lines of that silly song, 'Your *knee* bone's connected to your *thigh* bone . . .' It was all intended to add up. One thing followed another. '. . . your *thigh* bone's connected to your *hip* bone . . .' It was all quite rational, really, it made sense so long as the doctor – the hospital doctor – was talking, so long as the windows kept the noise of the drifting shoals of traffic on St Giles pianissimo and the sun wasn't shining directly into his disinfectant-odoured room, out of its imitation azurine sky.

It was a more melodramatic business than she could have foreseen, if she'd properly had any end in view.

Like a B-movie, a second-feature.

Yet her father continued to treat his misfortune with a degree of British phlegm and fortitude that irritated rather than shamed her, which drove her to exasperation sometimes, and she wished quite often that he would allow himself a show of proper histrionics. He still didn't discuss the circumstances of the fire with her. She had no doubt that he wanted to, but if he had then she would have been obliged to ask him questions also, about a period of their life further away and more troublesome to her than Umbria.

So silence reigned in the house in Oxford: silence the despot. At the same time she was assuming practical command of the situation, for the simple reason that she exercised control of her limbs while he did not, and what did it signify that he could out-think her on almost every point in their conversations. Oxford was Oxford, however, not the Los Angeles suburbs of *Whatever Happened to Baby Jane?* and she continued to be intimidated by the academic credentials and social proficiency of others, without learning how to trust them or herself. Her father's friends treated him as some kind of martyr to intellect, and she wanted to laugh in their faces, but because she preferred that it was she and not the nurse who let them in and let them out of the house she remained a model of reticence. This didn't result in *her* being seen as a martyr to virtue, but rather, in that sexist community, she was frequently overlooked almost entirely.

The years were diluting her, she came to feel, making her less opaque than other people. She would think back now and then to that portentous afternoon in sun-drenched Umbria, and recognise that she had been herself – to the limits of herself – as she had never been before or since: only for an hour or two, a creature of peerless bloom in that poisonous garden. The contessa was a *verboten* subject now, but she became nostalgic nonetheless for that place and that time: nostalgic for herself and her own unique serene certainty, for her blind disregard of the consequences, for her joyous immersion – without a single second's wavering – in the pragmatic laws of natural science.

In the restaurant they are on the far shore from all that. Aren't they?

She can't remember if he is asking her questions about her father, or if she is half in love with this stranger: half being any number of times better than not at all. (She dropped her rolled umbrella on the floor coming in, and he picked it up for her.) But he has a manner about him that puts her in mind of someone else. Even though there is no clock in the room that she can hear, chipping away at time inside her eardrum, like the Viennese stalwart in Tivoli Road, where Father first sent her, to try to have her little kinks – shoplifting was the easiest – straightened out. Today isn't umbrella weather after all. The things on the table glow, as if – who was it? – El Greco painted them, blind monkey and all. (Or was that Goya?) Someone on television said the pictures had brought him a perception of the holiness invested in the simplest objects like a burning light, which include man, in the sanctity of a world created by God. But she isn't convinced herself, and would rather put her trust in the processes of nature and science, which some say amount to chaos and not order, but which she has chosen to imagine as a mechanical intelligence, a superhuman computer terminal. That might only be what is meant by 'God' anyway, so it all boils down to much the same understanding in the end, but why is she going into all this now, in a restaurant, with a smiley and personable young man sitting opposite who may be less interested in her father's academic accomplishments than he is claiming to be. Well... The light contained in objects, of course, that is the point. God – an ashtray – a bona fide tortoiseshell magnifying glass. Sun like some atoning fluid, like the balm of Gilead. But on second thoughts, no, not forgiveness, she doesn't feel...

Or is all that is occurring a dream? She only has to think of space never ending, of infinitude, not to know how that could be, to doubt everything she's capable of thinking. Everything may exist in her mind only, and she is a grain of sand on the ocean's floor, and somehow time and space are boundless. Forgiveness is nothing, therefore, or alternatively it becomes the abiding purpose of all human experience.

She holds her head in her hands.

The sun is everywhere. The objects on the table are scarcely distinguishable from it. Silver stars are embossed on the crockery, but the silveriness is turning to white. Sun-spots trail slowly down in front of her eyes. Down and down. She snatches at a leaf on the stem of a flower in the glass. Someone laughs, close by.

When she turns the leaf over, staring at the underside through the sun-spot flares, there is the Mississippi. But only for a moment or two. It might be, Jesus, it might be the *Missouri*...

Why has it not occurred to her until now, did she get the two confused? Such a critical question of geography seethes at white heat in her mind, and suddenly, only further out this time, she is lost all over again.

'And now,' she hears the American saying to her, 'now you are your father's apostle.'

She gives him a smile as meaningless as his remark. It would wither anyone with a modicum of sensitivity. He considers himself wise, mistaking education for wisdom. Angels might weep for the time he must have served in campus libraries, accumulating all that dull and third-hand information from books. Books, and more books.

He knows nothing, this idiot, knows nothing at all.

Her eyes keep returning, though. To his face. To the set of his shoulders. His broad chest.

Wasted time, she wishes she could tell him, if she could trust the wine to let her. This, what we're talking about, academic drivel, *this* isn't real life.

With those shoulders, that torso, you could make someone happy, still, and what turns the world, always has and always will, is sex, SEX, the motor of life, a lesson so simple, every schoolgirl knows it, every squaddy, which I glimpsed the truth of once very long ago and haven't had the courage to discover since and learn again.

She became her father's secretary, his amanuensis. It was a suitable occupation to pursue in a Victorian house. After all, they belonged inside a Henry James short story.

She had no qualifications to do any other job of work. One thing had led to another. She couldn't think of a reason to resist.

She wasn't grudging about her new tasks, but she didn't enthuse either. She just did what was requiring to be done. It was made easier by discovering that she had a memory for the smallest details — individuals' addresses and telephone numbers, the minutiae of past correspondence, although not the finer points of classical literature and archaeology. She was never to be naturally fluent with these: the effect at the start was the same as if she had tried to learn to speak a language by correspondence course.

Most of those who dealt with her father were directed through her, so they assumed there was a closeness between them, an empathy, but it would have been too long a business for her to enlighten them — using, of course, the most neutral terms — as to what her true sentiments were. She was too indifferent to him now to feel spite for her strictly secondary role. A marked degree of pride caused her to conceal her other emotions, and to work instead at perfecting her skills within the narrow parameters of her job. She never made a mistake, and couldn't have been faulted, if anyone had had the face to do so. Her father humoured her, and didn't seek to create any difficulties. She developed a brief alphabet of expressions which would reveal nothing to him or to anyone of what she might be thinking, not smiling or scowling, not seeming to be anything except assured of her own inscrutability.

But that was just the exterior. Inside, she ran naked through the hot streets of a Mediterranean town — haunted the corridors of Oxford's Randolph Hotel as a *femme fatale* — reared children in a chintzy country house in the shires — presided over a table of business men at an everlasting board meeting — gained fame and fortune as an actress, or as a novelist of romances — was the inspiration of Roman poets — drove a white American convertible — was unflaggingly serviced to within an inch of her life in a cage-lift — uncovered a lost city in the dust of Italy's heel — and, most amazingly of all, found her mother to be alive and well, living in the very next road, and hardly a day older after all these so many and wasted years —

*   *   *

In the restaurant. She catches her. Breath.

Catches it. Catches it well. Swallows it down. Won't let it go, let it go again, whatever. Ever.

Could it have been that she had encouraged her father to make his move in Arles, but without having a glimmer of suspicion herself that that was what she was doing? Did she allow him to misunderstand that she was somehow sympathetic to his purposes?

The thought gnawed and fretted, and she could never kill it. It loped off into the shallows of her sleep, trailing its long caped shadow behind it, but its disgruntled appearance meant no more than that it was lying low, under cover of a troubled dream somewhere, in wily readiness for another ambush at some point in her working day when she could least defend herself.

She was exhausted by its returns, and by the pathetic job she made of grappling with it. She had as little conviction in herself now as eight, ten, fifteen years ago, when she had first been able to turn the sensation clouding her head – a massless dark contradiction – into a thought, by mentally speaking it in images, in common words.

It was guerrilla warfare, played out inside herself, and she was quarry to her own demon assailant.

She would watch her father watching his students from his wheelchair, watching them watching her. Cheroot in hand, balanced elegantly between his index and third fingers, within adroit reach of an ashtray, so that he never dropped the hot flèche of ash which she was certain he must.

Too much expertise. Too much dexterity, too much cleverness by half. Watching, with his mouth only just revealing the pleasure he was taking in the situation.

Laughing at them all.

Their presumption. Her embarrassment.

Their romanticism. Her craven spirit.

Their ignorance, bravely concealed by bluff. Her worldliness, shamelessly disguised as false innocence.

In their dining-room the oil portrait of her mother as a young woman hung above the sideboard, on the wall where the sun didn't reach.

She wore no engagement or wedding ring, so at that time the future must have appeared to be cast before her: *any* future of her choosing. She smiled, seemingly without a doubt that she might be disappointed, and without a suspicion that the seed of her disease was already planted inside her. Her face as the artist had shown it was clear and open, as if she believed that the best really must be possible.

What did it take, before you lost the will entirely? How bad did it have to get before there was no remission for mind or body and a sorrow or pain became unending?

Life – this life that comes to us once – it was for enjoying, she knew the wisdom of that. Friendships, places, food, music. Sensation. But the efforts it took some days just to reach the level plane of ordinariness were monumental, and a bugger on reaching anywhere else beyond that. Pleasure seemed selfish and blasphemous when the newspapers were chock-full of catastrophe and injustice, showing her that she lived in a world of callous cruelty and sometimes unimaginable horror.

They were extreme views, and equally valid, but she was stranded in the vastness of distance that separated them, dithering between the concepts of hedonism and morbidity and repelled by both, helpless to decide in which direction to turn.

After her father, she had never slept with another man again.

She liked cleanliness in the house. No dust. No smells, except polish and cut flowers.

She liked order, and her father had the lesson dinned home to him, over and over.

All the books on the shelves had to stand in alphabetical sequence by author's name. Certain cushions had to be arranged in the same certain way on their respective chairs. There was a routine by which the larger and smaller cups and saucers went into the display cabinets. The ornaments were here, and here, about the rooms – not there, or there, even if only a couple of inches out. The curtains had to hang straight, and when they weren't in use the blinds hadn't to come below – or reach above – a specific point of the window frame.

She had scores of rituals and superstitions to attend to in the course of a day, and she had attended to them so often she didn't give them a thought. She even insisted that the wheelchair follow certain paths between the pieces of furniture, on the runners of felt she'd had laid down on the carpet (and which she removed when their visitors came). The nurses who helped had to learn quickly just what was what, or – when her patience with them snapped at last – they were out on their ears.

If she was listening to music, the type of music corresponded to whatever time of the day it was. She tended to re-read books, and she would return to particular authors in their season and not out of it.

It was a house where nothing was left to chance: where everything, but absolutely everything, had its one and proper, allotted place.

She was a woman of a certain age. Forty-three. Or forty-four. An age when a woman, or this woman, was left gravely irresolute. How young to dress, how demurely to behave. She'd had her father's academic reputation to protect since his death, and she was in possession of his money (garnered from a string of his elderly maiden aunts), and she was caught on the stubborn horn of yet another and connected dilemma, between obligation and freedom.

She could walk out the door at any moment and take the first departing flight to, for instance, Outer Mongolia – or, better, to somewhere thereabouts with an expensive Sheraton or Intercontinental, like Katmandu – and binge herself for weeks on smoked salmon and caviar blinis and chilled Rhône wines of exceptional vintage, and let loose in the hotel discotheque or learn how to sub-aqua dive.

Anything was possible, theoretically. And in practical terms, she remained as crowded out by indecisiveness as she had ever been, hampered and cowed inside her own head. Physical movement was easier, a little easier to her, than opening up the landscape of her mind. That was still, away from the well-tramelled parts, undiscovered and forbidden – not virgin, but off-limits territory.

At some point the lunch ended, it was over.

She's on her bicycle travelling back to the house that is her home. She drifts into and out of situations like this. She doesn't need to be tipsy – is she? – to find herself in muzzy uncertainty sometimes of her precise whereabouts. At least it prevents certain things coming too close to her, which would smother her with their tedium. She moves by free association, and it is the safest and most painless route. The saving from pain should always be the ultimate consideration.

Tourists. Crocodile files of them. Open-topped buses. Packs of Latin teenagers with identical fluorescent back-packs, cutting across lanes of traffic and taking one-way streets in the wrong direction.

At one time the visitors were confined to summer, and out of season only the exotic specimens came: men in alpaca coats and women in long minks, transported to the sights in chauffeur-driven cars. Now, in a world of serious refugees, tourists too had the look of committed migrants.

The Sun on the Wall

* * *

On the Broad, twee baskets of flowers hanging on chains from the lampposts.

She lived in the Oxford which the tourists failed to search out. Some of them ventured to St Giles, as far as the outset of Woodstock Road and Banbury Road, and even up to the Cherwell, but they didn't know about the obverse side of the coin.

Oxford was too much a city of mind. What feelings there were in currency, from her vantage point, were the very worst ones, like jealousy and pride and fear, all hopelessly jumbled. Minds cracked, from too much introspection. In stripped-pine kitchens the last defences fell; lives were laid bare and remorselessly dissected. In conifer gardens women of a certain age picked up leaves and dead-headed, as if envisaged by a novelist of the 1950s.

No cardigans now, though, she had a rule about those. No sewing either, except vital repairs. Tea bags straight into the mug, no pots of brewing leaves and tinkling teacups. If she went under, it would be in polo neck and faded black denim, to something random on the radio, like a Nashville song of blighted love. What frightened her now was to imagine that after surviving so much she should become just another cliché at the end of it all.

She was pedalling on the last stretch when a metallic green Saab convertible with its hood raised passed in front of her at the traffic lights by the new wine bar.

She saw him through the glass. It *was* him – Dr Huxtable, she mentally called him – driving against the sun with the visor down.

She recognised the puffy profile. An academic 'doctor', which she thought pretentious, but that was the man all over. At his age, which was about her own, he ought to have known better. But she had stopped being surprised at the foolishness of clever people. Those who wrote books and papers on the humane arts had the most cramped outlook of all, in their steepled city partitioned for years by savage feuds and vendettas.

Last year it had happened. Or rather, had not happened. The scenario: He had been one of her father's younger departmental colleagues, a bachelor. He had rooms in his college, a set, to which he invited her. She arrived wearing a sale Country Casuals two-piece she had bought for the purpose. While he poured them both sherries, she gingerly seated herself in a battered leather armchair slackly stuffed with horsehair. He told her that it was his favourite chair.

'Ah.' Then she realised her faux-pas. 'I'm so sorry, would you –'

'Oh no.' He gulped. 'No. I should prefer that you –'

He went on to speak about his mother, who had died fifteen or sixteen months previously, not long before her father. A slab-faced woman stared at her out of silver photograph frames, and trailed her round the room with gimlet eyes that missed nothing, from the mantelpiece and the sofa table and the top of the grand piano. The eyes flushed her out of every corner she retreated to.

The rooms looked down on to the college deer park. She slipped on her spectacles to see. Timid spotted does cropped beneath bare lime trees, raising their heads and darting off at the first hint of disturbance. He indicated them with a nod.

'There's always talk of using them for High Table.'

'I'm sorry?' she said, not understanding. She removed her glasses. '"Using"... ?'

'Roasted. On a spit.'

She felt her stomach flip over. He was smiling at her. But then the silly smile stuck on his face. His fleshy, overindulged, really rather gormless face, and definitely undercooked.

She turned to find his mother's eyes and willed herself to stare back at her, with all the disgust she could muster on the does' behalf. But the nearest pair of eyes watched her from a more confident age, in monochrome black and white, when photographers were summoned to private homes and given their brief, and absurd women were wont to disport as if they were Diana Cooper herself. The stiffness of the gladioli in the background, though, and the cold formal hang of the window drapes behind the sitter's shoulder, she couldn't see that those were quite so harmless –

'You're looking at Mother?'

'What?'

(*Pardon*, she meant.)

'She was considered rather handsome. I believe so.'

'Ah.'

'In her time.'

He was like a man trapped out of his own time. She watched him reflected in the glass over a framed print – an antique map of some gnarled inland shire – and she caught him fidgeting with his bow tie (self-tie), then placing his hand on top of his nearly bald crown.

What oh what am I doing here? she asked herself.

When she turned round she had a composed, non-committal smile ready for him. His voice sounded under strain, as if a mechanism had been wound too tightly. The vowels were stretched, so that he had to twist his lips to say some of them. He pointed to the map, told her something about it, but she wasn't caring to know. She smelt not sherry but peppermints from his breath, or mint mouthwash possibly, and detected a defect, another one. She thought he had the look of a man who would become petulant whenever he was denied something he wanted: all his life he had been used to having his whims catered to. He didn't – he couldn't – want *her*. And she wasn't an accommodator of others' whims.

She looked away, towards the window. Bleak sunshine fell among the trees. An arc of light fell on to the golden stone of the arcaded Italianate building opposite, and she caught her breath. She was aware of a movement by her side, and she pulled her arm back instinctively. She applied another smile to her face, but it was a tack-on. She angled away, and noted a whiff of something else. She switched her eyes leftwards, and spotted what she hadn't before, white arum lilies standing in frozen poses in a white glass vase. They were an interior decorator's choice, or an undertaker's stock-in-trade, and she shivered at the sight of them, couldn't stop herself shaking.

He took her out to dinner on a couple of occasions.

The first time it was to a restaurant in Oxford, crowded out with media dons and their wives or bed-mates, all dedicated foodies slavering over their choices from the menu and eyeing the results critically, competitively. It was dreadful.

The second time he drove her into Berkshire, by the Thames, through a part of the world she could never get mapped out in her head, even though it was so comparatively close to home. The restaurant was housed in a converted watermill. In contrast to the brown paper covers and shared tables of the first restaurant, the décor here was plush and muffled, every blind ruched and every curtain tied and pelmeted and the flouncy covers on the chairs secured with twiddly ribbons. It was dreadful too, and she wondered how many unspeakable establishments just like them there were in the world, until now unguessed at.

In the watermill she attempted to eat crabmeat and avocado salad, then guinea fowl: because she wasn't hungry she had picked out the first items on the menu her eyes fell upon. Followed by a platter of tiny forest fruits, so-called, set among fanned leaves. She'd glimpsed the ornately cursive numerals of the prices: the intention must have been to make them difficult to decipher.

This time the tables were placed well apart, and the chairs had high backs and padded arms, and she felt they were ensconced like two grandee diplomats, he and she, engaged in some official transaction. Which, by his design, they doubtless were. More small talk, even though – she realised – it wasn't supposed to be that. Words exchanged as counters, as tokens, which

– unlike her companion – she was only permitting to carry their immediate, surface meaning. The conversation meandered, halted, found a new direction, continued with its deflections and diversions, hesitated, halted again.

They set off home, through deep woods where kings used to hunt for sport.

It was his habit to drive at speed, and who was she to interfere with the methods of a forty-four-year-old unmarried man? It was the season for headlights on main beam, and she lost count of the creatures that were sucked under the car's bonnet. The journey was punctuated with what seemed to be endless soft thuds beneath the chassis.

She might have fallen asleep in other circumstances, since it was so late and the interior of the car was so warm. But he was cross, irritated, afflicted with the sheer pettiness of the situation. She wanted, not to scream at him, but to do something mean and trivial, like – like take a pair of scissors to his tie. Then she realised she was thinking that because of the Bear pub, where he had taken her before a concert, and where they had commented on the infamous collection of snipped tie-ends displayed under glass – and she realised also that every thought in her head had its prompt, one previous thing leading to a subsequent other, by hidden pressures of logic.

A dire concert it had been too, in the Holywell Music Room, arch people sitting intently forward on hard benches to listen, and the music played on 'authentic' instruments and killed for her by its own purity and by his holding a manuscript of the score open on his lap throughout.

She turned on the radio in the fascia by reflex, and found it tuned to Radio 3. Soppy operatic voices were warbling away.

She snatched at the channel button, and found a French channel with some inane disco rhythm pulsing out. She tapped her fingers on the arm-rest, where he could see, aware she was behind the beat, or ahead, but always between.

She had read an article about High Disco of the 1970s as a 'cultural entity' now meriting serious academic study. (Of course it would have to be serious, what alternative was there?) But she couldn't be bothered explaining, she had no intention of justifying herself. The music alone sufficed, assuring him they were both of them quite incompatible.

Mission accomplished.

Back in the house she drinks her tea, staring at the postcard that's Sellotaped to the kitchen wall.

A photograph by Lartigue, the small boy and not the famous man he became.

The Sun on the Wall

'*1905   Paris   40 rue Cotambert   Bichonnade.*'
A young woman in an ankle-length dress is flying through the air. A moment before she jumped from the fifth or sixth step of a stone staircase. She will land on gravel. Her legs are tucked beneath her.

The pose always astonishes her, because the woman is dressed in neck bow and mutton sleeves for the stiff rituals of a drawing-room. Under the rolled hair she has the plainish features that make her believable: the expression of this willing accomplice is concentrated but at the same time light-hearted, and – taking loud sips of her tea-bag tea – she recognises kindness when she sees it, even at this other extreme end of the century.

She longs for some proof of grace, a clue to redemption, some unexpected sweetness. She feels that there should be a progress in life towards something better, for one and all, but she doesn't have the evidence of it, only a sensation, which is something less than a premonition.

In a Palladian city just now and then she runs along a ringing colonnade. She jumps over the jagged shadows, in and out of sunshine. There is no one to forbid her to run, and with her flights of aerial ballet she cuts the air as cleanly as a cutlass blade.

And back on the down, elbows on the table and nibbling at her nails, with the good going-out watch she bought herself removed from her wrist and with unseasonal redcurrant dye spreading on to the pads of flesh under her fingernails, she thinks ahead, a season ahead, inevitably, to winter.

Oxford winters.

Pristine drifts of snow in locked college gardens. Swirling blizzards on Woodstock Road. Icicles hanging from the gables of the house like a hagwitch's fingers.

The gas fire spluttering in the sitting-room, a sleepy orange glow. Summoning courage for the journey to the bathroom: green and white tiles, the coldness of every porcelain surface. Tea never staying hot in the wrapped mug, but drinking too much caffeine none the less. A cartographer's frosted continent plotted on the window glass. The crackle of puddles in the garden. The sad whistles of the trains, keening from across the Meadows. Loosened snow sliding down the roof, sending shudders through the house. The complaining whines and rumbles of the water-pipes behind the walls.

Cloudlets of breath appearing in front of her face.

Packed grey clouds, the strained gruelly light. She can cope with that. It's the sun that terrifies her in their quiet, becalmed, snow-smothered streets. That pastiche of Mediterranean sunlight, so stark and harsh. It's cold, and without the heat it seems even more merciless to her; it ranges like a searchlight into each of the back rooms, shrinking them, showing them to be primmer and somehow more enclosed than they appear to her at any other time of the year. In winter she realises how the fabrics have faded, and the paper has crinkled on the walls, and the carpets worn in the places where they've been oftenest walked on. From one winter to the next, however, nothing is done about the wear and tear, and the years hurry past and then are lost, and all that's left behind is the evidence of the running down, a whirring spiral of deterioration...

She returned to Dr Herzl after her father died. She felt she was doing something well out of its authentic period. The old cretonne armchair now nipped her around the waist, and inexplicably Dr Herzl had grown a wiry grey beard. But it was more important that she came, just to have somebody – anybody – to talk to.

Not that he hadn't been quite good-looking, once, then. She granted him that. So why oh why the beard? It did nothing for him. Not handsome, once, but quite personable, yes. And now. She smiled too broadly. Herzl's eyes homed in. Back to the beginning, back to 'Go'. The room felt quite familiar to her. New blinds, venetian. About time too. But apart from that. She smiled again, tried to get the tension right in her lips. Herzl was humming under his breath. It was her money now, and deserved, she could do whatever she chose to with it. Not *very* handsome, once, but moderately so, and manly, commanding, oh yes that.

She sits on the old swing in the garden. The wooden frame is green with dampness and moss. The seat groans on its shaggy ropes.

The sun is playing hard-to-find behind a haze of high cloud. She squinnies over at the windows of the house. Momentarily, even without her long-range lenses, she spots her mother behind glass, in the room that was her bedroom, *their* bedroom.

She has fair skin, just like her mother's. It seems to have got fairer with time.

She doesn't like to be out in the summer sun for long, because it leaves scarlet splodges on her face. Anyway, there are so many dangers now – three kinds of ultra-violet radiation – the spoilsport articles in the newspapers keep reminding them. She wears a sunhat when she's out of doors, an old one, and too small for her, but she remains faithful to her clothes, as if they are the steadfast friends of her life.

She used to swing so high on the ropes, once upon a time, that she could put her feet on the roof of the house, she could kick the steeple off the church in Hidcote Road. She was afraid of nothing as a child, until her childhood ended, in the sultry afternoon heat of an ancient city in a southern latitude.

She might be able to manage, except for the sun. The good Doktor Herzl doesn't understand about the sun, how significant it is, how it is the key to the lock in the door.

It slashes early through the trees. It blazes white on the old brick wall on the north side of her garden. It creeps across the tangled wisteria vine with its long-abandoned, fraying blackbirds' nests. It seeps upwards, through the garden, towards the house.

By the time she's up and dressed and in the kitchen making tea it has reached the window. An arc spreads on the wall. It widens and widens, including the pottery crock of spatulas and whisks, the calendar with its bleached photograph of Blenheim Palace and foreground fountain, the plug socket, a copy of *Cooking for One*, the rack of dusty spice jars.

She sits down at the table with her tea and two wedges of toast and marmalade.

She waits. Sits and waits.

For the postman, of course. But he is almost incidental. Her eyes return to the wall and fix there. In grim anticipation of the moment when the sun will reach one particular point.

It might be any point. But the one that matters so much to her is the top of the crack splitting on a diagonal across the plaster. It resembles the Mississippi River. When the sun reaches it – *if* it reaches it, because there is always the possibility that it may not – then she knows in her innards, in the gut, that the game is up and she cannot be reclaimed.

It is a superstition, but quite real to her, as utterly real as anything else in her life. *The sun mustn't reach the crack*, that river gouged in the wall. But it will or it won't without her being able to decide things either way. She is helpless to exercise a bearing. The situation eludes her, every time, and she sits at the table watching impotently, as if she is being judged. Her terror in these moments knows no limits. Damp rings form under her arms, her stomach knots, her hands grip the arms of her chair, her mouth – even after the tea – dries, her whole scalp itches. She panics, and as the instant of truth approaches her breath grows short and frantic.

Afterwards, when the sun has hit the exact demarcation on the wall, from there it is downhill all the way. There is no purpose in anything after that, it is all equally useless. An unending prospect of snow light, a white-out without dimension, mass, extent, limit. She is being sucked into it, the spirit in her is thinning and thinning, evaporating into that ice vacuum, into perfected absolute nothingness.

She doesn't have the feel of her fingers on the swing's ropes for cold. Maybe this is the process beginning?

She opens her eyes at last to the garden. She blinks through the lenses of her looking-away glasses. Only Yakov is missing.
Where is Yakov? Poor Yakov.

For as long as she could remember, Yakov had been their gardener. They shared him with two or three others scattered about the city. In Oxford regular gardeners were jealously guarded by their employers, and her father had said and done all the right things to placate him.

Much of the man's existence had been a mystery to them. He may have been married, once or twice, in the time since his Russian one. No one had seen where he lived. He had never mastered English, and some of his procedures at work were surely on the eccentric side: little mirrors in the greenhouse to turn the sun on to sprouting plants, pinning a photograph of Queen Mary to a stake to scare away birds (with great success), weighting branches of the fruit trees with bags of stones so that they wouldn't grow over neighbours' walls, and – quite advanced thinking for its day – tipping their leftovers of food into an oil drum colonised by grubs and worms, to produce a very rich plant feed.

There had been an easy communication between Yakov and herself, indeed a rapport. They hadn't needed to speak to make themselves readily understandable to one another. Their silences were comfortable, unlike the ones that would sometimes open up around her and her father in the house when there was no one else there, suddenly isolating them among household trivialities, with the unspoken and unsolved a constant menace.

She liked to hear Yakov in the garden, going about his work. That aspect of routine and normality was always a solace to her, when he was scything the long grass or wielding the old diesel mower or raking leaves to burn or staking the trailers or setting to the finicky job – which he did under duress – of potting out. Labouring work pleased Yakov best: it didn't matter how hard it was. Her father tried to oblige him, cutting down the number of rose beds and grassing over the annual borders which her mother had made her responsibility, or else attending to the horticulture – not very successfully – by himself.

In a Latvian forest, in 1943, Yakov and other men from the village had been taken to a scene of execution. Women gathering mushrooms had heard a barrage of gunshots some days before. When the men were brought to the place, they saw heaps of bodies thrown into a pit. At gunpoint they were ordered to pick up shovels from the ground and to fill in the long trench.

'Who dug it?'

Yakov shrugged at her.

'Who were they? The people who were killed –?'

Yakov shrugged again. Nobody had dared to ask the Germans questions, not when nervous fingers were being flexed on rifle triggers.

For weeks after he told her, or tried to tell her, she wondered just how many of the strangers she passed in the streets had such terrible shaming pasts of their own which they were struggling to keep the lid tight closed on.

A de Chirico print hangs on the wall behind Dr Herzl's desk. The picture draws her eyes every time. It interests her but simultaneously it irritates her.

The painting shows a white colonnaded building receding sharply into the distance. A green sky. A little girl running with a hoop and stick. Across the street another building stands in sombre shadow. A long wooden box on wheels, like an empty cattle truck, is angled into the darkness of shadow with both its doors wide open. Halfway down the ochre street a man's shadow falls on to the ground, from some concealed point behind the gloomy building.

The painting's title appears beneath on the print. *The Mystery and Melancholy of a Street.*

Happiness was the problem. It took so much more application and mental effort. She often saw a tiny old red-cheeked couple who went shopping together, and they always seemed to be chirpily smiling, or laughing, and she was quite mystified as to how it was done.

She didn't care to be how she was. If she'd not had the evidence of the wee folks' merriment, their *joie de vivre*, she would have supposed that in real life there was no disposition left for such transforming miracles.

She wasn't stopped, though, from dabbling around the edges of the problem.

For the past seven or eight months she had been going to fortnightly Russian Orthodox services at the ecumenical centre in Pink Street. The idea ought to have come from Yakov, but he had never heard of the place, and anyway he had disavowed religion long ago.

She so badly needed another perspective on things. It was somewhere else to try, another last resort. She required saving. That seemed a sterling reason to her why she should go. She was desperate, to be saved from desperation, and she would avail herself of every opportunity to be enlightened.

After her father's death she had found among his academic effects an incomplete essay, still in its handwritten first-draft form and replete with crossings-out and arrowed inclusions. The paper it was written on might have been – she guessed – twenty years old, or older; the ink, once black, now had a red-rust tint to it, and some particles started to flake off when she passed the tips of her fingers across several words.

She could decipher her father's script, as college secretaries had rarely been able to do. It required knowledge of his vocabulary, and the combinations of terms he used. She would always read what he had written at speed: that yielded most, rather than picking over particular words. She had never cared to ask him, and sheer exigency over the years had developed a sixth sense in her. With practice and perseverance she had become better acquainted with the content and still more so with the mechanics of his train of thought and his prose style, so she certainly hadn't surprised herself by her later capacities.

It was fast, fluid script, with a bias to the horizontal. There was no break within words, and separate words were frequently joined together. Stalks and loops and cusps were minimal; 't's were rarely crossed or 'i's dotted. A graphologist would have remarked on the introspection and mercurial intelligence of the writer. Her own script by contrast was cramped, and italicised, written very precisely – and artificially – with an oblique nib. His had much more *élan*, and always seemed to have been dashed off, with – deceptive – aristocratic nonchalance.

It was another cause of envy to her, and further humiliation, and she had concluded yet again that 'attitude' – most specifically, the bludgeon power of will – was the essential difference between them.

The paper's subject was a community of the second century BC settled in the flatlands of Lower Puglia, between modern Brindisi and Taranto. Its people were immediately descended from colonists who had made the journey west from an isthmus on the southernmost tentacle of the Greek Peloponnese between the Gulfs of Messania and Laconia, some time between 230 and 210 BC.

They had been an especially homogenous and exclusive, self-sufficient society, mostly belonging to one of three families. Each family exacted particular loyalties from its members; the families were all distinct from one another, and while they co-operated together in the community's defence it came about that they founded sub-communities – which became something like townships in time – within that locale of thirty or forty square miles. Family remained the basis of the way of life there, and a democratic process of self-regulation in their province ensured that serious disputes and contests were avoided, to the greatest mutual advantage of all parties.

It was the strength of the original family bonds in this land of exile which was the prime matter of significance to her father. Her eyes sped-read the major part of an analysis of the structure of authority inside the family sub-groups. It was the later sections, about personal relationships, which slowed her down on that first reading of the long-lost material.

Apparently there had been no proscriptions against incestuous pairings. Mothers lay with sons, fathers with daughters, siblings with one another, and uncles and aunts and grandparents were free to take their pick. Although there was no evidence extant that this behaviour had been practised so freely in their Greek homeland, here the spirit of democracy seemed to have been taken to an ultimate end. For a couple of generations the relationships were essentially recreational: child-bearing remained the prerogative of husband and wife, as in general society. Later that freedom went to their heads and the original strictures were dispensed with – a father of children might make his own mother pregnant, or a sister might deliver a baby to two brothers in succession. Incestuous offspring – say, the two children of that one woman by her two brothers – then mated with one another, as early as the age of eleven or twelve. At which point 'the community discovered that incest is the only common taboo in nature: it only had to study the quality of the current progeny to be convinced.'

Various charts and diagrams of family trees were provided, but she no more than glanced at those. The entire essay, in this rough form, was really only a kind of historian's footnote. It was her father's interest which interested her in turn – and the remark, expressed without any qualifications as an established fact, that incest is the principal instinctive prohibition among the natural species on the planet.

While he drew – with copious details, which she glossed over – a picture of an Edenic society for its first two generations, he also recognised the hazards that were already built into it.

Had he believed that the damage could be limited if the situation was treated cautiously? – or was a calamity predestined to happen, at some prospective juncture, resulting in a tragic and brutal pay-out?

If self-destruction was endemic in the system – how long ago had he understood this, before or after what had happened for the first time in the midsummer siesta heat of vertiginously antique Arles?

It was the single item of her father's work which she suppressed.

She knew at once that it had to be sabotaged.

Accordingly she tore up the pages and was going to set fire to them in the kitchen sink when something stopped her and she blew out the lit match, after it had nipped the ends of her fingers. Instead she took the debris to the cloakroom WC, and dropped it into the bowl of the toilet, and pulled the cistern handle.

She stood watching as the pieces of paper were first spun around in the tumble of water and then flushed away. After another tug of the handle she pictured them being carried through the sewerage ducts of this city of fabled learning.

Subterfuge, subversive thoughts: but capable perhaps of spreading contagiously, and seeping back into the communal order of things? She doubted that, although it was an appealing fancy during those moments of imagining so, how she might come to infect an entire population with this damp but seditious, anarchistic confetti.

Yakov had attacked a man in the Spar shop in North Parade. He told the police afterwards he recognised him, he'd been one of the officers in the forest.

Which forest? they asked him.

The victim spoke English with a German accent, but his passport stated that he came from Poland. It didn't make any difference to Yakov: for him the man was guilty. When she went to see him, she said to him, 'But how do you know he's the man?' Yakov told her, 'I remember.' That was his favourite English verb, and he repeated it in that cheerless grey room in the police station, over and over like a charm. *I remember, I remember, I remember.*

'But I don't see how you can.'

Yakov closed his eyes and shook his head. That was her misfortune, he meant, not his.

How do I tie in with this, she asked herself on the way home, how is it that I connect? With Yakov, with Latvia, with what happened in the forest? She went into the Spar shop. The tins had been neatly stacked up the way they'd been before the fracas. Yakov was in custody. Maybe that was safest for him, she thought, and for the other haunted types who fetched up in this city, at this crowded crossroads of spiked destinies.

There was a repetition of the incident, eighteen months later, involving a different man, in St Aldate's. Yakov was taken away for 'treatment'.

She half wanted to visit him, but she wanted just as much not to. She went to the first of the church services instead, in the hope of finding a resolution to her indecision. The sounds of Russia, spoken and sung, washed over her, and she was oddly soothed, quietened.

She tried to accept that she was sitting on the hard pew for Yakov's express benefit. She was meaning to bring him to light. In the hospital it wasn't possible for him, among all those messy and fractured lives.

She was listening to the chanting when it occurred to her why she hadn't gone to visit him. She'd been too full of fear: in case any of the staff should think they recognised her, on an instinct, as one of the kind who belonged there.

There was a third assault, shortly after Yakov was released. As a consequence, he had to be taken out of circulation. This time his victim was Dr Herzl, who chanced at the time to be giving his surname to a sales assistant in the garden centre on Banbury Road.

Yakov had earlier been tending a bonfire in her own garden, which was why he had been in the area on that afternoon. She felt implicated therefore. She wondered if she should make herself known to Herzl, but didn't betray herself by so much as a bat of an eyelid when the man's name was repeated to her by the policeman.

Maybe God was telling her that she wasn't attending the church services regularly enough, or not bringing proper conviction to the business of prayer, or wasn't giving with sufficient generosity when the plate was passed round.

What she needed, she felt, was faith. To her way of thinking that wasn't quite the same as belief. Faith was a preliminary, an attitude. She should be able to surrender herself without comprehending why. Which would be nothing new to her. It is only – so she would have told the priest if he had spared her more than a paltry, sixty-watt smile as he spied out the well-heeled in his congregation – it is only the story of my life.

Her fellow-churchgoers – she doesn't yet count herself a worshipper – are mostly in their fifties and sixties, and older. There are exceptions: a haughty-looking young man for ever in profile, a girl with a ballerina neck and overbred features and a bitter mouth, twin sisters with flat, very northern European faces and a fur-edged rug which they share inside the chilly building.

She doesn't really understand much of what is going on. She goes for the chanting, the slow singing of responses in bass voices, and for the spicy warm mist of incense from the swinging censer. She goes because she has no reason to be there except wanting, and because she can forget for several minutes on end that she is in Oxford.

The commands translate as 'detachment', 'purification of the heart', 'attentiveness and watchfulness'. The Dormition of the Virgin; Anastasis, or the Harrowing of Hell. The Feasts of the Exaltation of the Cross, of the Transfiguration.

The faces of the icons – Gabriel, St Sergius, Christ Pantocrator – radiate peace and wisdom in the shine of candles, and she longs to give herself to their solemn mystery, to be admitted through their doors of perception to that which is beyond.

They creep out of church into daylight, and usually – as if God were testing their devotion – into rain. Most of them stand about for a while, under cover of those telescopic umbrellas that spring up into the air, if only because it might seem uncharitable to hurry off home and maybe because they truly don't have anything better to do with their time.

She has heard it said – safely behind his back – that Pyotr Vasilievich Tsypkin comes to church to repent. She sits two rows behind that solid back, watching it for indicators, for a spasm of guilt perhaps across the shoulders. But so far, no sign. Comfortably into his middle age and with too evenly grey hair, Mr Tsypkin may not be there to atone after all.

Certainly he is wealthy, from causes which nobody has worked out. She suspects he is a landlord, with umpteen properties across the city. If he is repenting anything, it must be a mortgage swindle; she learned from the radio not so long ago just how it's done.

Mr Tsypkin arrives and departs in a large silver and black American car piloted by a chauffeur in livery. After the service and a confab with the priest and a little loiter outside, he gets into the car, hand-kissing to the last, and always with a final look over in her direction, even though he may be calling across in Russian to someone who is standing close by her. She would see better if she was wearing her glasses, but she leaves them off; she soon twigged that this is his ruse, not to look at her directly, and she is careful to do nothing that might help to give his game away.

She knows – simply *knows* – this much about Mr Tsypkin, that one day he is going to invite her into that two-toned car which slithers about the road as the driver steers on heavy soft suspension for the kerb, and inside the rear cabin – or at his home, whether it's up in Headington or on top of Boar's Hill – the goodness of God and her own endurance will be acutely put to the test.

In the kitchen she washes up her tea mug.

Anyway, what novelists forget is how much of life turns out to be trivial and tedious. She doesn't want to read about that, but it is surely the sober background which helps to define those big dramatic explosions in people's lives. For everything untoward there has to an accounting. In the end she knows more, much more than the novelists do.

In the kitchen she washes up her tea mug. If she thinks hard, thinks hard enough, she will start to forget, she will be left in peace.

Nothing ever quite finishes. One thing leads to another. People either don't die, or when they do they persist as their own ghosts. There are no neat underlinings beneath the facts of the past, the purported facts. She is still a spectator of what others choose to preserve as her reality.

– and thinks hard enough, she will start to forget, she will be left in peace.

A smile to be distinguished from other smiles. Movements that strangely correspond to her own. A sense that out of all the babbling babel of chatter words are being prepared, to be spoken by him with his head inclined towards her in that unmistakable and fawning way.

Every year there used to be another two or three of the students who would try. Sometimes it had been done as a dare, but mostly the intention was genuine, as they supposed in their naïvety. She would hurt to appear so insensible towards the handsome ones, because she felt they should be under no illusion, since it gave her stomach flutters even to think about it. The plainer ones used to trouble her conscience less, and their faces seemed to subsume their disappointment more readily.

It was too late, always too late. In this charmed, sugarspun city. Lewis Carroll had dreamed it all on a riverbank, as an alternative condition, reality turned out of itself by unreason's spurious but dulcet logic. It felt quite real enough to her, but she had to work at it, touching the warm medieval stone with the palms of her hands, letting her feet ring on the cobbles, making her voice hollo down a dark alleyway or soar over a garden wall as she cycled past. She picked up evidence as she walked along: leaves on the pavements, beads and pennies from the gutters, the flattened wet pages of textbooks – fallen from bicycle baskets – which she unpeeled before the lettering of poems and mathematical principles and biblical exegesis became impressed for ever in the grooves of insignificance between the cobblestones.

Seven weeks ago she saw Nanny Chisholm in the covered Market, from her table in Brown's café.

She was sitting in that democratic meeting-place, among the traffic wardens and antiques dealers and tally-collectors and the pairs of earnest students discussing philosophy and analysing the state of their love affairs.

She hadn't a thought of the woman in her head and then, suddenly, she spotted her passing by, shuffling past the window and weighed down with a shopping basket.

She had turned into an old crone, but it *was* her.

Even without her seeing-away glasses on, she knew.

The same hat-pin eyes in their deep sockets, under a profuse and untidy ginger wig. Eyes that had always confronted nothing and nobody directly, but at sly angles, malevolently.

The woman didn't look in, or seemed not to. But the sighting left her shaking in her chair. Some tea slopped out of her cup on to the table's Formica. She was being studied by her neighbours, she felt: they were pitying her. She reached into her pocket for a paper hanky to mop up with.

She had supposed Nanny Chisholm had just disappeared. Instead it had just been the case that for years they had chanced not to meet. Taking different roads and turnings, rounding this corner and not that, kept apart by fate and luck. What was the point of their tracks now – almost – crossing, running parallel for these several heart-stopping seconds?

Her hands continued to tremble, and she placed them under the table. She couldn't trust herself to lift the cup again without spilling, although she had such a thirst, her mouth was baked dry. It had been by mere flukes and fortuity that they hadn't met, she and Nanny Chisholm. What was the import to be read into this rainy Wednesday morning, serendipitously raising her eyes to a point in a window where the condensation allowed her to see out and to glimpse another of the monsters who stalked her wood?

She didn't want to stay on in the house, but how much more courage was it going to take to leave it?

One day she'd gone to look at a flat in a newly completed block, in a cul-de-sac off Banbury Road. It was over-priced, but she knew the current value of complete and undivided houses in her own road, so the cost wouldn't have been a problem. The estate agents had insisted she had to see it for herself, *by* herself, that she should find some time to inspect it at her leisure, and so – with a view to a killing – they had given her a key. She chose to cycle over one morning, just after breakfast, before the postman arrived with the demands of another day's correspondence.

Unfortunately the sun was shining and, worse, the flat was angled the same way that the house was. Standing in the kitchen she recognised that arc of sun spreading on the pristine blankness of white wall. Here, though, the ceiling was lower, and the kitchen – for all its up-to-the-minute concealed conveniences – was narrow and incarcerating. The double-glazing might have been triple, because she could hear nothing from outside of traffic or other people or such nature as there was trapped in north Oxford. She felt her breath wrapping itself into a tight puffball inside her chest.

Breathlessness.

Breath. Less. Ness.

Suddenly. It would happen.

Her head started to feel light. She put an arm out behind, stretched her hand, touched the door jamb. Held on to it. Any second now a crack would appear in the unblemished white paintwork on top of the wall's smooth plaster. She had to close her eyes. It was a nightmare, at twenty to ten in the morning. She could only smell headachy paint, and a mania for newness, and no air at all in this flat that was too exorbitantly priced to sell.

Did Pyotr Vasilievich Tsypkin have anything to do with the agents' browbeating her into coming?

She turned. Ran to the front door. Let it slam behind her. Went scrambling down the stairs – cold, terrazzo-faced, and a 'feature' – in her panic, just to flee. To get the hell out of the place.

She took the shadiest roads back on her bicycle, but the sun was racing her home. It reached the house before her. It was waiting for her in the kitchen. She sank down on to the chair at the table. Inside she felt nothing except the judders of her heart – no thoughts, no emotions, no recollections – as the river on the wall turned to sea and prepared to wash her away in the calm rage of its flood.

At lunch, remembering the incident, her glass toppled over and sent wine spreading across the linen cloth.

The circle of wetness spread and spread.

One thing leading to another.

She sat staring at the mess, with her head in her hands. Her young host was trying to dam the wine's progress with his napkin.

'Don't worry, I'll clear it up,' he was telling her, in his transatlantic twang. 'I'll attend to this.'

She allowed herself to smile, a small smile.

From little things greater things come. But at the same time her breath was growing hard and sore in her chest, and she knew she had been here before at this impasse and would be here again.

She squeezed on the smile and closed her eyes against the source of light. In the pinky dark behind her lids the sun repeatedly faded to dying and then was resurrected. Over and over. A succession of identical suns.

'I meant to ask you, about when your father –'

The same sun, falling and flaring to life, a pinhead of exploding light.

While meantime –

Her head was floating off, helium-head, and one thing was leading to another. To.
Breathlessness.
Breath. Less. Ness.
Suddenly. Suddenly it would happen –

From the landing window she hears a noise. Car brakes squealing to a halt on the road outside the house. She runs, as if understanding, to the front door. She goes out on to the front step. There he is, her sturdy well-formed young American, in a white low-slung open sports car.

'Are you ready, my love?' he calls up to her, laughing.
'Yes,' she hears herself reply. 'Oh yes.'
'Bring your things then, jump in.'
'Please – please wait for me –'

From under her bed she pulls out the crocodile travelling-case given to her by her father, which she has never used. She is packed in no time. She runs downstairs, grabs her shoulder-bag, and lets the front door slam behind her, not checking whether she has a key with her or not.

He puts her case into the boot while she lowers herself into the passenger seat. He gets in beside her and revs up. She knows there will be faces watching, but she doesn't look for them.

And then they're off. Along the road and round the corner. Then round another corner, and the present and the past are slipping behind her. Only the future matters now.

She sees a sign – a footpath – to Tivoli Road. But what the hell? she thinks. None of it concerns me any more. She lets the wind blow out her hair. She feels young and light, and susceptible for the first time in many years to prettiness.

There is only the sunshine to trouble her. It's everywhere. Then she remembers that something else is needed, and she fishes in her bag to find them. A pair of dark glasses. She takes off her spectacles and puts the others on.

The sun can be no hazard to her now.

He turns up the radio. Softly sexy voices, over a quiet but insistent beat. Soul music. It seems to be coming at her from all directions, all at once. They will be able to travel for miles just like this, for miles and miles.

He places his hand along the back of her seat. She feels, not intimidated, but protected. Everything is going to be fine. Not a hint of breathlessness. Her story, her long long story, is going to have a happy ending after all, she is travelling towards its conclusion, into brilliant sunshine and it doesn't matter.

The grandfather clock struck on the landing. Seven protracted chimes which seemed to be never going to end.

The Sun on the Wall

She took off her looking-away glasses, and sighed.
Then she thought she heard sounds in the clock's echo. Footsteps.
She spun round. Peered. Peered hard to see.
But there was no one. Only her shadow where it was stuck to the nearest wall, shaped out of the waning glow of the evening's cold sun.

The Broch

PART ONE

The house is full. Doors opening and closing, water-pipes gushing, children calling from windows. Wardrobe doors being prised open on squeaking hinges, disobliging drawers rattling stiffly on crooked runners. The sounds of so much urgency suddenly. Sandals slapping, high heels scraping. Shouts from the shore, Chinese Whispers played on the upstairs gallery, and incidental whispers from the adults that their speakers wouldn't want to be overheard.

Everything is in motion. The house heaves and creaks.

However it has come about, it has happened, and here they all are, with their lives to hold from unravelling.

Mrs Meldrum

There was only one photograph of the seven of them taken at Achnavaig, on the beach, all caught in the one frame. She, Ming, and the five children.

Ming was fixing the spar of a box kite; she was holding the string herself, and Lewis and Struan were helping to disentangle the ribbons. (At the time Lewis couldn't have been any older than ten, and so there weren't the distractions that came later.) Moyna was standing by her side, and Nicol was crawling about on the travelling rug. Ailsa's head was turned to look out of the picture – towards the first of those external attractions about to intrude: trust Ailsa, when it was probably no more than a momentary lapse of concentration, but that was her fate as she saw it, always to be misunderstood.

Lewis is serious, as befits the eldest. Struan has muscular legs already. Moyna stands in her mother's shadow. Nicol is following his instincts. Ailsa's mind is wandering. Ming is doing what fathers do, while she is left pulling the strings, because someone has to.

Who took the photograph? She forgets. Only – on closer inspection – Moyna appears to have noticed what's afoot, eyes homing in on the camera.

No smiles, no formal and fey sentiment. It may have been a freak moment, but they're all present in their essence, that's the curious thing.

Ming, herself. Lewis and the others in due order of age. Ailsa. Struan. Moyna. Nicol.

The snapshot shows them unmistakably as they were.

As they now are, with one exception.

She keeps the photograph out of her family's reach, in a drawer of the tallboy in her bedroom where it cannot be found.

It's two years since Ming died. Rather, it's two years exactly since the day of the funeral. This seems the only place for us to be.

By hook or by crook, by land and sea, they've come. We haven't all been together since then. That was in Glasgow, before I sold the house and moved for that short interim into the flat. Maybe they saw how itchy I was to leave Glasgow. It was Lewis who persuaded me I should keep on The Broch, that he would assist me with the expenses of living there – living *here* – if I decided to uproot myself and go north, and that the others would chip in as well.

How many years is it since we were under this roof? Every summer we came: and at Easter, and – weather permitting – at New Year. It's such an extravagance. I can't imagine it would sell quickly in this day and age, such an impractical mish-mash of styles – a proper mongrel of a house – and too big for anyone's peace of mind.

It can just about accommodate us all. I wanted the grandchildren to be included, although they are further away from the experience. The Broch was their great-great-grandfather's indulgence. The firm has gone now, since Ming's death, so the purpose of the house can't be clear to them: they were all bound up, the work and the four generations – when Struan was involved – and the houses and this manner of life. It did make a kind of sense, not a great deal, but some. At least they'll have their own recollections of it, before it is finally sold, experienced one hot August, a little less hot than the August before that but, even so, an untypically fierce spell for the west of Scotland, for a sea-facing unenclosed stretch of shore. Memory will transport them back, when all this has gone from us, when The Broch is a hotel or time-share apartments or is the crumbling evidence of one further owner's defeated aspirations.

The funeral in Glasgow took place on a day of stunning, heartless heat. The cars had to travel with their windows open. The flowers were wilting on the wreaths. Handkerchiefs mopped at, not tears, but perspiration runs. The pall-bearers' hands were so wet that their grip would slip on the coffin handles; their faces showed the full strain of the weight on their shoulders. The organist was in desultory form, and stumbled on some of the notes, which set him trying harder, so that the veins and sinews stuck out on his neck like whipcord. The high plate-glass windows of the crematorium chapel revealed a prospect of washed-out heavenly blue, without a cloud anywhere. The doors had to be left open at the back. Service programmes were waved as fans. The curtains – maroon velvet, with gold tassels – parted and closed stickily on their rail. The silence for reflection was filled with lots of tiny sounds – of insects, of women's shoes being stepped back into, of an ice-cream van's bells a couple of miles away.

Outside, hands – hot palms – had to be shaken. Fingers ran round the insides of shirt collars. Phials of spray-on perfume were applied, as discreetly as they might be, on ear-lobes and wrists. Damp circles had appeared under the arms of dresses. A drinking fountain was ignored with difficulty. The birds were invisible in the trees and hadn't the energy for song. The next party had already arrived and were circling the car park, looking for available shade; the faces watching them from the cars seemed irritated.

Stockings and tights were wrinkling. It was as much as one could do to keep up ordinary appearances, never mind seem sorrowful and remember the appropriate, rehearsed words to say.

The drive back into town was a muddle. On the motorway a couple of sheep transporters became confused with the procession, and some cars lost contact with the ones they were supposed to be following. A few travelled too fast in the outside lane to keep up, so they were carried past the turn-off – and others were too slow and, anxious not to miss their signpost cue, departed at the junction before.

They showed up when they were able, those who managed to find their way at all. More windows had to be opened in the house. The food looked a little less than fresh, although of course it was, or had been, very. The plastic cling-film was a devil to remove from the rims of bowls and plates. Gradually suit jackets were taken off and women loosened cuffs and collars to ventilate themselves and ditched handbags and consulted coiffures and complexions in wall mirrors and the glass of picture frames. The house was much as it customarily seemed during 'At Homes', and it *was* easy to forget the circumstances... Ming might only have been gone from the room, as would happen on those occasions, presumably to find and uncork a bottle. (But even on that score there had been rumours in circulation afterwards to those with a disposition to hear.) Conversation was respectful, or so the widow and her eldest son sincerely hoped. All the family did their bit, and nobody who had come was intentionally overlooked. There was some light laughter, then slowly – over the couple of hours – it became more voluble, until the afternoon started to sound like old times. The rooms were in continual movement. The burbles of laughter signified the general relief. If the reason for their being here on a weekday afternoon could be temporarily forgotten, in these little spurts of good humour, then that – their hostess knew – was in the way of a little victory.

Lewis shadowed his mother, without encroaching. Moyna, even with her husband Jamie there for support, was the one among them who seemed least herself, and Nicol came to her assistance whenever he could. Ailsa was on office-party automatic pilot; Greta was busy being 'Mrs Lewis Meldrum' and very talkative indeed, while Struan ensured he was always somewhere else than near his former business colleagues.

The widow smiled at the bland, evasive sympathies that came her way, and Lewis was at hand to rescue her from any fraying holes that opened in the exchanges. Greta removed her diary from her shoulder bag (Etienne Aigner) to check on her future availability, but noticing Lewis's corrugated brow she put it away again and committed to memory possible dates for lunch or dinner. It wasn't easy to think in the heat, to be unfailingly correct, and the wisest were able to make their departures before etiquette and decorousness could be put at risk. Some stayed on too long, but Lewis was adept at tactfully administering hints, and the dangers were minimised.

Even when they had the house to themselves, the party voices remained behind as echoes, along with the faintly treacherous laughter. Everyone found plenty to do, and there wasn't a minute for Mrs Meldrum in her mourning to be left alone. They all flitted about her, with their underplayed concern. Objects were for ever being retrieved which their house-guests had left behind, and the telephone was in constant use, and the forgetful owners didn't seem especially surprised to be called, as if the oversight must have been intentional all along. What a day, what a hot day, and thankfully so little time in which to think straight, or to think laterally. The heat lingered, and now not so unwelcome as it had been earlier: indeed, the drift into evening, from light to dusk, was balmy and even comforting. An archetypal summer twilight followed. The flowers in the herbaceous beds glowed, and the warm air smelt of their accumulated sweetnesses. The birds suddenly found their voices, and the blackbirds and thrushes ventured closest to them with their songs, as loud and uninhibited as reveilles. There wasn't to be a moment's true peace surely, and no one could be sorry about that. Some of them were staying on – not Ailsa, and not Struan, who both had commitments that couldn't be cancelled – so even Greta and Moyna found a sudden plenty of matters to discuss, in no great depth, as they helped to spin out the long evening with distractions.

The Broch

Eventually Mother must be alone, when they were all in bed and the lights went out around the house. That didn't necessarily mean she was more lonely than she had been in her married life. She would adjust to the unapologetic space in the room, the licence to let out breath heavily, or to hold it in without Meaning Something by it. She was her own woman now, and the condition was unrestricted by euphemism. It was an unconditional state of being, an incontrovertible truth.

She slept not badly, what's more. A light sleep, perhaps, but it carried her, and she floated into the morning, past half-past five, even past six, long past the birds' confused piping-in of the new day. Washed and dressed she looked much her usual self. Maybe her brightness was exceptional, because as a rule she required several cups of coffee to fire her up. The first mention of the previous day was a long time in coming, and that also distinguished their behaviour as a performance of ordinariness. There are actually degrees of ordinariness, and some must be more self-conscious and theatrical than others, and so their lives continued to be as ever a rondo of comparatives and comparisons.

The Broch was a hybrid, a sprawling confusion of architectural styles. Scots baronial, English country house, French Provençal. A thick squat turret and stepped corbie-stanes; lozenge-leaded windows, studded oak doors, rain barrels; a square keep with peaked roof at the centre of the building; rustic stonework and paved loggias.

Six public rooms including a small library and a billiards room. Eight bedrooms. Scattered staff accommodation. Mounted antlers in the vestibule. A straight forty feet of tartan runner in the downstairs hall.

It was patently a house for another age. It ought to have been sold a generation ago, but its temptations were irresistible. Lawns, a woodland walk, the collection of rhododendrons and azaleas, the two terraces, a three-hundred-yard stretch of private beach, and the nearest houses further than that and dextrously screened by trees.

Its impracticality was part of its appeal. It had an expansiveness that seemed much more American than native: with something of the film-set about it too in the naïve jumble of styles and the free and easy manner – given this unpredictable Atlantic climate – in which the indoors consorted with outside. The original builder, an Anglo-Scottish ironmaster of cosmopolitan interests, had taken delight in the complexity of the enterprise; at the last minute stones had been salvaged from the ruins of an Iron Age tower fortress further along the shore, to give a homelier feel in the New Englanders' style of construction. The fortress had lent the house its name, The Broch, inscribed at numerous points and most emphatically of all on a massive red sandstone lintel – like something very ancient itself – raised above the entrance vestibule, along with the date 'AD 1910' and the first owner's name, 'Archibald McAllister'.

Mrs Meldrum's husband's grandfather had bought the small estate in the Depression years, when the prices of property nearly two hundred miles from Glasgow plummeted. It wasn't the time for indulgent gestures either, but the buyer had been so intent on the purchase that it was supposed some reason – of pride, or self-gratification, or oneupmanship, even revenge – had overridden all other considerations.

The Broch was to prove a great drain on resources. But it caused several new houses to be built in the area, and a small community developed, and it was judged only proper and deserving that The Broch should retain its primacy. Priorities, then as now, were always having to be decided upon: a tarmacadam surface for the driveway or renovating the lodge, improved plumbing or better drainage in the garden, rebuilding the perimeter wall where it had fallen away or reroofing on the sea side, replacing salty window surrounds or widening the steps down to the beach, reguttering or building up the dunes. Decisions would be arrived at, and otherwise postponed, and some matters were lost sight of completely. It was all part and parcel of the history of The Broch, and literally of its fabric.

By Menzies Meldrum's time, when he had inherited the house, guardianship seemed an obligation and due. It was inconceivable to him that they should think of leaving, simply because of doubts about the expenses entailed. They had to justify its maintenance, so all the family holidays were taken there. Inevitably its condition deteriorated, and they were advised – when they once enquired – that if they were intending to let out the property, a long list of repairs and 'upgrading' would have to be attended to first. The Broch therefore remained theirs and theirs alone, and by their example the parents educated their children not to notice the indicators of age and running down. They both wanted the house to seem somehow *inevitable*, and their being there a 'rite' if not a 'right'. It was an outmoded way of living, ridiculously so, but Elshender Meldrum's grandson was quite determined – with or without his wife's assurances – that they had to hold on to it: for his grandfather's sake, and his late father's, and the firm's, because time and endeavour sanctioned it and because he couldn't be seen to be betraying them as the one unequipped to cope.

Mrs Meldrum

From the Round Room that obtrudes on the south side, she is glad.

From season to season she can follow the sun's progress, rising and setting, in each of the five windows, and she has never tired of the spectacle.

The Broch

The room is a mess. Newspapers and magazines and books have spilled from one surface on to another beneath, or finally on to the floor. When she wants to sit down she has to clear a space for herself on the sofa or on one of the rattan chairs. There are forgotten tumblers and cups and saucers. Dropped handkerchiefs. Biro pens minus their tops. Tennis balls. A folding alarm clock, which loses several minutes a day. A broken straw hat. Weeks-old crosswords cut out of the newspapers. Urchin shells. A bottle of hand-lotion. A magnifying glass.

She wouldn't mind never moving out of this room. (She has retreated indoors for half an hour even when the house is filled with her family.) From here she can look across the side lawn right out to sea. A lumpy divan lies under two of the leaded windows and she can prop herself up on cushions and pick up a book, whatever's to hand, and listen to the turning of the waves and, in no time at all, be gently lulled asleep. There's a grandfather clock, but it stopped years ago; the alarm clock has a habit of toppling over on to its face. From her private sitting-room tenses glide into and out of one another, and she can perform all sorts of magical experiments on her life.

The pretence was that The Broch was a country cottage merely expanded.
The walls were pine-panelled; the fireplaces were of plain angled stone or arched with brick. The rooms were sparely furnished; the furniture was good but simple in its lines. In the dining-room they sat on wheel-back chairs at a gate-legged table. There were side-tables and stools that had been worked out of storm-battered driftwood. Table-lamps were preferred to the cartwheel centre-lights: squat Chinese vases or pieces of bulbous and possibly nautical treen, carrying deep shades of old silk, spotted and faded. Some barrels had been ingeniously converted to hold books. The seating was comfortable rather than elegant: well-worn armchairs with layers of cover thrown over the original chintz, and cane chairs and loungers. A Lapp sledge of indeterminate antiquity had been fitted with an upholstered cushion. On the walls there were a few still-lifes, by artists very reputable in the twenties, but mostly the pictures – oils and watercolours – showed views of the Western Isles, unchanged over a hundred years. There were several cases of stuffed birds, posed in simulated habitat. Other items of decoration had a practical function: the stands of walking-sticks and crooks, the skates suspended from hooks, the tree of hats and scarves in the hall, the rack of folded newspapers hanging from the sitting-room ceiling which was in fact a ship's ladder of cable and wooden rungs giving access to the Round Room's attic.

Mrs Meldrum

She has always preferred The Broch to Glasgow. At the end of his life Ming claimed to be indifferent to the house, which surprised her. She had tried to argue its case, but she felt she hadn't convinced him: or that he was defying himself not to be convinced by her. It had seemed very odd to her, so untypical of the man. He had become quieter in general, but not any less agile mentally: distracted certainly, but sharp and alert when he needed to be.

For some reason The Broch failed to please, but he denied – urgently – that costs were a factor. He wouldn't say why, and that kept her guessing, which was the worst that could have happened. From the windows of the Round Room, her command post, she would look outside, scanning to where the grounds ended and other properties began in search of some authentic answer.

The Broch had continued to be theirs. Or maybe Ming had died before he could begin to implement any plans he might have had for its future. She had sold the house in Glasgow, moved into a small modern flat for a while, sold that, and then made the second and final move, to Achnavaig. She shrugged aside everyone's concern. 'The winters will be a challenge,' she told them, and knew she recklessly understated. Two winters had come and gone, and she had survived: milder winters, admittedly. Lewis was always at the other end of the telephone in Glasgow or Edinburgh ready to deal with problems that occurred, and she had learned to stop censuring him for his deeds of generosity to her. Why so much, she would wonder, why so much when you were always uncomfortable with Ming – but then she would switch her thoughts to Greta, with those superior airs and untrusting eyes, and she would start to lose the original riddle a little, of why Lewis was so solicitous and how could she better express to him her gratitude?

Lewis

He knew they all thought him supreme in his confidence. But he envied them all something: Struan his physical prowess, Nicol his sensitivity, Ailsa her elusiveness, and Moyna her unashamed domesticity and Jamie his enthusiasm and practicality.

He picked up his book. A paperback Maigret. He liked the unteasing of a case, the detective-inspector's immersion in the details of the suspects' lives. He looked for orderliness in the fashioning of the story. Sometimes, though, the later Simenon suggested a situation might not be so cut and dried, which was disappointing even if it was truer to life. At least the atmosphere of the books was evoked with a consistent economy, you took a sort of mathematical pleasure in the minimal manufacture of these descriptions.

But today, this afternoon, the familiar spell wasn't working for him, he couldn't concentrate.

Greta

They had brought only Toby with them. Hugo and Claudia had prior claims: a music course for her, and for him a sailing holiday with a schoolfriend's family. She thought that Toby, being the youngest, should see the house, just in case an opportunity like it didn't come his way again. She wanted him to have a memory of its down-at-heels opulence, its illogicality for these times, its having existed at all as a private dwelling-house. In the future he would be able to weave fantasies around his recollection of the place, and find himself unable to distinguish fiction from equally improbable fact.

Ailsa

She hadn't meant to come. She could have found pretexts for staying away. She had thought long and hard about it. In the end she *had* come. She didn't feel good about it. Or even bad. Merely impassive.

Well, maybe what had persuaded her was the prospect, the certainty, of seeing her mother's astonishment, that she'd actually joined them. And the pretence that it was no more than she expected.

She was conscious of her smiles failing more often than not, her top lip catching and sticking on the top right front incisor. Yesterday her face had soon got raw with the effort of it all, and she'd been irritated with herself that she felt obliged.

One more night. Supper or dinner, then breakfast. If another lunch was mooted, she'd call a taxi. She'd have remembered something she had to do. Something pressing, urgent. And Mother would look thoroughly sceptical at the mention of the word.

Struan

He told them that Cat hadn't been able to get away. Pressure of work. She was very sorry, sent her apologies, etcetera.

In fact it was he who had talked her out of coming. He knew she found Lewis rather dry, so he informed her that only he and Lewis would be there – and possibly Ailsa – with their mother, discussing some outstanding business about the will. She offered to accompany him, for company's sake, but he dissuaded her. The distance, the time it took: having to make conversation with Lewis once she got there, Greta having to hear about it, Ailsa eyeing her up and down. She took a few moments to consider, then agreed, but he sensed that she was disappointed.

She would have gone in order to feel she was being included in the family, which was precisely why he wanted to keep her away – not for her sake but his own. He didn't mean to save her for himself: more immediately he preferred to deny her a visit. His engagement to Kirsty and the ritual steps towards their marriage had had a frightening inevitability about them, as if others were doing his thinking for him. He didn't intend giving Cat any further opportunities to make claims.

He needed to be sure that she required just him, or even his money, but not his family too. The more she discovered about him as a unit of that organism, the less personal the relationship would become. He was alarmed also to think of them both consumed by domesticity. Somehow the situation was easier when there was just themselves, the two of them, being purely selfish and using their joint income to pay for those services that attended directly to their needs – housework, food, dry-cleaning, cars. He was trying to make this new life – his second chance at adulthood – as different as he feasibly could from his first with Kirsty. No more mistakes this time round, and no occasion for the bad habits to begin.

Moyna

She is cow-heavy. She hardly has the energy to keep smiling. The smiles are deflections. Greta thinks it's vulgar to have so many children, and ecologically unsound. Ailsa can't understand the longing at all. Mother is amazed, and maybe a little vexed because her own tally of five will have been matched.

Now *she* is 'Mother'. She feels for her own children in a less inhibited way than the generation before did; she can believe she lives in part inside each of them. This coming birth will subtract a fifth portion of her. She isn't greedy to keep it: she is served best by what she can give of herself. Now she is a dispersed life, and she is – more or less – reconciled.

But, oh, she is cow-heavy. She is dragged down by the necessity of everything, loaded down with gravity. It's her role in life. She forgets if the role originally came to her quite spontaneously or if she made it come. With this child – who will be Daniel or Alice – she knows the impulse is less ambiguous. Jamie did his best to persuade her that four was a tidy sum, a sensible size. She chose not to protect herself, as Jamie realised as soon as she told him she was pregnant, but he hasn't once spoken a word of blame. He thinks of himself as a pragmatist; at the clinic they want him to go over half and half to administration, and as a student he had a head for facts – memorising them and regurgitating them. A self-evident matter of fact such as this isn't going to stump him now.

But someone is calling to her. Ben this time. Calling not urgently, repeatedly none the less. She focuses on the cry, comes closer and closer in on it. The whelp, the mew. Cow-heavy as she is. She concentrates her thoughts, with laser precision, on what she defines as the need. While Ben waves an arm from the shoreline, hopping on one foot, with the other touching ground only when his balance wobbles. A cut, conceivably. A sprain, perhaps. But there are no tears, so she whittles down the possibilities, takes a guess at sticky black tar.

Where's the bottle of eucalyptus oil?

Mrs Meldrum

When they were thirteen or fourteen – and Nicol fifteen – the children were sent away to their boarding schools. She had never been quite comfortable about that arrangement. They should have gone earlier, so they might have adjusted more easily, or she should have argued that those who preferred to should remain in Glasgow and attend one of the day schools there.

It was a rather indeterminate, wishy-washy policy, she always felt. It might have looked as if they were trying to get the best of both worlds – the English tradition of communal life and the Scottish one of stay-at-homes – while in fact they committed themselves to neither.

She forgot how it had happened. Decades of a country's bitter-sweet flirtation with Sassenach ways, a small nation's envy and defensiveness leaving her and her own boarding-school kind with this mealy-mouthed way of talking, half-heartedly stretched vowels feigning an acquaintance with southern attitudes – while their minds reverted in the awkward little matter of morality to those tight-lipped and reproving reticences of such very long instinct.

Nicol

I don't know how the place holds together, but it does.

The rattan loungers still take my weight. The linings are still attached to the curtains, and the sun hasn't yet totally faded the patterns. The ornaments perch on the same spots, the lamps light the same corners. The rugs cover the same dark shadows on the floor, and the shadows seem no darker than before against the honey wood that surrounds them. Even the doors rasp in the same dependable way.

Somehow the model sailing-ships on their stands don't topple over, they don't go crashing on to the reefs beneath them. The piano sounds just as blithely out of tune as ever. The books of music are propped up open, Schirmer editions with their yellow covers bleached, the same ones we used to practise from. The carved wooden goose suspended from the ceiling remains airborne, the black pupils in the bird's orange irises are still just as manic at the confinement. The clutter of letters and bills and shopping lists on the bureau is instantly recognisable.

It's an intense relief after all to discover everything is the same. I've been half hoping to find things different. But only because, maybe in that case I should find we too have mysteriously altered. There is even less chance of that, I think.

Meanwhile the sun blazed in the sky, a bluey-mauve sheet-metal sky. The gulls had temporarily vanished, and the waves. Even the miasma of midges had faded away to nothing. The sea lapped at the line of shore lethargically. The rocks seemed to have turned redder, to the colour of boiled crabs.

How was it that, elsewhere in the world, waves hissed and foamed and fish even had the energy to fly? On the continent's rim, the will had gone, on this untypically hot and sapping August afternoon.

Mrs Meldrum

The Broch had been beyond their station in life. At least it was so at the outset, but the longer they lived in it the more inclined she became to forget. Ming had been careful not to divulge how much things were costing, and she had been weak and persuadable enough to let the matter – such a major matter – pass. She had allowed his ambition to carry her, and it was like being driven very fast, in a powerful and silent and cossettingly comfortable car. The familiarity of speed, and the sound deadening, they tranquillise you into ignoring just how fast, and how dangerously . . .

Ming wanted their schoolfriends to visit. 'Invite them up to stay.' So people would come, not always mutually compatible company, and she suggested that, please, a week should be a maximum. 'In case they're just saying they're enjoying themselves.'

It didn't happen very often in fact. Bringing someone was an embarrassment for them, she came to feel. She asked too many questions, 'Are you enjoying yourself?' 'Will you let me know if you need – ?' Their friends felt they had to reciprocate, and there was the problem of transportation, getting up to Achnavaig and away from it. Lewis was jealous of his friends, and Moyna a little forgetful of hers, and it was all too easy to discover that away from school your interests didn't coincide as closely as you thought, or as they did the year before. Friends could also surprise you by defecting to other members of the family.

Ming liked to show the house off. Driving back from the station he enjoyed watching their passengers' faces for a first reaction when they turned in between the gateposts. He enjoyed their confusion as to where all the rooms in the house were. He didn't seem to see that Ailsa's and Nicol's friends tended to notice things like peeling paint and scuff marks, and that Struan's guest one year was diligently working his way through the decanters in the drawing-room.

'Sitting-room' she had preferred to call it, but Ming opted to use the other, because – he implied – he was only being faithful to the old ways. The term lacked warmth, but Ming swelled a little at the sound of it in others' mouths. He made a point of not being surprised to hear them use it, affecting for their benefit the casualness which they – invariably with a suburban experience – could not.

Lewis

He felt they were the last detachment of a generation who had been brought up in the old ways. Over-disciplined and under-indulged, possibly over-educated but as individuals understated.

He often wondered what their strict education had been in aid of when he saw the can-swillers in the streets, walked past video shops and entertainment arcades, confronted the vista of trivia served up at home on the television screen as he pressed the channel buttons in turn, read about pornographic computer software, heard on the radio about people's bad debts.

It was a populace out of control. Everyone whining about their 'rights', when there are none preordained in the world, not even the right to a job of work. Money, however gained, was held to be an open sesame to instant gratification.

He hadn't been equipped by his education and upbringing for any of this. Preparing his cases for court he was conscious of slipping into the mental habits of an older man. He couldn't feel the alarm about it which he felt he should. It suited his tailored three-piece, three-button method of dressing for work. When he looked in the mirror and caught the features of his father floating beneath his own in the glass, his attitude of mental déjà vu made a shadowy kind of sense to him.

Ailsa

At school they had been so sniffy about trade. Yet she came to believe – having to form the opinion completely from scratch – that there was something honest and necessary, noble in a way, about making things. Her father, after all, was only a middleman, a whisky broker like his father and *his* father, and there must be a high degree of risk and expendability about what they did. Even true professionals lived off others, and frequently profited from their misfortunes, so they weren't entitled to get uppity either, although they usually did.

She quickly learned to see through the self-protecting conspiracy of people in groups pretending to a merit and grace which they did not possess.

Greta

Yesterday, in quarter of an hour Lewis had had the bedroom colonised. It was their territory now, and was staked out by his exemplary tidiness. Her drawers, his. Her hangers, his. Some tissue paper she had dropped from the suitcase he picked up and folded twice, three times, four times. He straightened the curtains where they didn't hang to his liking. Hitched up a little painting an inch or so on one side. Checked that the bedside lamp was working. Uncoiled its flex.

That was Lewis. Everything accounted for and in its place, and nothing left to chance.

Ailsa

It did occur to her not to fly up with Nicol as they had arranged. She could have found an excuse for a delay. Or, more simply, she could have failed to arrive at the airport on time.

But there again, maybe it wasn't going to be so bad after all, and they would prove to one another that they had a capacity for change.

It turned out to have been a forlorn fancy. Nicol was as he always was, only more Americanised. Asking her – of course – to check if she had her ticket with her. If she knew where her boarding pass was. Advising her that she shouldn't take her shoes off on the plane in case she couldn't put them back on.

'It's just to Glasgow, Nicol.'

'Even so...'

On the plane she shook her head when he suggested coffee, or tea, and she requested the hostess to give her two of the small bottles of gin with some tonic water.

The robotic girl fished out second helpings from the trolley.

'The bubbles'll go straight to your head up here,' he told her.

'All the better then.'

She leafed through the complimentary magazine and looked out of the window, at a glowing antarctic of woolly clouds, their whiteness firing to orange. Ice and flame. She shook her head again, this time at the splendour of purified life at thirty-seven thousand feet, and she briefly forgot that Nicol was sitting right by her side, the last member of the family she would have chosen to share this quarantine with.

In the hire car she had the excuse of dozing. Nicol couldn't get used to right-hand driving, but she didn't want to start nagging him. The frets had to be all his.

Later, on the new dual carriageway after Loch Lomond, they discussed their business lives, willingly enough so that it kept them off the personal. She envied him the experience of New York, but she wasn't going to admit that to him, so she zoomed in on the negative aspects. Nicol agreed with her about the prohibitive cost of living there, and also the creeping illiteracy at all levels; they spoke for a while about this American epidemic of stupidity dulling even intelligent people and inducing so many new kinds of isolation. She thought that might be taking them too close to an accidental revelation, so she yawned in an obvious way and laid her head against the headrest and closed her eyes to the drowning of purple light in the sky. He turned on the radio, switching channels. Fragments of talking, Scots' voices – first carping (as ever) about a Glasgow painter's international success, then something about a nuclear dump proposed for the Outer Hebrides. Then music, under the crackle of interference, one of those shamelessly sentimental native wallows, thankfully orchestrated to exclude the words with their clumsy geographical rhymes, 'Highland glory . . . Tobermory', 'straveighl'n . . . Dunvegan', 'I cannot tarry at Invergarry', 'I must set sail for Armadale'.

Jesus God, she was back home, and no two ways about it.

Struan

All the time he was growing up, his father could do no wrong.

Where Lewis sometimes disputed him in his school prep, and Ailsa later quizzed him on moral points as practice for her school debating team – why he held to this or that view, which he clearly accepted as 'inherited credo' – *he* had been happy that his father's word should be final on any matter.

Inside and out, mentally and physically, the man was one, a constant and consistent presence, and he considered that compared with his friends he was exceptionally fortunate to have such a father.

He had noticed the mothers at school functions taking sly glances at him, drawn by his hale good looks, his athletic build, his easy air, his tailor-cut tweeds. He wouldn't have wanted a father as intelligent as Professor Duguid, who appeared to delight in inflicting put-downs in front of his sons' friends and discovering what the cleverest of those friends didn't know about their subjects. Too much intelligence, he suspected, made you restless and discontented, always needing to know a bit more and a bit more after that.

His own sporting prowess at school was general, and not concentrated on one activity rather than others. He ran, swam, golfed, skied, played rugby and cricket and tennis and basketball. He was good at them all, better at a couple, but not so surpassingly able at any one of them to have practised exclusively at that and only that. He was a team stalwart at school, and represented it against other schools, but knew he didn't want national recognition. That knowledge was something in itself. When he felt comfortable in his body, at what it could achieve, he was happy also in his mind, and – frankly – that proved sufficient to him.

He would be fulfilled, he used to believe, just to follow in his father's footsteps, trying to turn himself into a second version of him.

Moyna

She always used to be the last back to the house. Hers would be the final sandcastle of the day. Even when Lewis and Struan had dug the trench to the sea and the floodgates were opened, she built just one more on top of the crumbling edifice. The others would go and she would be left alone, while a voice called her name repeatedly from the house.

She didn't know why she should have stayed on there, with the beach suddenly cold. She was overseeing the fall of a sand empire, of course, at the same time as she was patting out from her bucket one more sandcastle that was going to seal the fate of the others stacked beneath it. Water swirled along the trench, and even if she dammed it with her spade she was only building up a tidal force.

Why had it been she of them all who resisted the summons back, to the predictable comforts, to lamplit rooms and supper and then a bath before bed?

Now hers was the voice that marshalled everyone home. She had charge of the routine which was obeyed – and on occasions disobeyed – by instinct. It might have seemed like full circle, but it wasn't, not quite. When she was a girl she could have been postponing the satisfaction until the very last minute, knowing that home was no further than sixty or seventy yards away. She may have required that sense of isolation, the creeping chill on her skin giving her goosepimples, to send her scurrying home all the quicker.

But this was an adult thinking back to then, and perhaps she wasn't being as truthful about the past as she ought to have been.

Nicol

Dad's ideal would have been Lewis's brain inside Struan's sportsman's body. He came so near to it, having the perfect son he wanted, and yet – by another view – he didn't come close at all, and fulfilment was as far from him as before any of us were born.

Somehow Lewis eluded him and Struan lacked something essential. I was a last chance, but I only reminded him how little I resembled either of my brothers. It didn't matter that *I* felt I was a kind of synthesis, to Dad I offered no combination of elements that he could recognise. I was my mother's favourite, and that seemed to confirm the matter for him – as if I required to be favoured because of some vital absence of talent or will.

I understood that much, Dad, and early on, even if I wasn't able to explain it to myself.

Mummy would place her arms around my shoulders and, from behind, fasten her hands at the front on my chest and laugh, making a serious joke of my constriction. Dad's reactions grew less irritable, more resigned, sadder maybe, and he would just let the business go and leave her and me to extricate ourselves from our cosy, useless complicity.

Mrs Meldrum

The cups and medals were kept where they always had been, in the china cabinet in the sitting-room. Some were Lewis's, prizes for his work at school and university, and others were Struan's, for his sporting victories. Nicol had come third in a national essay-writing competition when he was fifteen, and there was a photograph of him receiving his scroll and cheque from Princess Alexandra; the citation said the essay was entitled 'The Broch', but he had never allowed them to read it. His graduation photograph was kept on a different shelf from Lewis's: a Princeton 'Cum Laude' and a Cambridge First ought not to be directly comparable, she felt. Ming had come second in a regatta at Tarbert one year, and been presented with a small cup. Moyna's gymkhana rosettes were included with the trophies, although none was for above fourth place.

Hard to imagine Moyna on a horse now, and maybe she had forgotten herself. It was Struan who would pause in front of the cabinet doors and peer in. Lewis by comparison was more furtive, sneaking sideways glances, for his own reasons not wanting to be seen acknowledging evidence of their achievements.

Only Ailsa wasn't represented. She had helped her House win a silver debating cup, and once won a medal on her own account at school, for 'Citizenship', but she had 'mislaid' it – she'd claimed – on the train journey home at the end of that term, the one year when they hadn't been able to attend the prize-giving. The school didn't find out – just as well – and maybe she wouldn't have told them that she'd won it if they hadn't chanced to hear from one of her friends about the loss. Ailsa had admitted to them what had happened, mouth nipped but with her face expressionless. After that she had never again referred to either the award or its disappearance, and in all the years since she hadn't once allowed herself to be caught as much as inclining her eyes in the direction of the china cabinet. That took some doing, and couldn't have been accidental: rather, it must have been grim resolve on her part, to ignore her exclusion – which she had helped to bring about, after all, by her own heedlessness or uncaring.

Everything that happened had a way of proving, finally, to be only too typical.

Lewis

A couple of the pines were in bad shape. He suspected they were dying on their feet, so to speak. A neighbour had blamed acid rain.

'*Here?*'

But why not here too?

It wasn't worth consulting an expert, bringing him out this far for the sake of two trees. Two trees might only be the start, of course. Maybe the others would simply catch the spirit of death, like a contagion.

He felt briefly how he did when he had that dream in his sleep, finding that all his teeth had dead roots and the teeth then starting one by one to fall out of his mouth. He had the same dismal gnawing sensation in his stomach. At this point he normally resurfaced out of the dream.

He shook his head. The trees were still standing, though. They were the trees he used to watch from his bedroom as a small boy, imagining them as people. Tall spies at twilight, exchanging secrets in that Cold War age. Now they were rotting away. He wished he could save them, but he didn't know how, except by having them sawn down and planting others in their place and merely hoping the best for those, a long growing, at any rate for the duration of his own life and his children's.

Mrs Meldrum

Having the children had been the main work of her life, and also the greatest pleasure it had given her. She had even, unbelievably, enjoyed the births, because the house had been filled with women, with relations and friends and midwife. No men, and it was perfect. Then the cry, the first cry, and the question, and the answer, girl or boy. She was pleased about the boys for Ming's sake, and the girls for her own, but the years had brought their turn-about, their disappointments (more with Ailsa for never seeming to do as she anticipated than with Moyna, who grew up rather colourless) and revelations (of Lewis's slightly brusque thoughtfulness and Nicol's sixth sense for knowing her likes and anticipating her wants).

Lewis's Greta, she felt, was two different persons: a mother sometimes, and not a mother. She could look quite startled when one of the children materialised from somewhere or other – as if she had forgotten all about them. She was good with them, in a brisk and efficient way, which her fastidious appearance didn't suggest she would be. She seemed put out to have to talk about them; or perhaps she was afraid she would be caught out by a question, and so give an impression of ignorance. Child-talk could have been a point of contact between them, but it was a lost opportunity, another one.

She had felt pleasure when each grandchild was born, being put in mind every time of her own happiness, an aching joy that used to seem as if it was splitting her apart. She would concentrate on thinking back, so that she might recall that original sensation of supreme but clear-headed delirium, that pure ether of hope in transferring life from herself to another.

Ailsa

She had gone looking for a windbreak to take down to the beach with her. A rugby ball rolled off a shelf at the back of the cupboard and landed at her feet. She bent forward and picked it up. The leather was battered; she examined the puckering along the seams. It had been well used.

There had been nothing quite like the game for the girls, nothing institutional in the way that rugby was. Rugby was solidity, respectability, sociability, it was the acme of normality and middle-classness. Even tennis didn't match up to rugby in the eternal scheme of Scottish things. She had played with them a few times, but only because she had been allowed to, and because they were playing more frivolously than their usual, her father and Lewis and Struan and anyone else from roundabout. Passing, kicking, maybe line-outs, tackling down on the beach.

She still remembered how much she used to envy them the earnestness of their rough and tumble. She wanted to join in, and what prevented her wasn't the will but the stupid accident of her gender. Girls in those days didn't play rugby except by their indulgent brothers' say-so, not unless they were prepared to acquire a reputation for being a tomboy – which once acknowledged was almost impossible to shake off in later life.

She stood holding the ball. She felt its weight, its balance. She thought of the beautiful arc Struan used to manage with his kicks. How hard Lewis had tried to carry it off, but only ever straining. She closed her eyes, to bring it all back to mind. Her father's exuberant good humour, when he seemed to forget the matters that could cloud his face without warning: wearing summer shorts, strong-thighed but trim-waisted, running for their touch-down lines on the lawn.

She found she was swaying on her feet. It was so long ago, and it was no time at all. Holding the ball into her waist, how her father had shown the boys, she crossed over to the window and looked out, just as she used to look out whenever they played and she heard their shouts. High spirits, and the disturbance – which her mother was usually so sensitive about – didn't count, because it was all in the cause of rugby.

Down on the lawn Nicol stood with one of Moyna's brood. They were examining something held in the child's hand, an insect. Nicol had been born too late to be included in the best games, the vintage ones, but – give him his due – he had tried to keep his end up, when her father had explained the rules and demonstrated the moves afresh every time. For Nicol, though, there were subtler ways of assertion than chasing and claiming a ball; and there used to be something patronising about the way he received the information, with that saintly tolerance of his. Well, *she* would have welcomed the opportunity to learn, if she could have had it instead. On Nicol the time was all wasted.

Bloody lacrosse was her lot at school, locking sticks and those swipes – not always accidental – across the backs of her legs, and such a tiny insignificant ball slithering about like a pesty little rodent, and the girls either sexless boors or stand-back sissies. A rugby ball was *worth* pursuing and possessing. Stolid, dense, a crafted object, to be hugged close in to the chest or waist. In the muddy primal contact you would have known who your teammates were, and how dependable, which somehow you didn't on the lacrosse pitch with your eyes turned down for so much of the time in that untidy, clumsy skirmish of schoolgirls' sticks.

She would have taken Nicol's chance gladly. The curse of 'tomboy' would have been worth risking, since she now knew femininity was such a slight and clichéd utility by comparison.

Struan

It was Lewis that his father had wanted for the business. But Dad was torn between one form of selfishness and another: whether to have his eldest son working with him, or to allow him to make a name for himself in one of the professions. Once Lewis had won his exhibition to Cambridge, though, he was assumed to be on a conveyor belt to prestige and fortune. It became inconceivable that, with his qualifications, he should regress, and that's what commercial life would have amounted to. His father didn't stop hoping, against hope, but wishes can be unreasonable and disobliging things.

By contrast, his father had never entertained very high expectations of *him*. It was merely supposed that he should join the firm, and that would be that. He would be a welcome recruit, as additional family firepower, and his loyalty not seriously doubted for a moment.

Jamie

He had been staying with the McArdles that summer. He became confused as to who was called 'Ailsa' and who 'Moyna', and when he was finally introduced to them he called Moyna 'Ailsa'. Moyna smiled as she corrected him, but when her sister overheard and looked over her shoulder from where she was lying, on top of the terrace wall, her mouth was set quite straight, and he was struck at once by her judgment of silence. The frown above her eyes might, of course, have been disapproving: or equally, on that first afternoon, it might have been caused by the glare of the sun.

She was to remain inscrutable to him, although he did become aware of a certain frostiness on several occasions, from her gestures and from what she didn't say. When she asked him questions about himself, she considered his answers with care, and more critically than Moyna ever did. His responses appeared not to satisfy her; it embarrassed him to refer to home, or his ambitions to become a doctor, and he tended to treat the enquiries lightly, smiling and shrugging and making puns. Sometimes she would disagree with him, almost with impatience, as if she was meaning that he wasn't thinking clearly, not nearly hard enough. When she was quizzing him her eyes didn't let him go, which irritated him but also indicated a degree of curiosity he found flattering. Eventually her interest would wane during those conversations and he would be left with the impression that she felt he wasn't being true to himself, somehow selling himself short.

He wanted to win Ailsa round, but there were days – that year, and the next, and whenever their paths chanced to cross in Glasgow – when she wouldn't give him a single inch. Her easy movements and her laughter with others disturbed him. At the same time he couldn't convince himself that she disliked him, because he imagined there would have been some more obvious chemical evidence of reproach in the air. She continued to give him her time however, and that encouraged him to think he could actually come to understand her, and she him.

With Moyna there were no such problems. She was on his side from the beginning. By contrast she gave every encouragement to his ego. Her prettiness stayed constant, while Ailsa grew into a striking young woman: a long face with fine features and a high brow that gave her an aloof and overbred European look he later saw resembling Marisa Berenson's in *Cabaret*. Maybe the frizziness of her darker hair had something to do with the similarity, while Moyna's was sun-streaked and, being cut shorter, wavy.

Moyna gave him sympathy every time he needed it, and assured him his intentions were the correct ones whenever he discussed his future with her, and always concurred with him if he was criticising the faults of others.

Her sister wouldn't commit herself in that way, and he had many opportunities to be grateful that Moyna was so different.

Yet Ailsa's behaviour drew him irresistibly. Why was she so non-committal? Why the sceptical air? Even when referring to his exam results, then later his university progress, he always had the sense she believed he could do better. Now and then she would recall something he'd said previously, quoting back at him his very words, and it was always as if she was making an unfavourable comparison by implication – showing him how an earlier idealism had weathered into a lesser enthusiasm, become tempered by what she chose to read as complacency or apathy.

He became tetchy when he felt she was unjust to him. More bizarrely, however, he became irked with Moyna also, for falling in so closely to his cause, for so invariably shadowing his own declared opinions with hers and interpreting all his actions and motives as the best ones. If he was being unjust to Moyna in turn, maybe she was being less than fair to him by seeing him as much through a distorting prism as her older sister did?

Nicol

The gardener had come back for something. He had supposed it must be the gardener's boy, but his mother told him he was 'the man himself'.

He watched him from the terrace, the best he could manage in the sun without placing his hand over his eyes, which would have given the game away.

He was never not ready to notice meat, to suss out a promising-looking crotch. He amazed himself, and sometimes he was ashamed. Did it mean he was abnormally horny, or was it just the nature of the condition, that sex stayed so fresh on his mind? During the first years of concealment guilt had bottled it up, pushing it back down inside, so that sex occupied him like a virus. He still mentally undressed his quarry, although now he was more selective. He had never come to tire of imagining what he would find, how the stud would be hung: the greatest thrill with a stranger was postponing the moment when – slowly, slowly – you removed his briefs. It felt in cooler moments like a mark of his immaturity: but it didn't stop the want taking hold of him again, obsessing him, placing him – metaphorically and literally – where he always found himself, on his knees making his surrender.

Mrs Meldrum

She fanned the photographs in her hand, like playing cards, then she laid them out on the table. They all showed her other family. Mother, father, brother, sisters, two sets of grandparents, three aunts, two uncles, two great-grandparents, a great-aunt. She recognised the narrow, close eyes on her mother's side and the thin noses on her father's.

She sat staring at the faces. She had begun with the intention of remembering them. But now she found herself experiencing the reverse – she had a sensation that she was being remembered by *them*. It was as if they were all concentrating on the memory of her, as if their existence depended on their remembering and on her being retrieved.

Her hands hovered, she silhouetted the faces with her fingertips. But when she took her hands away again, the eyes continued to watch. Even when voices from outside in the garden disturbed her and she gathered the photographs together, sweeping them up into a pile, she saw the faces still on the mahogany of the table top. Their ghostly impressions floated in front of her as she stood up and pushed the chair back and turned for the door. When she looked in the oak-framed mirror she saw them there too, but living in her own face. Time passed in and out of focus as her own features moved into and out of theirs.

It was the sound of laughter that caused her to realise a hand was being passed in front of her face. She stepped back, seeing the hand in the double-distance of the mirror, behind the cold glass. Ben's, was it, or Fanny's?

Once, in her youth, her mother had been pretty. Gradually a patina of experience settled on top. The looks remained – but not the spirit of them, the gist. Without their good cheer, they seemed somehow hesitant and steeled at the same time. 'Hardness' wasn't the right term, but there was definitely a defensive outer layer – a firmness about the mouth and an extra tightness about the eyes.

Her mother's retreat began before she was into her teens. She came to recognise when she was saying one thing and meaning quite another: it was a kind of acting. Father started to drink to keep himself hopeful, the semblance of his younger self when he'd thought he might be cut out for farming, while her mother performed to keep that former self – hopeful in its own way – suppressed, being for ever on the lookout for new faces who wouldn't be able to recognise her from the person she had been.

I find myself doing things as my mother used to do them, small and insignificant actions. How I stir tea – with back and forth movements instead of circular – and how I comb my hair, from the back over the crown to the front, how I read a newspaper from the last page to the first, how I pare dessert fruit on my plate into a series of thin exact slices, how I need to sleep with a glass of fresh water by my bedside although I never take a sip of it.

I don't know how long this has been going on, and I can't bring myself to ask. It should be second nature to me, but at certain moments of the day my behaviour feels to me second-hand, unoriginal and dictated. I am secretary to an invisible arbiter, who provides me with my menial instructions, and I just do as I am bid.

How I place my left foot splayed behind my right foot when I'm sitting down. How I sketch the air with my pen when I'm stranded between sentences writing a letter. How I always press my nose to the pages of a book whenever I open it, to devour its smell.

Small and insignificant actions to the eye, and all secretly telling a different story.

Lewis

Nevertheless, there was something irrepressibly smug about Ailsa. He suspected she wasn't the most confident of them, but that she needed to be seen as that.

He remembered her terrible capacity for spoiling. Sometimes at the very last minute she would back out of getting ready for a party, or any occasion she was meant to enjoy: she denied herself the pleasure, and he didn't know why. Perhaps it was only to confirm to herself that she could. She may have supposed also that she didn't deserve it, that she had to feel the reward was earned, but her perversity wasn't something he could have hoped to make any reasoned sense of. It just was. A persistent hazard he had learned to steer his way around.

Struan

She needed loosening up, of course, Greta. She was much too much the professional wife. Much too Edinburgh.

That hairstyle was wrong for a start. Expensively cut to sweep across her head in vaguely windswept fashion, but actually stiff with spray or lacquer. Oddly, the incipient greyness appealed to him. And it was to her credit that she hadn't attempted to disguise it. She retouched her face, and clear-varnished her bitten nails, and wore tasteful but distracting jewellery. Her heels were low, her choice of clothes faultless. But she habitually erred on the over-formal side. He always had the sense that she was wound up tight. Her voice was pitched rather too high for comfort, with a slight mechanical harshness to her honed and shapely vowels. As if she was speaking on a very stretched tape.

There was something else about her, though... He had an inkling that she wasn't wholly as she tried to appear to be. Occasionally when she was with him the voice hesitated, and her motions became a little disjointed, and her eyes lost their purposeful focus and flitted from one object to another without being held. Then he would be amused and intrigued by her.

She looked him out, he was aware of that. He let her see that he appraised her, and whenever she noticed she didn't turn away. Beneath it all there was quite an attractive woman, and (even if she didn't realise) one more sexual than she was able to be with her husband.

Ailsa

She hears voices from the terrace. Some of the children appear.

Fanny's flip-flops slap on the crazy paving. Ben is cradling something – another specimen – in his hand. Molly is brushing her hair. Toby spins several circles anti-clockwise, to a dance beat through his headphones.

She stands at a window and watches. Watches with envy and a little fear, as if – she's guessing – as if they carry with them both naïvety and a vast potential for inflicting guilt. If she were the mother of any of them, she would be trembling to think what their minds were storing up through their eyes for future years, she would be helpless against all a child's expectations of what she must provide. A child must be an endless responsibility to the conscience.

Moyna

She had never known where she was with Ailsa.

She realised Ailsa was obliged to speak down to her, and that she didn't like herself for doing so. But if she hadn't forced herself, and come down to her level, then how else would they have communicated except in their jerky way?

She didn't have Ailsa's confidence. She envied her that air of efficiency, and the luxury of switching between styles of behaving with different people.

So, then, why have any doubts?

It had occurred to her, though, that there was something not right. More 'why's . . . Why was she not in thrall of her sister's social life? Why didn't Ailsa have more friends than she did? It was she, Moyna, twenty years younger than now and ungifted, who'd had no shortage of offers, no gaps in the week out of school term-time for unhealthy introspection.

Nicol

Ailsa was intelligent, but she had always lacked suitable outlets.

He had tried to let her see that he understood, this socio-historical plight of hers. She was too sharp not to notice, and he realised he was being rejected by her. The more coyly he attempted to win her round, the less inclined she was to capitulate.

It was stalemate between them, he felt, through no complacency or neglect of his.

***

She was wearing tartan trousers. Not their own clan tartan; but maybe they were difficult to find, and anyway that was Ailsa. He always forgot she was only an inch shorter than him, and two or three inches taller than Moyna. Her height must have helped to intimidate when she wanted it to. Her hair was darker than last time, just as it used to be, and there was more of it. Her face seemed longer and thinner. (He might have thought she was working public relations out of her system, but she was ploughing away at the same job.) Two years ago she'd had that contrived, blow-dried leonine hairstyle of breakfast television presenters, and outsized pearl studs in her ears, and a boxy little businesswoman's jacket, and print culottes. Now there was a striped cotton shirt with the cuffs folded back; she left the (real) pearls to Greta and wore a thick brass Third World clasp round her neck instead.

She was still finding herself, and he wondered if she might actually be starting to get there at last.

Mrs Meldrum

Ailsa could give you an impression that she was criticising you. All she needed to do was raise an eyebrow a fraction, or let her mouth stretch a little at the corners, into the skin that was stretched so tensely and inflexibly now over her cheekbones. She unsettled.

She had wanted Moyna to be, if not clever, then happy. She had blamed her for a while that she didn't work hard at school like her sister, but to want to work harder she would have had to be curious and – maybe – malcontent in ways that she was not.

To be satisfied with your life was to reach a state of grace, take a mother's jealous word for it.

Nicol was an afterthought, a coda. Fairer than the others, he didn't have their 'look', derived from Ming's high brow (his was more forward, broader) and from her own slightly pinched eyes (his were wide, candid). It had come as no surprise to her to see those differences develop from birth, but she wasn't sure why. She had simply had a notion that her fifth child was going to be different.

Because he was the last, she watched over Nicol more intently than she had the others. With him she tried to correct the mistakes made earlier. Ming thought it was going to make Nicol too dependent in later life, but she intuited how intelligent he was, quite wise enough to live how he wanted to. Five children had been one too many for Ming, so she didn't listen to his caveats. Nicol was *hers* as the others had been *theirs*.

Ming went through the fatherly routine for him, and Nicol responded with perhaps more courtesy than affection, making a kind of show of his appreciation. There were no major tensions, however. Lewis and Struan had different and unmistakable personalities, and it was unlikely that he would turn out to be like either. A new model was required, and Nicol would become it by his own endeavours, with the assurance of her protection and approval.

Lewis

He hadn't thought that so much of his father would be left behind.

Here he had taught him to catch a mackerel with a line and hook, and there he had shown him how to fly a kite. And over there was where he had explained, haltingly, the physical effects that the sight of an attractive girl was likely to produce upon the body of a gawky adolescent of the sort he was then.

It was his father who had patiently given him swimming lessons all one summer, 1960 or 1961. It was his father who had persuaded him to believe in his own abilities, and who let him see the extent of his pride at his achievements.

Suddenly the scene shimmered, wobbled. Started to melt. Two hot, peppery tears oozed from the ducts of each eye, so readily that they must have been formed and only waiting for their moment. Then two more.

Land turned to sea turned to sky.

Greta

The furnishings as they were had class and tone. She recognised that. But she preferred softness herself, lots of fresh fabric, pretty papers on the walls instead of the gloomy fumed panelling she'd had to live with growing up in Royal Circus. A home should be a little unreal, she felt, but only in a pleasant way: a retreat from the complications of outside.

Lewis had never denied her: more for the sake of good relations, she sensed, than because he felt enthusiastic about her continual innovations. When he walked into one of her revamped rooms in the house for the first time he would look a little panicky to discover that she had replaced tired curtains with ruched improvements, and that those were co-ordinated with the chair covers and cushions or a bedspread.

Co-ordination was a recent illumination to her, giving a room its 'theme'. Each room should have its own 'theme'. Every room was meant to be a different ... well, experience ... and as far from the memory of Royal Circus as she could contrive. In time Lewis would come to appreciate better what she had achieved. In the designers' boutiques of Glasgow and Edinburgh she was well known, and was offered Lapsang or a sherry whenever she dropped by to leaf through the manufacturers' latest catalogues. It required 'an eye', her advisers told her.

The Broch offered untold possibilities.

Struan

Moyna was in a rust corduroy pinafore dress. And floral blouse. With those yoked shoulders and mutton sleeves Kirsty had favoured when the style first came out.

Cat had asked him to remember what everyone was wearing. Maybe she felt obliged to interest herself, because she rarely as much as glanced at fashion articles.

Moyna could have made more of herself. You expected women to have a sixth sense for that kind of thing, whether or not they read the fashion spreads. With four children, though, and with another well on the way, there must be priorities. Moyna had them, and so he supposed that he should admire her for sticking to them.

But pictures would come into his head, sort of memory flashes from the *Rocky Horror* period, of how – he heard from gossip – she used to tart herself up when her family weren't going to see, away at school but skulking off, in face-whitener and lurid make-up and slashed black fishnets. The fad may only have lasted for a couple of terms, but that had been Moyna at a particular time of her life. How did you travel all that distance, from stilettos and hot pants to a pinafore dress?

He felt he didn't speak much to her, and his own reasons eluded him. Parenthood bored him and alarmed him, and yet – more than that – he didn't know the verbal shorthand that would connect the two of them as they were now with the persons they had been then. Moyna had always (officially) 'fitted in' as Ailsa had found it less and less easy to do, and like him she'd had no shortage of friends. Their friends hadn't been the same ones, however, and the legacy was a surfeit of ignorance between them, about one another, which he still had great difficulty coping with in words. The children had a tendency to get in the way, literally, making it awkward to proceed from one sentence to the next. It was simple by comparison just to graze cheeks with a kiss and to smile harmlessly, exchanging pleasantries about the weather, the garden, the tides running or dragging on the shoreline, the return of the beach tar.

Moyna

She smiled at Greta: who must have thought at first that she was making a judgment, and so took up a defensive posture, until she realised that it wasn't Ailsa who was smiling at her.

She envied Greta her stylishness. The details changed from year to year, and yet the effect was unvarying. When people looked at *her*, they were calculating whether she had 'made an effort' or not, and puzzling how to respond, while with Greta they all of them knew exactly where they were.

The frosted hair. The expert make-up. The classic clothes, which actually had to be bought new every season, since 'classic' is being perpetually redefined by the designers. The authentic pearls, which somehow never seemed to be the same arrangement of pearls, lending their pricey Tay lustre to her skin. The shoes with their untrod soles.

She, Moyna, noticed. She wasn't supposed to, but she realised she was as alert to Greta as either Ailsa or Nicol. She took private pride in her deception. It was also politic of her to notice, so that she could arrange her own appearance accordingly, to seem to be the opposite of her sister-in-law's faultless and pristine look. Bluff and – touché, Greta! – double-bluff.

Nicol

Greta doesn't know what to make of me. We can discuss certain things – colours, films, flowers, even fashion – and while she thinks it's all a bit superficial she knows Lewis can't do that in the same way. She enjoys my being humorous about myself, but of course she isn't sure to what extent I may be tempted to send her up too.

And inevitably there is the problem with the children, the boys, Hugo and Toby with those ludicrous names that outdo even Moyna's lot. They're at an age when, she supposes, I must start to show something more than an avuncular interest. She thinks she is being alert, protective even, yet she also does everything to encourage me into having conversations with her, even when Toby is in the vicinity.

She talks of all their friends, Lewis's and hers, but at the same time she knows she is absurdly lonely for someone in her position. Maybe she realises *I* will realise this, but that I'll also sense some other potential in her – for slightly patronising sympathy, for instance. She thinks she is being open with me as she properly is with no one else, but I have still to be convinced.

She is starting to lose touch with whatever might be true and certain about herself. She is waiting for *my* sympathy too, in exchange for what she supposes is her own.

Mrs Meldrum

So, sometimes I came up here alone. Ming didn't try to dissuade me. 'I want to go away for a few days. To be by myself.' He nodded, and made the right sounds in his throat, which I was free to take as his approval.

The house would be cold and airless, but I was too glad to have reached it to care. I lit gas fires where I needed them, and made tea which I flavoured with whisky, and just walked about for the first hour or so collecting myself together to be calm. If the phone rang, I let it ring. I opened windows and closed them again. I let the rooms grow dark. The long drive would have left pains in my arms, and I always realised too late that I'd forgotten to turn on the hot-water tank. I had to wait until much later to draw a fairly tepid bath, which took me well into night and almost through to the morning. That was all right too: I enjoyed the contrast with custom. When I sat down on a chair and rearranged the cushions and closed my eyes, incidents and images from the journey replayed themselves behind the dark pink of my eyelids. Sometimes I drifted into a light sleep, where I didn't have to trawl far or deep for snatches and wisps of remembered dreams.

After the bath I returned to the bedroom: one of the single rooms, on the landward side, smelling a little gassy but warm. I would already have made up the bed, in approximate fashion, and lay down with a hot-water bottle. I would watch the play of moonlight and shadow on the ceiling and walls. Everything settled around me, into its proper shape and sound. The house was silent, but not quite. The walls twitched, the timbers shifted above me in the roof, a tile rattled, and of course the water tank gulped and hissed. The freedom from responsibility was alternately frightening and enervating. I worried one minute, and the next I was telling myself, oh well, what the hell? I wove my way into sleep eventually, by meandering roundabout routes. I shook off the long day and its long, long night. Sometimes the mementoes would be there, casting beneath sleep waiting for me, but I was too tired for it to matter. The restive arabesques on the ceiling and walls melded to ivory or to silver and stuck there as I closed my eyes to them, to consciousness and conscience.

Once in that interlude of three or four years when I had the need to get away by myself, I was wakened by a sound like nothing I could recognise.

I did understand it in the first few seconds as being a cry of terror and pain, although it was inexplicable to me.

I got up and crossed over to the window. I stood on the cold carpet and pulled up the window sash.

There was a din of galloping feet and dragon's breath, an animal shriek followed by a metallic wailing. Clouds covered the moon but I could distinguish some movement or other on the tennis court. I thought that the perimeter wire netting shook – then I became certain.

Something moved behind it. A beast of some kind.

My body froze.

The thing reappeared. A creature with horns, impossible gilded horns, like neon scribbles against the dark.

The Broch

I heard the cantering hooves, the slithering horny feet on the cracked asphalt.

Quite, *quite* ridiculous —

I dressed quickly, though, and went out armed with the heaviest walking-stick and a torch. I approached the tennis court with care, keeping to the shadows.

The wire netting rattled as the thing landed against it, slipping or hurling itself at it. Another of the wooden support-posts was dislodged.

Violet clouds. Moonlight. I strained to see.

Inside the tennis court, excited to panic because it couldn't get out, was a full-grown stag.

Back and forth, back and forth, it took the same measure of asphalt. The clattering hooves thundered out a tattoo. I was mesmerised, by the motion and by the sound of it. To and fro. Back and forth.

The stag's pain — it was injured, although I couldn't see blood — came rumbling up out of the pit of its belly. An occasional scream would provide a desperate, chilling top note.

To and fro. Back and forth.

The incident ended disgracefully. I couldn't think what to do, and watched helplessly, and could finally do nothing. The stag caught sight of me, halted for a few moments but only to recover breath, then it started again. Now it had added resolve — or despair. More of the wire netting fell away, ripping from the posts. Instead of that helping, however, it complicated everything even more. The stag might have trampled over the wire and escaped, but when it tried its legs became entangled, and it stumbled, and its body became impaled on one of the upturned wooden staves, on the spiked end.

It died slowly and horribly, screaming at me, and there was nothing I could think to do. I was too shocked and too weak. I should have tried to club it, to end its agony. Its eyes rolled in their sockets, and I couldn't read anything in them, and I was petrified in my own selfish extremis.

Its death seemed to last through a dawn. Probably it took an hour or so until it breathed its last — while I wound my way around the garden, past untended beds, in circle after circle.

I only started to cry then, at the very end, standing over the twisted and crumpled body. I found I was shaking violently, and my knees gave way, and I dropped on to the grass banking. I was exhausted, in my own way. But, I reproached myself, I was alive. Alive, *alive*. I held my head in my hands. I thought of the stag's stupidity, or its pride. And still I couldn't understand — as I have never understood — how it got into the tennis court, that magnificent and formidable and proud and stupid creature of the high hills.

In the house there is a Victorian oil study of a stag cornered in a bracken brake. The painting still hangs in Ming's old business-room. The stag has halted and is facing you, implicating you, but it's impossible to determine just what it might be thinking, or rather which instinct it's obeying at this one particular, arrested, unfinishing instant. It's such a haunting image, and I notice almost every time, and I hasten past it, because I prefer to.

I needed several years to be able to approach the tennis court with even the pretence of ease. Ming didn't suggest I could have done anything when I told him the next day, when he arranged by telephone to have the carcass removed and the damage repaired. If he felt that I could have shown some courage, he had his reasons – of pride, I should say, and not stupidity – why he chose not to. He realised I required my space, and maybe – more muddledly – I perceived that he was asking me to acknowledge a similar requirement in himself.

But still I didn't comprehend, as I have continued not to, how it was that even by way of an unlocked gate in the wire fencing a stag could have entered the tennis court and become trapped there, in its killing place.

PART TWO

Mrs Meldrum

This was the second evening. Tomorrow her guests would be gone, back to their busy lives in Glasgow and Edinburgh and London and New York.

She had asked Mrs McKay to push the boat out, just for tonight. There was salmon poached and smoked, cold silverside, salads. Vichyssoise, mussels. Atholl Brose and a rum baba. Wines and spirits, since no one had to drive anywhere until they'd slept it off.

She didn't go in for elaborate tables. The food looked appetising just as it was, with the complete dinner service stacked for a buffet and the good glasses, marshalled according to purpose. Crystal water jugs. The florist's flowers that Greta had brought, and some – on the sideboard – from her own garden. The lamps switched on. Chairs distributed about the room. The windows open, and the doors, so that they could step outside if they wanted to, on to the terrace.

The room was at its best, because it was going to be full. The signs of wear and tear didn't really matter, although they would be noticed by one or two. She was counting on the voices and the shadows distracting the rest of them. (There was a contradiction in her thoughts at this point, since she knew it was her condition they were bound to be considering, how she was holding up in the solitude of The Broch. The truest reason she'd had for inviting them was so that she would have company, on this day of all days.)

Now – now everything was ready. She walked slowly round the table. Here and there she repositioned a dish, a glass. She lifted a silver serving spoon and stared at her upturned reflection in the bowl, then she replaced it. She picked up a peony petal that had shuddered silently on to the waxed mahogany.

As pretty as a picture, she decided, wincing at the turn of phrase. Which reminded her – and she crossed the room to one of the watercolours she had spotted from the doorway, and straightened the frame on the wall. She caught the tepid smile of her reflection in the glass. She would have to do better with her mouth than that. She tried.

The smile was in place when she heard footsteps and turned round. Nicol was standing at the door. 'Looks great!' he said. She didn't need to will herself to smile for Nicol; she was easiest with him of her children. She could have put money on him noticing. In his case she was glad she was able to predict, to have the confidence of his support. She put an arm round his slim waist as she directed him towards the bottles.

'I need a boost, Nicol.'

'No problem.'

Struan – in casual blue shirt and loose white chinos – was next. He nodded to Nicol, awkwardly. He came across and kissed her first on one cheek and then on the other. It was a little like a gesture in a play. He didn't use to kiss her twice in Kirsty's time. Did she have his girlfriend to thank for the innovation? But she wasn't here, and of course she'd had to wonder why not. Could she be quite so busy at her work, this business Struan had set her up in, as he'd told them she was?

Moyna sauntered in, just ahead of Jamie. She smiled vaguely, and ambled over to the window, in that rather flat-footed way she had quite suddenly acquired four or five years ago. She looked out, listening for children, letting them all see that she was. She felt her own eyes narrowing as she watched her. Then she started as she felt a hand on her arm. Jamie's. She smiled into his face, drawing back a little. He was paler than he ought to have been: too much application in his lucrative surgery, although where the money went was anyone's guess. They didn't *look* rich, but then she didn't know what houses in Putney cost and what school and kindergarten fees are for four young children – to be five by the autumn.

Ailsa was in the room, she discovered, without her having been aware. She thought she turned her head away in anticipation of her noticing. One of the pictures was preoccupying her.

'Ailsa,' she said, 'have a drink, won't you?'

'I just stick to mineral water nowadays.'

'Yes, of course. I'm sure we have –'

'Or something soft would be fine.'

'Well, just tell Nicol what you want –'

Her daughter's eyes sped past her, to fasten on Nicol. Intelligent eyes, shrewd and canny, but a little daunting sometimes in their intensity. As if, in this low sunlight, they were lit behind by little electric bulbs – not quite what you wanted to have studying you. She touched Ailsa's elbow, because she didn't know what else to do.

'Will you find yourself . . .'

The arm seemed to chill, and she removed her hand. She had been hoping Ailsa might have come to Achnavaig accompanied. She thought she looked at the same time alert and wearied: the bulbs were lit, but under heavy lids. Her perfume had a dry, almost antiseptic smell, although it was bound to be up to the minute and expensive. Even the under-dressed look she now sported couldn't have been arrived at casually. Nothing was accidental about Ailsa.

She had told them 'five past eight', half intending it as a joke – after the name of the variety review at the old Alhambra Theatre in Glasgow – but also letting them appreciate that she had planned the evening to be a little special. The theatrical atmosphere didn't displease her, although she hadn't foreseen it quite in this way, as a sequence of arrivals at the door and rather stilted entrances. Or alternatively, as a finale of curtain calls.

She would have expected Ailsa to be last. The rear, however, was brought up by Lewis and Greta, and an instance of 'but not least' if ever there was. Greta had a star's timing. She preceded Lewis, so that she wouldn't be eclipsed. She was dressed for dinner in a hotel, or at a smart restaurant. She had the knack of never quite over-dressing; her clothes were discreet, but – contrary to the old rule – they still somehow managed to advertise their cost. Befitting his seniority Lewis was turned out in a blazer and flannels and black steel-tipped Oxfords. A second, lunching-out chin was partially disguised by a silk cravat patterned with horsey paraphernalia (the donkeys in the Innes' field used to scare him as a boy), and he looked as comfortable as he ever did, which his mother understood quite well was a double-edged compliment. He seemed a little less careworn than yesterday, at least; Greta remained her invariable self, with her face a mask of very brittle affability. Already they were the centre of attention in the room, but complicatedly, with nobody speaking to them for several moments and eyes directed past them to the food or the paintings or the views framed in the windows.

All home to roost, and no one but herself to blame for the consequences.

Mrs Meldrum began, tapping for silence from her chair.

'This is the first time we've all been here – been here at Achnavaig altogether, I mean – since . . . since the accident . . .'

Nobody spoke.

Mrs Meldrum passed her hand across her neck, fidgeting with the collar of her blouse.

'Well, of course, you know that. But . . .'

She looked away from their faces, across the room to one of the windows.

In the silence some limbs shifted in the chairs. A glass was placed on a window-sill. A throat was cleared. Outside, the children's voices sounded like the cries of the gulls.

The Sun on the Wall

'We *wanted* to come,' Lewis said.

Mrs Meldrum's eyes lost their focus on the view. They turned slowly to where her eldest son sat. Her mouth shaped some words, or they might have been his words, which she was repeating to herself. Lewis had an ability to sound convincing, but that – they had all tumbled to – was a lawyer's trick.

She stared at the rug, as if she was trying to remember what she'd meant to say next. More shuffling silence. One pair of eyes squinnied back, Ailsa's, and Moyna turned suddenly in her creaking chair, always remembering the children.

For the evening Greta is wearing immaculately pressed and pleated flannel trousers, beneath a tunic top with shawl lapels and braid and brass twist buttons. She is perfectly narrow and straight, and she appears taller than five feet five; she is dressed to go out somewhere, but the terrace is as far as she gets, plate in hand. In her other hand she holds a glass between thin, pliant fingers; her hands have a wide grasp, and her mother-in-law has noticed over the years how acute her reflexes are for reaching out to catch a falling object. She has permitted herself one-inch heels, and on the fronts of her pumps the squared-up black satin bows are demure and tasteful as satin bows go – this woman would know never to put a foot wrong. It's best foot forward in fact while she slowly circumnavigates the terrace, keeping them all in her sights as she parcels out little gifts of attention for each one of them in turn. She keeps smiling for the most part, and she is surely a heroine in her own way.

Greta

Of course this was all very...

She thought of an adjective.

... *civilised*.

Yes.

Or it would have seemed so to a stranger's eye.

The surroundings, the drone of voices. The chiming sounds of good china and glass. The unhurried pace of the occasion, an air of well-mannered formality.

It might have seemed quite enviable, looking from the outside in. Politesse, smiles, restrained laughter. No palpable tensions. Even the children, up so late, knew to keep to themselves and not to interrupt or provide distractions.

Elegance and decorum, perhaps.

The sun had embarked on its descent, and was slanting lower now across the bay. The air was cooler.

The other houses receded. There were just themselves, at the centre – the selfish heart – of their own concerns. The chatter and bright amusement of their mutual evasiveness. The gentle but unflagging choreography of their movements. While their eyes cut across the necessary charm with the precision of steel knives.

Lewis

He sometimes felt he and Nicol were the two poles of the family, the north and the south. It was time's doing that they had failed to get to know one another any better. There were seven and a half years between them, too many to make up. He had no hard feelings that Nicol had been his mother's favourite. Much had been expected of himself, which had been his spur to ambition. Nicol had been under no such pressures, and yet that comparative freedom to make his own life had been *his* incentive to construct one by his own talents. They had more in common after all than he used to think.

He envied Nicol his ease. The cashmere jacket, the pressed blue jeans, the Brooks shirt with the washed-out yellow stripes, the tasselled black loafers. He envied Nicol his rapport with women, which he had never had. (Never mind Greta saying he must be gay, never mind her presuming you couldn't grow out of that. He'd had to be circumcised as a baby because of an infection, could that have anything to do with it – ?) Mother had incidentally taught Nicol to recognise umpteen aspects of feminine feeling, and he would never learn those for himself. Greta was a foreign land to him in many respects, still exotic occasionally but chiefly a compendium of puzzling manners and customs.

Struan

Although Ming Menzies had two brothers and two sisters, only he and Torquil – Uncle Torquil – worked in the firm of whisky brokers founded by their grandfather.

Uncle Lachlan had been 'war-mad' since he was a boy, and his family granted his wish to be allowed to join the army, a Highland regiment naturally; he rose to become – finally – Major-General Meldrum, and he sometimes appeared on television, speaking from his Pitlochry home on the history of war with a limited command of vocabulary but with the mannerisms of a fanatic which the medium so appreciated. Uncle Torquil was a bachelor, and only his sister Seonad – married to a minister with a fashionable parish, who became Moderator of the General Assembly one year – had children, two girls. The major-general's son was left crippled by a car crash, at Brands Hatch, and of the assorted uncles, aunts and cousins, no one apart from Aunt Mhairi's husband, Uncle Maurice, was to have anything to do with the company, attending to its accounting until there occurred a falling-out with his brother-in-law Ming.

Uncle Torquil retired shortly after he joined the firm himself; perhaps inspired by his own year-long jaunt around Australia and New Zealand after school, he decided he wanted to sail the Norwegian fjords, and sold his house in Glasgow to finance the purchase of a forty-foot ketch. Nobody in the family contested Menzies's taking on the responsibilities of The Broch (he let them be in no doubt that it was a considerable financial strain), although Aunt Seonad – never an admirer of her sister-in-law – occasionally expressed concern that her daughters weren't able to appreciate the fruits of their great-grandfather's labours. Her brother didn't have much truck with that, and implied she had surrendered her rights by marrying a churchman. Nevertheless he invited his nieces to spend a couple of summers at Achnavaig, where one patently didn't fit in and the other was only too accommodating, as her mother was subsequently to discover, losing her virginity to a village boy in a bracken bosk.

It hadn't been supposed that Struan Meldrum should do anything else *but* join the firm, when the time came. His school results weren't good enough for university; if he'd gone he would surely have worked for a business degree, but nobody – least of all he – decried the lack. He learned the ropes, and his father gave him to expect nothing less than his unqualified dependence on him. He wasn't presented with the option to fail. He worked as diligently as he was able to, and he didn't sense any hostility among the management personnel. He wasn't the type of person to prompt such feelings anyway, offering very little for others to be antagonistic about.

There was a mute presumption that he would stay there in perpetuity. He became adept, and popular, and was trusted inside and outside the company as a man of his word. Even if he didn't declare as much in words, his father could hardly have hoped for better. Yet after several years with the firm he retained the notion that his father still regretted Lewis's non-involvement. Lewis might have been tempted to take more risks, using his intelligence to browbeat others less confident of their capacities, while *he* was content that they should carry on slowly but surely consolidating. Quite possibly the company could have been made more profitable, but at least this way they were saved from the hazard of over-extensions and false compromises.

Things might have continued in like vein. Intermittently, however, he would sense that his father wasn't being wholly honest with him, that he was being selective in the information he gave him. He kept an eye on the books, through Uncle Maurice, but unless his uncle was in cahoots, there was no evidence of cover-ups in that respect. Rather, his nagging unease concerned more trivial matters. About whom his father might have been meeting in

Glasgow, or failing to meet. Why he went off about Scotland and the north of England on business trips but promptly altered his timetable when he got to his destination, telephoning Glasgow to cancel or re-fix and sometimes to fit in an extra night's accommodation elsewhere. It was untidy practice, and somehow clutter-headed, and only in his thirties did he discover for himself the value of Lewis's manner of precision and order, attempting his own imitation in respect of his business diary as if to compensate for his father's bouts of vagueness, a lax and slipshod attitude towards colleagues that sometimes bordered on cavalier insouciance.

Along the way Uncle Maurice, for no very clear reason, ceased to be involved with the accounting, and persuaded his brother-in-law – who wouldn't consult anyone about it, although his secretary was overheard putting through a call to Lewis in Edinburgh – to transfer the work to another firm of accountants, not his own. Uncle Maurice became a host of Christmas parties instead, and while he consistently failed to ask Struan questions about the company, he seemed to know exactly how much water Lewis liked in his whisky and which food Lewis was permitted on yet another of his exclusively personalised diets.

Still he held to the notion of his father's knowing best. He realised he was consulted less often than he might have expected to be, even as second-in-charge, but he had never at any juncture in his life disputed the sovereignty of custom. He went along with the flow, as he always had, and if life at work or at home with his wife threw up no great surprises it failed to disappoint greatly either.

Ailsa

All those model boats in the house. She saw the sadness in the sleek prows and spread canvas sails. The impulse to escape: to be anywhere else but here.

The boats on their stands irritated her. They took up too much room. They were dust traps. Sometimes one would topple over, for no obvious reason: a dry drowning which caused her to jump right out of her skin.

They were snobbery pure and simple. In later years, when they were becoming adults, Daddy would return from his sailing weekends pickled in gin, with the smell of it oozing out of his pores. (Had everyone else forgotten?) If he had a weathered complexion, that was accidental. He loved the idea of it, but less and less the practice. *She* had noticed what the others must not have done, that after those later jaunts with friends his hands showed no sudden calluses or rope burns. (How come? How charming do shirkers and lingerers-below-decks have to be to get themselves invited back?)

All it had been was vanity, inherited from an age more confident than their own. There was no excuse – or she didn't accept so, in her current frame of mind – and the pity of the situation gave off, so to speak, a mouldering whiff of an essential dishonesty.

Anyway – what was it that took men to sea?

Moyna

Motherhood had taught her certain virtues. It had also subjected her body to ravages, which left her feeling resentful and made inroads on her willing capacity for selflessness.

Since Jamie was the father of her children, it was maybe only appropriate that her attitude towards him should be so equivocal. There was gratification for his never refusing her anything, and irritation that he understood so little as to imagine her fulfilled. In the end her responses, if she was lucky, cancelled out. She could depend on him, but he saw her as somehow less than the person he had married. So what did that all amount to?

She had the children, *their* children, and even if he was working all hours to provide them with their material advantages, she believed that she was fettered by them – by their physical needs – in a way that *he* was not.

She was trying to fend off bitterness. Against the world for its expectations. Against Jamie for his unthinkingness. Against herself for having allowed it all to happen.

Mrs Meldrum

Her father had always liked the idea of being a gentleman farmer. The practicality, however, defeated him. The gentleman thought the farmer was beneath him, and left the farm to run itself. The farmer distrusted the gentleman, deflating his pretensions and finding it hard to offer respect.

He was a very contrary man. He didn't know which he was – the amateur scholar (who had dropped out of Oxford Greats after two years) or the gumboots-in-the-Perthshire-mire yeoman (who moved from milk cows to arable to sheep to fruit to pigs to poultry, looking – nothing daunted – for his milieu). He read Virgil in the evenings, reviewing an occasional book for, not *Horizon* or *Scrutiny*, which he probably aspired to, but the *Scotsman*, which all their friends read. When pricked by conscience he would be up at first light with a summons to the latest farm foreman, leading out the cows ahead of time and then planning the combine-harvester's rota for the coming day.

He meant to be honest, two different men living inside one person, but he couldn't keep himself resolute, and was easily distracted.

We were spectators, never confidants, not (I suspect) even Mother. As children we mucked in, helping to walk in the cows or picking rasps from the canes or shelling peas, and we rewarded ourselves by lying low in byre lofts or in the lee of corn stooks in the fields.

Later Father wasn't so keen for us to lend a hand. He pretended he was concerned about us neglecting our schoolwork when really he was ashamed at having our friends discover how we really lived. We always did return to school, even though Colonel Mair the bursar's glacial looks *en passant* in the corridors signalled to us that the cheque to cover last term's fees was late again. None of us was academic, but it wasn't the school's fault. We were there to acquire some compensatory measure of ourselves, to gain confidence and a hand of other small skills, and of course to work at the companionships that would last us all our adult years. Perhaps that was the sole reason to hang on to the farm, to keep us at school and my mother in cashmeres, which she bought once a year from a shop at Gleneagles Hotel, and so what that the tedium of putting off his creditors yet again drove him to drink. He was the provider for his family, and we weren't on any account to be disappointed.

It was as simple in its theory, and as complex in the discharging, as that.

Lewis

'But no one would buy the house,' Greta had said again on the drive up. 'A house like that.'

She was fishing, in the way she did it, by suggesting the opposite of what she meant.

'Probably not,' he replied to her, intending to be unhelpful.

She was watching him, while he watched the turns of the road.

'The Albatross,' he heard her say, not for the first time, 'would have been a better name for it.'

'I suppose so.'

'Or The Millstone,' she added, and again it wasn't the first time she had suggested it.

He didn't know if it was the house or its furnishings that appealed to her, in spite of her denials. She would be content to have it rented out, he guessed, just so long as it wasn't allowed to be taken from them with no one making the effort to resist.

'Your mother will consult us all?' she asked, as if she had read his mind.

'Yes, I'm sure she will.'

'You *can't* be sure, though–'

He leaned forward in his seat, so that she could see he was trying to concentrate on the road. There was silence for thirty seconds or so. More was to follow, he sensed.

'So long as she's aware, Lewis.'
'She seems quite compos mentis. In control of herself.'
'So?'
'She doesn't even need to think about it. What she'll do.'
'The time will come.'

He let her have the last word. She was correct, he believed. It wouldn't please Greta to be acquainted with the actual facts as he – only he – knew them to be. The longer his mother kept her health, and her mind, the longer he could postpone her own and Greta's discovering.

Greta's head meanwhile must be full of plans, of imaginings and hypotheses. She was stripping the walls already, only to refurbish the rooms in her rather over-stated and precious way. They were harmless enough fancies, but just while they remained where they were, inside her head.

Struan

He wasn't sure if he loved Cat. His feelings for her were negations rather than affirmations. He lived with her in the hope that she could cancel out Kirsty. Everything about their manner of existence was due to a counter-reaction to what had happened earlier in his life. It was a more complicated matter than love alone could ever be. He was only learning now that adulthood required the wide-angled view and a very deft lightness of touch.

Cat had never mentioned a wish for children. He was relieved. But at the same time he couldn't suppress a notion that it wasn't quite natural, in a woman even more than a man. Why else should the company of children agitate him, except as rebukes? He couldn't think how he might have coped with his nephews and nieces *and* with Cat.

As it was, he felt irritated with himself: for not knowing how to conjure up paternal sentiments even here, in the very thick of it. He had transferred some of his irritation on to Cat, by deciding he wouldn't phone her after all. He'd keep her waiting, guessing, imagining. It would give him a little more purchase on her mind, and he wasn't apologetic about it to himself. By not phoning home, he was briefly denying that it was his home.

'Home.' The word should have enclosed him as it once used to, the simplest expression of an ideal of comfort and security, as trim as a glove. The term didn't really apply to that open-plan converted grain-house they shared, white-tiled and furnished with Cat's eclectic choice of chrome and leather minimalism. From this distance – standing on the dining-room's sidelines – it seemed an especially inappropriate term to him, and just as much so when he tried to whisper it on the back of his tongue, casually and hardly audible at all, into the old, dusty, faded William Morris fabric of the curtain by his shoulder, with the yellowed cotton lining along its fingered edge picked to tatters.

Ailsa

Moyna and Jamie would invite her out to Putney every couple of months or so. They seemed oblivious of her own failure to reciprocate.

Several birds were felled with one stone at a family brunch. The children would be playing under the table, dogs sniffed around and barked, there might be some unsuitably high-brow music as far-away background. Her own conversation was always the most stilted. No one appeared to notice, however. She would be invited back when they thought they had got their next Sunday social mix about right.

She usually had to repeat the information – over the noise, and contending with her fellow-guests' incredulity – that she was actually Moyna's sister. No, it didn't sound a likely truth to her either. It was the only reason why she was sitting here, amongst these hearty medics and their child-proud wives, and it was hardly a proper reason at all. She was conscious of a tiny tug of familial obligation inside herself, but it was invariably beforehand – in anticipation of these get-togethers – and not during or after. Also, she noticed, they didn't entertain her alone, and she supposed that they were too daunted by the prospect: having to footer about for topics by themselves. They were brave enough to have her to the house, but not that brave. Sometimes she felt she ought to have been grateful to them, but it was a twisting and slippery emotion. Instead, she tried to feel no feelings at all.

Mrs Meldrum

Mothers know. Well, maybe not all mothers know, but this one did.

There was something different about Nicol. He was ironic where the others were not: and, not least, he was ironic about himself. I only hoped that, since this was so and unchangeable, he could continue to behave in a spirit of healthy scepticism, curious and wondering, and not as often happens with those of his persuasion, with bitterness.

Acidity comes about when people feel they are rejected. He wasn't a self-dramatist, really – a parodist, certainly – and he joined in as much as he could. He didn't stand back and allow others to decide for him. If we had produced a homosexual, I was determined that he should be a level-headed one.

Moyna

Between having her third and fourth children, she developed pains in her back. Jamie sent her to so-called experts he knew, who diagnosed nothing wrong with her. He advised against osteopaths, closing ranks with his own kind perhaps, but she went to one nonetheless. She went to two. And to a sports-injury physiotherapist. She tried an acupuncturist. An aromatherapist. Then, more nervously, a hypnotist. She wasn't comfortable with him, however, and wasn't sure if she had really felt his hand placed on her bottom during his second session. She read up about crystals, and bought a couple, but their vibrations weren't strong enough for her.

The pain persisted, although it wasn't constant, amassing and then waning. It was difficult even to explain, to put into words, and she found herself floundering once she attempted to, which she was obliged to do whenever she embarked on a new course of treatment. It was in her shoulder, and her lower back, and occasionally in her abdomen, just – oh God – above the groin. 'Psychosomatic' she guessed they were wanting to tell her, and they hummed and hawed, some more tactfully than others.

In the car, just driving about London, the pain became a cleaner but duller thing, it thinned and compacted instead of seeming pervasive, edgeless. She could live with it then, because she started to forget that it belonged to her. It slunk away, sort of, and by doing so it only (problematically) confirmed that the verdict on her was a just one.

Jamie

In the evenings his height contracts by an inch or so, he's quite sure of it. He doesn't show up in a very good light then. It's lamplight usually: centre-lights depress him like nothing on earth. His mum and dad always used to have the centre-lights on at home, making the already small rooms seem still smaller, with no corners that let you be properly by yourself.

Somehow, though, he'd been able to shut it all out when he needed to, to be able to study. Somehow he had won his scholarship to boarding school, and even though he learned the knack of sharing study desks with others in the communal prep room, the problem of home wasn't remedied – how to introduce his friends to the fact that his family lived, by comparison with theirs, so modestly. He could call himself 'Jamie' instead of 'Jim', acquire a more refined accent, polish up his manners, become more outward-going, talk about the world in general, and yet – for a few years – everything returned to that vital matter of his parents and younger brother at home, in the shrinking bungalow.

The problem became a lesser one, by virtue of his confecting excuses and staging various 'accidents' that kept his friends away and which took him into their social territory. Developing flu at Ronnie Cole-Watson's house in in the run-up to one Christmas and having to stay there until Hogmanay. Declaring a sudden interest in sailing and being taken by the Naysmyths for a ten days' jaunt round the Outer Hebrides, the following August. Coming to Achnavaig and meeting The Broch set had been part of another summer's exercise in adroit distancing, when inadvertently the Meldrums had caught him at what was becoming his most typical.

Ailsa

In their schooldays the other mothers seemed staid by comparison with their own, and that too had been a performance – to allow herself to be distinguished from them.

To her it was a no-no, having a mother who watched *Top of the Pops* over their shoulders and who swam in the sea at any temperature and who had the gardener take her on the back of his motorbike for a trial run and who wore – for the whole of one memorable season – a shift dress of swirly lemon and tangerine blobs. She once kept dancing reels until dawn at a ceilidh, and for a spell tried to teach herself the Spanish guitar.

But if she had really been that kind of woman, they should have grown up wild and without any flushes of embarrassment at all.

It was a very disciplined sort of esprit, though, on all counts.

Mother had an eye for presentation, and that involved her children having the meek manners – the famous Meldrum charm – which ensured *she* was kept to the foreground.

All their lives they'd had the courtesies, the rituals of politeness, dinned into them. How to sit, how to hold cutlery, how to speak to strangers, when to stay silent. Make your own bed. Don't lean on your elbows. Open doors, offer precedence.

Sometimes Mother used to give herself away. Keep your best clothes best. Thank your host for having you, and then write to say 'thank you' again. Change out of your outdoor shoes inside. Brown paper covers on the most-used books. Segregating the chipped cups on the left-hand side of the kitchen cupboard, for family teas only.

That was a little different from the insistent, endless economies. Eat all the food on your plate because the starving children in India can't. Use a pencil down to the stub. Save string. Switch off an unused light. There was a self-denying aspect – use up the first pencil before you eye the indulgent luxury of a full lead on the second – which was merely Scottish. If it was perverse, it was quite understandable. Lewis would work a single stretch of two or three hours at his university work in the holidays before allowing himself a mug of coffee. When Struan went swimming he confined his legs with a float, to make the exercise harder on himself; she used to think he actually preferred a round of golf in the wind, because he had to put in double the effort to be accurate. Moyna only really enjoyed cutting out and making up a dress from a pattern that was technically too advanced for her. For a long while Nicol denied himself a newer kind of camera – when his father would have bought him a good second-hand one – because he thought he had to push his skills further to acquit himself well with what he had.

What it actually amounted to was selfishness, while simultaneously believing yourself virtuous and persuading others of the same. An artful dodge, in other words.

The middling middle-classness was more problematical to her, because she half-recognised its tenets. She knew what they were about. About being amenable, making yourself wantable, steering conversation away from home, making people think you only watched nature documentaries on television and not *Top of the Pops*, justifying yourself as socially adept. About your becoming semi-invisible, in fact, and un-hazardous. Which was where she lost the trail a bit, not seeing how that accorded with the scatty, quirky but smiling, always smiling, impression she felt her mother preferred to make.

Mrs Meldrum

Something about the way Lewis swells his chest, then slowly lets the breath out.

It's Ming. Again he's standing in the room and my own breath gets all caught up in my chest, forty-odd years later, and I have to open my mouth to ventilate.

How ridiculous. I try to steady myself. I become gradually calmer. It's just been a silly fright, that's all, because of the way my eldest son chanced to be altering his posture.

Lewis

He didn't blame his father. After the war openings were limited. Coming out of the navy he couldn't have had full confidence in his skills, whatever his skills were. He had no experience for any work except war.

Grandfather Meldrum had had a reputation for sledgehammer methods. By and large they had created commercial success. He lacked the finesse of touch which personal matters require, and probably knew so: in business affairs he would delegate where necessary, but with his family he had to suffer the consequences of his own insensitivity. He ensured that his son was faced with a diminishing number of choices, so that there was really no alternative except to come into the firm. Once in, he couldn't be transformed into whatever his nature prevented him from being. At first young Menzies had the moral satisfaction of fulfilling his father's expectations, but it must have become clearer to him – even if he disguised the situation from his father – that he didn't have the turn of mind, or maybe the ambition, to make the sort of impression which two previous generations had done.

He took stock, built up a base; he acquired some fat against possible lean. He didn't generally look forward, however, which his own father preferred to do. When Struan joined him later he would recognise in his son attitudes similar to his own. But Struan had an opportunity subsequently to assert himself, with others showing a more judicious appreciation of his abilities considered against the lesser fact of his limitations.

Menzies Meldrum didn't have that opportunity to prove himself, positive over negative, to his contemporaries. He remained under *his* father's thumb for too long. That was unfortunate, and also as impartially authentic as history. Menzies had taken care not to reveal his accumulating weariness with his responsibilities, which only helped to create for later years a morass of problems left too carelessly unattended. Reasonably efficient managers did keep the business in sound credit, but they and their achievements weren't given their due, and several departures in quick succession left him holding the reins, without appropriate advice on directions.

In hindsight it was all quite inevitable. It didn't become a more avoidable situation, however, because Menzies Meldrum would always have been much the same, with his father's will watered down into obstinacy and that blend of personal confidence and insensitivity transformed into petty point-scoring and a blind disregard of his own weaknesses.

He would only have had to look inside himself to find his fate. It was sealed, ready and waiting.

Greta

She watched the two of them together, Struan and his mother. Only Lewis and Nicol knew the knack of handling her: she seemed a little timid with Ailsa, and condescending with Moyna. With Struan she didn't declare herself, but mostly looked at him when he wasn't looking at her. There was an oppressive formality between the pair. Small words prettily candied: nothing much said, and far too much to say, but how to begin?

She saw Lewis watching her watch his mother, and she smiled back brightly, to confuse the issue.

At one time Struan had given her butterflies in her stomach.

Even at her wedding she felt the breath knotting in her throat, exacerbated by the tightness of her dress, her mother's dress. It would happen in spite of herself, which was what most concerned her. She didn't like to feel she wasn't in control.

But once they were away, in their suite at the Turnberry Hotel before they took the train south in the morning, her excitement could hardly have been owing to Lewis, who showed less enthusiasm – surrounded by the expensive debris of room service – than he had in the past in their snatched moments. Then into her head without warning strolled Struan with his sportsman's gait...

He had never been less than chivalrous with her, and brotherly, a little distracted indeed as he tended to be in his dealings with Lewis. I'm me – I'm me, she wished she could tell him to his handsome face, I don't belong to anyone. Oh yes you do, his silence always seemed to be answering her. But she had mistaken that habitual silence – so she was starting to appreciate now – for something less than the man's sound common sense.

Oh God, sometimes she wanted to do her living intensely. That was why Struan attracted her. He wasn't an intense *person*, but in his sports he acquitted himself dramatically. His leisure was as important to him as his work. She liked the craziness of that.

Frankly, Lewis lived somewhat too much for his brain, and she would have welcomed what Struan gave to others of his simpler, more mellow view of the world. Thus, into her head over the years strolled her brother-in-law, looking slightly placeless admittedly, and yet with a clear and unmarked forehead permanently tanned. The tan, the physique, the co-ordination, and an undignified uncontrollable oozing between her legs, of a sadly unassuaged want.

Lewis and Struan got along, not well but sufficiently so. There was little socialising other than at these obligatory family gatherings. Neither of them, she could guess, had fully recovered from his boyhood envy of the other's abilities, so that now they remained cautious and reserved with one another.

But behind it all, she couldn't help feeling, there was an understanding that went deeper than the envy: a truce about something or somebody, in that past which they shared without her.

Moyna

No one had asked her where she'd gone in the afternoon. Technically, in geographical terms, she wouldn't have been able to tell them. They remained none the wiser. And neither was she.

All she had wanted to do was get into the car by herself and drive off. Drive anywhere. Here the choice of places to go was limited, very. In London, when it happened, she was spoiled. The degree of privacy was the same, however. The car itself was the same one she used for the afternoon drives she took, say, two or three times in a fortnight.

She didn't know why she did it. Why she *had* to do it, with her back aching. But she wasn't the sort to go in for rationalisations. If she felt a strong enough urge to do something, she was taken up by the compulsion, and that was that. She didn't require to get to the nitty-gritty of what it meant. People generally enquired too much. She preferred to keep a few mysteries in play, especially to herself. She couldn't help it if that was how she was made.

In the car she listened to music cassettes. Rather, the music filled the silence of the space. The very familiarity of the music enabled her not to give it a thought, and a tape could reach all the way to the end of its second side without her being aware. Only the renewed silence told her that things weren't how they had been before.

In London she clicked into the sequence of traffic on the road. Like one of Struan's Scalextric model cars they used to send hurling round the chicane track set up in the billiards room. In the afternoon she had encountered hardly any other traffic at all, and she had realised that she was missing it. Traffic carried you, you were engaged in a game, and it all kept your mind occupied. At home, in their red brick and Dutch-gabled corner of Putney, the unremitting concerns, questions demanding their answers, worried away at her confidence that she could cope. In the car she was just kept busy, and she didn't have a spare moment for any of the usual welter of queries. She became liberated; an enthusiasm infused her, pulsating through her feet from the pedals.

Round about London nobody saw her. Hereabouts she was bound to have been noticed. News would get back to her mother. She would search her brain to remember what excuse Moyna had given her for that temporary absence. But it would hardly have registered, since Lewis and Nicol were the ones she occupied herself with, and Ailsa – of course – because she failed to make sense of her.

What Moyna did mattered much less, if at all.

At one time she had been grateful to have that disturbing intensity of attention taken off her and transferred to Ailsa. Neglect was an ingrained habit by now. This was just the true cost of an ancient bargain. They probably all imagined they knew Moyna, and could read her like a book, a not very distinguished book ghost-written to a formula.

Mrs Meldrum

The war was just newly over, and so their lives were no longer in jeopardy, far away as they had been in Perthshire and at Boat of Weem where the family went to school. But her morals were considered to be in distinct and immediate danger from her elder sister, Lindsay, and so it was decided that the two should be separated for a while.

The Sun on the Wall

Her Aunt Bunty might have taken Lindsay with her to America instead, in the hope of a reformation. Her nerves weren't up to that challenge, however, and there was a risk that in New York Lindsay might even regress, to something wilder than obtuseness.

Through the offices of friends a place was found for her at a small girls' school on their side of the Park, the West, on a corner off Columbus Avenue. It turned out to be a more snobbish sort of establishment than she was expecting to find in the land that called itself the 'home of the free'. Still it helped her to know where she stood, and she played on Scotland's romantic connotations quite shamelessly.

Through the same friends Aunt Bunty was introduced to a family in the Upper East called Cauldwell, who took an immediate liking to the pair. There were three children in their teens, and Aunt Bunty judged the double coincidence – their being contemporaries, sort of, and having a surname of remote Scottish provenance – a lucky one.

It was also lucky that they met up at the start of summer. Her own holiday plans were settled in one fell swoop when Mrs Cauldwell suggested that, while Aunt Bunty fulfilled her obligations with cousins in St Louis, her niece should come and join the family in Massachusetts, by the sea.

Amersham was a small resort town, grown from a fishing village, on the nibbled Cape Cod coast south of Waquoit. Mrs Cauldwell and the children were residents there for eight or nine weeks of every summer while Mr Cauldwell worked on in the swamp heat of Wall Street and came down every second weekend.

It was perfect, really.

Sherry was her own age. Green was eighteen months older, going on seventeen, and Bip one year younger, although his precocious gravity had a confusingly ageing effect. Sherry had a creamy skin and fair hair held with a band: a tartan band, by accident or design. Bip's appearance was darker – or maybe it was just that his eyebrows met in a trail of little hairs on the bridge of his nose, and made his features generally seem a little lowering, concentrated into thought. Green, thankfully, had inherited the same glamorous richness of his sister's colouring, which she envied for its air of – what?

Of privilege, she supposed. Of freedom from concern. Why else should Sherry have that faintly languid air, which struck her as being – again – surprisingly un-American. Green had his own style, of a more conventional sort. He could sail, play tennis, dive from a highboard, knock up the runs in a mean game of rounders; he could even water-ski, and furthermore he was the possessor of a driving licence.

She adored her tennis lessons, having Green's firm arm and sure hand to steady her and show how she should be holding the racket. She was fascinated by the blond furze on the flawless skin, on his legs too. He exuded mastery and control, seeming to know so much about the subject, with his practical skills and his eye for local form and his encyclopedic memory for the big international match results. On their own lawn court he was unfailingly patient with her. She thought he had the most perfect teeth she had ever seen. She asked his sister an endless number of questions about him, behind his back, and didn't doubt that Sherry would be discreet in her turn, by not letting on.

It was perfect, really.

Tennis, swimming, waiting for the lobster and clam catches down on the old wooden jetty, negotiating a bicycle with a cross-bar, forgetting sometimes to think of her family back home on the farm in Perthshire. On Kerrix's grass and sand tennis court with the sun going down behind the red spruces and pitch pines. Sipping at a mint julep (what else?) at Blinkey's, where Green drove her with Sherry to meet their Crag Bay friends. Listening to scratchy Hot Club de France records, smelling Bip's palette of oils and turps bottles from the room under the roof where he painted, being a very willing audience while Green recited lines of Ovid and Whitman for his school exams.

It was perfect, really.

She supposed that she and Sherry could have no secrets from one another. They would sit out on the side-stop of the shingle house, or lie side by side on one of the beds, or hide in the airing cupboard sweet with the fragrance of apples, and together they would talk Amersham and West Sixty-Third and East Eighty-Seventh Streets out of their systems. When they went walking, along the dunes or up towards the creek, Sherry linked their arms at the elbow. The familiarity made her toes tingle, and she knew she never wanted to forget these times, just as she was living them now. In this safe place everything melodiously harmonised, everything chimed.

Even when Sherry teased her, she knew there was no edge to it. Sherry was protecting her, she guessed. Her American education had bewildered her – trailing chiffon scarves above their heads during eurythmics sessions up on the flat sooty roof of the school, brisk chaperoned walks past the nude (always nude) statuary in the Metropolitan, the brief history and vast geography of a country she was quite ignorant of – but here at Amersham she could feel she was getting her bearings again. Even the subject of boys fell into place, comparatively, when she had Sherry to tell her – and several times to show her – how boys kissed and how a girl should kiss back. She asked Sherry how she knew, and her best friend shrugged in a way she found shockingly, exhilaratingly casual. She didn't understand how she could contend with that degree of worldly experience, but Sherry continued just as before, speaking knowledgeably but taking no advantage from it.

Sherry suggested they try on one another's clothes. It was a funny sensation of closeness, and a slightly perfumed one, and exciting. She didn't think Sherry could be interested in *her* clothes, which lacked softness and shape by comparison, but it turned out that she was, and very much so. She realised Sherry's only consistency was in being unpredictable; it was that, though, which constituted – perplexingly – a significant ingredient of her charm, which prevented one's holding any final certainties about her. Sherry was her very best friend in the world, and yet now and then a doubt would form – a passing high cloud inside her head – whether she did in fact know as much about her as she assumed she must do.

Bip's attention for her on the other hand was tangential, coming at her by way of various reflecting surfaces. She was unsettled by his expressions, which struck her as disapproving. Sherry only laughed when she mentioned this to her, which didn't confirm or deny her suspiciousness. Did Bip think she was being too intrusive?

She was Sherry's friend, and Green's. Not his. In her mind she felt closer to his brother's age. She found Bip too intense, watching her from his sly angles. She pretended not to notice. On several occasions he caught her out, and by the time she had calculated where his vantage point was, damn, she had lost the moment.

While all the time she was being drawn to Green, she could have no doubts about it. A mute impulse was directing her. She felt deliciously somnambulant. The decision had been taken out of her hands, and she was drifting, drifting –

She is dazzled, she permanently has sunlight in her eyes, that clear crystalline sea light.

His hair, his teeth, his blond furze. The confident way he talks about the future. His strength and agility on the tennis court.

When he's not speed-reading for his cramming course, Green takes her for walks, out past his friends' homes. They leave Sherry lying, suncreamed, on a lounger and Bip hammering away at another of his sea collages. She allows Green to hold her arm and to point her, gently, in the direction he intends to go, to Crag Bay again perhaps.

The Broch

* * *

So, content as she was, she found it was becoming easier for her to say things to Bip that caused him to smile his thanks. She knew nothing about painting, and couldn't pretend she did. He took her at her word, though. She wasn't sure herself just what it was that she ever meant.

Smiles notwithstanding, Bip still struck her as needlessly intense, reading more into a situation than it deserved. Sherry had told her he was the most intelligent member of the family, but that gave her grounds to be wary. Clever people, she knew even then, are never at rest; for them, happiness is a case of life serving short measure.

Now, she thinks, anything might happen with Green. She earnestly believes it. She is wanting something to happen so much, and at the same time she is afraid, that none of this is intended, that she is far from the cursors which have marked her life up until now.

She is waiting on the edge, a threshold edge.

One evening they're sitting, all of them, on the steps of the stop.

In the slow fading of light the three dimensions are clearer than ever, and the colours brighter. That's the funny thing.

Very lightly a breeze blows in across the fields. The grass sighs, the trees rustle. She realises that Green and Sherry and Bip are attending even more carefully, with their senses primed. She means to ask why, but she has only parted her lips to shape the first word to speak when she remembers having been told about the grey nightjar, the goatsucker and, at the same moment, Green catches her eyes and shakes his head, no, no, no.

He looks away, and she follows his eyes, towards those out-fields that lie beyond the garden, to which the garden must have belonged once.

She hears it, for the first time. A disembodied sound. Birdsong. A peculiar call. *Whip-poor-will*. It has the effect of freezing the others. She keeps perfectly still herself, to hear better. *Whip-poor-will, whip-poor-will*. She can't tell how far away the bird, or birds, must be.

Eventually the bird or birds fly off. Silence, of a sort, is restored.

In these parts, she has been told, the bird's old bad and disproved reputation – for leeching on goats – still colours people's attitudes. Its darting movements, like a swift's, seem to have some supernaturally charged, manic quality. Always the bird is heard at the day's end, as a harbinger of night to come.

'When whippoorwills call,' Sherry is singing softly at her side, 'and evening is nigh –'

The rest of them join in, even Bip, at their various pitches.

'I – hurry – to – my – blue – heaven.'
And that is what it is.

Then one day – in the falling of the coastal daylight – there was a sea-change, a clarification of a different sort.

She didn't like to suppose that Green might have set out intentionally to deceive her, by seeming to ignore those Crag Bay visitors whose names she had never quite got to grips with. There was a brother and sister among them – called (if it could be credited) Jonty and Delta Hayden – and she hadn't been able at first to hit on a connection between them and Green. She had imagined that the boy must be the link, until one afternoon she started to watch the girl, observing her fly and well-timed watchfulness from beneath that straight fringe of black hair whenever Green happened to be playing on the court. If she had been better-looking, then she might have merited notice earlier; she was quite plain indeed, but she accepted her plainness matter-of-factly and without either the bullishness or meekness that affected others; she even seemed to make a kind of virtue out of it. It was suddenly obvious that Green was intrigued by her, and that he played better when he knew one certain pair of eyes (yellowy-fawn, like amber stones) would be attending to him from the shadows of the pines.

The days cooled on her skin after that. She felt edgy, and couldn't settle. She was irritated with herself. When she was partnered with Green she missed easy balls and stopped saying 'Sor-ry!' in her famous drawly fashion, because she didn't have an ounce of apology in her.

Everything was pulling apart, she now knew.

Green carried on as if nothing whatsoever was wrong, which was one way of confirming that it was. Sherry seemed friendlier and more accommodating than ever, and that made it more difficult for her to keep her distance. She tried to ignore the look of uncomprehending dread that she sometimes saw in those peppermint green eyes, but it resolutely stuck in her mind.

She tried to shake off Amersham, to view the place without people or even houses, and only as its elemental constituent parts, which the first Puritan settlers must have done – bitter soil and black primeval rock. She stood on the shore looking back to her old life, and found herself lacking courage, unable to decide. Several times she came upon Bip drawing the same sky; she stared at the improbable crayoned streaks of lime and vermilion dashed down, still in her mind confusing accuracy for verisimilitude and rating an impression as distinctly inferior to the real thing.

She could believe, just, in a 'real world', but Amersham was not it.

She didn't exactly grow sentimental for Scotland at last, but it did fill her mind more and more. She smelt it, felt it on her skin; she could imagine its rain on warm and sultry days, and she heard its far-away winds when the bay below Kerrix was still like glass.

Cycling along the lane out to Rebekah's Rock with Sherry one afternoon (there had been no more walks with Green of late), they crossed a stream. A car happened to pass them on the wooden bridge, spluttering petrol fumes. In that one instant the smells of water and oil combined uncannily to evoke another smell, of a pleasure steamer. The Firth of Clyde: smoke: the rumbling engines beneath the wooden decks. She was a child, and she was crying about something – crying so heartily that the other passengers were turning to look at her, amused. She knew she didn't want to go anywhere on this boat; she screamed herself into hysterics, and in the end her father had to take her off at the next stop while the rest elected to travel on without them. He and she took the train instead, and she calmed herself remarkably in the compartment of the carriage, crouching in the window corner and watching for a glimpse of the steamboat in the sound. She couldn't remember if she spotted the steamer with its two plumes of smoke and froth from the paddles, but what she *did* see was a stag – a fully grown one – swimming offshore. Her father, for some reason not angry, had pointed it out to her and she stared at its awkward but majestic progress through the water, head raised and antlers like eccentric trees, like exotic candelabra.

Why should she have remembered, so vividly, something she had so nearly forgotten about? On another continent flints scattered beneath the wheel of her bicycle, and a thin little fragrance of dusty dryness rose up, and sunshine reddened her knees and arms and hurt the back of her neck, and still she could retain the memory of what had happened such a large portion of her life ago.

Already Amersham, even on afternoons like this one in their Indian summer, was receding from her, at a rate of knots, faster than any humdrum paddle-steamer. Already the possibilities ranged ahead of her were diminishing. Fewer and fewer, and the angle of her vision was tapering, to a precise and sharply illuminated track that seemed to offer no alternative but to follow this straight and narrow, in its wake, to wherever it was leading her.

Before she left for home, Sherry took her into Bip's den at the top of the house and showed her a sketchbook filled with images of herself. They were recognisably 'Nancy Chalmers'. In each of them she was appropriately oblivious that she was an object of study, and just as natural as her cute flirtatiousness with Green had allowed her to be.

The Delta Hayden business still gravely disquieted her. But that hadn't been her only misreading. She had supposed Bip to be a dreamer, and somehow not as capable of feeling as she and the others were. The sketches' attention to detail, quite unlike his swirling landscapes, it was that which now alarmed her. He knew the appearance of her like a mirror, down to the little gestures of her mouth and eyes which she used to solicit his brother's attention.

There and then she asked Sherry who this Delta Hayden girl was, from Crag Bay, and Sherry answered with more knowledge than enthusiasm. She was caught again in a conspiracy of innuendo, the web of a past spun as neatly and tautly as spidersilk threads. She was excluded from what had seemed so desirable to her, a density of reference she had thought would be a comfortable cushion, a means of showing off her own novelty by comparison. But the world was organised into tribes, and they were each of them true to their own lore and language.

They would become like a dream to her, those fifteen months: except that dreams felt more real to her than her memories of living like that. She would forget how desperate she must have been to begin it, asking herself only how *had* she begun, embarking on such an unlikely and far-fetched enterprise?

It was Nicol whom she had told most about Amersham. He was furthest from it in time, so she thought that she could take the risk. She wanted *somebody* to be made aware that she'd had a different life, with unexpected expectations, and Nicol was the most sympathetic listener in the family.

She tried to be exact and literal, and she guessed that she mostly was. She sensed that she was also invoking a spell, defying the past to stay there in place, steadfast and perennial, unyielding to change as to misapprehension. She repeated herself, many times, but familiarisation was part of the process, an indispensable element of this as of all ritual.

Moyna

Away back, back at the beginning, when she couldn't be sure that Jamie was going to ask her to marry him after all.

She had been waiting for her moment, and now she knew that it had come. For days she had been planning what to say. Suddenly the words were spirited into the ether.

Jamie laughed to see her watching him so intently.

'Trick or treat?'

'What?'

'I thought –' He clasped his hands to his face. 'I thought I must be wearing a hallowe'en mask.'

'Oh no,' she said, not as lightly as she should have done.

He laughed again, good-humouredly.

'I don't get it, Moyna.'

She attempted a smile. It didn't really work.

'Well...' She swallowed a deep breath. 'Something... something's kind of happened...'

'Yes?'

She stared at him.

'What, Moyna? What's happened?'

She tried to remember how she'd arranged the words, but she had forgotten. What did they say in films, on television? All those times she'd watched and listened and now she couldn't even –

'About what, Moyna?'

She stuck a grin on her face, but it was hopeless.

'Oh...' She shrugged. 'Well, actually...'

'There's something you want to tell me?'

'I...' She nodded. Then she realised she'd let the grin go. Too late now. She couldn't retreat from where she'd got to.

So she told him, haltingly, and in no very sequential fashion. About going to see her doctor. ('The woman doctor I mentioned to you, remember? Dr Strachan?') For an examination, a going-over. No, not just a general one. (He had asked the question, as if he had a premonition –) An internal examination. Down—She pointed where.

'I see.'

It took her another few moments to find her verbal bearings again.

'I had a feeling –' she began.

'A pain, you mean?'

'Oh no. Nothing like that. Well, not a pain, no. But a feeling. Something physical *and* in my head.' She tried tweaking out the smile, but it refused to come. 'An instinct, I suppose.'

'What about?'

His eyes fixed on her. Oh God's teeth, she thought, it's something else he's imagining. Ulcerous, cancerous.

'She's always been very good,' she explained. 'She's got ESP about some things.'

'That's what you said the last time.'

'So... she took it all very... calmly.'

Why should she be so terrified? And why should she be so bo-peep now? She had been as close to Jamie – in that intimate way – as to anyone in the world.

Her eyes looked past him, to the turquoise of sea. White spray. A bluey blue sky, lapis lazuli, and a perfect and unadulterated horizon.

'She – she told me . . . that I'm pregnant.'

A few seconds later her face squeezed out a smile. She wanted to smile wider, grin, seeing his face so shocked, paralysed of any movement at all.

'Seven weeks,' she said. 'I wasn't counting, though.'

His face remained rigid.

'But she worked it out. From what I told her. I just let her know everything.'

She struggled to keep smiling, even though the sudden deep lines creasing his forehead were alarming her. Wavy warning lines.

'She's so good to tell, you see. So underst . . .'

The words expired on her tongue. She felt her mouth underneath it quite parched. Momentarily she experienced a surge of anger. But it abated, evaporated, leaving her as before, uncertain and forgetful. What to do now, which were the words that came next?

Mrs Meldrum

Lindsay wouldn't speak to her when she got back. Never mind.

Returning to school at Boat of Weem she was conscious that she brought a measure of glamour with her – and a slight twist in her accent.

She was generally welcomed back into the fold, although a couple of the mistresses who didn't teach her had a way of speaking out of the corners of their mouths when they passed her in the corridor.

She had developed some interesting spins and a deep penetration in her tennis game, and – precociously – ended up captaining the school team notwithstanding that it was only her second term of belonging to it. She might belatedly have become a Hearty, but tennis was her single team sport, which she kept up for the sake of Green, who occasionally wrote to her and helped to sustain in his letters (which made no mention of Delta Hayden) the memories of those warm Amersham afternoons turning golden in her recollection.

Otherwise she settled back into the old Laureldene ways, with Rosalind and Fiona and their new protégée Marcia Ralston, and of course with her Jewish friend Naomi, whose dusky complexion and Baltic connections were still exotic to her, even after America, but whose longer silences and troubled eyes intrigued her, to know how to shake her out of such a curious new inwardness.

After having been so close to the Cauldwells, she couldn't account for her finally losing touch with them.

They had communicated until she sent them news of her engagement.

Then the letters became intermittent. She married Ming, and sent Sherry her first Christmas card as 'Nancy Meldrum'.

A card came for her, but her new surname was spelt incorrectly on the envelope, and somehow that was like a premonition to her. There was another card the following Christmas, but it was to be the last. She wrote to Eighty-Seventh Street. The letter was redirected back unopened. When she sent it again, in a fresh envelope to Amersham, she hoped for better luck.

She waited patiently. No reply came back. Then she got rather out of the habit of expecting to hear. She knew that Green was down in the south, Louisiana way, and Bip out somewhere near the Rockies, so she assumed that Sherry must have been leaf-blown too but had forgotten to notify her of a change of address. Or perhaps one or other parent was unwell, or finances were straitened, and they'd all had to take to a different manner of life elsewhere?

She could only connect them with Amersham and Eighty-Seventh Street, though, and sometimes she had to remind herself that all that was history: the only history that had stuck in her mind after her expensive and inadequate education on the west side of the Park, corner of Columbus.

Struan

Then at some point, with his mind not on the words he was speaking, he referred to Cat as 'Kirsty'.

Ailsa wrinkled the end of her nose, and her brow furrowed.

'Don't you mean Cat?'

'What?'

'Cat. You said Kirsty.'

'Did I? Hell—'

Ailsa smiled, in a dry way. He shrugged. She looked past him, but he could tell that she was thinking of the mistake.

Several times since he'd got here he had thought he was seeing Kirsty. On the rocks. Sitting in the long grass on top of a dune. Looking out of this or that bedroom window.

To begin with, she had been one of the beach set. Most summers, from the age of ten or eleven, she had come to Achnavaig with her family when his holiday and hers happened to overlap. A rumbustious relationship had changed to a more respectful and then, finally, tender one. There had always been an element of parry and thrust between them, which they couldn't have done anything about, but they had got to know what liberties they could take with one another. Marriage had thrown them, having to play by different rules and needing to be adultly responsible, and it was only when there had been an end in sight to it that – he felt – they were able to resume the friendship he was starting to remember with some fondness.

By contrast his relationship with Cat was very recent. It dated from just after his break-up with Kirsty, from the night of a party to which they had both been lured by well-meaning friends. (Very well, he'd decided, I'll do what you don't really expect me to do, I'll walk straight towards this trap you've all sprung for me . . .)

Ailsa

She smiled at Struan's mistake, in a dry way. She wasn't disapproving, if that's what he thought. Presumably he didn't know that she'd kept up with Kirsty since the divorce. She knew more about Kirsty's present life than he did. From midway through the marriage she had been on Kirsty's side. It *was* a contest, a skirmish, even a little war. She had only started to comprehend Kirsty after she'd let her independent spirit show.

She could identify with that.

Good luck to her, even if it'd been the marriage that had to suffer. At least the two of them had known not to make it an imprisonment.

Good luck to both of them, but especially to Kirsty, who had still more fortitude to find from somewhere. Struan would never be quite sure of what he was about, but maybe his pickle – now, for instance, his fancy that he could reconstruct something of the past with Cat, as a kind of business partnership this time – maybe that would keep him (just) on the side of all the bravely smiling optimists.

Lewis

The telephone had been ringing outside in the hall. Mrs McKay put her head round the corner of the door. His mother pointed to herself, but Mrs McKay shook her head and nodded over to him.

He immediately felt his skeleton stiffen.

'For me?' he asked Mrs McKay in the hope that he was mistaken. They had left Dominique in the house, so it could only be an emergency: an act of God, or an accident she'd had entertaining one of the boyfriends whose existence she so stridently denied.

He walked out to the telephone and picked up the receiver. The stiffness was settling into his bones, into the marrow. He hesitated for a second or two, listening down the line for a clue.

'Hello?'

'Mr Meldrum?'

Instantly his stomach started collapsing in on itself.

'Is Mr Lewis Meldrum there?'

'Speaking –'

'Is that you?'

'Ye-e-es. That's right,' he said, trying to win himself another few seconds' reprieve, to think how he could treat this intrusion. How far could he allow himself to object? 'This is Meldrum speaking.'

'McAleese here.'

'Yes?'

'Surprise, surprise.'

He didn't reply. Couldn't think –

'Quite a game of hide and seek I've had.'

A little silence came ricocheting after the words. He listened, to discern some sort of menace concealed in them.

'I – I'll be back tomorrow,' he told his caller.

'Sorry. I'm seeing folk in Birmingham tomorrow. So I thought I'd track you down before I go.'

It was a coarse voice affecting some refinement. His wife was supposed to be a cut above him. The man's money would have helped to salvage her conscience about demeaning herself.

'I find this getting about a bit of a shag, don't you?'

Maybe he really was trying to be – what? – matey.

It occurred to him that someone could be listening in on a party line elsewhere in the house. He looked behind him, too late, to see if the dining-room appeared depleted. Or one of the children perhaps –

'Just wanted to have some more of your' – there was a momentary pause – 'expert legal advice, Mr Meldrum.'

No doubt he did. But he was perfectly able to let a note of facetiousness intrude too. He could afford to, God knew.

McAleese's original timing might only have been accidental, but it had been easy to discern a pattern of opportunity in events, as if fate was taking a hand. He had just completed his examination of his father's finances – that is, if there had been a proper end to the complexities of ineptitude and evasion – and his morale was at its lowest ebb. His mother was clearly dissatisfied with her new life in the flat. For some reason his thoughts kept returning to The Broch and, particularly, to his teenage years there – now the favourite period of his life – when he had become much more receptive to his surroundings.

A colleague had put McAleese on to him. Rather than coming to see him, the man had taken him out for an expensive lunch, out of town for discretion's sake, to explain the predicament he was in with the authorities. It was a complicated story, concerning two sets of development grants and the construction of a couple of factories in Grampian parts, disputed export licences and the alleged but undeniable 'inefficiency' (which was to prove a euphemism) of book-keeping methods in McAleese's several companies. He had sensed straightaway that the bloke was a crook, but quite a charming one. It was oddly flattering to see how McAleese was studying him as a man of refinement and good taste, and – when they met for a second lunch – remembering so much from last time, verbatim, with unerring recall.

McAleese wanted to be represented in court, through his own offices. He ought to have known better of course than to take him on. But McAleese dropped several hints that he would be handsomely rewarded if he could pull out all the stops and have the several charges dropped. Under informal questioning he proved vague on a good many points, and didn't conceal the fact of his concealment from him, leaving him free to draw his own conclusions. (At the back of his mind all the while, he was reliving those long summers of his earlier, unshadowed teenage years in the welcome shelter of the bay's crook and The Broch's garden, which had conjured up a whole alternative world to their imaginations – Outback, Spanish Main, Wild West, Monza, the Moon . . .)

He didn't expect to, but he won his case, by a combination of his persuasive skills and a certain unanticipated reluctance on the prosecutor's part to engage. McAleese was as good as his word – on this occasion – and expressed voluble thanks, via an assortment of shares and bonds transactions which he was able to redeem through a mutual contact in the Glasgow Stock Exchange.

He had mentally shut off from that portion of the business, just as he had tried to disregard McAleese's equivocation on matters that ought to have been established beyond all doubt. It was sailing very close to the wind, and may have become something more serious than that, but he was vastly tired, stressed out, still reeling from the disclosure of his father's debts and unable to decide what to do with his mother – in every sense, his poor mother.

No bargain could be so straightforward, though, and he found he had McAleese hanging on to his coat-tails, foraging for 'advice' he considered himself entitled to without further remuneration offered. He attempted to oblige, but taking care to decline any more lunch or dinner invitations, and finding sound reasons why he wasn't in a position to propose him for membership of the New Club and Muirfield. Sometimes the amateurishly refined accent slipped, and he was left listening to a man from longer ago and (socially) much further away, and that fissure of credibility caused him to panic. True breeding would have saved him from the prospect he now imagined and dreamed about in his sleep, a show of gross bad manners, a shower of guttural invective directed from the back of a metallic silver 600 SEL Mercedes – McAleese could still repeat conversations of six months and a year ago, as if he had committed them to memory on the spot or (a more intensely alarming possibility) as if he had reacquainted himself with the contents of concealed micro-tapes which had recorded all their exchanges since the very first.

Voices were reaching him from the drawing-room. He heard Greta's forced laughter, and Nicol's more placid sort. He looked back, wishing he was there with them: where he belonged, with his own tribe, and not speaking to someone like McAleese whom he could so little predict. A renegade, a social gaucho. But in the next instant he reminded himself that they were only here in this house courtesy of a rogue business man none of the others had met, who had travelled his own Outback and Wild West, from a Dundee council estate to three primped acres in the holy of Edinburgh holies, Morningside.

'Maybe,' he heard himself say, 'it would be better if we got together.'

He hadn't yet caught the drift of McAleese's enquiry.

'Time's my problem, Mr Meldrum.'

'For both of us, I think.'

'I'm not interrupting you?'

The negative said it all.

'I *am* a little tied up at the moment.'

It came out sounding like a bishop-to-the-actress remark, but McAleese wasn't tempted to make a joke about it.

'Tuesday then? Don't think I can make lunch.'

'A drink, Mr McAleese? The Horse Shoe, say?'

'Don't want us to be overheard.'

'I see.'

'You'll be in Glasgow, will you?'

'Yes,' he lied. 'Yes, I–'

'Could you drive through for coffee? Tuesday morning? The Sheraton, eleven. No, make that eleven fifteen. They'll keep a quiet table for me.'

He listened to himself agreeing. He forgot what he had on in the Edinburgh office – his 'chambers', as he had never learned to call them but which Greta did – for Tuesday morning. Whatever it was would simply have to be put off, no two ways about it.

'Eleven fifteen,' he repeated.

A few pleasantries followed. Equally false on both sides, he was sure. Then he was able to replace the receiver.

He felt his skeleton was being squashed down inside his skin. He was a sagging sack of bones. His knees were shaking. He leaned against the wall for support, and felt an obscure twist of pain in the lining of his stomach. An ulcer, that was all he needed: although he didn't know how he had survived from his schooldays without one.

'Lewis –'

245

His head spun round on his neck, and a joint cracked loudly.
'Greta?'
'Who else?'
'I –'
'Is everything all right?'
'What? Yes. Yes, fine.'
'Who was that?'
'Just – just something to do with work.'
'Ringing *here*?'
'Dominique must have given them the number.'

Greta delayed, tellingly, before nodding. She didn't usually enquire about his work – except to discover something about the social arrangements of his colleagues.

Why this show of concern? Did she suspect he'd been talking to the ersatz New-Tory voice she had once lifted the phone to in the house? She turned away, but just to examine her reflection in the wall mirror behind her. A hand went up to her hair, how his mother's used to: the same gesture in the same mirror, where she would stand waiting to receive those colleagues and acquaintances of her husband who were now and then entertained in the house. Again he was caught on time's loop, with its grip as vicious as a strangler's noose.

Mrs Meldrum

Mostly she had forgotten about Delta Hayden. She registered in her memories of tennis afternoons as only a shadow among shadows, in the far and dim background, as an audience for her own skills taught to her by Green.

She meantime has become impossibly athletic and inspired, and plays like Mo Connolly, or like a Helen Wills Moody from the baseline. Thwack! Plung! She races to the net and smashes and volleys and puts away like Alice Marble at her peak. She covers the court as if she has six pairs of limbs; there is nowhere she cannot be in an instant. She is at her gilded best during these games, and least like the person she either turned into or – in all probability – always was. She is caught in the glow of the others, of Green especially. He made her feel like a dancer, all lightness and grace. He is inseparable from the sensation which she has, accurately or not, retained. She is vastly grateful, and hoards the experience like the secret treasure she needs it to be.

Ailsa

'I was talking to George Lightfoot the other day,' Jamie said.
   That name.

The Broch

She opened her eyes and looked up from the terrace wall. She had realised he was hovering about, while Moyna was upstairs checking on the children.

She stared at him.

Was he drunk?

She didn't speak.

'We – we know one another. George and I. We go back a while. To . . . oh . . .'

She shrugged, pretending casualness.

She still didn't say anything. Couldn't think what to say. Was he bluffing? Or could he be meaning nothing at all?

But she noticed his eyes were sliding off her, down to the crazy paving under the wall. He knew. He *knew*.

She felt her heart was up in her throat. She opened her mouth, suddenly remembering that she needed air to breathe. She lifted her hand to cover her eyes. She thought his eyes passed over her breasts before looking away, towards the shore.

Of course. Her breasts had never fed, had never been unbuttoned in maternity rooms and in quiet corners of motorway service-station car parks, to do as nature intended. That was poor Moyna's lot.

Of course.

She closed her eyes. Her breath was crammed inside her chest. Her heart continued to palpitate wildly somewhere it shouldn't be.

'Nice chap, George. Big in obstetrics. Very good workman.'

She sat without speaking. He wouldn't force her to, however hard he tried.

'Very discreet too. Just about the best.'

At the prices he charged, he bloody well ought to have been. (They were a company of rogues.) Momentarily the thought distracted her, then she recalled her predicament.

Was he guessing? Or had Lightfoot spoken to him, supposing the name Meldrum meant nothing to him and that the disclosure was bound to go no further?

What the hell was all this about?

She got up from the wall. Stretched. Walked off. She wouldn't look at Jamie, but she was aware that his eyes were on her, following her at every point. She wasn't going to give him a chance, not a goddamn chance.

She lit a cigarette, although he disapproved, and let the smoke drift in his direction. He probably saw through that, the ruse and the cloudlet. He probably understood why she was even finding something to say to Nicol. So long as she could stick it out until they left.

Greta

She pressed the lipstick into the flesh of her lips.

Her solution to all her lapses of confidence was to open her portable suede and leather vanity box (Loewe of Madrid, by way of Bond Street).

In the end it was what she couldn't forgive Lewis's mother for, that she had looks which weren't better served by cosmetics, because they didn't need them.

It sometimes seemed to her that unfairness was the basic premise of life.

Mrs Meldrum

Ming, with his slight clumsiness and his shy straining after elegance, proved quite different from Green Cauldwell. She must have understood that subliminally, but at the time she was more struck with certain explicit similarities to Sherry's brother. He hadn't Green's throwaway confidence, or his ill-defined ambition either, but he was about the same height, agreeable-looking, had good teeth and soft down on the backs of his hands, was the best tennis player Achnavaig and the locale had to offer, and he let her see how everything about her at that interim fascinated him.

When he spoke, she started to lose the recollection of Green's accent, so she would encourage him to talk on, flattering her with his absurdities – and it did occur to her whether in fact she was the first girl he had said these things to. He was throwing himself into the business, and she had some instinct that he was doing it for a reason, and not just because he was afraid that she might slip away from him. Did *he*, as well as she, have a ghost at his shoulder? Sometimes she thought she caught a more desperate ring in his voice, as if he couldn't be certain that words alone would be enough to hold her.

All that talk between them, concerning the surfaces of their lives, and still – really – neither he nor she knew the first and essential things about one another. Not that she understood the oversight then, when it was important that she should have done.

They passed beyond their demure words and amiable letters, until on one of his visits to the farm they reached the Point of No Return. It happened too quickly, and messily, and in the minutes afterwards her mind ventured far away, across an ocean, high above tiny steaming liners, to alight on a corner of a New England field where a boy and a girl are sitting under a tree, a yellow locust tree, waiting for something else to happen, something that will be mysterious and harmonising.

For the moment, however, the deed is disposed of. Ming doesn't tell her that he loves her, but he is gentle none the less. When he looks at her she recognises that his gaze, even with no others to see them in the byre loft, is proprietorial. Nobody is going to take her away from him now.

Ailsa

When Moyna phoned, only doing Jamie's bidding, she would find she wasn't available for any future Sunday brunches in Putney she might be invited to. She might discover Jamie waiting for her outside the office building but she would conspicuously fail to notice him and brush past. She would twig that he was tailing her home in his car, parking opposite Belsize Underground station, but she would carry on not quite regardless and maybe hit on a route home by back lanes where a car couldn't pass. The telephone would ring, later at night, but she would have the answerphone switched on and – since Moyna always issued the Sunday invitations – he wouldn't dare to speak after the buzzer tone.

She foresaw in those seconds just how it would be. The Celts' third eye and all that. Jesus, she'd drunk too much of that strong coffee.

She blew out more smoke, a little meandering blue fog of it, to give her just some brief cover. She sighed at the predictability of even allegedly brainy men.

Nicol

An Old Boy who came to distribute the prizes at school one year turned out to be not such an *Old* Boy after all, and was introduced as a Professor of French at Princeton University.

It was his second last year at school. As a prize-winner he was introduced to the man at a tea-party afterwards. He found Professor Henshaw friendly: but he became aware as they chatted that there might be a little more to it than that. Before they spoke he had been conscious of the professor's eyes turning to his corner of the room. The eyes had caught him out, and he'd felt his neck heating inside his tight collar. The professor was good-looking, he couldn't help noticing, and very much so as Old Boys went. When they got talking he had a pleasantly soft voice, its polite Scottish vowels overlaid by American inflections. At the prize-giving ceremony the headmaster had announced that Professor Henshaw was donating a generous sum towards the future tuition fees of a pupil from the school at an American university, and that it was hoped several boys might benefit over the next ten or a dozen years or longer. The man gained a definite allure from such an association of money and privilege, and it was inevitable that others should also be drawn to that spot in the headmaster's sitting-room. Yet none of them was being singled out for the attention that he was.

Next term a Princeton prospectus arrived for him at the school, accompanied by a three-page letter handwritten on Princeton faculty notepaper and signed 'With my best wishes, Howard Henshaw'. The writer apologised for his forwardness, but suggested he might be interested in perusing the contents of the booklet. The rest of the letter was very chatty, and talked about a vacation spent at Key West, and a summer school he'd taken at Williamsburg. No mention was made of a Mrs Henshaw. Rather, it was always a 'friend' – male – whom he'd looked up in Greensboro or who'd invited him to have lunch down on the Jersey Shore or had him to stay out in Roanoke Rapids.

He was delighted to receive the letter and its enclosure. No one else in the school had been contacted, he discovered, and he was twice as intrigued. He had a congenial memory of the man in his navy cashmere jacket and soft flannels and tasselled black loafers, with his lean good-natured tanned face, the evenly grey hair – a thoroughly well-cared-for look altogether.

Princeton seeded itself in his mind, from the (to him) picturesque particulars photographed in the handbook. He heard the sales spiel spoken (not quite aloud) in Howard Henshaw's confidential tone of voice, in his sophisticated international vowels. The man was esteemed a great success, and in turn he was very flattered by his declaration of a professional concern. Additionally, though, he found himself entertaining other mental pictures of the man, which had much less to do with his status at the university: as he saw him on vacation at Key West, in sports wear, or lying in front of a log fire in the chilly Virginia night talking softly, softly to another of the 'friends' he conjured up, unexceptionally young and suntanned, lithe of limb and with good muscle definition.

He got into Princeton, to major in English. Maybe a few strings were pulled, but he never found out for sure. Some of his classmates at school thought he was getting a little above himself, and sounded sneery. He couldn't understand their snideness, or didn't want to understand it.

'Aitch' – as they both decided he should be called – made a contribution towards his fees, although he had more worries initially about the likely bills for board and lodging. But in that respect also Aitch was to prove helpful, arranging that he stay with the widow of a colleague who principally wanted the company, someone to house-sit when she went off visiting relatives. Once installed, it wasn't long before Aitch was invited by Mrs Friedriksen for lunch or dinner, and he made no attempt to avert his eyes from his hostess's lodger. When Mrs Friedriksen had gone south, to Charleston, Aitch invited himself round.

The two of them ended up on the floor in front of the electric fire in his room, and then on top of the narrow single bed.

Once a French boy at Achnavaig had sort of led him on, but this was his first time at going all the way, and not a great surprise. Practically it was a little sticky, and a shade disappointing technically. Aitch seemed obsessed by him and now he was less flattered than puzzled. The polished accent slipped, twenty years of American living was peeled away. Embarrassingly the man spoke of all they had in common, places (he confused their names), interests (he was guessing), even a Scottish education (truer, but these things change as well). He found him looking deep into his eyes, then he was fingering his face, his neck, his shoulders, but backing off a little as if he were touching marble. His mentor seemed afraid that he was losing somebody he had supposed he was recognising – himself, maybe. Meanwhile he was trying to keep his own head as empty of thoughts as he could, scared of recognising the implications of the situation, for the recent history that had brought him here and for his future at Princeton.

The affair cooled off inevitably. It would have proved too exhausting if it hadn't.

They settled not for routine but for haphazardly occasional couplings. Some sessions worked better than others. He managed to be not always available, in order – paradoxically – that he shouldn't disappoint and also to make himself *worth* waiting for. He was correct in his surmises, and he felt he was being appreciated better because of the ploy.

It wasn't in his nature to hold grudges, so he accepted that the past could not be changed, and that the future must be made as simple and reproach-free as possible. Every knot that started to develop he patiently unworked. Maybe Aitch was really needing someone less considerate if not more available, he couldn't be sure.

Finally, but only much later, he saw that the relationship was an entrée. It marked his introduction to the meticulous imponderables of something that wasn't quite love, full of careful and determined imbalances and a generous abundance of makeweight concessions.

Moyna

Maybe, though, she couldn't have done anything else. But that was a hypothesis.

'Could you help me finish the coffee, Moyna?'
'Thanks, Mum, I think so –'
Their bright smiles were instant: unlike the coffee.
She felt her mouth a little sore with smiling. The muscles were on overtime. But it was only until tomorrow.

She put the cup to her lips and sipped. It was good coffee, but – she remembered – Mrs McKay was responsible, not her mother. She couldn't be Mrs Perfect all the time.

Hmmm.

Maybe, though...
Where was she?
Ah...

She had told Jamie she was pregnant. That first year of knowing him. And if she hadn't, they might just have drifted apart without the mutual will to keep together. Or long enough to contemplate getting married.

Unlike Lewis and Struan she didn't have an engagement: there wasn't time for that. A medical student should have been the last type to get a girl pregnant, but she hadn't been completely certain that he was the one to blame. She had always liked to have two boyfriends in play at any one time, something Ailsa had disapproved of and which she may have done more to spite her than to pacify herself.

There had never been a period of her life until then when her mother didn't intimidate her. She had grown jealous of her being so necessary to everyone, more so than their father. The birth of a child seemed to reduce the threat offered by her mother. She felt that her second child was a further indicator to her mother, I can do this too, I can teach myself to do it every bit as well as you.

The children took up all her life. She gave herself – not quite willingly, but entirely – and had hardly a moment free to think about herself. She was aware, vaguely, that Jamie found he was under pressure to provide for them, and that some of his fine hopes for his work had slipped. But she could believe that that was just 'what happened' to adults under their altered circumstances, so she didn't fret needlessly about his lost opportunities. After all, they were better off, and he had his faithful hypochondriacs in his smart new practice, and his BMW-driving colleagues included them on their social circuit, so what had he really forfeited?

She didn't hide behind her children, not altogether. They weren't under an imposition to shine. She wanted them to be happy, or as nearly so as they could manage. Certainly, by having so many she was hedging her bets. By the law of averages there would be a pushy one in the hatch, and at least a couple of quite contented plodders at life. Success should be what *they* wanted it to be, not she or Jamie. The parameters were to be of their sole choosing, with just a little essential direction-providing as part of the inclusive parental service. That, to her, sounded not at all a bad revenge on her own past, with its evergreen familial fictions: her father's dependability (why did he have to go and die on them?) her mother's motherliness, the siblings' talent, the God-given right signified by The Broch.

Nicol

After Princeton doors had opened. All he had needed to do was be himself, which was a revelation.

Persuasiveness seemed in-built, but it was an unconscious talent. Some of his interviewers were men of his own sort, some weren't: he couldn't make more of it than that. Women too recommended him wholeheartedly in their references.

Certainly he knew in particular circumstances, walking into a room, just how the table spun. It pleased him that he barely needed to sell himself sometimes, and his guilt was less than he feared. If anyone declared an extra-curricular interest after he had gone to work for him or with him, then shit, play life just (pun wholly intended) just as it lays.

Mrs Meldrum

Whatever her own existence had amounted to, she had been the conduit of life between long-dead people she had never known and her own children and *their* families. She belonged to a cycle of being, and that had been her purpose. It was why she sympathised with Nicol so much, because he had been the exception to prove the rule of normal instinct.

She had acquired her character through the accidental combinations of others, and had passed it on – tempered by Ming's – to the two generations beyond her own.

Now she was disturbed to think of the sort of planet they would inherit. But she recognised that she was as responsible as anyone else for turning her hand towards making it a better one than it presently was. At school they had for ever been reminded it was their 'due' to give back, to add to the world for others' sake and not to take, to subtract for their selfish own. Even if such advice could only have been offered to them from an attitude of complacent overview, its message wasn't lost to her half a century later.

For years, until only last summer, she had been in the habit of reminiscing about her schooldays with Rosalind and Fiona. Once every four or five weeks they had met in Glasgow for coffee. Latterly they had frequented a patisserie in the Princes Square shopping mall. The atmosphere had alarmed her a little: the turn-of-the-century Viennese décor with luxuriant swirls of tracery ironwork, the echoing hush, the tumbling greenery and plashing from a fountain somewhere, the constant vigilance of the security guards with their walkie-talkies, the shoppers' concentration on enjoying the experience, the determined politenesses, the awful narcissism of the young with their eyes turned to every reflecting shop window.

The proceedings never varied, from one visit to the next. The trio sat on a mosaic terrace, under the escalators, and inevitably – after filling the others in with private news – they returned to the inexhaustible subject of the past. Years after the events their own laughter went wafting upwards, to be caught in the queer muffled musliny net that voices and movements became in the place. That had the effect of compressing them further into themselves, into the saga of the past which they shared. Although to an untrained eye quite different (if, however, of an age), she had still been able to spot the little tell-tale mannerisms that were common to all three of them: the elongated vowels and rolled r's, the tidy manners of hands and feet, even the preference for shades not too far removed from the olive and navy combination of their school uniform – and also the slight lean-to forward stoop they had developed since meeting as if they were conspiring cabalists, and the trick they had of picking up the thread of one another's thoughts and continuing to wind back and back.

As Rosalind and Fiona did, she valued – *had* valued, until last summer – these get-togethers, like beads looped on to a string of days. She felt that the continuity was a very comfortable constriction. It was something to be admitted to and accepted as a limited but required element of 'self'. It wasn't to be despised as it had been by those girls who had married so ambitiously or else shrugged off in the way she had witnessed several times over the years when someone she recognised from school – usually encountered in Edinburgh – nippily switched her eager eyes away and concerned herself with the display in a shop window, with what the weather was doing in the sky, with what a chattering child or wilful teenager or taciturn husband might be meaning to communicate.

Ailsa

From behind, Jamie's hand alights on her breast. It fits over quite surely, as if he has always known how this will feel.

She leans against the wall, side-on. She closes her eyes. His fingers knead the breast through the cotton, but very gently. His fingers are so dextrous, utterly professional, she might only be his patient. Even when the pads of his fingers pass across the nipples.

She concentrates on her breathing. Taking deep and regular swallows.

His breath is hot on the back of her neck. She feels the lightest, tenderest contact against her skin on the nape. His lips. Then the tip of his nose. She has never suspected him capable of such sensitivity.

She doesn't move. She concentrates on not moving, not a single inch. She feels, briefly, endlessly prodigal and benevolent: giving away so much to him like bountiful charity.

The feeling leaves her with a fuddled head.

She leans against the corridor window. The children are asleep in another part of the house. Thank God – for once – the place is the size it is. She glimpses falling darkness between her eyelids, across the bay. She opens her eyes slowly. Everything she sees is utterly familiar to her but without any precise meaning to her now. There's a glaze of unreality over it all. It moves in and out of focus.

PART THREE

Nicol

The others have drifted off, but Mother and I sit on. I have the cover of the purple half-light, and stare at her.

She has always had time for me as she hasn't had for the others. We don't say much, or we don't need to. I've always presumed that there is a special bond of sympathy between us. But maybe what it has been all along is her remorse – about the aspects of my private life which I don't discuss with her – and thinking she has to make me some atonement. Five children was chancing her luck, that they would all turn out to be holding a full deck of cards.

She doesn't want me to tell her about my going to Amersham, so I won't. It's too long ago for her to revisit, and it's too fixed and complete in her head to be changed. She asks for the silence instead, and that's easy enough to give. I imply I only drove through the town anyway.

In our creaking chairs we both settle to watch the sea. That, at least, is the pretext. Everything that's done here is a pretext for something else.

If she is afraid, I don't blame her. She has much more to lose from knowing than she could ever gain.

Her face takes on that mask-like opaqueness I've watched it revert to all my life, from a time even before I knew what it was.

Struan

If Lewis had come into the firm, he would probably have turned it around and saved it. He would also have put *him* into the shade, so in the end he couldn't regret that Lewis had gone off and made a different life for himself. Events had worked out finally to Lewis's benefit and his own. The pity was the human cost – the scandal of their father's sacrifice.

Mrs Meldrum

On television in The Broch one evening she had watched a news item about the population who live underneath New York City, in a vast network of vaulted tunnels built for railroads that were never laid. Drop-outs, thieves, junkies, winos, but also delivery men, mail men, lift operators, even office clerks and store assistants. There is only occasional daylight, filtered down from miles above, and many stretches are in complete darkness. Here and there, apparently, the stench is foul.

Did that underworld exist when she was a Manhattanite and blithely walking the sidewalks above it? The sights on the screen had – curiously, at this remove of forty-five years – undermined her memories of that time.

The elegant trees on Park Avenue South like flaming torchères in fall. Car headlights in sleety streets on winter afternoons. The florists' brilliantly yellow daffodils set about the St Regis terrace for an Easter Bonnet party. The crazy heat of summer with the tarmacadam buckling and, in their rich and safe enclave, the propellers of the ventilator fans mesmerically turning, stuttering on apartment ceilings.

She felt she was trapped in her mind – stuck fast – between what she had seen and what she hadn't, between the known and the unguessed, and both authentic in their equally exclusive fashion.

Ailsa

The point was that she was Moyna's sister. It was the only point, really.

She turned the old key in the lock of the door, and had to have several attempts before she heard the reassuring shudder of the mechanism.

For tonight at least she was safe.

She leaned back against the door. In her middle teens the key had gone missing, and remained lost for years. She had suspected that her mother had simply appropriated it, to deny her privacy. As a clumsy consequence she'd had to move furniture about, to block the door, whenever she was in urgent need of solitude.

Now lo and behold.

But it was going to take more than doors and locks. She was too tired after a long and very trying day to fix on the problem.

She caught sight of herself in the mirror on the other side of the room. The career woman! It was a joke, wasn't it? She smiled into the back of her hand. A silly charmless grin. Then she tried to wipe it off, but it wouldn't rub, wouldn't work loose at all.

It was her one achievement in life. A job and 'prospects'. Two hands gripping the ladder of promotion. The flat, the car, expenses, holidays.

It meant – didn't it? – that she had won out over her mother in the end.

Skill and adaptability, and ambition of course, had got her where she was.

Hunky dory, fine and dandy. And so far she hadn't had to forfeit anything she would have preferred to have instead.

That was the gospel about Ailsa Meldrum. According to Ailsa Meldrum. And then, on the other hand, there was George Lightfoot.

At the name's recall she watched the smile fade in the mirror glass. Slowly her face acquired another ten, fifteen years of experience, and it wasn't a pretty sight. She closed her eyes.

It would only necessitate a confidential word from Jamie in Moyna's ear, and Moyna in turn was bound to let it slip. Stupidly or maliciously, it would be impossible to say which. Moyna was, enduringly and stubbornly, unreadable.

She opened her eyes again. Blinked at the stranger in the mirror glass. Envisaged the mirror smashed and cracked.

And it would happen, certainly, it would come to pass *unless*...

Greta

'I think your mother's wandering. Lewis? Did you hear what –'
'Yes.'
'Well?'
'Very likely, I'd say.'
'Don't you care, Lewis?'
'Why shouldn't I care?'
'You don't sound as if you do.'
'She's all right. No financial worries. There's this house –'
'I wasn't talking about that.'
'No?'
'I'm sure your reaction is a very proper lawyer's one.'
'Good of you to say so.'

She heard him sigh. She rubbed harder at her cheek with the ball of cotton wool. In an instant she saw herself in twenty years' time, with the children gone and alone with Lewis. By then she would have forgotten what her justification had been in marrying even a Meldrum. They would have one another's company more than now, and with fewer topics to engage them than they had at present. But more frightening to her than that was the thought of what it would be like not having him here with her.

How on earth did his mother manage, surviving just by herself? It must be the most thankless and selfish calling, widowhood. In these moments she started to feel something peculiarly like sympathy for her condition, If it was family tradition that sustained her, truths which she cobbled together out of baser matter, the same mythology had magnetised her as a young woman.

They might be at their extremes, Nancy Meldrum and herself, but they were set on the same axis.

'What's amusing you now?'

She looked up at his question.

'I'm sorry – ?'

She waited, but he didn't repeat his question. She continued sitting in front of the dressing-table mirror watching him as he tidied up. She couldn't have had a more orderly husband. She started when she realised he was looking at her. She forgot momentarily that she didn't exist in that looking-glass world, and it was when she lowered her eyes that she saw the debris of cotton-wool fluff on the rug and realised she must have torn the dabs apart with the strength of her fingers.

Struan

He only discovered two days later that the meeting between Middleton and his father hadn't taken place. Middleton told him over the telephone.

'Why not? What happened?'

His caller said his secretary had been informed that something urgent had come up. He couldn't recall any urgency in the office within the past two or three days. Another appointment had been made apparently. Middleton hadn't taken any offence, no harm had been done.

But to himself it was puzzling. Very.

He chanced to overhear a call going out from the office to another client. His father's secretary was offering her apologies that Mr Meldrum would be unable to get away this afternoon, something urgent had occurred requiring his immediate attention. When he spoke to his father later that morning, no mention was made of any especially pressing business; his father looked quite unruffled, in positively buoyant spirits.

In the middle of the day they happened to leave the building at the same time. He was starting his car when he saw his father step into a taxi. Curiosity got the better of shame and he tailed the taxi.

It stopped right in the middle of town, but on Argyle Street, hardly Meldrum country. He watched his father get out, pay, and make off down Jamaica Street. Lunchtime pedestrians crowded the pavements. (Kirsty would have called the area 'louche'. 'Seedy' was the word that came into his own mind.)

He pulled into the kerb and stopped the car. He got out just in time to notice his father turn into a side street. He ran to the corner. His father's mackintosh allowed him to keep track of him. With his eyes he followed him to his journey's end, a doorway under a dirty torn awning.

The Broch

When he'd crossed Jamaica Street and walked the fifty or sixty yards to the door, he had a presentiment of what he would find. The attraction advertised was 'ADULT FARE'. The films' titles were listed behind grimy glass.

Frauleins of the Reeperbahn
To Sir With Lust
Sexy Smiles
Kinky Kapers
Oriental Spice
Six of the Best, Miss!
Stockholm Steambath
Monte Carlo and Bust
My Uncle Randy

As he stood outside several men singly passed through the plastic strip curtain of the doorway. They looked ordinary enough – a couple in suits, all of them shaved, no bad smells, none slobbering or slavering. Some of them did seem rather hunched, and it was a mild day for topcoats with deep pockets.

The crinkled photographs under the streaked glass were losing their colour. The top-heavy 'lovelies' were fading into their backgrounds of sauna pine and padded headboards. No nipples were on display, no pubic shadings: just the high thighs and dipping cleavages.

'WE GIVE YOU MORE'. the handwritten bills announced. And more cravenly, 'YOU'LL KEEP ON COMING!!'

A tramp was hovering close to him. A man's hand parted the plastic curtain and a thin foxy face was visible behind, eyes trained on them both. He looked away, up at the sky. The sun was directly overhead, between the sooty walls of the narrow street. The effect was suddenly – say – Neapolitan. Flies rotated round an open dustbin. A dog scratched itself, sniffing at a wall. Something unspeakable – a portion of an animal's interior, but also fur-topped – lay in the gutter. Decomposing potato chips were stuck in a drain. The sun observed, he could believe, with Latin *insensibilità, apatica*.

He walked back towards the car, taking his time about it. He buried his hands in his trouser pockets, then realised what he was doing, and took them out again. He felt – inexplicably – empty, without any emotion to carry him. He crossed the road, following a straight line. Already the location was quite familiar to him, he might have known it all his life. He stood by the car when he'd reached the pavement. He looked back the way he'd come, and in those weightless moments let the sun warm him with all that unseasonal Mediterranean unconcern.

Back in the office he didn't refer to what had happened, he had no idea how to. What could he have said? 'I just chanced to catch sight of you from Union Street . . .'

His father seemed as uncomplicatedly buoyant as he had beforehand. The surface of his day continued to be unruffled. He smiled dispassionately to one and all. The whites of his eyes were clean and unveined, as if he hadn't been sitting cramped in a hot darkened smoky room. But this afternoon the pupils were seeing nothing of what passed in front of them.

Mrs Meldrum

She'd had the broken walls in the garden rebuilt, patiently, by a man very careful about his craft, who advised her to use slate as well as stone.

She put the lawns and beds and pergolas into some kind of order, after the years of indiscriminate neglect. She had a screen of mixed trees planted.

She worked at it herself, alongside the gardener. Using a neighbour's collection of books on fruit husbandry for reference, she set about making the old orchard fertile again.

Some of the house's structural problems were attended to as well, although she supposed that the family wouldn't imagine that she had tried as hard as she had. It was an unending task. Lewis knew better what was entailed, because he saw the accounts, or those she chose to pass on at his persuasion.

Greta

She had always suspected that she couldn't have escaped Lewis, even if she'd tried to. She could picture him with a list of Scottish High Court judges, and details entered in his exact and regular script of their unmarried daughters – and that he'd been working his way through them, ticking them off one by one. At last he had reached her own name, under 'O' for 'Oliphant', and . . .

Girls of her sort had seldom ventured from the trodden path of rectitude. The virginal Lewis had been irreproachably down-the-line, to a fault. Happiness then as now was considered rather a plebeian fancy, according to the prevailing philosophy of his sort and hers. It was much more important not to sell yourself short. Happiness was unreliable, whereas material possessions remained a relatively stable commodity.

She'd had to be very adult, even at twenty-three years old, thinking by some primal instinct of her long-term consolations.

Ailsa

A cry. Running footsteps, a child's. The squeaking of a trolley's wheels. On carpet, not linoleum. All the deadening sounds of that place, which her money – but more importantly, the so-called 'privilege' (Lightfoot's term for it) – could buy. As if a sin smothered was a lesser sin.

But the voice wasn't silenced, nor the footsteps. However faint they were, she heard. She picked them up beneath conversation, beneath music, beneath sea swell, beneath breathing. She had bat sonar for them. That cry, which was always the same, a suppressed yelp. The little girl's footsteps running, either away from her – from this paranoia as she knew it to be – or towards her, to a myth of maternal love and protection.

Nicol

None of them could sleep. They weren't meant to be sleeping. It was only one night out of a lifetime.

All the times had come together, criss-crossing. There was a tension in the air: not to do with awkward anticipation, but with the simpler fact of an inevitability about everything. Here they all were, and whatever was bound to happen *would* happen.

And it wasn't the moment, he was doubly certain, to tell his mother about Amersham. He wasn't making it impossible that she might know eventually. Of course not. Now, however, was not that occasion.

Everything meanwhile hung together in the night, in the slow course of this exceptional night, but it cohered fragilely. The balance was precise, precarious, achieved with gossamer finesse. What right did he have to subvert this parlous harmony, and all for the sake of a cause so trifling and will-o'-the-wisp as truth-to-tell honesty?

Lewis

His father sat crumpled in the chair. He stood over him. He couldn't remember having ever seen him despondent. Preoccupied, yes. In the past, pride would have channelled any brief dejection into anger turned against others.

Now everything was different. After what Struan had told him, about the blue films and about the mess the company's books were in, he was experiencing feelings in himself he hadn't encountered before in his life. The occasion was a cue for pity, but he couldn't dredge up any to offer. He felt distaste, disgust even, welling up in him, from everything that made his own experience.

It was only fitting, that his father should have educated him to feel no sorrow for him. He had been brought up to imagine himself gifted, superior, as capable as ambition demanded, and also invulnerable. Invulnerability came through denial. (He had never been allowed to feel pity for himself, so he had no knowledge of it.) Appearances had been paramount to his father, which was why he now found himself despising this lamentable, unforgivable lack of form, the helpless forgetting of a principle.

He continued to stand over the man. Within the hold of the armchair, his father shrank further into himself. His shoulders – those famously developed swimming shoulders – drooped. His neck craned forward, suddenly exposed. If he'd chosen to, he could have encircled the gullet comfortably in the span of both his hands.

He put a hand to his forehead, melodramatically, where his father couldn't see. He couldn't believe this was happening. His own part in it alarmed him, it was drilling a hole in his stomach, his back was a ladder of pain. When he looked down again, his father was staring up at him. The man's eyes had lost their fear, now they were vacant and far removed. Then he really did want to strike him, to lash out at him with claws. He let his revulsion show, he didn't care. He let him see what he was thinking, that the whole business – the dirty films, the woman he was keeping, the company landed in Queer Street – it revolted him, all of it. And everything had come about like this just because Lewis Meldrum's father couldn't keep his prick inside his trousers –

All his own life he'd taken every precaution, he'd trodden on eggshells and nobody could have had a soupçon of suspicion. He narrowed his eyes with the concentration of disdain. He hated having the responsibility visited on him. His father should have been down on his knees before him. He was furious, and he was already bored and indifferent, sick of it all.

Then he remembered his mother. He thought of their name, the family. The firm; which was what it was all about, of course. The sodding firm.

His father lowered his eyes and turned his head away as if he could read his thoughts quite well. He hadn't meant to hide them from him, but he couldn't permit his own front to slip; his invulnerability shouldn't for a second be brought into question. He dug his hands deeper into his pockets, fixed his mouth, clenched his teeth behind his closed lips, began – without at first realising – grinding them together.

His father spoke. He missed what he said.

'What's that?'

'I – I wondered – how you saw –'

The words died away. His father's eyes slowly travelled his height – from his knees, his thighs, to the waistband of his trousers, his lapels, the tightness of knot in his tie. They were an actor's eyes, only feigning concern. Behind them was such a casual, lofty failure to get involved, to believe himself answerable, to be brought down to the humdrum and demeaning level of others. And, implied in it, there was such disdain of *him*, for being a man of small concerns after all.

'Christ Almighty!'

The eyes merely blinked at the words, spoken from on high.
'How in *Christ's* name –'
'I understand how you –'
'The hell you do.'
'Please, Lewis. We –'
'Don't tell me!'
'– we have to be adult about this.'
His hands grabbed the wings of the chair. On a reflex his father edged forward. The frame of the chair shook.
'*I'*ll do the talking.'
It was gangster-speak. Hollywood scripting.
'You've caused enough bloody damage –'
'I thought you'd be a calming influence,' his father spoke over him. 'You'd be able to put everything – into its right perspective.'
From above, in his own turn, a contemptuous sigh of exasperation rolled over the words. There seemed to be no end to this cycle of folly. He was furious that he'd allowed himself to speak as he had, exposing his feelings when his instincts warned him off. He saw how his fingers were bunched into fists, indenting the fabric of the chair's upholstery. His mother's choice of pattern –
His fists didn't unfold. There was a force in them that had nothing to do with his own intentions, which merely *was*. He stared at his hands, half in wonder at himself. He felt he was swelling with rancour, with the surfeit of gall that was inside him.

Nicol

It wasn't that he was becoming more conservative. But in his publishing work he did feel that the manuscripts he bought and edited should not add to the glut of cynicism and denigration, even barbarity, fed to the world in books. It seemed a much easier option for writers to reduce than to celebrate. He didn't mean that they should be complacent, or incurious: but they should use their gifts, he sincerely believed, for finer ends than most of them did.

It was a difficult and very unfashionable position to take. Maybe he would start to incur scepticism at editorial meetings, and his colleagues' impatience. He dreaded being thought smug. He knew that he wouldn't change his mind, though. He could only become more determined.

It was one thing to write about the passions, as Balzac and Simenon did. But he wasn't persuaded when sometimes very observant authors pitched lower, at depravity, and suggested that was the level at which the majority of men and women operated. His education had insisted on standards, on personal expectations of self. In that respect smugness *was* a risk, being holier-than-thou: yet even that was a lesser vice than the wholesale doing-down that he encountered every day in the manuscripts that were dropped from the post trolley on to his desk.

Lewis

He turned over, and the bed springs sang. The same arguments, rolling over and over again.

He was irritated that he had to carry this burden of knowledge. He was irritated that his mother retained that easy air, as if everything were right and well. He was irritated with himself, that he couldn't express himself to anyone. Greta wouldn't have been the person to confide in, because she required the romance of the Meldrums just as much as she had at the beginning: she was better able now to size them up than she'd been then, but in spite of her achieved knowledge she needed to believe no less than she had, so as not to prove herself deceived all those years ago.

Mrs Meldrum

She was only one woman, past her prime, and yet she knew that by creating purposeful thoughts and actions she was helping to change the world.

Until she left Glasgow she had helped out in a hospital shop two afternoons a week. Up here, in her new life, she had preserved a house from neglect, and she had caused walls to be rebuilt that would last a hundred years, and had begun to husband an orchard. The donation of fruit money, like that from the collections of old newspapers she made locally in the car, served a charitable end, in a remote hot country she would never see. She pickled and baked for bazaars at the church which she didn't attend, and potted small heathers in peat. She was going to have a couple of handicapped children to stay next Easter, a trial operation that would let her decide if she should continue. She assisted with transport (catalytically converted) whenever Cancer Research put on a musical evening at the Cally Hotel. She used only recycled paper and the truest green of household products, and was helping to organise a bottle-bank for their neck of the woods. She kept a worm bin to decompose kitchen waste. She kept abreast of the news on television and might watch a documentary, while bearing in mind that there are two sides (at least) to every story; but she had long ago given up on that pap diet of publicity-greedy purported 'personalities' favouring one another, innuendo-strewn sitcoms, the wallowing self-pity of dramas that claimed to be true to life. It was a shallow rill, and by not watching she kept a clear head and retained for her other occupations the commodity she could now least afford to fritter away, her time.

Ailsa

When she was young, she wanted to do everything as well as her brothers. It became clear to her that her father didn't think she was in the running with them. That had annoyed her, but what annoyed her more was finding she could win his approval by being merely feminine instead, smiling and slightly simpering – by cheating, in other words. Her father was happiest with her when she pretended to be powerless and submissive.

To carry it off, she had to think herself into being Moyna, in that quiet interlude before her sister's troublesome phase away at school. She felt the need of her father's favour, and was prepared to be not quite herself to win it. His approval meant more to her than her mother's, and she accepted that she didn't have an aptitude to foretell his reactions. One day he could be very interested and on another very preoccupied, either demanding of the abilities she did have or alternatively all too uncritically easy to please.

Moyna bored her, but she had a winsome charm. So she copied the charm, not bothering to work out if Moyna's was bona fide or not. A little later she would see Nicol trying to prove himself, rather as she had done, and she studied the peculiar responses of her father, how he struggled to be impressed and couldn't make his praise sound quite genuine. His ready approval of her came to seem a little glib too, like a token response only. She might have felt sorry for Nicol, but confusedly and inexplicably it was envy – for his rejection – that took hold of her instead.

Mrs Meldrum

She'd had her circle of friends at school. Rosalind Drummond, Fiona McArdle, Rhona Irvine, a girl called Verity Dalrymple, and another – Janet Fleming – whose father's job removed them all to Dublin. She couldn't have guessed that it would be Naomi Srebnitzki of them all who would exercise the most potent influence upon her, and even thirty-five years after she died.

To the others she went on meeting in Glasgow, the name always prompted some discomfort. There was still something shameful to Rosalind and Fiona (and, for a time, Mary McGregor-that-was) about dying young. They came to mention her less and less, gliding about the subject. The name was all they used, attached to a person of twelve or fourteen or seventeen years old, who had betrayed them by failing to offer any clues as to what was going to happen in the time ahead, her ultimate forgetfulness of decent good manners.

It was Naomi, she was conscious, who was going to miss her most when the time came to leave for America with Aunt Bunty.

Her father was a professor of physics, a second-generation Lithuanian

Scot with strong bonds to his Jewish family in Kovno. His parents and he had retained their original surname. Yiddish and a little Russian were spoken at home along with English, and their Jewish customs – as she heard about them from Naomi – followed the same ritual observed in (moderately) orthodox households in Poland or France or America. Friday evening synagogue, Saturday afternoon sabbath walks, eating bled shechita meat, saying grace after meals.

During the war everybody had a response to the surname, from impudent delivery-boys on bikes who thought it was German to teachers who tried too hard to favour Naomi, which turned her against them. It was evident as an end to the war approached that her parents were concerned about the safety of their Kovno relations, confined for the past three years in the ghetto of Slobodka and at the mercy of native Lithuanian mobs; there had been forced evictions to labour camps in Estonia, and deportations of old people and children to camps in Poland ... Naomi had taken on herself some of this burden of worry, and seemed to regard it as merely rightful that she should.

This sharing was something new to her own (lapsed) presbyterian-based experience, according to which 'family' existed to be a stubborn, wilful impediment to self and pleasure. In some respects the anxiety appeared to go deeper with Naomi, or maybe she wasn't able to conceal it as well as her parents. At home she sat by the wireless to hear the news broadcasts, and pored over large detailed maps in a gazetteer to plot the war's progress. If she hadn't visited Kovno – four times since she was six – and hadn't had the clarity of her memories, then it might have been less immediately vital to her to know how the various Allied campaigns were succeeding or failing.

'You *will* come back, Nancy, won't you?'

'Come back?'

'From America?'

Naomi didn't reproach her for going in words or looks. Her friend's perfect acceptance took her aback for a while, until she realised the effort of control that was being made not to disconcert her with her feelings. She intuited them, however, and recognised that Naomi had selflessly forgiven her any unthinking remarks in the past, just as she comprehended why she was New York-bound. It wasn't because she was running away from the country's privations, but because the alternative was deemed to be the ruination of her morals by an older sister no one could cope with.

History moved on, for everyone.

A couple of years after victory and with the worst truths still to be uncovered, she once asked Naomi the question, 'But what could you have *done?*' when she'd thought they couldn't keep on talking about this war just finished for ever, as if it was still going on. At that, however, Naomi's face had paled from its customary hazel colouring, as she had never seen before. She couldn't tell if her friend was wordless with anger or with terror. Her brown eyes set in their gel, and the question echoed interminably in all the muffled air of the Srebnitzkis' thickly carpeted, over-furnished sitting-room in Portobello.

She had turned her eyes away, so as not to be looking any longer into Naomi's, and they had alighted instead on the refined oval faces in the framed photographs serried on top of the sideboard, on either side of the seven-candled menorah.

'But what could you have done?'

Struan

He let his own discontentment show. He begged to raise objections to some of his father's decisions. He encouraged a mood of democracy in the office, which there had never been before. He grew more sociable but more secretive with his acquaintances in other firms; simultaneously he was eliciting more information from them than previously. He learned much in a year or so, and enjoyed his new mastery of private knowledge, gleaned from its various sources. Disputes continued with his father, automatically, and he didn't attempt to dodge them.

He didn't trail his father again. He sensed, however, that matters were as he had discovered them to be. He had never much considered questions which didn't concern him directly – adultery, abortion, and so on – but now he did. He found he was deeply offended. He thought a lot about his mother, taking quite an altered view of her, recognising that for most of his life he had put her in the lee of his father. He was disturbed by his own unintentional chauvinism. At the same time he became irritated by Kirsty's concern for him, by her observations of the changes she claimed to notice in him. She wanted a child, but he didn't, not yet. He kept imagining the presence of potential seducers, and couldn't know who was deceiving whom, she him or he her.

He was taken for an obscenely expensive lunch by strangers, and concluded not very quickly that he was being head-hunted. 'They' represented a newly amalgamated firm of London whisky brokers setting up a Scottish office in Edinburgh, and he was shortly afterwards offered one of the senior positions, which would entail his doing much as he was doing at present but on a larger scale and for two-thirds as much salary again. He accepted their offer without discussing the matter with either his father or Kirsty. The first person he told was Lewis, who supported him by saying it was the wisest step he could have taken. His father received the news as badly as he predicted, by speaking hardly a word to him and confining his response to curt head nods. Kirsty left him in no doubt that she didn't want to uproot herself from Glasgow and leave her friends; when he tried to entice her with Barnton or Murrayfield or Cramond, she was mightily unimpressed. He told her that in that case he would arrange to spend his weekday nights in a company flat. 'That's just fine by me, Struan.' He wondered which friends in particular she could have been referring to, and frequently at that time found himself – literally – with a bad taste in his mouth.

His mother was the intermediary with his father, although he couldn't ignore her disapproval of what he'd done, because he hadn't chosen to consult them first. Things were never satisfactorily made up on that score, but Christmases became survivable. His mother was unable to persuade him to trust his wife any better than he did. Since he guessed Kirsty was his parents' favourite among the extended family, he was further prejudiced. He sensed he wasn't being wholly reasonable, but Kirsty belonged to his perturbed recent past, and he needed a focus for all his discontentment.

Mrs Meldrum

At a certain point, after her return from America, they fell out, she and Naomi.

About a coat.

It was she who spotted the coat in Jenners' window, and who took Naomi on a Saturday exeat to Edinburgh to see it. A fitted blue alpaca coat with silver fur collar and cuffs. In their size. Beautiful, but somehow discreet also about the fact of its expensiveness. They had stood in front of the window on two successive Saturday afternoons, just to admire.

It didn't occur to her to envy the anonymous woman, younger or older, who would become the owner of the coat. It was enough for her just to daydream some of the physical pleasures – the soft touch of the wool, the warmth of the fox collar, the elegant sway of the coat's fuller skirt.

Naomi beside her was as silent as herself, but she had supposed that to be because she was less impressed and wanted, in her usual considerate way, to spare her feelings.

By Easter the windows had been changed, and there was no sight of the coat to be had on any of the rails upstairs. She guessed that it must have been sold.

She certainly wasn't expecting to see it again. For the first few instants after Naomi's mother – as ever – opened the front door of their home to her, she couldn't connect the coat draped over the end of the staircase banister with its circumstances.

Mrs Srebnitzki followed her eyes.

'Naomi told me what a wonderful coat she'd seen. That's not like Naomi at all, you know. She's been working so hard for the exams recently . . . just as you have, I'm . . .'

Her eyes filled with the coat. Then her gaze narrowed and narrowed.

'I don't think it's an extravagance. To keep yourself warm. Do you, Nancy? So many people in this world of ours, they never . . .'

Naomi came skipping down the stairs. Suddenly, with a foot on different treads, she stopped. Her face fell, then it went red. It was as if she was only now understanding the implications of the purchase, for the first time.

'Nancy –'

'I'll stop blethering and leave you two, shall I?' Mrs Srebnitzki said, surely sensing an awkwardness between them.

Once Mrs Srebnitzki had gone, Naomi didn't begin to explain. While they both stood avoiding contact with their eyes, she envisaged these long moments of waiting – for clarification, for a reason – being sucked through the narrow passageway at the back of the hall and becoming lost for ever.

Naomi was holding out the luxurious coat to her to try on. She shook her head at that, quite decisively.

'Please, Nancy, go on –'

'No.'

'Why not?'

'I don't want to.'

'Oh, *please* –'

What, only to make Naomi feel better about owning the bally coat?

She wouldn't even look at the coat. She stared at the clock instead, because the afternoon couldn't pass quickly enough for her. The house felt impossibly airless, with too much damned furniture, and foreigners' taste in furniture at that.

She decided suddenly she wouldn't stay. Mustn't stay.

She turned, and felt herself sinking into the pile of the carpets.

Treacherous sands indeed, but she was never to be clear whose the worse treachery was. Mrs Srebnitzki appeared, so surprised when she snatched her own coat off the peg. By genuine mistake she caught Naomi's coat with her elbow, and it fell off the banister post and dropped on to the carpet. She didn't make any attempt to retrieve it. It was Naomi's mother who did that, with a theatrically bright smile to conceal her confusion.

She looked down as Mrs Srebnitzki stooped in front of her. She stared very hard at the crown of the woman's head, at the thinning hair there, and smiled and then looked up and caught Naomi out with the speed of her eyes. Naomi seemed quite pained. Another flush reddened her toffee-coloured complexion, like an accident in a paint box.

* * *

Their friendship became a lesser thing. At first Naomi went on treating it as before, so she was obliged to transmit her disapproval to her by her wintry blasts of indifference. Naomi's dependence only made her thoroughly determined to teach her a lesson.

In a subsequent period of her life, when it would be much too late, she was to realise what Mrs Srebnitzki had been meaning, about the need to keep yourself warm and so to suppose yourself better equipped against adversity. The context – of a war and its inhumanities – made all the difference in sad and contrite hindsight. Perhaps in Jenners' Ladies' Department mother and daughter had had an inkling of what would prove to have been their Lithuanian family's fate. As yet it was kept from them, but soon enough the story of the Kevno Ghetto would demand that the world heard.

A coat, a blue alpaca coat with silver fox trim. She allowed a misunderstanding about so little to come between them. When a few years had passed, they tried to put it behind them, although they never quite did. The coat haunted them. Afterwards she appreciated it was a spectre of her own incapacity at that time to think herself into another person's mind, and to understand how to forgive.

Ailsa

If she hadn't been looking for love – who the hell was going to admit that? – she had certainly needed to feel she was approved of. But, with her, her mother had seemed to employ higher standards than she did with Moyna. *She* obeyed while Moyna, for a phase of her life, found ways of wriggling out of obligations, sidestepping. Yet whenever she, Ailsa, unwittingly erred, her mother was much harder on her.

Was her mother's unwillingness to excuse somehow a condemnation of herself too, for having failed to realise her own full potential?

'Good grief, Ailsa! How many times . . . ?'

So much was riding on good exam results, a university place, a career. She had noticed that no mention was ever made of *her* becoming a mother in her turn.

She remembered a time in Glasgow when they'd been going out for a family Christmas party. Her mother liked them all to appear in kilts, for her own reasons of oneupmanship where her sisters-in-law were concerned. The Christmas before she picked up on her Aunt Seonad's irritation and her Aunt Elspeth's twitchiness, and this year she decided to spill a little tea – strong tea, which would leave a mark – so that she would have to wear something else.

When she came downstairs wearing her more sophisticated green velvet dress, her mother stared at her and she knew ructions would follow. In the middle of the telling-off Moyna appeared in her kilt, but wearing it two or three inches shorter than last year. It looked ludicrous, preposterous, but her mother ignored that, because to her the only point was that a kilt is a kilt. A green velvet dress, even from Forsyth's store and however soignée, was not.

'We always wear kilts. Why do you want to be so – so *awkward* about it?'

'I'm not, Mummy, I'm not –'

'Don't answer back.'

'You asked me.'

'Yes, and you've got an answer for everything. I'm tired of it, Ailsa.'

Her father joined in, meaning to be amicable in a troublesome situation, but he was rounded on and accused of 'always taking her side'. He didn't deny it, even though it was less than the whole truth. What was clear was that they wouldn't all be going, and certainly not after the admission of a tea-stain slap on the front of a kilt. What kind of a house would people think their mother ran?

'Why didn't you say, for heaven's sake?'

'I thought I could wear this instead.'

'You know you don't at Uncle Roderick's.'

'It doesn't matter, though, does it?'

That was the last straw for her mother, who told her she was to stay at home. Moyna said nothing, not a word, and walked past with a shrug, hitching her skirt a tad higher on the waist and showing as much of her thighs as she dared to. The length, or the lack, only exaggerated the breadth of those hips, and she wanted to snigger aloud, so that Moyna heard. But the snort that came out was a preliminary to tears.

Only at that juncture, just visible to her in the corner of her eye, did her mother's mouth shape a small smile at her humiliation.

Mrs Meldrum

She remembered the day. March 15th, 1957. A Saturday afternoon in Glasgow, that dreadful drag time in her week.

She was getting Lewis ready for a party. Ming had jabbed a screwdriver into the fleshy part of his hand, which was spirting blood, and she was trying to keep an eye on the state of the cloakroom basin. The car was failing to start some days, and that was another worry, in case she'd have to call up Lewis's nursery friends' parents at the last moment for a lift.

Then the telephone rang. She must have been a full minute reaching it, and when she did she was out of breath, clutching a roll of bandage. The dog was barking in the garden, and the kitchen window had blown open, knocking a jar of whisks and wooden spoons into the sink. And now Ailsa was starting to cry in her pram, damn her.

She hadn't spoken to Naomi for several weeks, and here she was, and she was irritated with herself for her sorry, inadequate apology. 'Can I ring you back later?' She sounded far away, but no, she was at home, in Edinburgh. She would remember the strangeness of her voice later, hundreds of times: somehow faint and shrill together, assertive and – in retrospect – helplessly afraid. 'I'll ring you back, Naomi.' There was no reply, just an intake of breath, and then another. Could there have been a sob, or did she invent that? Might she have failed to notice it, or later was she meaning to load herself with all the blame that she could and weighting the facts perversely against herself?

That same afternoon Naomi's husband found her hanging from a noose of rope, above the spacious stairwell of their desirable villa in Braid Hills.

There had to be a post-mortem and a fiscal's report. Somehow her husband's powers of persuasion enabled the funeral to be held in a Church of Scotland church, the one where he was an elder, in the contrived form of a non-denominational service. No reference was made during the formalities to the mental distress of the deceased, but in conversation with Alistair afterwards she learned of Naomi's battle with depression over the years. 'It went back to the war. What happened to her relations in Lithuania.' Naomi, he said, had taken what pride she was still capable of in concealing her condition from their friends. The word 'friends' stung, not because Alistair had in any way intended it to, but because she heard it mock and jibe in the distorting echo-chamber of her mind.

What had seemed a dire but (presumably) accountable tragedy then became, for weeks and months, savagely abstruse.

She hated this having the comfort of an armchair in a warm sitting-room from which to look back upon the past. So she would stand out in the garden instead, in wind and rain, trying to come to terms with the calamity of crossed lives that had occurred – Naomi so deeply concerned with the terrors and guilts of the century, and herself so bogged down in the clamour of the domestic and the trivial.

It was music that eventually helped to rouse her from her grief. Bach. Firstly 'Jesu Joy of Man's Desiring' and 'Where Sheep May Safely Graze', which they had learned to knock out – no better than that – on the piano for Miss Dimmock at school. Then, the swelling 'Passions' and, by way of the more sombre and introverted Casals's recording of the cello sonatas, a piano version of the unapologetically reflective 'Art of Fugue', with its almost translucent repetitions. The music seemed to her eternal, destined to be always listened to. Before Bach put it on paper, it was only waiting for its audience – waiting as sounds and effects in those woods where the composer would walk for inspiration, to be transcribed from nature as a kind of shorthand for the endurance of the spiritual. Greater than the little time of household affairs, and transcending also the self-importance of historical time. Through the music she perceived that Naomi now belonged to a continuum of time where guilt and sorrows were resolved in a dense miracle of shared understanding.

She envied her, even the slow agonising torture of her egress into freedom.

Struan

For months consequently he had suffered from seemingly irrational flashes of anger because of his father. It happened less often in the office or in the flat than with strangers: shop assistants, commissionaires, other drivers. There had to be an incitement, however tiny and inconsequential in retrospect, which left him at the time wanting to lash out with his fists. Once in a bar he did, and on another occasion in a queue at a filling station. Things had improved recently, but he knew he was less predictable now than he used to be.

Mrs Meldrum

She had been how she was because she needed to be, but she couldn't expect her children to understand that. She'd had to become strong and resolute, with a confidence in herself. If she hadn't been those things, they would have had to depend on Ming and no one else.

Even before they were married, she saw his fascination for Lindsay. Maybe it was because Lindsay had become engaged to her big catch that she rushed into an engagement herself, supposing her sister had opted for normality when she was actually being more wayward than ever.

At any rate, Ming ought to have been out of bounds. And Lindsay too, to him. She had a sensation, however, when all three of them were together that the space between them was threaded with implications like a cat's cradle, and she was snared by her own ignorance. Lindsay was too clever for her, and too clever for Ming also, although he couldn't perceive that.

She had no proof until ten or eleven months after their wedding. One of her old Edinburgh schoolfriends called on her in Glasgow, and blurted out – or wanted to give an impression of letting it slip – that her husband had spotted Ming having lunch in the Café Royal with his sister-in-law.

She confronted Ming. She swept aside the evasions, told him she knew everything, and watched his mouth drop open.

'It's just mistaken identity –'

'Yes?'

'Of course. Why shouldn't I tell –'

'With *Lindsay*?'

'But – but it didn't happen – how you're saying –'

'It *wasn't* you?'

'Why should I tell you I wasn't with Lindsay –'

'I know Lindsay. She can make people do anything she wants them to do.'

'Really, Nancy –'

He wouldn't admit anything, but she did prise details out of Lindsay. She had to use blackmail, threatening to put her wealthy husband in the picture. They were only details of a meal, Lindsay made out, denying she'd had any other interest than a free lunch.

The second denial was as unbelievable as Ming's. But she already had a little plan of revenge in her mind, and the culinary information was enough for her purpose in the meanwhile. She didn't want to hear any more divulged, thank you very much.

On their first anniversary she arranged for Ming and her to go through to Edinburgh for the evening. She had booked dinner – naturally – at the Café Royal, for the two of them only, at the same out-of-the-way table Ming had known to ask for when he'd taken Lindsay. The meal, she explained to him, had been ordered in advance.

Each dish accorded with that of the lunchtime menu, as recounted to her by her sister. Hers was Lindsay's choice, and his was his own original selection. The wine was the same château and vintage, and the spirits that followed matched exactly, the blend of whisky for him and rather vulgar cognac for her. He must have had suspicions before the end of the first course, and definitely rumbled to what was going on at the appearance of the second. She didn't address the subject, and carried on as if nothing were untoward. He was having difficulties swallowing, but kept going, maintaining the pretence not bravely but in a blue funk. His appetite must have waned completely, as hers did, and the meal was protracted for that reason. For him, she hoped, agony was being piled upon agony.

She was letting him understand. I know. I bloody well know, and it's not going to happen again. Or at least I have no wish to hear about it through your clumsiness if it does. The Café Royal is off-limits, and my sister is most definitely off the menu. Somehow, miraculously, she managed to continue smiling. It was one of the most formidable things she'd ever had to do, but her life – the surface one – was depending on it. She felt herself hardening as the meal progressed: shell closing over flesh. He had been a fool, an idiot, a dupe, and she was giving him her verdict.

Still, audaciously, nothing was said. They played their supremely ingenious game. In and out between the words they did speak on other matters, ducking the inadvertent implications and double-meanings, smilers like half-wits, stickers to their lasts. An intricate revenge, but as subtle as she could make it: symbolic, after a fashion, and cheap at the not inconsiderable price.

He was quiet on the way home in the car. She switched on the radio. Voices burbled on, and she – like him – wasn't listening to any of them.

She was trying to read the future in the tracks of the car's headlamps.

Some features were clear, others not. She had this assurance for one, that their evening would not be referred to again by either of them. It was over and done with. Its significance couldn't be lost on him, however, and now he must realise that he was married to a more astute woman than he'd appreciated, even just a matter of hours ago. She wasn't conventionally clever, but she *was* armed with the basic arithmetic of distrust to be able to put two and two together and to hit on the unconsoling answer.

She had no more trouble with Lindsay, that she was aware of. They met infrequently, and only because family protocol required it. She would – very obviously – look the other way when Lindsay and Ming were obliged to acknowledge one another. The loss of an elder sister was no more to her than it had been since her adolescence, so very little had changed.

Lindsay at least had the tact to stay away from the funeral: which only confirmed to her that she had been correct to do what she had done so long ago, nipping a situation in the bud and (in a sense) never looking back. Lindsay's excuse was her third husband's bout of pneumonia, although since he was in hospital she might have spared them the time, but chose not to. Blood intuition, even between two such unsisterly sisters, was a uniquely expressive language.

I don't know what he was looking for: what it was those women were able to give him that I couldn't.

I was angry, and jealous, and mystified, but I was also relieved. Some of the pressure was taken off me, to provide complete satisfaction by my own efforts.

I said nothing. It didn't matter to me if he saw that I knew, but blast me to hell if I was going to confess it. I embroidered our deep silences on the subject with inconsequential remarks, only pausing to sniff at a fragrant current of air, or to straighten my stockings with the sort of pernickety concern which I supposed was that sort of woman's preoccupation.

And that, thanks to my commendably mature approach to the matter, was pretty much that.

Greta

She lay listening to Lewis beside her turning on the mattress, trying to find comfort and support for himself.

He had a bad back. She read all the articles about backache that appeared in magazines. Her diagnosis was that in Lewis's case it was largely stress-induced, acting on a not unusual leftwards bias of the spine.

He didn't complain much, but the problems were never far from his mind. He preferred modern hotels and newish beds, and holiday lets with their unpredictable furnishings were a thing of their past. After this sagging soggy bed he would have another two or three nights of fitful sleep at home, then he would start to settle again into his routine.

The stress wasn't constant, and he had good and bad spells. The prospect of the visit north had seemed to be slowing him down, and she'd noticed the stiffness in his back last weekend. She would wonder if there were any deeper reasons why it happened, if it necessarily always referred to his work. He had been raised to be the family's prime achiever, and when he talked about his growing up she could feel sorrier for him than she had words to express.

She turned her head and watched him as he trawled between consciousness and sleep. Two lines were etched into his forehead, above the bridge of his nose, and now – she guessed – those would be irremovable. His eyes were screwed up tight, and little lines fanned sideways at the corners. His hair was thinning, when that wasn't really the way of his family; he was *au fait* with barbers' disguising techniques and the careless spite of a breeze as he never used to be.

Changed days, and yet inevitably it had all been there from the beginning, waiting to happen.

She hoped quite sincerely that she didn't make his anxiety worse than it needed to be. But he had probably taken that into account long ago, selecting for himself the wife who would be no less and no more than the woman he might be expected to marry.

Nicol

He lay on top of the bed, bringing back to mind the vision of the gardener in the afternoon.

His right hand settled on the pod of his briefs. He pulled at himself through the puckered cotton.

Such a cliché. So obvious, and at the same time such a harsh proof.

He tugged and fretted. He kneaded his knob like dough, prolonging the build-up of a hard-on. One face became another face which became another. On and on. Like some rolling computer screen.

His hand worked away of its own accord while his mind travelled by towns and states, over the continent of his experience, across the years of his enlightenment.

Ailsa

A party of archaeologists descended on Achnavaig in the mid-1970s. Their work was a distraction for them that summer, when they had nothing else planned, or numbers were depleted.

She forgot what was found, after the fine sifting with trowels and teaspoons. The diggers interested her rather more, with their in-talk she immediately wanted to be a part of. She had been expecting pale and weedy specimens, but instead these academics and their acolytes were as fit and weather-bronzed and practically muscled as construction workers.

What she was to remember of their summer visitors she did so for reasons only very incidentally archaeological, but which helped to define her feelings for Nicol once and for all, as a brew of distrust and jealousy and just a little disgust.

One of the dig's crew, no older than herself, was called Fabrice.

She was stumped to recall later if he'd been properly handsome or not. He must have been passably so at any rate, for her to have given her time to him. He was French, definitely that. Or – no – it was possible he'd been Swiss, living near the border (perhaps). In more than one sense.

'AC/DC' they learned to call his sort subsequently, but when it was too late and she'd had to endure all the discomfiture and disappointment he caused. By then anyway she had come to see him (she liked to think) as a weak-willed individual, passive and vapid and a drifter between the vague points where other people were required to make choices.

He must have had a little more to recommend him to her, but again the trail always went cold in her recollection, and she lost her focus on what it might have been. Looks, conceivably, would have proved enough. And a certain romance about his presence, which she couldn't ever bring to mind exactly.

He wore long shorts, to just above his knees, and with turn-ups to them, and Lacoste tee-shirts in citrus colours she hadn't spotted in the magazines, and natty white woollen socks with a little green crocodile emblem flexing itself on the nubble of ankle-bone. He had Gallic charm, indubitably. She practised her French with him, and found his delivery of syntax she only knew from school French quite – well, sexy. God knows what they could have talked about, but at the time they had no shortage of subjects. He spoke in a breathy, confiding way that felt hot on the side of her head, and since she remembered a lot of breath from him and toe-curling on her part there must have been a lot of talk as well.

The old gang watched her from the beach, and maybe they thought she was tiring of them. She wasn't, not really. But she caught them saying things to one another under cover of other actions, and that only made her feel more obstinately inclined to linger on the roped-off fringes of the excavation.

It was a snigger from Lesley Campbell one afternoon that alerted her.

She looked back from the dunes, towards the dig, and saw Nicol lending a hand, doing navvy work with a spade. She didn't see what was so funny about that. Beside him, Fabrice was showing him how.

Should *she* have volunteered? It had crossed her mind earlier, but it seemed to her too much like hard labour, and she only had to look at the effects on the girls' hand. She'd had a year at university, and this was supposed to be a kind of reading holiday in any case, so she hadn't given much thought to the possibility of offering her services. Already she had a sense of grown-upness: how she now called her parents 'Em' and 'Eff', how she rationed her disclosures about the arcane customs of student life at St Andrews, how she was lightening her hair and waxing her legs. Fabrice responded to her as a woman, she felt, because that was the only way he'd seen her, while to all the others a bit of her remained the little girl of so long ago.

Nicol was a child by comparison with her. A handsome one, and – opinion had it – with a sweet and obliging nature, although it was easy for him when he was spoiled something rotten by Em. He wasn't a child, of course: she realised that quite well when she moved closer to the trench and watched him wielding the spade. It had recently become noticeable to her how he influenced some of the others of the beach set, those closer to his age than her own, just by the force of something or other: his looks, a way he had of seeming to take you into his confidence, an expression of imploring which his face sometimes took on, or else that damnably cajoling smile. Thought of like that, it dangerously resembled charisma, and she tried on this as on succeeding leaden dog-day afternoons to put her little brother as much out of her mind as she possibly could.

The Broch

* * *

Had she suspected, though, that there was something more complicated about Nicol?

It began to register with her that when she couldn't find Fabrice to talk to, Nicol was also missing. Whenever she asked one about the other, they spoke with a vagueness she felt was deliberate. Nicol would ask her questions about Fabrice. At first she clammed up, and then she started to elaborate on the facts, making out that they had a huge amount in common. Nicol just smiled at the information, in a disconcertingly knowing manner.

It was only through hearsay that she discovered they had tracked down a private patch of sand where they swam together: skinny-dipped apparently. She was in Nicol's bedroom one day when he was out, sent there by Em to retrieve some crockery, and in the course of her recce her eyes alighted on a single white sock dropped on the floor. She picked it up. It was woollen, not the thin cotton type they played tennis in.

A little green crocodile on the ankle bared its fangs at her, but with a sly watchful smile.

Fabrice took her to an archaeologists' night out, a houlie in the lounge bar of the Cromarty Arms. She had shamelessly angled for an invitation once she discovered that there was to be an outing. Fabrice agreed, but she felt when they got there that she had been brought along for appearance's sake. Over the evening he was peculiarly uninterested – in her, that is – for all his Frenchman's coyness. He asked her too many questions about Nicol for her liking, and she found that the things he did already know about him were oddly intimate – his shoe and collar sizes, his first shave, his chipped tooth. 'You should have brought Nicol along,' she said, with an icy laugh. 'Instead of me.' Momentarily his eyes grew very round and afraid. Then he remembered his charm, that badge of separateness, and he recovered the image of himself that was the one he meant her to have.

Maybe nothing did happen, either up there in the bedroom when the house was quiet, or along in their secluded cove where the road briefly parted company with the sea.

Nicol was only fourteen, and probably didn't know what was involved. Not that the chasing, if that's what it amounted to, was necessarily Fabrice's. She had spotted a circumspection, also – not cunning – a *canniness* in her brother, which served to put her on alert. At that age the connotations would have been demonic, for someone so young to be able to spot the weaknesses of character – since shirt-lifting surely came into that category – buried in others.

Had she helped to bring her confusion on herself? What was the good of a university education if you could be outwitted by a fourteen-year-old? When she looked hard at Nicol, very hard, she became confused all over again, unable to decide if she was seeing him as more worldly than the evidence allowed. The risk was that he didn't really know himself, and so his acuteness had no ulterior purpose, it was as unthinking as second nature.

Lewis

The girl wasn't the sort he was expecting, not to have been his father's mistress while he was alive.

For a start she wasn't a girl but a woman, in her forties. She was pretty and well spoken. The flat in Glasgow's West End was tastefully and unfussily furnished. The crockery which she produced for tea was very like one of the sets they used to have at home. A silver spoon was placed in his saucer, and he noticed that it carried entwined initials quite familiar to him. The heels of her shoes were a degree higher than his mother would have approved of, but they gave her legs a lift and showed them to better effect. She had dignified movements. Her long neck intrigued him. She had a distinct chin, but it didn't project and nicely balanced the other features of her face. Her eyes were very blue, and while their expression now was curious he could see how they might be gentle.

He was mystified. He had been imagining someone wholly different. When they started to talk, she spoke of his father without any embarrassment, real or false. He quickly discovered she had felt very close to him, very affectionate and appreciative of all the acts of generosity he had shown her. Her own husband, she explained, had walked out on her five years before, and she'd been left extremely confused, with so little confidence in herself.

'I just felt – I wasn't worth *anything*, to anybody –'

That had been his cue to say something hurtful – about her getting her own back on married men – but he couldn't bring himself to come out with any such thing. The occasion passed, and – as events proved – he wasn't to feel the impulse again.

They chatted. Only that. And reminisced.

Oddly, he was loth to go when he felt it was time to. He sat on. He was comfortable with her in the cosy, restful flat, three floors up among the trees of its quiet square. The gas fire purred in the old fireplace of white and blue Delft tiles. She poured them both drinks; she placed a cushion behind his back. 'The chair needs it,' she told him. 'Your father liked that chair best, though.' He smiled, but did it awkwardly. The malt was his father's favourite,

Glenlivet. She seated herself directly opposite him, on the small sofa, with careful but unaffected elegance.

'My life,' she said, 'didn't turn out as I expected. I was going to be a good man's wife, a dutiful wife, and I would have his children. That's what I thought was predicted for me. And here I am.'

He heard an ironical tone in her voice, that preserved her from self-pity. She sat looking out at the trees. The leaves were on the turn, from green to – variously – yellow and red and gold. A smile slowly appeared on her face. All her features lightened. He had a glimpse of her as his father must have been used to seeing her, leavened by a demure joy.

He found himself smiling in response. For a second or two she was perplexed by what she saw – himself sitting there, smiling as if he was quite content – then she looked away again, with her long neck reddening, to the distraction of the kindling trees in the square.

He went back. Ostensibly it was to enquire after some of his father's papers which he couldn't find.

She replied to his question with an expression of bafflement, as he knew she was bound to. It was a cold day, about half past four in the afternoon, and when he didn't make a move to leave she suggested she make them both tea. 'I should like that very much,' he told her, and she hesitated before smiling back at him.

He had come without any forewarning, but even in her house-clothes she had a simple and unselfconscious grace. Her face didn't require make-up, with those fine cheekbones and blue eyes and – he noticed better today – the Cupid's bow mouth. Her erotic capacities still puzzled him: she had been his father's mistress, after all, and they must have done more than drink tea and malt whisky and study the trees in the square.

He asked her another question, about her own future, adopting a businessman's manner to do so. She started, as if she saw – or heard – through that, to a recognisable tone of voice under his hesitant parody.

'My sister's husband died last year,' she told him. 'She's been wanting me to move in with her. Down in Seamill.'

'The flat is yours, of course.'

She nodded.

'Ming was a very generous man,' she said.

That, necessarily, was the problem. His unbounded munificence. And now, for his own part, having to mop up around that. Trying to minimise the losses for the family.

He studied the dignified composure of her face, called it to himself 'august'. That mouth, which a lazy author would have described as 'chiselled'. The blueness of her eyes. How her hair – copper-coloured – was pulled up and fixed at the back with silver clips, making her neck appear longer still.

While she poured tea his eyes explored her body, from the neck to her crossed legs, her slim calves, the neatness of her ankles, the ball of one foot which hung from the back of her shoe.

She didn't seem disturbed by him as she sat on the little sofa, evidently far removed in her thoughts, and not in a Seamill direction. He found the contours worked into the upholstery of the chair which he occupied suited him very well, for his back and buttocks and thighs.

'Do you – do you want to leave here?' he heard himself asking her, with consummate kindliness.

When she turned to look at him, she had tears in her eyes. Very slowly she shook her head.

'Then – then why should you?' he said. He was trying to make it sound the very voice of reason itself. 'Why should you leave the place when you're so comfortable in it?'

For economy's sake, quite possibly. Or on memory's account, perhaps. And who knew, maybe also because she was afraid she might attempt to relive the last few years with a replacement?

'Take some time,' he said. 'Please. Don't rush a decision. You need a chance to think about it. Don't be tempted to do anything you might regret later.'

She nodded her head. A smile, unambiguously grateful, came up on her face.

'You'll consider carefully?' he asked, before taking his hazardous next step. 'Will you promise me that, Alison?'

He hardly knew why he had used her name. He was shutting off the turmoil further back in his thoughts.

She did a double-take. She blinked twice in succession. But she didn't take offence, and this time it was his turn to let the gratitude smile from his face, a smile he could feel lifting his cheeks and stretching his nostrils and slipping into old creases of skin he got too little use for these days.

Nicol

The men he was picking up were getting younger, really boys some of them. They all conformed to a certain appearance. A full head of hair, sporty good looks, well built but without any fat, clear complexions, wide ready smiles, carefree expressions.

He didn't want introverts, and he definitely didn't need femmes. He picked a physical type that would have fitted into the life of Achnavaig when he was their age himself or just a little younger. They were idealised versions of himself, notwithstanding their New York accents and talk.

From the beaches of Fire Island he looked east through the smoke of barbecue grills and the fine spray of sand kicked up by a game of handball. He loved them as he wished he could love himself. He caressed their shoulders, their backs, their buttocks, their thighs, he moved into them with the gentleness he wanted shown to him – but which he disallowed from them, in case he should be disappointed, so that the advances were largely one way, and ultimately not as fulfilling as they might have been.

He didn't intend to risk disillusionment, though. Inevitably things cooled off, and they both tried to be reasonable about the matter, money included, and in another few weeks – or days, if he got lucky – he spotted someone else, in the likeness of the last, and the process began all over again, in what had once been a ritual of renewal and which was bound to end up soon enough as a travesty.

Lewis

He turned from one flank to the other, and the mattress springs wheezed under him.

He didn't hear them. He was back in Drumbeg Gardens, at any time during the past couple of years. Alison had served them tea. From somewhere, impossibly, the sound of breaking waves carried into the room. Alison was simply being herself, and he felt the simplicity as a relief from his life at home. For a moment, as she spoke, he heard the words – but losing the sense of them – delivered in Greta's voice. He shook his head at the silly confusion.

Alison lowered her eyes in that modest way he was so fond of. He waited with some trepidation, as he always did, for the eyes to be raised again. He couldn't bear to imagine that she might fail to remember him. Suddenly she looked up, and smiled. But then, when she started to speak – while he lost the sense again – he realised that she had used not his name but his father's.

He wanted to stop the conversation and rewind. Back to that point when she had first started to get away from him, with the wrong name used. She continued to talk, though, and he couldn't stop her. A mild and peaceable wash of words, as lulling as the sea.

When he looked down, at his lap, he saw – staring and staring – that his hands weren't his own hands. They were his father's, with their trails of sun freckles among the bleached hairs, and blue veins, and the nails hard like horn.

He tried to spread the fingers but they wouldn't respond. He said something, meaning to make them obey. The voice that came out of him at that instant wasn't his own, it was his father's.

He trembled to hear the exact timbre, the precise weight and pace of the words.

He was aware of wetness on his cheeks, a sensation that wasn't as exceptional to him as he had always supposed. The hands that he couldn't move wobbled beneath him, one blurred into the other; he was seeing nothing but a terrible liquid uncertainty.

Nicol

Maybe he was looking to find himself. And if he could have found himself... But the most dangerous illusion was to imagine that something might have been different from how it had turned out to be.

He had made the mental adjustments to being gay because there was nothing very much he could have done about it. This was how he was, and he had resolved to be honest. With his family he made an exception, because honesty sometimes consisted of reticence, which was one of the cardinal virtues instilled in the Meldrums. He was making it easier on himself, but also – so he justified his behaviour – easier on the others as well, by not causing them discomfort.

He didn't blame, and if that saved them it also saved time wasted on reproaching himself for what – then as now – simply could not be helped.

Mrs Meldrum

Naomi's Alistair eventually remarried. His new wife had been his secretary for the past six years. Rae was a chirpy, kindly disposed, mature woman who might have supposed herself earmarked for spinsterhood. Small, slightly plump, auburn-haired (dyed), she spoke with a soft southern Irish accent. Conveniently, Rae was most of the things which the tall, angular, jet-haired Naomi had not been.

She was invited to their wedding, but found a good excuse for not going, and declined graciously, offering profuse apologies and her sincere best wishes.

Every September she had sent Naomi's daughter a birthday card, and received a letter back. By choice she had arranged that they should not meet.

One June, when Judith was in her twenties, she received a postcard from a kibbutz near Mount Tabor. Since the annual birthday card and its reply were their staple form of communication, she wondered why Judith should have decided to notify her of the fact – this particular fact. In tiny packed script her correspondent mentioned her tiredness, her contentment, the weather, swimming in the Sea of Galilee, also the sense of community and common purpose.

She called in at her local library and read up about kibbutzim: 'farm collectives, in which all members are equal, and life is based on socialist principles'. She found a *Blue Guide* to Israel and took it out. In a bookshop she came across a Penguin on the origins and tenets of Judaism, and bought it. She went to a showing of Vishniac's photographs of a pre-war Jewish Romania that looked medieval and was no more, and in the gallery at Strathclyde University she was the only gentile in evidence apart from the attendants. Subsequently she bought occasional paperback editions of books reviewed in the newspapers, about the ghettoes of Lotz and Bialystok and the oral histories of that harrowing time. She tried to read some of Isaac Bashevis Singer's stories, ghouls and golems and brusque couplings and all, and thought the film of *Yentl* was better than the press it received.

She had no clear sense of being directed anywhere. Judith did call her from the station one day when she was in Glasgow, and they ended up having tea in the only place she could immediately think of to meet, the patisserie under the escalators in the Princes Square shopping mall. There, in the antiseptic atmosphere, Judith's narrative of her second life – the kibbutz, Jewish community work in London, her research into a genteelly fascist organisation called the League of Albion which flourished in Britain in the late forties, her engagement to a fellow-monitor of European anti-semitism, her recognising an unattractive strain of xenophobia in Israelis – it all had an unreal quality in the surroundings, with Judith sounding so earnest and dedicated about her work, even though she spiced the account with humour. As she listened to her, and realised how controlled a young woman this was, she felt herself succumb again to unassuaged guilt about her mother. She experienced it as breathlessness, pins and needles in her head that threatened a faint, and she had to allow Judith to take her to the back doors for some deep swallows of cold fresh air.

Back home that same evening, she decided what she had been meaning to decide for years, that she had in fact lived in the Glasgow house for too long. Its comfort oppressed her, and knowing every sound to be yielded by each floorboard in a specific place, and how sounds lost or gained, and where the currents of air crossed. She was too easy here, and took too much for granted. Her life since Ming's death had lacked texture. She lived it on the smooth and plain, and she was missing everything out there, outside, beyond this sensation of loss.

Firstly she moved into a modern flat; it was well appointed, and 'labour-saving'. She was restless, though, and she felt confined. She read a book about the Abkhasians of the Caucasian Mountains, and resolved to do what they did, which was to spend two hours of the twenty-four out of doors, in the open air.

Part of the problem was living in Glasgow, where her acquaintances didn't know how to treat her, talking too much or too little about Ming. It was time for a change, she concluded, but not for a severance. She discussed her financial situation with Lewis, and between them they arrived at the same conclusion – The Broch.

For the past few years the house had been let out for the middle portion of the summer, in a hush-hush kind of way through a solicitor friend of Lewis's. Ming hadn't known what else to do with it – the rental payments justified their holding on to it, and yet he wouldn't have contemplated putting it up for sale. Lewis assured her that it could be kept going without the income from rent; with careful costing and some family subsidy, he explained, it would support her, and continue to do so (he implied) for the duration of her life.

Her mind was put more at rest, and she got down to the business of restoring the property to some sort of order. She did finally succeed, on the whole, by dint of her determination and hard graft. Her tiredness felt as Judith's must have felt on the kibbutz. (She had an opportunity to ask her when the newly married pair dropped in on a visit north.) Her own family thought her quite eccentric as it was, so she didn't tell them that she quite often took a cold dip in the bay: the unseasonal bathing and the long walk every afternoon cured her of most of her ills, and on a diet much biased to the common-sense virtues of bananas and porridge oats and halibut oil capsules she felt more alive and receptive inside her skin than she had done for many years. She could never believe that she achieved enough, but it was some sort of accomplishment that she didn't exercise any negative influences, or any she was conscious of. She sought to be constructive, even if sometimes – she realised – that left her exposed and unfairly gave an impression to others of naïvety.

She had the blisters and calluses on her hands to prove that she had worked *something* with her energies. A diamond had fallen out of her engagement ring one day, into the sea when she was swimming, but there were four left in the cluster, which was surely sufficient to serve the ring's purpose, as a memento of who she had been. The money she might have spent on replacing the stone she used to plant Redsleeves and Rubinette saplings in the orchard for her successors to crop their fruit.

Lewis

Alison was modest, and without any 'side' to her, and she could laugh both at herself and – not unkindly – at the absurdities she detected in other people. She made the flat seem like a sanctuary, as comfortable and snug as a nest.

She had no false airs and graces, and he completely trusted her. He realised quite soon that he had deeply misjudged not only her but his father. He fell into penitent silences, and had to assure her that the fault was his and his alone. She seemed, somehow, to understand, but he preferred to believe that she really did not.

He went round for 'tea' one or two afternoons in the week, and for 'supper' on maybe another couple of evenings, with his alibis offered to Greta. Sometimes he drove them across to Edinburgh and they had a legitimate but clandestine lunch. He spent just a few nights with her, and those were on occasions when Greta's sisters had taken her with them to a family wedding or funeral.

It worked out, though, because Alison and he were sensible about the situation, and made no unreasonable demands on one another. He also knew not to take what was happening for granted, and to relish the secretiveness.

He was happy, more so than he had been for -- he forgot the total sum of years.

And with Alison he lost the self-reproach he'd had to put up with. He felt closer to his father, somehow more in tune with him. It was as if by doing what he was doing he was helping to keep the spirit of the man alive.

Alison seemed to come more alive too, between his arriving and departing, not that he ever fooled himself into imagining he was performing a charitable deed.

He couldn't be certain why he came. At the back of it all was his father, and Greta, and a not very loving life. Alison was giving him a course of lessons in simple affection, if nothing else.

There used to be a song played on the radio – 'The greatest love of all is to learn to love yourself' – and he hoped very hard that it didn't have one single iota of truth to it.

When he was with Alison he would find himself thinking more often of his mother than of Greta.

Taking his father's place, it was only apt that he should pick up the waves of thought left behind in the flat. He was accepting accountability for his father's guilt, and did so willingly, because it was proving the point to him that he really had been stung by his conscience after all.

It was as if, for his father, being with Alison had allowed him to come closer to his wife than he could do in her presence. Alison offered few physical similarities, but something about her – the forbearance, the calmness, the serenity – established an ambience of quiet introspection in which he could reflect on the qualities of the woman he had married, who was the mother of his children.

As for himself, it was more important to feel the closeness to his parents than to Greta: not because he cared less for her, but because she was a woman who presented only rare indications of weakness, who – when he pictured her once he was away from her – was always busy, in demand by others, far too taken up to be considering *him* in his absence.

Moyna

She realised Jamie wasn't sleeping. She sneaked looks. His eyes were shut, most of the time, but his mind was ticking over. She could hear the whirring of the mechanism.

She turned away on the mattress and curled her legs beneath her. Even a hot day at Achnavaig cooled in the evening, so they didn't have the excuse of humidity keeping them awake. Nor of too much light, since the curtains were heavy lined velvet. She stared across the room into the density of shadows. Shadows inside shadows behind shadows. Around her the structure of the house heaved and cracked, contracting after the day's expansions. She thought she could hear the bricks resettling, and dust sifting from layer to layer to layer through the tiny flaws and fractures opened up in the fabric of the building.

She sighed, into the sheet. Jamie would hear her. He would be distracted for a moment or two. She held her breath, waiting for him to get back on to the track of his dream. She didn't move, not until she heard the mattress gasping under him as his body relaxed. He turned on to his left, further side. That was her prompt, and she let herself be accommodated among all the fortissimo of sighing springs, easing herself inches over to her right so that there was now a chasm, a canyon, riven between them.

Mrs Meldrum

The charitable doings, the little optimistic acts of good faith, those her children might be able to understand. However, the long walks to tramp all the aches and pains and weak thoughts out of herself, and the foolish drives south all the way to Glasgow just to learn more of an ancient desert language from a man Judith had put her in touch with, whom she – *she*, just as unchurchy as their father was – had supposed from his calling in that insalubrious part of the city to be old and stooped and myopic and neglectful of himself...

But Rabbi Abramowizc had turned out to be a youthful man in his late thirties, hale and energetic and enthusiastic. She had made the mistake at first of letting her mind dwell on what she imagined must be all the absences and denials in his life, until she started to perceive from what he told her that these sacrifices were affirmations of a faith he'd first felt welling up in him from a deep, inscrutable source. They had been less than rational choices, admittedly, but stronger and more compelling, because intuitions of his being.

Greta

She has noticed what Lewis obviously hasn't, that sometimes he carries on him the perfume – the cheaper fragrances – of other women.

Maybe it's harmless enough. Maybe it's done by them – the contact – almost in the way of a little light joke, with its not-so-subtle after-traces.

She has tried considering Lewis in a new light, but most often she cannot. Just occasionally she sees that, yes, it might be possible. When she can think to eliminate her own experience of fifteen married years with him, she finds herself looking at just the outer form of the man, and she can't be certain that a woman would not be attracted. His manner has command and persuasion, enough to distract them from their ignorance about the aspects of his character which she is privy to – his self-discipline, his concern with appearances and their rigorous upkeep, sometimes a sternness and dourness that weren't there at the outset of the marriage.

She senses her own disloyalty in observing so closely. Yet the perfume clings to him, to the weave of several suits. Conceivably they just brush against him, *en passant*, in the corridors. A client or two may proffer a hand on his shoulder, but she cannot be convinced.

She has a sensitive nose. She has gone around the testers in Frasers' store in Glasgow trying to match her recollection of the fragrances with the bottles and sprays on display. At the cosmetics counters she doubts if she will be recognised swathed by a headscarf, but she is aware of the mixed horror and absurdity in her predicament, raising another tester to her wrist, running out of space on her skin. In the twiddly panels of mirror behind the displays she catches a frantic but dazed expression on her face, which visits her when she is most absorbed by the idea of Lewis's unfaithfulness to her. She'll go for a swim afterwards, to the leisure centre in Lewis's Glasgow club, at a time of the day when he won't be there, and she'll try – she *will* try – to work some of the stress out of her system. In front of the changing-room mirrors afterwards she will reacquire her composure for the journey home.

She has become infected with Lewis's attention to the surface, the outer form. People have to be reassured, lest – she supposes – misgivings be encouraged, speculations propagated.

In the windscreen mirror driving home her mouth remains closed, but it's set on a prim straight line that puts her alarmingly in mind of her mother and *her* mother. She looks least like her favourite actress Catherine Deneuve when she is alone in the car on those bad days of little faith, steering herself back home to Whitecraigs. Her hair is cut not dissimilarly from recent photographs of the star in *Hello!*, she has kept the facial bone structure of her twenties, she is regularly attractive, but she hates that mouth. The mouth *is* her, and there isn't a goddamn thing on earth to be done about it.

Moyna

The summer the archaeologists came, they made a gruesome discovery two thousand years after the event. The dig superintendent told them that the body they had unearthed didn't belong with the few others previously located on the site, mostly of old men and women in their late thirties and early forties. For one thing the woman was at least ten years younger; for another, she had met a violent and unprepared-for end.

That added a macabre interest to the business for the idle watchers. They stood about in their shorts and tee-shirts studying the shattered skull, which had been split from behind. The supposition was that the broch had come under attack, but the superintendent pointed out that there were no other bodies to prove conclusively that this had been the case. It was unlikely that the rest of the tower's inhabitants would have escaped, and certainly someone would have needed to remain to bury *this* body. Perhaps other bodies lay somewhere else, and yet the proximity of this shallow grave to the formal resting-places of the elders suggested that the death had occurred during the tower's occupation. Since the dwellers had been settled and peaceful types, it was improbable that the woman's life had been taken as punishment. That wasn't to say she might not have been murdered: and if that were so, the covering would have been furtively done, with fear or guilt of the consequences causing the murderer to place the body within rather than outside the familiar burial ground.

It sounded so vastly far from their own lives, they could only stand and smile politely. As they listened, though, the ancient past began to acquire a creepy, cold, dead hand's grip on their own time. Several of them turned to look over their shoulders, continuing to smile although less surely than before. The sun shone, but it had shone then too, on sinner and sinned against; a number of them experienced a chill on the skin, goosebumps, and – in Moyna's case – a sensation of having lived out this moment before. 'What's up?' she was asked. 'Someone just stepped on your grave?' She shifted a few steps away, puzzled by her own reaction when she knew next to nothing about history, compared to Lewis and Ailsa. The dig superintendent had told them that history was like a detective story, which made her think at first of something neat and even cosy until she had second thoughts and saw instead a crimson mess of gore and felt a rush of panic to remember that, once, there must have been a blood-crazed murderer on the loose in Achnavaig.

Mrs Meldrum

She didn't understand Zionist politics, although she felt a natural pity for the Palestinians in their camps and was disinclined to consider the predicament of the most radical, ultra-orthodox Jews living in New York City, the frenzied dancing Hassidics with their self-proclaimed messiah. In her American days Jews had been hard to find in Aunt Bunty's or Amersham circles, but the pace of life had gone up a couple of gears since then and now you couldn't get any reliable hold on developments, they moved so fast.

Instead she stuck to an incontrovertible fact, namely that the Jews were in danger, like the gypsies, like the migrant workers, like all who found themselves scapegoat strangers in this new Europe's strange lands. Now graveyards were being desecrated. She had to defy the tides of anger and self-righteousness and false-telling, the disposition for pure hatred.

The synagogues were mostly on Glasgow's south side, in the well-heeled suburbs from Giffnock to Newton Mearns.

She went to one in town instead whenever she made the journey south, giving kosher Whitecraigs a miss and preferring Lewis and Greta shouldn't find out. The area was run-down, but there were still delicate fanlights and later art nouveau flourishes to be seen among the neglect. She preferred to approach her enlightenment through this aura of decline and decay, negotiating the car along the potholed back roads, splashing through weeks-old puddles, avoiding the curly-tailed mongrel dogs.

One day, for no apparent reason, a wardrobe was standing in the middle of Rosebank Street. Dark wood, not pine, but faded by sun and rain and wind. Its door, containing an elegant oval of cracked mirror, hung open. Luckily there was room on either side of the object to pass. As she drove round it, slowly, she looked inside, but the hold – as she should have expected – was quite empty. A black dimensionless space.

She slowed and changed gears when she came to the cobbles. More puddles, although the sky was clear overhead, showing patches of blue between the glowering Atlantic clouds.

Sixty-three years had brought her here, in her shiny waxed car, to this. To a stretch of broken pavement, to a gutter clogged with a mulch of leaves. To a red sandstone Scottish recreation of a synagogue in mittel-Europa.

Nicol

Miss Cauldwell drove a nine-year-old Pontiac. Out on the road she hugged the wheel, and her vision was restricted by the dark glasses and headsquare she habitually wore. Her reflexes weren't so good now, apparently, and she would scrape fenders parking, steering straight in for the sidewalk kerb. Everyone knew her for an eccentric, but she was Old Amersham – or at any rate post-fishing village but pre-resort – and that gave her a right. She also had the right to buy her groceries on account, as she did the simple weekend clothes from Willy's Sea X Country Store. She worked for a couple of charities in the town when she remembered to, and always lent her support whenever a petition was got up, not to close the wooden bridge over the creek or not to widen Spink Street or, even, not to cut back the ground ivy which was such a feature of the place, never mind that it was a brick-chewing parasite. She sometimes dropped in at BJ's or Oceans Eleven, and either put it on the slate or paid by old-fashioned banker's cheque.

A housekeeper shared the house with her. It was common knowledge that this was their only piece of property, after Miss Cauldwell sold out her share of a New York brownstone to her elder brother's family. They must have had some means, therefore, even though the housekeeper helped her to keep tight hold of the purse-strings.

She was emerging from a hardware and chandler's shop as he made his way towards a wall cash-dispenser.

He took his chance to study her close to.

Her face had held together well structurally, but her skin was very lined by exposure to sun and wind. Her hair was white under the headsquare. She had small eyes, still brilliantly green.

She paused to speak to someone in the shop doorway, and her delivery was brahmin-lockjaw, the clench-throated Boston sort which she must have picked up from her vacation friends. Her clothes were plain and functional and hardly intended to flatter: a pair of very washed-out nantucket red trousers, a blue smock, scuffed and shapeless dirty-white weejies on her feet.

While she spoke she kept turning the car keys in her left hand, over and over. Her neck pulled as she smiled at something the man said to her. A smile for formality's sake, it occurred to him as he watched over his shoulder, a kind of feudal favour in this purportedly egalitarian society.

When she'd finished she crossed the pavement to the Pontiac. Today she was alone, without the prim-featured housekeeper who normally ran after her. Inside the car, the dark glasses went on, although there was no sun. Her long bony hands clasped the wheel in a five-to-one position. The gears crashed as she moved out into the road. No one on the sidewalk looked round, because the lady was just a custom of the place.

Mrs Meldrum

Recently she had started to remember what she had forgotten, the layout of the Amersham streets and their names – Ark Street, Light Street, Vinery Lane, Ladyfair Place. The white clapboard houses, the mixture of palings and Tom Sawyer fences, the sailors' church with the two walrus tusks raised on top of the gateposts to form an archway, the flagpole in the old Misses Lemon's garden.

It was easiest to bring to mind when she was in bed, trying to sleep. A part of her mind seemed to be more lucid then, but under the surface, as if it meant to shut her off from the full experience. She didn't want to be left behind, so she had to scuttle after the pictures in case she lost them for a second time: the canopied wooden bridge over the creek, the four different times on the town clock-tower, the stuffed German Shepherd dog that kept guard in the front window of one of the banks.

Nicol

He was in BJ's on his second evening in Amersham. He had decided not to make his call to the house called Kerrix. It occurred to him he was too late now, years and decades too late.

He started talking to the younger of the two barmen about Miss Cauldwell. The man was new to the town, and didn't have the same respect for its traditions and reticences. At their quieter end of the bar counter he saw no reason to be circumspect.

'It's not so lonely, though. She's got her visitors.'

'Visitors? Family –'

'Oh no.'

'Guests? Tourists, you mean?'

'They don't do much sightseeing. They're just here – well, to keep her company.'

'I see,' he said. He didn't. He supposed the barman meant they were companions of some sort.

'A man about the place –' he began.

The tender laughed. He couldn't see why.

'A man? Well, that'll be the day.'

'I don't . . .'

'How *I* look at it is, anyone who's going to get married *gets* married. Maybe they make a mistake about the person, but they wanna get married.'

'Miss Cauldwell – she didn't? Want to get married?'

'She's not the sort that does.'

The barman winked across the counter at him.

Then he did cotton on, he got the drift of the remarks. Who better equipped, after all?

'You're quite sure?' he asked.

'Oh, sure I'm sure. Miss Cauldwell and her girlfriends. Everyone knows about it. That's how it always was. From way back when.'

He nodded.

Life played the trump card again.

Mrs Meldrum

Where were they all? Sherry, Green, Bip? She could have tried to find out. She had suggested to Nicol he might drive down one short vacation, for somewhere new to see. But he was kept very busy at his job.

It would have been interesting to find out, and a little frightening too. Like opening a long-closed door, having to pull hard, against its resistance, not knowing what was going to be on the other side. She wanted to, but she didn't think that she honestly could. Feeling that first draught of old, cold, stale, astonished wind on your face...

Struan

In the days when he climbed mountains, before Kirsty forbade him, he had a different view of life – pristine, transparent, and very nearly innocent. Above the cloud line, in ice and snow, the world seemed to have been freshly made.

Now he was out of practice. He had a hankering, but he wasn't sure that his nerve would hold, or that his lungs had the capacity they'd once had. It might have come back to him. He hadn't been on a bicycle for a similar length of time, but from any of those white Alps above La Ville-des-Glaces which he'd tackled in his prime one single misjudgment would very likely prove to be your last.

Mrs Meldrum

Learning Hebrew was taking a stance. Committing a small good, against the tide of forgetfulness.

Here and there on this continent, the lights were spluttering. One day not so long off some of them might go out, and she wanted to offer some proof now of her solidarity.

She did it in memory of her friend, who had given up her life. Just perhaps Naomi had done so out of weakness, but she chose to believe that she couldn't bring herself to live falsely, in enjoying the pleasures of a life she had no more claim to than her relations who had been murdered. Naomi had sought to make sense of their end by showing that death could be invoked by something quite other than evil, by a not extraordinary woman's willpower. She was taking the sting from death, even though the process was irreversible.

That had demanded vast courage. To say 'folly', or even 'depression', was to misunderstand entirely. The action wasn't purposeless, because it signified a return – to family, to the original community of souls that had brought her into being in the first place.

There was, she judged now on Naomi's behalf, a sort of divine symmetry to it all. The gift of life was repaid with the supreme sacrifice.

Ha-Kadosh Baruch Hu, 'The Holy One, blessed be He'.

It was a pledge which she herself didn't quite understand, and that was why she valued it as highly as she did. If she had been able to think and argue her way all around it, then it would have been knowable and reasonable in a finite way.

Melech Malchei ha-Melachim, 'The King above all kings'.

By this means she too was included in a mystery, like Naomi, and so she lost her full consciousness of self, and she was grateful for more of this continuing discovery of humility.

Mi She-Amar V'hayah ha-Olam, 'He Who Spoke and the World came into Being'.

Earlier, during the second half of her marriage, she had ceased to be the supporting role and had become the fulcrum. Now here was her reward, shedding the rock tied to her back, being carried off on this journey through space and time – performing her little deeds of charity and decency, *gemilut chasadim* – to a destination which she couldn't anticipate.

'On that day,' Zecheriah declared, 'the Lord will be one, and His name one.'

Nicol

Miss Cauldwell was also known as the Congressman's sister.

For the past thirty years Congressman Green Cauldwell had been a figure about Washington, which saw rather more of him than his eastern home state. He was particularly evident in the bars of the Four Seasons and Sheraton Carlton Hotels. At weekends he could be found either at the Sequoia Hills resort or playing the tables at Anatole's casino.

He was married, with two daughters, but his wife didn't venture far from Baltimore, and on no account travelled to Washington, or to Amersham either. It was said that she didn't see eye to eye with Miss Sherry Cauldwell, who treated herself as sovereign of the family, quite irrespective of the fact that her brother was an elected member of the House of Representatives.

And notwithstanding that *she*, a cotton princess from Louisiana – from one of the oldest families in Lafayette – had been the one to finance his political dreams, way back in the days when they were courting in Baton Rouge.

The Congressman had a mistress in Washington. It was no secret to veteran observers there. His wife doubtless knew about it too, having a peremptory way about her but a grim determination to concede nothing: 'alternative arrangements' were par for the course, and she must have foreseen the inevitability from the outset of their most political marriage.

He had, once, been a man of some vision: not possessing a super-abundance of the stuff, but enough with which to have the makings of an early reputation.

The vision became diluted. In the capital he had seen less and less of the world. His sights had continued to narrow, to the range of his ambition and to others' encroachments upon it.

He did serve on committees and gave time to high-profile charities, and if that was going through the motions then better so than not at all. At least it identified in him a potential for some shame, a degree of awareness as to how far he had fallen from the magnanimous causes he blithely soapboxed about in his youth.

Mrs Meldrum

What learning amounted to was sympathising with the predicaments of strangers. Everything she had ever read in books had worked to widen her view of the world, so that she saw others as unique and yet in certain respects resembling herself. The drive of a person's life should be towards tolerance. Why live through the years just to become more self-involved and protective of what could matter only to yourself?

> Guard us
> from vicious leanings and from haughty ways,
> from anger and from temper,
> from melancholy, talebearing,
> and from all the other evil qualities.
>
> Nor let envy of any man rise in our heart,
> nor envy of us in the heart of others.
>
> On the contrary:
> put it in our hearts that we may see our comrades' virtue,
> and not their failing.

The Broch

* * *

Nicol

In his Colorado eyrie Bip did his own thing. It hadn't brought him a fortune – which is how success is estimated in that country – but he had made a living for three decades from doing only what he wanted to do, painting, and he was also able – just – to support a family. That was a triumph of resolve. He didn't have the onus of wealth, needing to devote himself to its preservation and reduplication. His working life was an odyssey, a map of discovery around himself, vital reroutings (metaphorically) to a succession of somewhere elses, which were always the next place he felt he needed to be.

The *Catriona* was found drifting, upright and empty. It was some forty miles down the chewed coastline, caught in a freak impasse between gentle but conflicting tides. Otherwise it might have been carried out to open sea, and then the search for its occupant could not have been started so comparatively soon as it was.

The house was uniquely quiet for those thirty-six hours. A vast stillness descended, and sounds didn't seem to register for longer than a second or two at a time. It was a silence like . . . like soft wax, like smothering honey. The telephone must have rung, but the sounds of that too were spirited away, or they were in recollection. The sea was quite calm in the bay. Everything in their line of vision seemed to be waiting, in breathless anticipation.

They already knew, before the police rang with the call they were dreading. This time the sounds of ringing cut through, because no one would pick up the receiver.

A body had been located, down at Carnbain, carried by the morning tide on to the strand.

Ming Meldrum had been a strong swimmer, so it made even less sense. He had taught all his children to swim, and had reminded them over and over to 'always respect the sea'.

His lungs were found to be full of salt water. His heart might have given out, but the post-mortem examination wasn't able to establish that. If he'd had a heart attack beforehand, then they could have told.

From wherever the boat had been, he could surely have swum to land, knowing how to float and how to conserve his energy. There was no evidence of injury to his body before it was washed on to the rocks; no blow to the head, no jellyfish stings. The weather had been fine. If he'd meant to save himself – Mrs Meldrum was left to deduce from the words which the police officers would not say to her during a private exchange in Ming's study – then inevitably he would have done.

The shock of the news, even after the hiatus, stunned them. In addition to everything else, they had to contend with the lack of explanations. They were left walking dazed about the house, colliding – quite literally – and meaning to think of ways out of this labyrinth for themselves. Over hours they grew exhausted trying to get a hold of the situation, unaware if it was day or night. Grief ebbed and flowed. Their numbness would relax, then again anaesthetise them. Their senses closed down, their minds locked, they went stumbling and fumbling back into that lightless labyrinthine place.

The unreality of what was happening threw them. It didn't belong to them, but to another family. Now they weren't quite a family any more.

That disorientated them too. Not being one and whole. In a sense they had been fraying at the edges for years, but arithmetically they had been complete. Now, literally, they could never again be how they had been.

In the immediate aftermath they only remembered the best of him. Their sorrow was properly for him and not for themselves, because he'd had the years stolen from him which he ought to have had.

There was no justice, there was no *point*. The unresolved circumstances only made everything worse, though, and led them back into the labyrinth. The same circuit of thoughts, and thoughts losing their definition. Imagining the bruised and bloodied body before it was cleaned for Lewis and his mother to identify. Envisaging the scene, where the waves roll in on the strand, slapping jetsam against the boulders that lie about like so much casual rubble. The rocks were the detritus of an ice shift, and the blood smears were as fresh as the day, and the man was sixty-eight years old (which was nothing), and time was in a vicious meaningless spin.

It was only what he did sometimes, going out in the *Catriona* alone, when he wanted to think. Or not to think. It was in the boat's predecessors that he'd taught them, with varied success, to sail. He had always been generous with his talents and skills, not hoarding them for himself. They lived on, in diluted form, in them. Their lives were testaments to his, memorials. They were carriers of his spirit, vessels of a much longer past than their own. It was humbling, and consoling, and terrifying. When they found themselves panicking at the knowledge, they didn't know how they could cope with it.

Lewis

Was his father's death an accident? The others seemed to accept that it was. His mother wouldn't discuss it with him, which must mean that she had her doubts. He had followed her example, and avoided phrasing painful questions.

Death is the very last *fait accompli,* and – he argued to himself without any of the logistical skill he was famous for in his court work – it was beside the point to determine the circumstances now. Maybe he was afraid of . . . Alone in his study in Whitecraigs late at night his thoughts turned back. He had to preserve himself from that long journey, to Achnavaig and Carnbain, so he floated himself off those dangerous rocks on another topping-up from the Johnnie Walker bottle, off – not very confidently – and away to wherever he could manage, courtesy of the CD player, buoyed up on a raft of digital stereo, Debussy's piquant Iberian gardens or Richard Strauss's echoing Alpine gorges.

Mrs Meldrum

She sat by an open window in the Round Room, waiting for the first signs of darkness waning. It happened imperceptibly, but there came a point when she realised it was happening, that sombre cohesiveness beginning to drain out of the sky. Somewhere beyond it, after indigo, came the blue hour, when night at last was on the run.

She had lit a log fire. It wasn't necessary for warmth, but she had another purpose in mind.

The envelope lay on her lap, with the folded sheet of paper inside. She knew the contents by heart; she wouldn't forget them, ever. She looked down at the envelope, crumpled from the contact of her fingers over the months after Ming's death.

She closed her eyes. Listened to the sea. Heard a branch of sweet apple wood splitting in the grate.

It wasn't chance after all, no mere accident. There were impulses, but also – more importantly – there were patterns and predestinations. She had the proof of it inside the envelope.

She opened her eyes. Got up slowly out of the chair. Stood in front of the window for a few moments before turning her back to the view and then proceeding across the room to the fireplace.

She paused briefly, because it seemed to her she was losing some essential touch with the letter's sender. But she had decided, and anyway Ming was going to be the gainer.

She opened her hand and watched as the envelope and what it contained dropped on to the burning logs.

Flames started to curl and char the corners.

She returned to her chair by the window. She leaned back, and the rattan responded with its familiar sequence of creaks.

She was exhausted. The letter was smoke embers, and its only existence would ever be in her head, until she began involuntarily to forget. Ming had left his note for her, and she'd judged that he was allowing *her* to decide what the others should know or not know about his death.

Suicide, she felt, demeaned him. The skill of the accident was that it made an open verdict possible. But *she* had understood, with the evidence provided for her alone in the lines of best-behaviour handwriting. She didn't believe he had been ill: she'd asked their doctor afterwards, and he'd told her he too thought it unlikely. Ming wrote of making a 'burden' of himself, which might have had a medical cause – but the letter was mostly a polite apology for the inconvenience of the action he intended and a very gallant, well-mannered acknowledgment of her thoughtfulness for him over forty-one years. (He had backed her up when she used to demand that the children pen proper 'thank you' notes after birthdays and visits to friends' houses. 'That's just what we Meldrums do,' he would remind any potential renegades, with a flash of that winning smile which Nicol had inherited.)

Remembering, she shook her head. The view of sea blotted, and she found she was crying. Sometimes she could be caught out like this, when she thought she was adequately prepared, with the grief siphoned out of her. It alarmed her to concede how lamentably little she had decoded of the man's nature, so as not even to recognise the hopelessness that must have been so much a part of him. She had only needed to ponder on why the levels were falling so dramatically in the bottles ranged on top of the dining-room sideboard, and – instead of bringing her father to mind – she should have concentrated on much closer to home.

Her tears receded, after a couple of minutes. The sea came back into focus. And the slow curdling of light in the sky. She looked over her shoulder, and saw that the letter had indeed disappeared.

She had been debating for weeks how to express herself on the matter, how to account to her children for its being in her possession. She would have needed to explain why she had failed to mention it before, and she couldn't fix on one single convincing reason. She had considered and considered what to do, until utter weariness finally settled the matter for her, unfinished business in the end.

They had raised a family who, for good or bad, had a capacity for keeping secrets. She hadn't been aware that that was what they were doing, but how could she deny it now? She had been afraid that her children might not have discipline, and secrets were the price of ensuring that they did. Maybe she had been afraid too of opening up to them, and of discovering more than she wanted to about Ming, so it was a measure of self-defence as well: necessity posing as a virtue, selfishness assuming a pious air.

The Broch

* * *

> I thank thee, O Lord, because thou hast put me
> at a source of flowing streams in dry ground,
> a spring of water in a land of drought,
> channels watering a garden of delight,
> a place of cedar and acacia,
> together with pine for thy glory,
> trees of life in a fount of mystery,
> hidden amid all trees that drink water.

She had lived with Ming knowing the tiniest domestic details, about how his clothes creased around him in the course of the day, and how often he was required to clip his toenails, and where the old freckles lay on his back, and how long he was likely to spend in the bathroom and when – by the clock, so regular was he – he needed to relieve himself, and which portion of his shoe heel wore down first, and which buttons on which jackets would have to be resewn and how soon after the last time. She knew as much about his diet as he did, and about the likings of his senses, for colours and music and autumnal smells. She had (unconsciously) learned to walk like him on their country hikes, and could guess from certain trigger words which she used what he was going to respond with in five or ten or twenty seconds' time, as if the words revolved on a spool of tape.

And yet, about other matters she had known next to nothing. He was reticent about his work, until she learned to stop asking. She could never decide what he really felt about those colleagues they entertained to dinner in Glasgow, and whose wives she dutifully chivvied with chat over a fatiguing evening. She wasn't able to fathom those silences he would fall into, which took him out for several hours at a stretch on to golf courses and around the bay in *Catriona*. She hadn't understood what his feelings about his parents amounted to, nor even whether he thought they had brought up their own children well or just averagely. She saw what engaged him with each of them – a little less so with Ailsa, and less than that with Nicol – but she wasn't clear how much was due to caring and how much to obligation.

> Let every made thing know thou made it,
> and every form comprehend thou formed it,
> and let each say that has breath in his lungs,
> the Lord God of Israel is King,
> and His Kingdom is in all.

She had asked Lewis if his father had had any problems, in the way of business. Lewis duly investigated, and reported back to her that the firm wasn't in a very good way. She guessed at the time that he was understating. She might have asked him more, but accepted his tactful summing-up of the financial situation. It was a closed book to her, because Ming hadn't wanted to involve her and because she had thought – insensitively perhaps, but only as her generation did – that that was a man's concern, while a wife and mother had her own. He should have told her what his worries were, and she ought to have persisted in asking him. She hadn't been able to think more modernly, though, not having been trained to. And so it came about that a historical cast had been put on everything.

Poor Ming.

But she needed to remain strong for him now, for the sake of resisting and neutralising hopelessness in herself – just so that she could keep going. Love had never ignited her; after the strains of the first year it turned into something else, tolerance certainly and a tempered affection. When the family were growing up it was easier to forget about Lindsay, and not to consider what might have been going on in the background down the years. Ming had learned not to bother her again: if that meant he gave less away of himself to her than he might, it also protected her from knowing too much.

Poor Ming. But no, she reminded herself, don't start. Sorrow can only degenerate. Into pity for yourself and, worse, cheap sentiment for a marriage that was just as complex as it needed to be.

At the end, when Ming was lying cold on the slab in that dripping room, she had studied his face for an expression. But there wasn't one. That was the final horror, so shocking that it kept her from crying then.

No pain, but no consolation either. Not a hint of a grimace, nor the ghost of a smile. He was free, and away from them.

On the drive back with Lewis, while he chatted away to distract her, she was trying to recall the time furthest off, when they'd first met. His face wouldn't come into focus. She tried to make it, to have the relief of a remembered smile, but the smile like the face eluded her. Then that time started to fade away too, receding into whiteness, not surely a condition of innocence but a mental white-out as her mind worked on an instinct to spare her more grief and more hurt than she could bear.

Lewis

The solution he'd hit upon was to buy The Broch himself.

He had several evaluations made and put the lowest of these to his father, who had no sensible reason in those last weeks of his life for objecting. He arranged a mortgage without informing Greta of the fact, and used the services of an old friend at a bank to grant him most-favoured-client rates.

The cost of the exercise was scary, even working on the evaluation most advantageous to himself. But he tried not to dwell on the personal inconvenience. He wondered of course why he was doing it. Perhaps – he decided – he was meaning to rescue the past from its disintegration. If the stories got out – about insolvency – and the house had to be sold, memory might not be able quite to trust itself. At least with The Broch still in their hands, all the past was somehow more feasible. Their father would be more believable too, as a man who once had the appearance of trustworthiness, someone to be considered a winner at life.

He was certain that his mother knew nothing about the house. His father would have been too afraid to tell her, for his pride's sake. The point of everything was that she shouldn't discover.

She would always have The Broch. She allowed him to contribute to the cost of heating and upkeep and a few improvements, and – because she'd let the matter slip once to his brother – Struan also pitched in, pricked by his guilt or besieged honour or whatever it was.

Only he, however, he alone understood how her affairs really stood. The secrecy was necessary, and in its way quite enjoyable. For so long, growing up, he had lived in ignorance, and now it was his prerogative to decide how much was to be disclosed and how much not.

Mrs Meldrum

Ming would be standing out on the terrace, by the portion of the wall where he always stood when he wanted to watch a sunset. How close he would be, and how far away. She might touch his arm, but if she did he would fail to notice: or if he was aware his mouth would smile only in an automatic way. He was light years removed. She would follow his eyes, to the melange of over-ripe colours in the sky. It could be a vulgar spectacle sometimes. Occasionally it would illuminate them like stage lights, in a lurid raspberry or emerald sea glow. It might have been a romantic moment. It had the makings of such. But Ming didn't seem to associate her with that sort of mood any more. She knew not to sigh about it. She wouldn't allow him the pretext for a rebuff, however gently the atmospherics might cause him to do it.

Ailsa

She only wished – genuinely wished – she could believe more fully in her mother's feminine accomplishments. But her memories were of a sly dominatrix. Now and then Eff would pass himself off as master in his own house, but it was Em who held them together, by some formidable strength of purpose. Her father was masterful on those occasions only because she allowed him to be – otherwise she could cut him down to size with a look, a glance at her watch, a hesitation in her speech or an unusual stress on a word, even an intake of breath at the back of her throat.

Maybe nobody else had seen it, but she had. It wasn't sympathy, of course, that caused her to notice: the opposite, rather, whatever that was. She still wondered, though, how she could have spotted the tendencies so young unless she'd already had a kind of premature obsession. A fixation was a weakness, and she preferred that shortcomings should characterise others and not herself.

Mrs Meldrum

No. Most of all she envied Nicol New York at Christmas time, in the life before Ming.

Car headlamps lighting up afternoon in the streets. The silly jingly carols playing from shop windows, relayed out on to the sidewalks of shoppers. Snow falling in the gulches between the canyon cliffs. Hot steam billowing from metal gratings. Dressed fir trees fastened above porticos and marquees. Running indoors from the taxi cab drawn up the kerb, ingénue as she was hungry for the warmth.

Ailsa

On the other hand it was too good to be true. A woman of their mother's age living in a house like this one. She had her health, and the luxury of space, when so many elderly folk were lucky to have the wherewithal just to get by. Welfare cost cuts, heating levels reduced, inferior food substituted for better, room-sharing in local council homes. It was all wrong, of course, that and this and the discrepancy: a screaming little outrage.

Mrs Meldrum

Naomi sits at the back of the room, a shadow among shadows.

She is almost afraid to look.

Why has Naomi come back, if not to tempt her? She says something to her visitor in Hebrew. *Zikkaron le-ma'aseh ve-reshit.* Slowly a smile emerges from the shadows.

She is almost afraid to look. It's a snaring smile, sparkly with the frost of some very cold place. Being very nearly forgotten is a state of deep refrigeration, and is that better or worse than a suicide's roaring hell, which is where she might have imagined her to be. But not even the trace of a roasting, not so much as a sun-bed tan. (She wonders how she is to explain an invention Naomi must be unaware of: she can't clog this situation with anachronisms.)

She puts a hand to her brow, which covers her eyes, and Naomi is out of sight although not out of mind. But ignoring the evidence is getting half the way there. The rest is up to Naomi, which is the problem.

She speaks the lines of a prayer. *Thou dost remember all that was done and no form is concealed from thee, O Lord our God, thou art he who looks and sees to the end of all generations.* She only hopes Naomi can remember. In her delivery she tries to evoke the mystery of the Torah. *Thou it is that hath taught all knowledge, and all things exist by thy will; and there is none beside thee to controvert thy plan; none to understand all thy holy thought, none to gaze into the depths of thy secrets, none to perceive all thy wonders and the might of thy power.* If only Naomi would appreciate that the living don't know enough to be unafraid . . .

She continues to sit there, in her tidy and composed fashion, but it is an imposition even so. I have a houseful of guests, Naomi, and I need to think of this and that, there's so much I have to turn my thoughts to, and so little time left to me. I must account for every single minute of it.

Unless for Ming it had been a way of getting back to somewhere else, or, better, of holding it all in his mind simultaneously? It might have been a desire for a total vision rather than extinction – to see how all the tenses fitted together, and how hypothesis and actuality were woven into one another. His action then became a rash, impulsive act of bravery, and not the thing that the cynics in the world took it for behind her back.

She opened the wardrobe door in her bedroom, thinking of that other wardrobe she had driven past, standing unclaimed in the middle of the wet cobbled street. She pulled the door back and stared into the dark hold while the hangers rattled. Ghostly music. A store of furtive figures, like puppet people, and all of them in the image of herself, memories and harbingers alike.

Faith was an attitude. Religious belief was an aptitude and would have to be worked at. Perhaps the prayers and incantations would bring her to it.

She'd read that the aborigines of Australia have no proper conception of future time, or a grammar to deal with it.

For herself, on the other side of the planet, the future is what she has to live for, the only thing, a saving life-line of sanity.

PART FOUR

The Broch had been dated back to the second century BC. On the early Ordnance Survey maps for the area it was called first the Picts' Hoose and then a Brough (a 'defended place').

It had originally consisted of a round stone tower fifty feet high and sixty-five feet in diameter at its base, within a low circular drystone wall and yard. The tower had an interior and exterior wall (the latter swelling at the bottom and then tapering inwards, in the manner of a waisted cooling tower). In the hollow space between the two walls were narrow galleries and, above a ladder to the first floor, cramped slab staircases to the upper levels. Entrance was by a passageway like a gulch – only one man wide – leading to a bolted wooden door. The structure was roofed, with either turf or thatch, and holes were provided to let out the smoke of fires. There were no windows in the outside wall; the thirty or forty occupants lived in darkness, and used the yard to do their sight-work, weaving and carding and making pots and shaping bone.

Probably few brochs in Scotland were attacked. The people who lived in them were not Dr Johnson's 'savages' but very capable farmers. They kept cattle, sheep and pigs; they hunted whatever could not be penned, deer and foxes and wild cats, and snared fowl – geese, ducks, herons – and trawled the rivers and sea for fish and seals. They spun and wove wool. Although they worked tools from iron, and manufactured bronze, they appear to have produced only a minimal supply of weapons. The inhabitants of the brochs knew to defend themselves by building as they did; occasionally there *were* disputes, over grazing or use of the seaways, but they chiefly respected one another's territorial rights, being units within a larger tribal structure. (The Romans were a different matter, trading where it suited them but also developing a cruel traffic in Celtic slaves.) Sited to allow safe anchorage, the brochs were protected homesteads rather than fortified castles. The economy was highly domesticated, and in every respect self-supporting.

Mrs Meldrum

This, she dreams, is the world after the end of the world.

A cold wind blows bleakly through an empty city. The husks of leaves rattle along deserted arcades. Shutters bang against walls; sodden curtains are stuck fast to the stonework of the house exteriors, faded where the patterns have taken to the stone. Here and there in the once-elegant avenues items of furniture stand haphazardly, where traffic used to flow. The cars remain where they were when the bombs fell; their charred drivers, turning to black skeletons, still clutch the steering wheels with their talons. Some of the cars have rolled over, in the pandemonium to escape when the sirens sounded.

The shops still display their wares – fancy cakes and hand-made chocolates, popular books, bespoke men's clothes, the newest fashions for the women. The cafés await, with their vacant tables, the tables and chairs that weren't toppled over in the stampede. Further out, on the allotments, a glut of vegetables and fruit suggest normality, but the tomatoes and apples have a perfection that is deceptive. Nothing is what it appears to be, nothing ought to be trusted, in this subsequent world. Beware looking down into the canals, or under bridges, or through any of those unshuttered windows.

The other survivors of the apocalypse have long fled, to far away, leaving their ambitions – of paupers, themselves, living in palaces – unrealised. What would be the purpose of eating off gold plates when the food is poisoned? There is no one to barter the booty with, and what would be available to offer back? A currency of the very finest luxuries would have no worth at all, and the craftsmen's handiwork is already destined to become a kind of frivolous memory.

The banks are undisturbed, because money means nothing now. The shop windows are unbroken, because there is nobody left to impress with what might be looted, and anyway the last foodstuffs without contamination were bought up weeks before the catastrophe happened. The heavy deposits of black dust would show tracks, and there are none. This is a city populated only by its restive and aching ghosts.

A vast classical structure of columns and pediments and domes, infused with references to a legion of other places. A receptacle of standards formerly considered civilised, before a barbarism worse than any previous kind informed the world – the world before the end of the world. Previously a metropolis of graceful vistas and meticulous perspectives, of stone and water, pink marble and gold leaf and filigree ironwork and green copper – now grimy, with drainpipes and overhangs spouting instead of the dry fountains, cracks gouged in plaster and roofs unsettled by the gales that blew up afterwards, flagstones dislodged in the chaos and glass smashed in upstairs windows which no one thought to close.

Once, though... What spectacular beauty and mystery pertained to this scene, overriding everything about it that should by rights have been too familiar and clichéd. Once upon a time...

Venice first for the honeymoon. Sexual afternoons. Then jumping over the shadows on cobbles into sunlight. Swimming in gondolas, passing under the ribs of bridges. Oh yes, very Proustian. *'My gondola followed the course of the small canals; like the mysterious hand of a genie leading me through the maze of this oriental city ... holding a candle in his hand and lighting the way for me...'* Then Trieste, and a mountain wind, and figures for ever disappearing round gusty corners. Colonnades, the rattling linen awnings, a three-masted schooner berthed in the harbour in front of the Piazza Duca degli Abruzzi, by the Riva Novembre. Their rooms at the top of a villa where the furniture in all the other rooms was shrouded under dust sheets. Waking in the night, long after their love-making, waking alone. Voices slithering up the walls, hands scratching on glass. While Ming sleeps, turned away from her on to his side. While she sits in the shallow trench worked into the mattress, knees drawn up to her chin and shivering. Down in the dark harbour meantime the schooner strains on its tarry ropes; she can hear them creaking ambiguously in the sudden vistas of silence. As capricious as the tendrils of dream in deep sleep...

Moyna

She remembers as she is getting dressed, and keeping an ear open for the children.

Nineteen seventy-four or 1975, about then. She would have been fifteen or sixteen. She had gone to visit a family over at Rubha Wiay, and she was cycling back alone. It was still daylight. She saw the figure ahead of her, sitting on a stone by the side of the road. A long-haired woman, very oddly dressed for the summer, wearing what appeared to be a long dark belted frock, but a shaggy frock, with open sandals on her feet. The person, whoever she was, continued to watch as she cycled up the incline.

She leaned forward on the handlebars to pedal harder. The sun reappeared, a blood orange far out in the bay and rolling along the line of horizon. She had to screw up her eyes as a red dazzle passed across the top of the road. Her eyes started to hurt looking into it, and she lowered them to her hands gripping the peeled rubber of the handlebars. She heard a lowing sound, like a cow but not quite, a long and disappearing moan. She closed her eyes, and her lids glowed brilliant pink inside. She sensed she was coming to the top of the gradient. She raised her head and opened her eyes again.

The woman who'd been sitting by the roadside wasn't there, she was gone.

At the top of the hill she stopped, tipped forward off the narrow saddle, and dropped her feet to the road. She looked all around her. The ground was open at this point, bracken and rough grass, and the nearest rocks three or four hundred yards away. She couldn't understand how the person – the woman – was able to conceal herself. How was it possible to lie so low?

A sigh went up from the bracken. Nothing unusual in that. But she shivered nonetheless, at a sound she had heard an uncountable number of times before. She looked for a betraying movement of the dark clothes among the swathes of green and browning bracken, but there was none. She stood searching. Waiting. She defied whoever it was that intended to trick her: she wouldn't *be* tricked.

But the minutes passed and she saw nothing more. A car drove up alongside, and she hardly noticed. When she turned round, she found a neighbour of the McMinns smiling out at her.

'Birdwatching?' Mrs Pirrie asked her, meaning to sound sceptical.

She couldn't have explained. Luckily she had a reputation only for dyed-in-the-wool normality, so she could appropriate the innocuous smile for herself. The car drove off.

Her eyes returned to the search. She rotated her head, one way and then the other. Three hundred and sixty degrees.

Nothing.

Why me? she thought. *Why me, of all of us?*

Greta

She had left her John Mortimer lying about somewhere. She scouted round the sitting-room looking for it. She spotted a hardback book lying open, face down, under a chair. When she got closer, though, she saw that it wasn't hers. Anyway, it was the chair Lewis's mother usually sat on.

She bent down and picked the book up. She meant to close it, but on a whim she flicked through it with her thumb. The right-hand pages were elegantly patterned with a very foreign script. Arabic, possibly, she thought. Or – or Hebrew. She was too ill-educated to know which. What was it doing here?

She peered up at the sound of footsteps.

'Lewis –'

'What is it?'

'– look at this.'

She showed him the book. His lips thinned. Then they puckered.

'Whose is it?' she asked him. 'Do you know?'

'Your guess is as good as mine.'

He handed it back to her.

'Your mother's?'
'What?'
'Who else's could...'

For a few moments his eyes shrank into their sockets, which was how she knew he was concentrating his thoughts. Then he smiled, in his most abstracted way.

'Funny,' she said.
'What's that?'

She held up the book and waved it before placing it closed on the chair's cushion.

'We'll never know –'
'It isn't our business,' he said.

He was talking nonsense. She didn't look at him, so that he would realise that was exactly what she was thinking.

'I've found it,' she told him.
'What's that?'
'*Dunster.*' She retrieved the book from beneath a magazine on the sofa table.
'Good.'

She took a last look at the other book's cover, with all its squiggles. The front cover appeared to be on the back: in which case the book would have to be read from the back page forward.

'*Very* odd...'

The Broch wasn't the safest place in which to be left alone. If Lewis's mother should start to lose the thread... The house should be enjoyed by as many as wanted to enjoy it: without their having to wait to be invited. She could certainly fill it with her children's friends. A family time-share arrangement would be best. They could do some of Lewis's entertaining here. More important than selling it was holding on to it. There must have been some point to having it all along – prestige, she supposed, although that was regarded as a dirty word these days.

She knew Lewis was aware that she had designs. She couldn't make sense of his resistance. It was *his* whole family she was thinking of after all. Why had his mother kept it on if it wasn't to maintain the allure that had drawn them all – like flies to sticky paper they couldn't disentangle from.

Mrs Meldrum

Combing her hair she suddenly caught the movement of her mother's arm in the dressing-table mirror.

She had watched her mother endure, sticking it out and always for appearance's sake, never getting anything back for herself. Her mind had atrophied years before her body ran down. For the last decade she was just coasting along, proper wing-and-a-prayer stuff, especially after the mastectomy on one breast, and hirpling at the hip with her arthritis. Perhaps she had resolved to see her husband out first, because how else could she have persuaded herself it was worthwhile to carry on?

She found it hard to distinguish any feelings for her mother. That shocked her. A person is defined – complicatedly – by the responses of others. Essentially her mother had existed apart; she wasn't one of 'them'. Her authority now happened to be accidental. She was a warning to her, as to what not to let herself become. No man, God knows, can be worth the denial of a woman's life.

She picked up the brush and tugged harder at her hair. Her mother faded.

She always thought of the one after the other. Father, in his suspiciously well-cut rural tweeds, standing in the middle of the stable yard with that lost look he sometimes had, as if he couldn't for the life of him remember how he'd got here.

At least *his* death was apt. Cyrrhosis of the liver. Its inevitability was a strange comfort to her now. Because, and because, and thus . . . If he'd died in a motor accident, say, that would have been cursed fortune. Dying as he did, he was only being true to himself, in those days before clinical drying out and rehabilitation. The manner of death wasn't proud, or distinguished, but it marked the rounding off, the dotting of i's and crossing of t's and the placing of the full stop at the only place left for it to go.

Then it was Mother's turn again, as she came downstairs on pleasant drifts of Mrs McKay's breakfast cooking smells.

Mother's entertainments used to be in the manner of salons. That was her gift, and her compensation for being condemned to Perthshire's outer limbo, and with Father in decline.

Minuscule smoked salmon sandwiches. Good tea or dry sherry. A pause in the middle of proceedings while someone played the piano, or someone else sang. Mother disguised the fact of her economies with another generation's elegance and savoir-faire, so that a luncheon or dinner party would have seemed déclassé by comparison with these Sunday afternoon At Homes.

Ming could never have got out of Mother's clutches even if he had intended to. She quite failed to see the squeamishness it was causing *her*. But Mother, carrying her silver-topped cane to support her but also as a totem of authority in her own house, was Mother. She meant to salvage something more profound than any of them ever supposed – the belief that it mattered more for her to have been alive in the world than not.

Ailsa

And then when breakfast was over, it would be over.

For a long, long time, she hoped.

She shook her head at Mrs McKay's offer of those salty, stinking kippers.

Status was her line of work. In London she could plug into that way of thinking. She had the excitement of buzzing around at the centre of things. She encountered cunning and stupidity, and like the wealth and poverty and refinement and squalor she saw in the streets it contributed to the atmosphere of a dangerously simmering melting-pot. All human life was there, so much of it that you could scarcely particularise, you just submerged yourself in the variety.

Away from it, she became somebody else. She felt wise, and sad, not quite a hypocrite and yet hardly honest. After a time the introversion disturbed her, and she longed to get back, to be able to forget about her scruples. She needed to be busy, to have her life taken up, so that she couldn't reflect too much.

She tried harder, harder than she ought, to have some faith in the purported truths of her clients' publicity. She pledged herself to the dissemination of others' talent. There were always new customers queuing up for the treatment, so she couldn't get too set. She was bound to develop ideas burn-out eventually, but she hadn't reached that point yet.

Best not to brood on it. In her line of trade you didn't consider how you'd got to where you were, or try to work out where you might be headed.

Nicol placed a cup of coffee in front of her. Milky coffee, not black. She sighed. Nicol's smile wavered. Very feebly she shaped a smile to offer back, and was irritated with herself both for trying and for allowing trivialities to matter to her so much.

When her mother was dead, she would no longer be a weak person. That was what it would take, though, to discover the courage contained inside herself. She had no special pleasure in thinking it but nor did she suffer from any qualms.

In the most neutral sense, she was only biding her time.

Tailgates sighing open and creaking shut. Car doors slamming. Voices calling. Things forgotten, double-checks.

This is how it ends, in a non-stop welter of activity. Everyone is too busy pondering on the implications. Indoors the plumbing is working overtime. Belongings are still being found, behind doors and under beds, while others continue to be overlooked and will only be found later. It's difficult enough to put your thoughts into order, with the unruly din of adults and children and dogs and, more times than is usual, the ringing of the telephone.

Invitations, promises, evasions. A family goes about its business. The bay is its own shining paradigm, aquamarine under an active sky of high speeding clouds. The rocks have lost their bloody redness, and look merely ancient and protective. The sand is dry and white, as the adults all remember it. Their eyes keep looking over between the arrangements and goodbyes of differing degrees of sincerity. It's nothing so much, not compared with the Mediterranean or the West Indies or even coastal Massachusetts, but of course they see it each in their own way.

For the five grown-up Meldrum children, the weekend began here more than three decades ago.

Ailsa

Even when all Moyna's children had been accounted for and packed into the space-waggon, she had a sense...

She turned round suddenly to look. She felt a chill on her skin. There was nothing to see – naturally – up on the crest of the dunes. But she continued to look, straining her eyes against the sun haze. She held the view in the narrow space between her lids.

Sand, grass, cloud, sky.

She jumped as a hand touched her arm. It was Greta's. A smile exposed an expensive expanse of capped teeth. A tip of crimson flicked between them. It could have been an obscene gesture, in another context, if she hadn't been Lewis's wife. There was all the difference in the world, though. Some fatuously unspecific remark followed, about the two of them having to arrange to meet one another. Sometime when she and Lewis were down in London. Yes, yes. If, but, maybe. Whenever.

She looked round again. She was being reminded, by a featherlight voice even softer than a child's calling down the breeze to her, not to forget... not ever to forget...

Struan

On his way out he was passing the phone as it rang, so he picked it up.

'Kirsty?'

Asking when his mother was next coming down to Glasgow. He wasn't aware that she did go down, Lewis hadn't said anything about it.

They chatted. She didn't sound surprised to hear the family was there – as if she had known that already. She asked him if the secret mark was still on the window glass where she'd scratched it with her ring.

'You remember, Kirsty?'

It was the first thing he'd looked for. He'd never have guessed she would remember.

He let her voice trickle into his ear. It was softer than Cat's, when it chose to be – and it was humorous again, how it had been before they were married. He always used to find it a come-on, a *turn*-on.

No mention of a child. Was she still looking for a willing father, one she wouldn't have to be a wife to?

'I'm coming over to Glasgow on Thursday,' he heard himself suddenly say.

'Oh yes?'

She laughed, but with Kirsty there were laughs and there were laughs.

He suddenly realised Fanny was standing beside him, looking up at him. She was risking a smile, but she really wasn't sure. He smiled back, a broad and – for once – mirthful smile. The effect was quite electrifying all round.

'It's an afternoon appointment,' he spoke into the mouthpiece. 'But say I came through eleven o'clock-ish – d'you think Rogano's still do that turbot dish you used to like so much – ?'

Moyna

She bedded down into the noise in the Renault, into the smells of children and dog and husband. She kept busy, and included Jamie in the busy-ness, hardly having to look at him. She was never done turning round, asking the children, had they remembered to bring this or that with them. Who had given Luke his juice? And water for Folly, and was his drinking bowl there? That wasn't *their* nailbrush Fanny was playing with, was it? – then it must be Grandma's, and what would she say when she noticed it was gone? ('Grandma' – the name still jarred when she said it, after four children.) Please leave the side window clear, Ben, Daddy has to be able to see out. Seat-belt on, please, Molly. Why are you wearing odd socks, Fanny? What happened to your Elastoplast, Ben? No, I can't feed you just now, Luke; hold on a bit, will you? I can't find the road map; do you know where it is, Jamie? You ought to let Lewis go ahead, of course you can keep up with him. (Jamie had talked about getting an Audi estate, but an Espace – she falsely argued to herself – let them off the silly 'status' hook.) Would anyone like a piece of barley sugar – if you promise not to swallow it, Fanny. (Jamie disapproved of sweets, but he was saying nothing as she sat with the tin open on her lap; his thoughts were far away.)

She suddenly pulled down the windscreen visor with powdery, sugared fingers and examined her reflection. Hmmm. Up went the visor again. In the side mirror she caught a glimpse of the Whitecraigs Jaguar. Nicol's hire Ford must be somewhere behind, but the road bent and meandered. Struan in his two-seater sports job had got pole-position, and blasted off like a bat out of hell. It was such a godawful long way, and nothing was solved. She looked out at the patches of pine, and – closer to – the skerries of bracken on the grass that never seemed to grow. Outcrops of rock. On the other side of the road, inlets of sea. On the shore, black cows standing morosely in the water up to their knees. A trail of blue smoke rising from a lone cottage chimney. Bushes of prickly yellow broom. The old red road winding ahead of them which they travelled every time, thinking on each departure of what hadn't been achieved but clinging still – by fingertips – to hope.

Ailsa

She had told Nicol she wanted to be dropped off in Glasgow.

'I've decided to look around.'

'I'll drive you about – '

'No. I'll play it by ear. Stay on a day or two probably.'

She had no intention of doing any such thing. But if she got out there, in the city centre, she'd take a taxi out to the airport later and catch an evening plane back. So she would only have the car journey with Nicol this time, bad as that was, and then she'd be shot of him.

She thought America had afflicted him with blandness. Which ought to have made things easier, but instead he seemed not to acknowledge his faults. His success allowed him to look out on a largely wrinkle-free world: in another ten years he would be casting back on his past through very rosy spectacles. (No doubt, she mentally adumbrated, chic preppy-framed ones.)

She didn't care if he did latch on to her little dodge. She was doing this, she assured herself, to spare them both.

Mrs Meldrum

The whole point about brochs was that they were defences. Ordinary life was conducted elsewhere, outside, and it was to the round tower that they came at night, or when they feared an attack from raiders. The society was a highly ordered and peaceful one, whose virtues were more feminine than masculine: not assertive or aggressive, concerned with status and territory, but geared to cultivation, dependent on human energy and nature's cycle of supply. They were gatherers, that is to say, and not hunters.

Greta

She thought she had snagged her tights on the picnic hamper before getting into the car, so she wasn't really concentrating on the business of leaving as they set off. A run, or a dropped button, and suddenly you started to feel like a bag-woman. It was so maddening, when she had two unused pairs in the suitcase and a drawerful at home. She knew she shouldn't be bothering herself, but she couldn't help it. Appearances *are* important, inevitably, because they indicate your attitude, and her attitude was always to present the best aspect of herself: as a vindication of herself, and as a courtesy to others.

No, it was infuriating. Not trivial, as someone like Moyna might have thought. And yet – about Moyna she still wasn't sure. Her eyes observed more than she wanted you to think they did. A weekend of it was, frankly, more than enough. Ignorance was exhausting.

On which line of thought – what was she to make of Struan haring off like that? She had knocked against him coming out of the dining-room, and without seeing who it was he had – momentarily – clasped his arms for protection around her waist. A firm body, kept in tip-top shape, and hard she couldn't help noticing in a place which no machine in a gym was designed to assist. His face had burned scarlet...

She took a long, last, careful look at the house. She felt her eyes wide in her face, with admiration. She turned her head away from Lewis. She permitted herself a little smile. The Broch deserved it. A bond, she felt, had been established between the two of them, it and her: a complicity of need on its part and desire on hers. (Honesty was a private thrill in itself; she settled back into the ergonomic curves of the seat.) She kept her eyes fully open, meaning to lose nothing of what she was seeing.

Mrs Meldrum

They were a family, a community. But also, every one of them was alone in the end. There was the contradiction.

It was the final secret, preserved beneath layers of wadding to safeguard and conceal and deflect.

One is one, and for eternity is one.

So, what to do in the meantime?

Epilogue

Leaf

She can dream things to happen, or not to happen. She hears the stories in places and objects. She skims them off the back of the wind, and tells them, and she doesn't know where they come from. Sometimes she can say where the seals are to be found, or the otter nests, or the shoals of fish, and when that's where they're discovered to be the men come back to the broch singing her praises.

In the old days she walked on shingle, not on sand, and she used to fill herself with the raging sound of pebbles dragging under waves. In that place the waves and the wind and the fire in their home all roared with the same breath.

The sand here has dangers for them. How could they hear an intruder in the night? Where they are now, the Family considers it to be safer, even at the level of the sea. The tower is built on a promontory, on a tongue of land, with the bay on either side of them. But the sand is soft, and she worries about that, as she feels it is becoming her right, to worry, for the collective sake of the Family.

She realises that words are spoken against her too, inside the broch. *How does she know these things, when we don't?*

Wall-Eye speaks against her, although he smiles in her face. He ought to guess that she would know such a thing for herself, if she knows as much as she is claimed to do. What Wall-Eye says passes among the others, it takes fire in their thoughts. Their eyes glow in the tower's smoky darkness as they study her. She sees them watching from the windows in the galleries. That way they are all around her, even the women she has taught some of her skills to.

Being the Young Mother she should be respected, but the order of things has been upset. It is Wall-Eye's doing, she is sure of that, although he continues to smile in her face. Long-Leg won't take against his own blood brother, so she has to defend herself, with more silence than before.

Wall-Eye bears her ill-will for Moon's dying, for not foreseeing what happened on the crossing. And if Moon had survived their journey and lived on, then *she* would have succeeded Wing as Young Mother. She feels his anger. He is angry with the Spirit of the Cloud Glen, where Moon took her fever, but the Spirit cannot be touched. He believes that she has the gift to read the Spirits' minds, and that they may be harmed through her. He has forgotten that she took the fever herself, and it was only then that she started to receive the voices in her head, which have remained with her but not constantly, like the clouds that chilled them in the high place of echoes and falling scree they wandered into.

She has sensed dangers coming to them, very soon. While they travelled, Long-Leg heard of the men with red hair, who go by the sea-roads. There have been rumours of their violence.

Dangers are approaching them, they will be here very soon.

If she could only dream them away . . .

The voices come to her – by way of the Cloud Glen, and the soft green ground, and the rocks, and the sea. She is listening to hear the most important message of all, about the hazards threatening them. To manage that, she may have to promise to hear first – and then to give her gift away.

Inside the tower meanwhile they will have to do without her. For one day, or two, or more, for however long it will take. She has chosen a spot, within sight of the tower but on the next unguarded promontory. Between the rocks she can lie out of the lash of wind and rain and, when the sea stirs, the white spray. Those don't allow her to hear anything. A command stronger than her will is directing her to the place. Going there involves turning out of herself, into a chilly vapour of cloud. When she has had so many other responsibilities, it will be a strange freedom. The summons comes from the Spirit of the bay, and while listening for voices she is distracted – several times – by the honking cries of summer geese travelling north like slow arrows across the wide sky.

Hazards and dangers. But there are patterns, she senses at odd moments. Everything, she can vaguely understand, is determined by devices and designs that go unseen, and by repetitions and coincidences. The geese are no different from themselves, setting out on their long journey and following – just as the Family do – a road as hard as iron.

The broch will be a different broch, once she has dreamed away the perils.

The Broch

She will no longer be Young Mother, she is able to predict, but there is already an Old Mother. There cannot be two Old Mothers.

She goes to her sheltered crevice between the rocks and lies under the whip wind.

She tastes sand on her tongue, it sticks to her skin, she breathes some of it through her nostrils. Gritty particles coat her tongue. In her mouth it makes a noise, although she has always supposed it to be a silent element. She closes her eyes, but even so a few grains must have worked beneath the lids, she feels the soft skin smart. She tastes loam in the sand, as well as the distance of sea that brought them here.

They came with their hopes high of living undisturbed. The journey has separated them, though, from the living ghosts of themselves, as surely as sea does land from land. They were simpler people then, perhaps. But it isn't in her mind to be afraid.

Briefly she glimpses something she has never seen before. Hundreds and hundreds of brochs, just like their own, collected together and darkening the sky. She sees none of their inhabitants. A cold wind is blowing. Rain lies in puddles, the colour of an ox's heart from the old country. There are no Spirits in this outlandish place, even though it is present to her. She is puzzled, and disturbed, so much so that the place turns back into sky and rock: the rock that she can touch now with the tips of her fingers, against which she is lying.

She has to think of nothing first, so that she can concentrate better on her task, which is to undo what is otherwise bound to happen. For that she needs to lie low, as low as she can get on her front, wedged between the rocks so that she is defenceless. She has to show herself unafraid, so that the force of harm can recognise her determination to conquer it.

But when she is trying to think of nothing, why is she seeing Wall-Eye? He has crept into that space behind her eyes which she is keeping quiet and clean.

She shakes her head sharply, so that he will roll about and drop out. But he holds his balance, he doesn't slip. She tries again. He continues to resist. He can't be removed.

To try to forget him, she digs herself deeper into the sand, using her elbows for leverage, and then scooping with her hands.

Lying low in the crack of rock, she realises that for the first time since she started to receive the voices she has been guilty of a wish. Her sightings are visitations, she is only the bearer of messages. Wishes should have no part in it.

Wall-Eye has moved back into the space behind her eyes. He walks on

The Sun on the Wall

. Now he's carrying something in his hand. A stone, a big stone, pened at one end.

Sand blows past her ear. Once they lived beside shingle, in the old days, and they heard the footsteps of strangers for miles. In the softness of sand, in its treachery, smilers have the slithery killing grace of poison snakes.